MW00354919

THE
CUP of CHRIST
and the
FORGOTTEN
DISCIPLE

A Mystery-Thriller

JACK HOLT

The Cup of Christ and the Forgotten Disciple

This is a work of fiction. Apart from the historical figures, any resemblance between fictional characters created by the author and actual persons, living or dead, is purely coincidental. Any theological views or philosophies are the opinions of the characters and not necessarily those of the author. Any factual errors are the responsibility of the author.

Holt Publishing ™
For information, questions, or comments, contact
jackmholt.com
jackmholt21@gmail.com

ISBN: 978-1-7355283-0-4 (hard cover)
ISBN: 978-1-7355283-2-8 (paperback)
ISBN: 978-1-7355283-1-1 (e-book)

Cover and interior design
Deborah Perdue, Illumination Graphics

The High History of lé Sangraal and the Forgotten Disciple

is Dedicated to My Patron

and

Brother-in-Law

Comte Gautiér de Montbéliard

—Lord Robert de Borron

Introduction

The high history of lé Sangraal has never been told by any mortal man since Saint Joseph de Arimathea wrote these sacred words about our Lord and Savior. However, I declare to all men and women who wish to own this book, if God allows me to live in good health, it is certainly my intention to bring his story together. If God blesses my holy quest, these parchments will be found.

—Lord Robert de Borron
Anno Domini 1190

The Bible

But there are also many other things that Jesus did; if every one of them were written down, I suppose that the world itself could not contain the books that would be written.

—Saint John the Evangelist, 21:25 NRSV

Acknowledgments

I would like to acknowledge author Stephen Lawhead, for inspiring me to write my first book in The Cup of Christ trilogy. His tireless research in Celtic lore and the legends of King Arthur motivated me to create my own ideas.

Dan Brown, author of *The Da Vinci Code,* provided the inspiration for me to use symbols, codes, and arcane terminology.

I am grateful for Joanna Penn whose success as an independent author contributed to me taking the same route.

Thank you to my indefatigable graphic designer, Deborah Perdue, from Illumination Graphics, who used her artistic abilities to capture my book's vision. My sincerest gratitude to Reverend C. Allen Colwell for his counsel.

I offer my humble thanks to my great taskmaster, Pam Johnson of Pam the Editor. Without her helpful advice and developmental editing, I would not have accomplished this writing journey. Also, to my copyeditor Joni Wilson who kept me in the proper boundaries of literary grammar.

My printing company IngramSpark that offered great advice about getting my book published for all those who love historical fiction and mystery thrillers.

Dedication

To my loving wife, Carol, who had patience for the last twelve years listening to me speak about my book. Also, to my late mother, Charlotte, who gave me the interest to write, and my late dad, Jack, who had a great thirst for history.

The Principal Characters from Frankish Gaul and the Levant

Anno Domini 1190

Abbé **Jean de Saint Gaudens**—parish priest of Gavarnie, old friend of Grand Master Gilbért de Érail

Baroness Marie de Borron—wife of Lord Robert de Borron, mother to Robert's sons, Brian and Henri, sister to Count Gautiér de Montbéliard

Cardinal Folquet de Marseille—archbishop of Toulouse, former troubadour, head of the Roman curia

Chevalier **Marcel de Tournay**—seneschal to Cardinal Folquet, archbishop of Toulouse

Commander Armound de Polignac—Templar leader at the commandery of Carcassonne, old friend of Grand Master Gilbért de Érail

Comte **Gautiér de Montbéliard**—former Crusader, writing benefactor to Lord Robert de Borron, brother-in-law to Robert de Borron

Grand Master Gilbért de Érail—Iberian grand master of the Poor Fellow-Soldiers of Christ (Knights Templar)

Hughes de Montbard—Templar squire, great-nephew to Saint Bernard de Clairvaux, under the command of Grand Master Gilbért de Érail

Lady Marguerite de Borron—sister of Lord Robert de Borron

Muhammad Nur Adin—former emir from the Levant, constable of the Templar horses in Gaul, scout.

Rémy de Dijon—expert bargeman, fighter, and has two sons, Baudouin and Benoit

Robert de Borron—Lord of *Château* Borron, poet, writer, troubadour, swordsman, from Northern Burgundy

Sergeant Guy de Béziers—Templar scout, former seaman, under the command of Grand Master Gilbért de Érail

Sergeant Jacque de Hoult—Templar scout, under the command of Grand Master Gilbért de Érail

The Principal Characters from the City of Jerusalem and Palestine

Anno Domini 33

Alein Yosephe—son to Yoseph of Arimathea, partner in his father's business

Claudia Procula—wife of Pontius Pilate, granddaughter of Roman Emperor Augustus, deceased

Eli of Yerushalayim (Jerusalem)—camel and cloth merchant; with two sons, Eliyah and Isaiah

Enygeus—sister to Yoseph of Arimathea, husband to Hebron

Gaius Cassius Longinus—Roman Centurion guard, at the cross

Hebron—brother-in-law to Yoseph of Arimathea, overseer to Yoseph's merchant business, husband to Enygeus

Herod Antipas—tetrarch of Galilee-Perea, one of the sons of Herod the Great

Herodias—wife of Herod Antipas, she had Yohanan the Baptizer beheaded

King Arviragus—ruler of the Celtic Silures

Miriam of Magdala—land owner, mystic, student of Rabbi Yeshua ben Yoseph, a new friend to Yoseph of Arimathea

Miriam of Nazareth—niece to Yoseph of Arimathea, mother to Rabbi Yeshua ben Yoseph, and widow to the late mason and carpenter Yoseph of Nazareth

Nicodemus—member of the Jewish Sanhedrin ruling council, scholar, lawyer, old friend of Yoseph of Arimathea

Philip—disciple to Rabbi Yeshua ben Yoseph, a new friend of Yoseph of Arimathea, has daughters purported to predict the future

Pontius Pilate—Roman *procurator* of Yehudah (Judea)

Rabbi Yeshua ben Yoseph—itinerate preacher, mystic, biblical scholar, son of Miriam of Nazareth, rumored to be the foretold *Maishiach* (Messiah)

Shimon ben Yona—fisherman, nicknamed *Cephus* or "the Rock," disciple of Rabbi Yeshua ben Yoseph, brother to another disciple called Andrew

Shimon of Cyrene—follower of Rabbi Yeshua ben Yoseph, becomes friend with Yoseph of Arimathea

Yohanan Marcus—writer, student of Rabbi Yeshua, his two-story home used for the Seder (Passover meal)

Yohanan the Writer—disciple of Rabbi Yeshua ben Yoseph, biographer, a close friend to Rabbi Yeshua

Yosa—daughter to Yoseph of Arimathea

Yoseph ben Caiaphas—high priest of the Jews and head of the Sanhedrin

Yoseph of Arimathea—richest merchant in the Mediterranean region, member of the Jewish Sanhedrin ruling council, uncle to Miriam of Nazareth, great uncle to Yeshua ben Yoseph of Nazareth

Yudas Iscariot—treasurer, disciple for Rabbi Yeshua ben Yoseph, rumored to be a member of the Sicarii (daggermen), a group who assassinates Roman officials

Zechariah—orphan son of Yohanan the Baptizer, toddler second cousin to Rabbi Yeshua ben Yoseph

Anno Domini 1190

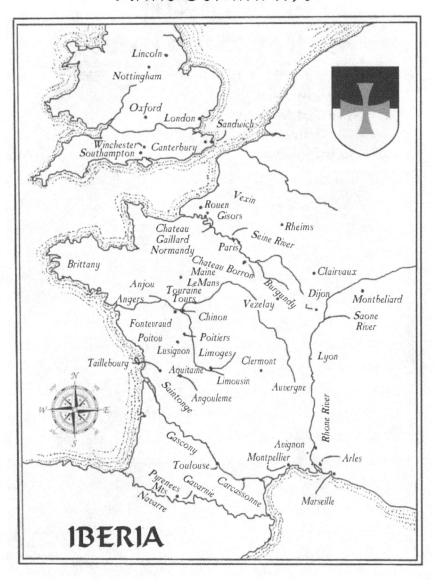

Jerusalem
in Roman Times

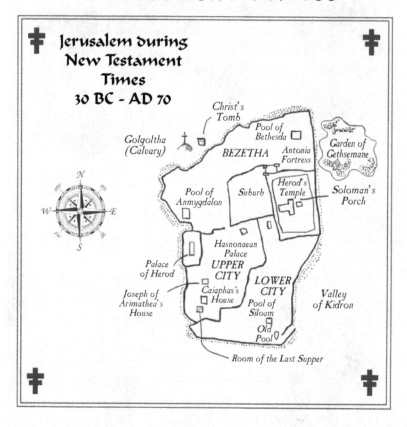

Jerusalem during
New Testament
Times
30 BC - AD 70

Christ's
Tomb

Golgoltha
(Calvary)

Pool of
Bethesda

BEZETHA

Antonia
Fortress

Garden of
Gethsemane

Pool of
Anmygdalon

Suburb

Herod's
Temple

Soloman's
Porch

N
NW NE
W E
SW SE
S

Hasnonaean
Palace

UPPER
CITY

LOWER
CITY

Palace
of Herod

Caiaphas's
House

Valley
of Kidron

Joseph of
Arimathea's
House

Pool of
Siloam

Old
Pool

Room of the Last Supper

Jesus Christ
Map of Life Events

PART ONE

The Beginning

CHAPTER I

Northern Burgundy
Early Autumn
Anno Domini 1190

The instant I saw the holly bush shake, my anxious steed reared, and it took all my strength to steady him. Fearing a large wild beast, I cautiously dismounted with my sword drawn. Using my free hand, I tied my horse's reins to the lower branch of a chestnut tree and crept toward the still rustling sound of leaves. Suddenly, from out of the dark forest came a hissing sound. I felt a rush of air as a crossbow quarrel struck a limb next to my head.

"*Mère de Dieu!*" I shouted, as three human-shaped shadows sprang from the bushes and ran into a tangled grove of high thorn shrubs. I cautiously took a step toward where they disappeared when unexpectedly three horses carrying the men galloped out of the woods and down a trail.

Did these men try to warn or kill me and why leave in such a hurry? Indeed, my one sword didn't outnumber them.

Creeping through the holly bushes to investigate, I stumbled over something and fell forward, catching myself with some branches. There below me, in the underbrush, a man lay face down in the dirt. His back had numerous bloody puncture wounds seeping with fluid. I turned him over to see if he was still alive. He wasn't, but fresh pools of oozing blood made one thing clear: he died just before I arrived. Maybe those men were robbers? But why didn't they strike me down?

I surveyed the man more closely. His black-colored surcoat had a large red-splayed cross embroidered on the fabric. His frame resembled that of a large bear, muscular and stocky. He belonged to one of the warrior-monastic orders. This ruled out robbery as a motive; most of them took vows of poverty.

I stood to search around the body for an explanation and sensed a shiver shoot down my spine. Just on the other side of the thicket lay an arm, a bodiless arm, with blood still oozing out of the clean-cut stump. With reluctance, I crept around the thicket for a closer examination. I noticed one of the swollen fingers. The third finger from the thumb held a gold signet ring. The setting revealed a black onyx stone inlaid with a golden-colored eagle and a crescent moon. This forearm and hand didn't belong to the murdered monk; he still had both his arms.

What had happened here? To whom did the signet-ringed hand belong? Did the ring's symbols indicate the owner's rank or station?

A sudden tree-rustling breeze caused me to flinch and interrupted my thoughts. This man's body and another man's bodiless arm had left me edgy, and any sudden noise meant danger.

The sun began its descent behind the forest, leaving me little daylight to bury the body.

Whoever murdered the monk, might revisit under the cover of darkness. Whatever their motives, I didn't want to delay and suffer the warrior-monk's same fate.

I dug the shallow grave with my helmet. The dry sandy soil gave way fast to a finished burial pit just as the sun fell behind the trees. Before placing the monk's body into the shallow pit, I examined it for any further identity clues. His right forearm bulged with muscles, indicating a swordsman, yet, so far, I hadn't found a sword. The murderers must have grabbed it when they left, along with his missing belt dagger.

As I pulled the monk's body into the grave, one of his boots slid off, dropping a folded parchment note onto the ground. My fingers reached for the note, hoping it might answer some of my unsolved questions about this man. The paper bore a red wax seal embossed with two men riding the same horse. How odd, I thought, as I broke the wax seal with my fingers. I read the note's contents, then I let it fall in disbelief.

The missive mentioned my name and said,

> *Lord Robert de Borron, meet my sergeant at the Abbaye-Église of Sainte-Marie-Magdalene. He will escort you to our fortress at Montpellier after Sunday worship. Your family is at risk don't hesitate or refuse him. The Holy Mother Church is in danger too. I am a commander of the Poor Fellow-Soldiers of Christ. Lord Robert, I know your facial features even though you don't know mine. You have auburn-colored hair and a small scar above your eyebrow. I will seek you out at the fortress—come at once.*
>
> *Non nobis Domine non nobis sed nomini tuo da gloriam*

With trembling hands, I reached down once more and grasped the missive.

Why were my épouse and *fils* at risk? Whatever the answers, it didn't bode well for me and my family.

CHAPTER II

The sun sliced into the horizon as my horse galloped the final hill road into the village of Vézelay. The trail in front of me revealed the *Abbaye-Église* of Sainte-Marie-Magdalene which appeared as a nesting bird perched on a hillock.

My *soeur*, Marguerite, born two years after me, requested my appearance after making her annual pilgrimage to Sainte-Marie-Magdalene, which I now regretted. She stayed with some of our cousins a short distance from the village and enjoyed coming on the saint's feast day. After visiting for a month, she'd written to me complaining about not visiting her more often.

A sudden warning of quacking ducks caused my horse to whinny as he trotted too close to some waddling ducklings. He appeared just as edgy as I did, yet our angst didn't subside. From a dense stand of trees, I saw movement, causing my hand to reach for my sword. For a brief moment, I thought the killers had followed me, but, to my relief, out of the forest ambled several spotted cows. A short distance away, somebody called my name.

"Baron *Seigneur* de Borron," shouted a familiar voice from the entranceway of the local stone-built inn. "It is me, François. Your *soeur* has been expecting you."

"*Bonjour, mon ami*. I think the last time we spoke, we observed the feast day of Saint John the Baptizer," I said, while sliding out of my saddle.

"*Oui*, that's correct," François replied.

My *soeur* used François as her overseer, chamberlain, and groom. He had many other responsibilities too, though I didn't recall all of them. François shuffled toward me with his crooked foot and embraced me.

"It is *bon* to see you once more, Robert." He released his grip and peered into my face. His cow-sized brown eyes seldom missed anything, and his physical infirmity wasn't a hindrance. He fought and leaped with the best of men.

"Robert, have you finished writing any of your tales? Or, are you a troubadour for the count?"

"No, to both questions. Yet, I am almost finished with the tales of Merlin, the prophet for *Roi* Arthur."

He nodded. "Did you have to use any of your excellent sword skills on the road to Vézelay?"

I hesitated to answer him at this moment, waiting to tell him my misfortune later.

"So sorry for the many questions. Your horse looks tired and your face looks drawn after your journey." He pointed to the white lather coming from its withers. "Let me lead him to the local stable for some rest. Your *soeur* is upstairs, the last door on the right, and eager to see you."

"*Bon*, and when you return, we'll speak some more. However, ask the local authorities what this symbol might mean." I drew my dagger and marked the image in the sandy dirt. "Remember it and duplicate it to authorities, then afterward meet me in the tavern."

At once, François reached for my reins and led my tired steed toward the village blacksmith.

The large inn had many windows, reflecting its spacious accommodations for the throngs visiting the *Abbaye-Église* of Sainte-Marie-Magdalene. After opening the door and stepping into the tavern foyer, several patrons stopped drinking their *vin* and glared, seeing me as a stranger. The waffling odor of sweet wine combined with body sweat left me queasy. I half ignored their stares, yet my eyes still glanced at their faces. Did any number of these men murder the poor monk?

I proceeded toward the wooden stairs, which the large *vin* casks somewhat concealed. At once, I trudged up the wooden treads to a large landing where a long faded lit hallway appeared as a gloomy, narrow cave, except it had numerous doors on each side. Remembering François's directions, I walked the entire length of the inn and knocked on the last door.

"Marguerite, it is your *frère*, Robert. Please let me in." There came the *clanking* sounds of latch bolts against metal, and the door flung open.

"Robert, *mon frère*, it is so *bon* to see you once again." Marguerite stood there on the tips of her toes. We hugged and then she kissed me on both of my cheeks.

"Come in and sit near the warm fire. I know you're tired after your long trip. Please come and tell me about my *belle-soeur*, Marie, and my two little nephews," she said before I had a chance to sit.

I removed my chain mail and sat close to the fire. Then I turned to gaze fondly at Marguerite. *Mon mère* had a difficult delivery with *mon soeur*. She never recovered after her birth but stayed in a weakened state for ten years. She died on my thirtieth birthday.

"*Mon frère*," she said, interrupting my thoughts. "Please tell me about my nephew, young Brian. Is he big enough to hold a sword?"

"*Oui*, but when he raises it overhead, he falls backward."

We both laughed, with my *soeur* revealing her dimples, upturned nose, and full lips reminiscent of our *mère*.

"Did your journey go well?"

I dreaded her question.

"Robert, did you hear me?" She questioningly tilted her head.

"*Oui*, I am just tired from riding all day and need some rest. Besides, nothing unusual occurred . . . even the weather behaved itself." I hesitated in my lie to her.

"It's quite uncaring of me to keep you from your rest. Please, accept my apology. I had the proprietor of the inn prepare some bread, cheese, and white *vin* for your comfort. It's in your room next to mine. In addition, your bed is ready too. However, the inn is full of pilgrims, so you must share your bed with François. I hope you don't mind?"

"*Non*," I replied. "It doesn't matter. My tired body won't know the difference. After our reunion, I must meet François downstairs in the tavern. There's an important matter concerning our vineyards in need of discussion before we retire."

"Is it anything to which I might contribute?"

"*Non, mon chér*, we'll speak some more tomorrow. Right now, he is waiting for me."

We both rose from our chairs, with Marguerite handing me the key to my room. Once again she kissed me on my cheek.

"*Bonsoir*, Robert. Sleep well." I opened her door to leave, then stepped into the hallway and closed it.

Lying to my *soeur* made me feel guilty, because of our close relationship. We didn't keep secrets from each other. Yet, fearing for her distress, I thought it prudent not to tell her the truth.

The faded lit hallway caused my palms to sweat as I passed each of the numerous closed doors. Along the floor, I spied a long black cloth similar to my attackers' head scarves. Might the murderers at once appear from behind one of these many doors? To my right one door edged open. I reached for the pommel of my sword. After which, I pulled my sword out of its scabbard as a meager-clad woman appeared.

"*Bonjour* pilgrim, fear not," said the sultry-sounding woman. "I see you just arrived, and I know you're tired, *oui*?"

"*Oui*, it's true, but who are you?"

"Have no fear, stranger, my body is here to help you relax. You look lonesome and in need of companionship. Please come into my quarters, and for a few pieces of silver my pleasures will lift your spirit." The woman's numerous ringed fingers gestured for me to come into her room as her other hand held out a large-nippled bare breast.

"I have no need of a prostitute for I am happy with my marriage." She came closer and rubbed both her bare breasts against me, still trying to lure me into her room.

"You know, stranger, Sainte-Marie-Magdalene prostituted herself," she whispered into my ear as my hand pushed her aside.

I detected my lips curl with anger. "Can you read?" I inquired still trying to avoid her advances.

"*Non*," came her weak reply.

"Then spend some of your silver to have a priest teach you and leave this life of sin."

"You are a damn fool, *mon ami*." Then a slight laugh came from deep down in her throat and she further spoke, "There aren't any other women of pleasure for leagues around."

She retreated into her dark room and closed the door, locking it. I proceeded down the stairs and met François in a well-lit corner of the tavern.

"Was Lady Marguerite pleased to see you?" François shoved a cup of *vin* in front of me. "Of course, she missed you; silly of me to ask such a question. Let us now talk." His eyes searched my face.

"Have you seen any unusual strangers here in the tavern or on the road?"

"*Oui*, but *non*," François oddly replied. "This village is on a pilgrimage route both to the *Abbaye-Église* of Sainte-Marie-Magdalene and Santiago de Compostela. Most are strangers seeking to view holy relics of our apostles. Their dress will look different just as the kingdoms they come from are different. Why do you ask?"

"Follow me outside so we can speak in private, for what I am about to say is disturbing."

We both guzzled our *vin* and then strolled toward the door. Once outside, the breezy late-night autumn air cleared my mind.

"Promise me, François, you won't speak of our conversation to Lady Marguerite."

"*Oui*, I promise, *Seigneur* Robert. Anything you tell me stops right here." His brown eyes grew bigger in anticipation of my forthcoming words.

"*Très bien, mon ami*, you are a loyal member of our family, and you will keep this a secret."

He nodded in agreement, and I told him every gruesome detail, including the note and the harm it proclaimed toward our family. After I had finished my recount of the terrible event, François's forehead broke out in small beads of sweat. He stood there looking at the dark ground in silence as if preparing himself for questions.

"What does this warrior-monk at Montpellier want of you? Why did they murder the man?"

"I don't know. His note has forced me to leave earlier than planned. Tomorrow, after Sunday mass, I will tell Marguerite about leaving early. As soon as you wake, ride to the local warrior-monk commandery, show them this note and tell them what has happened."

He took the note from my hands and with trembling fingers shoved it behind his surcoat belt.

"However, after you visit the commandery, prepare to leave at once. Convince my *soeur* to leave without alarming her. She can't know the truth. Tell her any manner of a lie, whatever it requires."

"But *Seigneur* Robert, I can't lie to her." He shuffled one of his boots in the dirt.

"Telling her a lie will act as a shield to protect us from evil. Besides, I command you to do this, *mon ami*. Both you and Marguerite are to travel directly to my brother-in-law's *château* at Montbéliard. Soon a letter will arrive from me for my épouse, Baroness Marie, also instructing her and my children to do the same. I will send another dispatch upon my arrival at Montpellier. Hopefully, this letter will contain details of why I am there."

"Damn these men who threaten us. Do you want me to try a less-traveled road to *Château* Montbéliard?"

"*Oui*, but better yet, search for any navigable river and barge that will transport you there faster. I plan to do the same when leaving here tomorrow. Now let's catch some sleep, but first you check the village for dark-dressed strangers." My right arm slipped around his broad taut shoulders and gave him a tight hug.

"God and His Son will protect us until we reach our rightful destination," I said. I then proceeded back inside to my room for some much-needed rest. At once, I wrote a quick note to my épouse, Baroness Marie, telling her to take our *fils* to her *frère's château* at Montbéliard. The next day, I would entrust my dispatch to one of the *abbaye* monks to deliver to my *épouse*.

Even though my tiredness pressed on my chest as a triple set of chain mail, it didn't help me in falling asleep. Also, my thoughts bounced and raced similar to a herd of deer. The unknown day ahead made my stomach stiffen as a twisted rope. Lying there, the morning seemed far distant to me. All of a sudden, my body flinched from a light rapping sound coming from our door, followed by the familiar whispering voice of my *soeur*.

"Robert, are you ready to leave for the *église*?" Marguerite asked.

"*Non*, not yet," I replied. "Let me dress first."

"All right, but hurry, mass starts soon. Don't you hear the bells?"

"*Oui!*" I murmured through the wooden door. Even my dressing commotion didn't disturb François from his steady snoring. "Wait for me in front of the inn. It won't take long for me to don my clothes." At last, she left as her soft clicking heels diminished on the wooden floor.

I glanced out the open window and witnessed the early morning sun's rays bathing the *abbaye-église* in shades of gold, yellow, and orange colors. Its honey amber-colored brilliance enchanted me and then beckoned me to come at once.

In haste, I fumbled with my clothes, yet cautious to hide my dagger in the sleeve of my aketon. I left François and his snoring and tiptoed down the corridor. Once I reached the stairway, my feet scrambled down the steps, after which I trotted toward the front entrance, grabbed the door, and hurried outside.

To my right paced Marguerite. "Robert, let's leave now, there are just a few bell rings left before the service starts." She grabbed my arm as we ran the uphill road toward the *église*.

"Oh, Robert, François forgot to give you this message yesterday. Instead, he gave it to me."

I quickly opened the note and read its contents.

Seigneur Robert, I talked to numerous people in the village and commandery. None of them were familiar with the ring's symbols. Though, one peasant said he saw three dark-dressed riders go by his hut yesterday.
Your obedient servant,
François

"What did François say?" my sister asked.

"Nothing, just about our vineyard production." Quickly, I stuck the note into my sword belt.

The urgency of the constant *gonging* bells made me scurry even faster. My longer running strides caused me to yank Marguerite behind me.

"Slow down, Robert, you will cause me to fall," she said, while huffing as we approached the *église* entrance.

"You said we needed to hurry, and here we are just in time. Listen, the *église* bells have stopped ringing."

The front of the *église* had three downward pointing half-moon-shaped tympanum entrances, with each funneling people into its interior. "See, we aren't the last arrivals," I said, experiencing a slight grin. While we waited to gain entrance, I looked up toward the face of the *église*. The archivolt, over the larger central doorway, held a bas-relief of Christ with his outstretched arms passing judgment over our final days. Once we entered, I knew why we had gained entrance with such ease. The narthex itself appeared the size of a large *église*. As we stood there waiting to enter the nave, my *soeur* pointed to an archivolt over the inside doors.

"Look, Robert, this carved stone scene represents Christ and the Pentecost." I turned to see. "He and his apostles are preaching to the heathens. Notice the heathens' heads are akin to animals or monsters on the lintel."

However, I saw something more. The mandorla surrounding Christ started radiating a snow-colored light. His form seemed to move out of His shell-enclosed surrounding, and one of His hands pointed toward me. At the same time, several stone-carved apostles did the same. With sweating palms, I rubbed my eyes in disbelief and staggered forward. At once, the archivolt now appeared stone still, and the bright lights disappeared. What had I just imagined?

"Where is the chancel?" I asked my *soeur*.

"Robert, don't you see it?"

I turned toward a central interior entrance, which opened to a long narrow Romanesque arched nave. The long crucifer-built *église* extended with unbelievable length, making the altar table a stone speck in the distance.

We proceeded into the nave while hoping to sit as close to the chancel as possible. I counted more than a hundred stone columns supporting the long narrow nave. Each column had an elaborately designed capital with stone-chiseled biblical scenes. One column capital, in particular, caught my eye as we searched for a suitable spot to observe the mass. Two stone-carved men milled grain, one of them poured his contents into a hopper while the other held a sack with one hand and turned a grinding wheel with the other.

"Robert, I see you're looking at those two stone-carved men." Her smile indicated she wanted to explain.

"One is Moses pouring the grain into the hopper, which symbolizes the Old Testament. The other man is Saint Paul holding the finished product, the New Testament."

Her explanation of the two holy men looked plausible, but I didn't care. It left me wondering if she had spent too much time at the *église* imagining such things.

We found an excellent location to observe the mass near the presbytery. This gave us an unobstructed view of the altar. The sudden jingling sound of bells, which came from a swinging sandalwood-smelling incense burner, announced the beginning procession of religious officials. After reaching the altar, they seated themselves in their choir seats, and the service began.

We knelt to pray, and, to my disbelief, an unseen female voice started speaking to me, which forced me to sway forward. I looked around for that person, but all I observed were many bowed heads and clasped hands. The voice kept saying my name. I seemed to hear it above the droning sounds of the priest's liturgy. The words emanated from under the altar or so I thought. However, many other hidden places made it possible for the voice to come forth. All of a sudden, my vision turned black. That caused me to whisper. "Oh, *mon Dieu*, I am losing my mind."

Marguerite punched my ribs. "Robert, hush. You are disturbing the others."

Swirling red and blue lights replaced my sight. Then a blurry image formed of a fortress *château* followed with a door carving of a splayed-shaped cross. The tender, feminine voice gave me instructions. "Seek out the city of Montpellier and the commandery of the Poor Fellow-Soldiers of Christ," in her soft, distinctive tone. "Robert, there is a book about our Lord's cup, which is kept at the fortress *château*. Pursue a battle-scarred *chevalier* of Christ. He's the holy keeper of the book. Beware, an evil man aims to use it for his own gain. Afterward, he will destroy it and now its future is in your hands."

CHAPTER III

The voice and vision ended. Kneeling parishioners surrounded me as they did before, acting as if nothing happened. My eyes surveyed the chancel and nave, and not one person seemed disturbed. Even the priest continued his uninterrupted droning liturgy. Then it struck me with certainty. My mind has failed. The devil now possesses me. How am I to obtain his release? How odd, my whole body stung with a sense of incredulity, leaving a prickling sensation over my entire skin. However, the bodiless voice sounded angelic. My mind ached to know its identity, demon or not. She had smothered me with her sense of urgency and left me with a sacred task. This didn't sound demonic in nature, but my mind wasn't right.

I never questioned the veracity of such visions from others, yet considered myself far from the saintly hierarchy of those worthy enough in such spiritual matters. However, this day appeared different.

After the service had ended, we walked back to the inn. I made my excuses to Marguerite. I didn't mention my vision or the female voice to her. Instead, I lied yet again and said that unexpected financial matters waited for me in Montpellier. I knew François expected me to tell the truth to Marguerite.

She was obviously saddened by this announcement. "Robert, when will I see you next?" Tears started to roll down her cheeks.

"Maybe in a month; yet expect a letter from me sooner."

"Our cousins expected us to visit them. In your honor, they prepared a large banquet. You disappoint me, Robert."

"You have my pledge when I return, we'll spend a fortnight together and the same with our cousins." I hugged her, wiped the tears from her eyes, and kissed her on her cheek. My pledge and embrace seemed to calm her displeasure, for she kissed me the same and held me in her embrace.

"Robert, I will pray daily and light many candles in the chapel for your safe return." She stepped away as her green eyes welled with more tears. "*Au revoir, mon frère*, travel in peace."

"Same to you, *mon chér soeur.*" She grabbed the door handle to the inn and then vanished inside. I used the sleeve of my aketon to wipe away my own tears, which helped me see clearer as I walked to fetch my boarded horse.

The blacksmith's stables sat behind the *abbaye* hidden from the road. A monk from the monastery supervised the shop.

"Are you *Seigneur* Robert de Borron?" the monk asked.

"*Oui*, I am."

The blacksmith monk gave me the reins to my horse and continued.

"François, your *chevalier*, directed me to prepare your horse while you were at mass.

He let me pack a sack of oats, a skin of our local *vin,* and I informed him of an honest bargeman in Dijon by the name Rémy. This bargeman is noted throughout central Burgundy for his speed."

Afterward, the *moine* said a blessing for my safe travel. I grabbed both of his coarse hands, slipped several silver coins in them, and thanked him for his hospitality. Then I mounted my horse to leave.

François had packed my saddlebags with pungent smelling Roquefort cheese and several loaves of crusty-grained bread for my trip to Dijon. In the other saddlebag, my fingers touched my writing quills and sheets of crinkled parchment. At the bottom of the leather bags, he had placed extra clothing to wear. I spurred my horse's flanks and then galloped out of Vézelay. I looked back from another hilltop, and the *église* caught my eyes, comparable to a green and yellow-colored jeweled stone on a bent ring finger. It reminded me of *mon épouse's* ring.

The monk told me the travel time to Dijon might take me three days on horseback and then another half-day for me to reach the Saône River. He said a capable bargeman, steering the swift currents from the Alps, might transport me down to Lyon and the river Rhône in record time. From there, the mountain feeder streams accelerated the river toward the Mediterranean Sea and Montpellier. If I used a barge, most of my river travel might keep me protected from any brigands or murderers and anyone following me, besides offering a degree of stealth.

I used deer paths instead of roads. Even though the thorny hedgerows hugged the trail, my sure-footed horse still galloped toward Dijon. We stopped just a few times to slake our thirst in the woodland streams. The first day, as the sun sank toward the horizon, we stopped in a stand of beech trees, which afforded me a broken view of a vineyard-covered hill road. Here I constructed a camp for the night. What daylight remained left me a view of the circling road below the hill.

After unsaddling my horse, I rubbed him down, and then fed him some oats. As I reached into my saddlebags for some cheese and bread, my eyes caught sight of distant movement. To my horror, I saw three dark-dressed riders galloping down the hillside road. I fell forward into some musty smelling leaves and then crawled toward a web of saplings to obtain a better view. They appeared similar to the three men who had murdered the warrior-monk. Not taking any chances, my trembling hands grabbed my horse's reins and yanked downward for him to lie down. Well trained by me, in past instances he could lower himself to the ground with little noise, thus mimicking a graceful dancer. If my eyes deceived me, I had nothing to fear. If the same killers, my secluded spot protected me, I hoped.

The sun dipped behind the many hills surrounding the forest, leaving me with just one fear. I knew my horse smelled my angst and might whinny, thus exposing our hiding place in the quiet forest. I grabbed his forelock and rubbed it several times. I whispered into one ear, hoping to keep him still.

The sole noise we heard came from a family of chattering squirrels, followed by the hoofbeats of the three horses. The riders sped by my hidden position, didn't glance in our direction, and disappeared down the dense forest road. Maybe these men weren't the monk's killers.

With an exhale of my breath, followed by crossing myself, I finished my cheese and bread and washed it down with a third of my skin of *vin*. Riding all day and now a full stomach caused my eyes to flutter. Yet, before falling asleep, my fingertips grasped my sword pommel and my other hand my dagger hilt.

The next several days my lathered horse raced on while stopping little, other than feeding and watering him. The constant fear for Marie, my *fils*, and Marguerite's safety left me sleepless each night. Lucky for me a full moon guided my way at night.

Late afternoon my horse trotted near Dijon. Suddenly, a thick stone wall appeared that deceived my eyes. At first, I thought it a small circle of stone cliffs, which at once became the fortress walls of Dijon.

The blacksmith at Vézelay told me to see a bargeman named Rémy, who lived in a wattle and daub, two-story house on the other side of town. The snorting of pigs and the bawling herds of cows indicated market day, but the animals created obstacles for me to reach Rémy's home. As my stomach grew tighter with each passing delay, the immediate threat to *mon soeur, mon épouse*, and *mon* children increased. Toward the horizon, the sun fell closer between the town's chimneys. Just as it disappeared, his house came into view with its crisscross-timbered design. Its large size reflected Rémy's wealth.

A rotund woman opened the front door just as I dismounted my horse.

"*Bonjour,* stranger. Look for Rémy in his garden; that's where he'll see you. Please, follow me." She escorted me out back near his herb garden.

"*Merci beaucoup,*" I replied, thinking she had today escorted numerous people to Rémy.

"*Bonjour, mon ami,*" came the voice of a narrow, tree-limbed shaped man, yet his shoulders didn't match the rest of his thin stature. They appeared as large wooden knots perched on top of each of his arms.

"One of the blessed *frères* from Vézelay has sent you for transportation, *oui?* Most of the strangers to my house are referred by the monks of the *abbaye.*"

"*Oui,* you're quite right, *Monsieur* Rémy, and now the shortage of time is my worst enemy. My name is Baron *Seigneur* Robert de Borron, and business calls me at once to Montpellier. Your barges are noted throughout Burgundy for their speed and your boating expertise, I hear tell."

"That's true, but Montpellier is quite a distance from Dijon." He rubbed his chin as if to deny my request. "It will take about a fortnight to arrive there, and that's with excellent weather. Also, there are other clients who desire my services in the next several days. How much are you willing to pay?" Rémy further rubbed his stubby whiskers and paused speaking, then continued. "We'll come across some portage, for this is the dry season, and river levels are much lower. Is this a problem, Lord de Borron?"

"*Non*, and if you transport me there in fewer than ten days, I'll give you a bonus of twenty silver coins."

"Before you commit yourself to give me a reward, first hear my standard fee for such a trip. With such a long journey, my two grown *fils* must help. Otherwise, your time of arrival is impossible to meet. My fee, including food, totals fifty silver coins and that isn't negotiable."

The old bargeman's firm demeanor indicated a parsimonious man of business while knowing all too well he had me at a disadvantage.

"If I don't reach Montpellier in ten days or less, you can keep my bonus. Besides, I have a reputation to uphold."

"We have an agreement, *Monsieur* Rémy. However, I demand that we leave tomorrow at first light or sooner."

"Do you have half the total agreed payment before I leave to buy the horses and supplies?"

"*Oui,* let me pay you now." My hand reached down into my boot to obtain one of my pokes of coins. Afterward, I counted out twenty-five silver coins into *Monsieur* Rémy's hands. He, in turn, placed the coins next to his surcoat sleeve and rolled them up tight against his arm muscle. We both shook hands, he bowed in respect and started to leave.

"*Monsieur* Rémy, grant me one final request. Please, don't say anything about me or our destination to anybody, not even your sons. My business in Montpellier is of a secret nature, and I prefer to remain anonymous."

"*Non* problem, *mon* Baron *Seigneur* de Borron. Every married man of business must have his secret *amant*, even if she's quite far away." He then gave me a wink. "I'll return after you are asleep and obtain your horse from the local stable. In the meantime, tell my *épouse* you're lodging with us tonight. She will fix you some supper before retiring. For now, *bonsoir.* Before dawn tomorrow morning, meet me at my front door."

He left through a back-garden gate and disappeared down a narrow tree-covered lane. I thought it best for maintaining my secrecy, even though a tinge of guilt stuck in my throat. His wrong assumption helped further my actual purpose.

Turning around to proceed inside Rémy's house, once again his *épouse* met me at the back doorway and hustled me into a first-floor bedroom.

"*Monsieur,* I hope you enjoy our accommodations. Listen for me a little later. You'll have your supper upon my return."

My eyes gazed at a large feather bed and from an open window came the sound of *clopping* hooves of sheep traveling to market. My exhausted body stumbled to the bed, just making it in time before I fell over. After riding for days, I readied myself for a long, long nap.

Without warning, loud bangs came from my door and then the voice of a young boy.

"I am Gabriel, and I have your saddlebags."

I used every bit of my remaining energy to retrace my steps and then opened the door.

"*Monsieur*, here are your saddlebags," the boy said, as he handed me both. "I saw in your saddlebags writing quills, ink, and many blank parchments. Some of it fell out when I unloaded your horse. I didn't spill any of the ink or damage anything. You'll find it just as before. Do you know how to write?"

"*Oui*, I am a storyteller and poet. Though, other serious issues have kept me from further writing."

"Your horse is bedded for the night. Tomorrow, if you need him, tell the madame of the house you want Gabriel to prepare your horse. The blacksmith is my *père*."

Gabriel stood there still and silent, obvious to me he wouldn't leave until he received a tip. His noticeable ribs and deformed hand, which pointed toward his wrist, didn't deter his energy. His right hand reached out quick as a striking snake, further insisting on his tip.

"Gabriel, here are two silver coins for your effort." I placed the coins into his small hand. "When you come back tomorrow morning and help me load my horse, you can earn another two."

He started to leave but stopped before closing the door. "*Merci beaucoup, monsieur!*" He then gave me a large grin. Just as he began to close the door, my supper arrived. Gabriel held up his coins for the woman to see and vanished. She smiled her approval and placed the large tray on a small table. After finishing all my food and *vin*, sleep beckoned, but my worries concerned my *épouse*, Marie, *mon fils*, and Marguerite's safety traveling to my brother-in-law's *château*.

Before leaving *Château* Borron to visit Marguerite, my writing about the Celtic legend of Merlin occupied most of my time. Now it seemed my worried days came with little time to finish his story. I hoped in the next couple of days to start writing once more. I looked forward to a peaceful barge ride down the Saône and Rhône Rivers. Finally, sleep came. Then, without warning, a spine-tingling scream awakened me from my slumber.

CHAPTER IV

Was the scream a nightmare or real? Darkness still surrounded me as shrill sounds further reached my conscious mind, followed by numerous thumping feet.

"It is Gabriel, the blacksmith's *fils!*" a voice cried out, as I bounded from my bed. My room glowed; however, not from my lit candles, but from the considerable hand-held torches flashing past my open window. Hearing the young boy's name hastened me to dress and then with dread I left, wanting to investigate. I ran toward the front entrance door and grabbed my padded aketon covering and sword belt off the bedpost. At once, I met people coming out of their homes holding candlelit lanterns.

"What's happening?" I shouted to several sprinting men.

"To the blacksmith's stables!" One local villager yelled in reply. "Are you the *seigneur* staying at Rémy's house?"

"*Oui*, but how did you know?"

"The young blacksmith's boy said you were from Northern Burgundy and a writer and poet. *Monsieur*, follow us, for it appears something terrible has happened!" the second man exclaimed while motioning for me to follow.

As I followed their lanterns, we raced toward the center of town and the blacksmith's shop. Up ahead a narrow line of undulating torches blazed a path for all to follow. We arrived at the blacksmith's stables a short time after six men and two women had gathered around one of the stalls. At first, the shadowy light from several torches didn't reveal much. I shoved my way closer to the inner circle of people. Then my eyes caught the slight swing of an object in one of the small horse stalls.

"*Mère de Dieu!*" The words blurted out of my mouth for all to hear. This evoked an immediate response from the entire crowd to cross their chests. There in front of me hung the young boy, Gabriel. A tied cloth bound his mouth; both tied feet dangled in the air, which measured about an arm's length from touching the stable's straw-strewed ground. Both of his bound hands held a long rope thrown over a large wooden beam in the blacksmith's ceiling. His contorted palms faced backward, yet his deformed hand had come forward resting on his forearm. His eyes bulged with fear. Buried in the middle of his chest protruded the hilt of a dagger and a note. His torturers had used "strapade" before stabbing him. I remembered several tales of this heinous practice from the inquisitors to force confessions, but I didn't realize its aftermath until now. My mind pictured the young boy pulled up toward the beam, with both hands tied behind him, and then repeatedly dropped. His shoulder joints now protruded from dislocation, and both collarbones did the same. Pure diabolical evil had motivated this terrible act. However, to my horror, the note had my name written on it and where I stayed.

One man, who rushed in after us, appeared the boy's *père*. He cut the rope and stared at the note while holding the small limp body with his muscular arms. Large tears rolled down his cheeks and he gazed toward me. The crowd of villagers now turned from their whispering prayers of salvation to grumbling sounds of revenge. Just as I turned to leave, I heard Rémy's familiar voice.

"Lord de Borron, we must leave at once before the crowd's blood lust becomes indiscriminate and suspects you, a stranger, the culprit."

Monsieur Rémy grabbed my arm and motioned for me to follow him.

"Why would somebody do such a horrible act and place a note with my name on the dead boy's chest?" I asked while I ran alongside Rémy toward his home.

"I don't know, Lord Robert," he replied, gasping for air as we approached his house.

My horse stood packed and saddled, with my bargeman's rotund *épouse* holding the reins to the horses. It appeared Rémy had told the young boy to saddle my horse earlier. Her turned-down mouth sobbed with grief, and one hand wiped tears from her eyes with a lace-edged cloth.

"Rémy, *mon mari*, please, guard your back," she said, as he gave her a kiss *au revoir.*

To my surprise, for an older man, he leaped up onto his saddle.

"Baron *Seigneur* de Borron, please mount at once so we can ride the hell out of here," he demanded, as a torch-lit angry mob approached.

Rémy was right, they were coming for me. Yet I hesitated to leave.

"Please, wait!" I shouted above the cries for revenge. "Madame, please accept this purse of silver coins for Gabriel's burial and have the priest to say prayers for his salvation." She reached out a hand to grasp my small sack of coins, made the sign of the cross with her other.

"Bless you, stranger. You are kind. I will give your donated purse to our priest as soon as mass starts. *Au revoir, mon ami.*"

Our horses raced out of town.

We galloped our steeds for half a league before coming to a halt.

"Why are we stopping?" I asked Rémy.

"There are some pack horses with our supplies hidden at the bottom of this deer path to your right. I brought them here after dark yesterday. It's not always safe to leave town in the light of day, for robbers have followed my travelers and me."

"What about the villagers seeking revenge?"

Rémy tied the packhorses to each other and said nothing.

"Do you think I killed the boy?" I asked while looking straight into his eyes for an answer.

"*Non*, you didn't murder Gabriel. Whoever killed him wanted you confined."

I sighed in relief.

"I heard you snoring when I brought the horses from the stable to my house. Gabriel had just helped me load and saddle our horses. He hoped to acquire his bonus from you the next day. That's all Gabriel spoke about as I left him alone in the stable. He never feared any stranger, above all in knowing the possibility of earning some spare coins. His livelihood depended on hanging around my house. I am the one who caused his death."

Even in the dim light of the morning, I saw Rémy's face had turned white from his self-imposed guilt.

"Did any of the villagers notice strangers lurking near the stable after you left?"

"*Non*, most slept. However, Gabriel's *père* said yesterday he saw three dark-dressed riders pass near his shop at sunset. He did notice one rider missing an arm."

At once, my stomach clenched, knowing these killers came for me. Yet, the dead monk and young boy turned it even more, knowing I caused their deaths.

"How long will it take before we reach the Saône?"

"The villagers are still following us, but there is a faster path to the river. My *fils* are with the barge at Saint-Jean-de-Losne waiting for us. I know a hidden trail that will save us several leagues but it's difficult for us to travel. In addition, most of the villagers aren't familiar with this route."

"*Bon*, let's start now," I said, as we mounted our horses to leave.

The horses stepped gingerly onto the trail of thick tangled wild grape vines and flank-high dense thorn bushes. My mind doubted the quickness of Rémy's trail, yet after a short while, I heard the distant sound of rushing water. Our horses approached a small meadow clearing that overlooked the river Saône. Below I viewed a long shallow barge with a large sail flapping in a strong river breeze.

Rémy pointed toward his barge and called to the two men on deck, who waved in return. "Baudouin and Benoit, prepare to shove off," he shouted. "Our traveler is in need of arriving at Montpellier in less than a fortnight!"

The horses started their slow descent down the steep riverbank. For some unknown reason, my mind told me to look back just as my horse started its downward path. There in the tree line, from which we had just emerged, I saw movement. Fear struck my stomach comparable to a striking fist, indicating the appearance of my unknown stalkers. I knew it wasn't the revengeful town mob, but the three dark riders or maybe more.

"Rémy, look! They are here. And it's not the village mob." I spurred my horse to move faster.

"Grab the crossbows!" he yelled to the men on the barge.

At once, both men disembarked, each clutching a crossbow and a fist full of quarrels.

"Hurry, *mon ami*, so we can board the boat. My *fils* will try to stop them until we load all the pack horses. Head for the boat ramp at once!"

Our horses slid down the steep bank on their hindquarters. My horse did the same. Their hooves made loud *clopping* sounds as they moved up the plank leading into the belly of the barge. Right away, my horse hesitated, but not from entering the barge. His ears twisted toward the hissing sound of the quarrels *thudding* against the hull of the barge. Then I saw the whites of his eyes rolling in fear. From my angle, our ambusher's quarrels came from the dark forest. Their aim changed at once, telling me the killers drew closer with the thought of outflanking us.

"Rémy, tell your *fils* to concentrate their aim between those two chestnut trees," I hollered, as he leaped on shore to untie his barge.

"*Oui*, Baron Robert, hurry and grab the boarding plank and pull it into the barge!" He raced toward his *fils*. I jumped off my horse, landing on the top of the plank. Then I bent down, grabbed the plank with both hands and jerked twice, and at last, it fell inside the barge. More quarrels hit the hull and I didn't see Rémy or his *fils*. Were we to die here on this barge reminiscent of old Viking warriors?

CHAPTER V

From the woods came the piercing scream, which caused a momentary lull in the crossbow arrows. This left just enough time for both *fils* to retreat and race toward the barge. Rémy's arm motioned for them to hurry faster as he made a giant leap over the left gunwale. Afterward, he grabbed the tiller of the barge. Both *fils* made a hurried jump, collided against the hull of the barge with their hands clung to the gunwale.

Rémy steered his barge so its sail caught a stiff breeze, which caused it to lurch forward to midriver. After each *fils* had struggled to climb into the barge, a barrage of quarrels struck the port side, sounding similar to hail pelting a wooden roof.

Rémy maneuvered to the opposite bank and out of the range of our attackers. After a quarter league down the river, a smile came to his face and then he spoke.

"Just another day in an old bargeman's life. Baron *Seigneur* de Borron, let me introduce you to my two *fils*," he said as he calmly manned the tiller. "The tall skinny one is *mon fils* Baudouin and the stocky young one catching his breath is Benoit. The name Baudouin means 'brave' *ami*, which he is to all he meets. My other *fils* Benoit, born later, represents 'blessedness.' My *épouse* almost lost him at birth."

I shook hands with both, noticing each had the grip of a swordsman.

"You and your *fils* move and fight as soldiers, *Monsieur* Rémy."

"*Oui*, the *duc* enlisted us as soldiers, but later we purchased our service to him. The *scutage* tax we pay is far less than the profits we earn from the barge work. Besides, our past fighting experience for the *duc*, as you can see, protects our flourishing trade. Yet, I must ask who is trying to kill you? It's important for me to know so I can meet our agreement's time arrival."

"These pursuers are just as unknown to me as they are to you. Not until several days ago, did I know they were stalking me. However, there's some more information I must tell you." He listened to every detail with my emphasis on threats to my family. Rémy rubbed his black beard when I mentioned these men hadn't yet killed me.

"So, you're not traveling to see a distant young *mademoiselle*, but traveling to a Templar fortress at Montpellier. Anyone who murders a Soldier of Christ, above all a sergeant or *chevalier* is quite vicious. From what you have said, these men must have a powerful supporter. It appears they're well-paid executioners and their benefactor desires something of value. Relax, *mon ami*, they can't catch us. If the wind, fast currents, and water levels stay the same, we'll arrive in Arles in less than a fortnight. Even if they hire a bargeman to chase us, I am the fastest bargeman on any river in Gaul."

His reassurance helped me some, especially he and his *fils'* abilities to fight. Yet, an unknown tingling danger crawled over my skin.

"Here, Lord de Borron," Benoit said as he handed me a skin of *vin*. "Take a large swig of a *bon vin*, it will steady your nerves." I grabbed the leather container, stuck its spout between my lips, and took several large swallows. Benoit seemed interested in what I just divulged to his *père*.

"*Mon ami*, one thought has gnawed at my mind while we threw them off our trail. Why didn't they kill you when you came upon the dead warrior-*moine*?"

Benoit had used his idle time to reflect on my past dire situation and came to the same conclusion, which had troubled me.

"Your question has several possible answers, *mon ami*. They didn't recognize me at first, or I have something they want, and they will kill me later. My thoughts have struggled with their evil motives since leaving Vézelay. My family concerns me the most. These monsters are capable of any manner of heinous crimes and don't forget what happened to poor little Gabriel."

"*Oui*, you're right about their evil intent. For your sake, maybe the commander at Montpellier will answer your questions," Benoit commented, as he used a pole to push the barge from the muddy bank.

A full moon rose above the tree line, casting its long narrow finger of white light across the surface of the water. I reclined against the hull of the barge, taking several larger gulps of *vin*. We sped faster downstream as I eased into a deep slumber until sunrise.

"Did you sleep well Baron *Seigneur* de Borron?" Rémy asked awakening me, as a glistening thick morning mist covered the river.

"Not satisfactory under yesterday's circumstances."

"Here." He handed me a soft rag. "Use this cloth to wipe the dew off your chain mail and clothes, not until we reach Chalon will this fog disappear. For now, it will slow us with little visibility to see. We'll dock at a secluded location at nightfall near there that my *fils* and I know. We're always cautious, not just with the threat of highwaymen, but also from river pirates. At the landing, you can stretch your legs while Baudouin sees after our portage downstream."

I didn't want to hear this. "Damn it, Rémy. I can't afford any delays." My foot then kicked the side of his barge. "And I don't want to stretch my legs."

"I understand your distress, but one of our trusted *amis* helps resupply our barge. Hopefully, we'll pick up some extra wind and regain some time."

As the morning progressed, the mist disappeared, and I used my spare time to write. It wasn't until late afternoon that we sailed into a small wooded cove. Benoit leaped over the gunwale, landed on the shore, and tied the barge line to a large willow tree.

"We'll rest here tonight while Baudouin meets our *ami* near the outskirts of Chalon." Then he pitched the rope to his *fils*.

"We must continue. It's still some time before sunset," I said, once again voicing my fears. "This is a perfect place for our pursuers to attack us in our sleep."

"It might look that way," Rémy responded. "The cove, the large rock canyon, and the brush-covered entrance you won't see. It's similar to a stone fortress surrounding the inlet so the rock walls will protect us from attack. The river is too shallow up ahead, and we can't afford for my barge to ground on a sandbar at night. Once my *ami* has my second barge ready, the portage to it isn't far, maybe a third of a league. When we arrive, we'll pick up speed with the stronger currents."

I knew I had to trust them, so I set my mind on other things. I used the afternoon light and cool shade of the inlet to further my writings about the mysterious seer, Merlin. He'd always fascinated me ever since my boyhood and *mon mère* told me stories and legends from her Kingdom of Brittany. My *épouse's frère, Comte* de Montbéliard, encouraged me to write them down.

"What are you writing about?" Benoit asked. "But if it's personal, please, tell me. There're plenty of duties that I need attending to."

"*Non*, it's not personal. Let me read you some of my written words." For some strange reason, I always felt compelled to tell Merlin's story. Even now, more so. The closer I came to the Templar fortress, the more obsessed this sensation took hold of me.

He sat down on a wooden keg with his green eyes focused on my lips. He listened to each of my spoken words and commented not once. The grin on his face spoke approval of what he heard. After reading a small portion of what I'd written, he spoke.

"This legend sounds similar to what I have heard about the great Merlin. However, in my story, he predicts to his *mère* that a man and confessor named Blaise, will author a book about the *Sangraal* or the 'Cup of Christ.' Merlin had the ability to see into the past and predict the future. The Celtic seer spoke of things no mortal man dares comprehend, so the legends say."

"That part is interesting, my *mère* never spoke of this man, Blaise. Did your story say what happened to his holy book?" My piqued curiosity now came forth, above all since my new written narrative lacked additional stories.

"Nothing particular, though some say the devil destroyed his book after he saw his Heavenly *Père*."

A sudden thumping of boots coming from the dense forest distracted my thoughts, which caused my heartbeats to jump into my throat.

"Who goes there?" asked Rémy. "Answer my question at once or suffer the sting of my crossbow."

"Don't shoot, it's me, Baudouin," came his *fils'* immediate reply. "I have urgent and terrible news." With one quick leap, his boots found their mark on the wooden planks and he started speaking with exhausted gulps for more air.

"Our *ami* is dead," Baudouin said, trying to catch his breath. "Whoever killed him took our supplies. He had just died, for warmth still came from his hand. It appears they are tracking us along the riverbanks."

"How did they kill him?" I asked, fearing his answer.

"I observed several dagger wounds to his chest, and they had slit his throat. Then I spied a large sword puncture mark on his back. I didn't have time to bury our *ami*, for fear they might see me. Afterward, I hid my horse in a thick grove of hedges not far from here. I didn't want the three riders to see me enter the secret entrance to the canyon."

Once again, the three riders.

"So, you saw them, and they followed you?" I asked.

"*Oui* and *non*, I didn't recognize their faces, nor did they see me, for they were masked. And *oui*, they didn't see me for I used stealth to sneak away. Though one of them limped as they left. I spotted several beached logs up the river, which I noticed earlier. After hiding my horse, I crept toward the logs and used them to float down the river."

"We must leave at once, Lord de Borron," Rémy ordered. "We won't stop anymore, *mon ami*, other than picking up Baudouin's horse. These men are smarter than I thought. Our next stop is Lyon.

The river is most difficult at Gigny. We might have to use our poles to push the barge past the low spots. *Seigneur* Robert, are your arms and shoulders strong enough to help?"

"You know I am a writer, yet my shoulders and arms are strong from using a sword and dagger."

"*Bon,* now catch some rest for you'll need it." He pushed the barge away from shore with a tall pole.

The full moon made navigation easy to see, thus reaching the village of Gigny sooner than expected. Our arrival came with a sudden scraping sound and thud from the bottom of the hull, followed with an unexpected lurch. The stern of the barge turned at once toward midstream.

"Grab one of the poles; we're stuck on some rocks," Rémy said, motioning to all three of us. "I'll seize the gangplank and afterward unload the horses until the barge is pushed to midstream. Lord de Borron, you're in charge of the anchor. Once the barge is free of the rocks, anchor it so she won't drift toward midriver."

I reached for one of the poles. My hands and arms held its heavy weight, which made it difficult to keep upright. After he had unloaded the gangplanks, followed by the horses and supplies, he gave the signal to start pushing with our poles. A persistent creaking sound issued forth from the riverbed that seemed to last an eternity, as the bow drifted toward midstream.

"We've hit some rocks. There's a crack in the hull!" screamed Benoit.

To my horror, water gushed forth from the bow and the barge tilted to the starboard side. My stomach surged with fear. If the barge sank, I envisioned us as speared fish unable to escape.

"Lord Robert!" shouted Rémy. "Drop your pole and grab two wide boards, some nails, and a hammer. They're in that large wooden chest at the stern of the barge."

I raced back and then opened the chest, followed by running to Rémy with the materials. Just as I handed them to him, the barge tilted farther. This caused me to drop them.

"Lord Robert, we're going to sink. Here, take over this pole."

The water surrounded the tops of my boots as both of his *fils* bailed the hull water. At once, he nailed the boards to patch the leak.

Slowly, the barge stabilized itself as Rémy and his *fils* bailed out all the water.

We reached midstream and the anchor held steady as Rémy reloaded the horses and supplies. After dislodging the anchor, the current pushed us forward and, once again, we sailed down the river.

All night we traveled and most of the next day before we stopped to feed the horses. Rémy announced we'd made record time and were far ahead of schedule to reach Lyon.

"The rushing water flowing from the Alps will speed us past Lyon and on to Arles," he explained. "After we leave Lyon, there are no shallow river bottoms. What I fear most, besides who murdered *mon bon ami* is the lack of obtaining supplies. Any place we stop and show our presence will signal the murderers who are trailing us. Several of my major suppliers of food and horse feed are downstream from here." Rémy at once smiled. "I just now remembered a secluded spot where Baudouin stored some dried food and grain. Baudouin, didn't we store some food and horse feed on our last trip down the Saône?" He shouted toward the bow, where Baudouin fished for food.

"*Oui, mon père,* it's in the same barrels we hid in some rocks near the village of Pont-de-Vaux. We'll arrive there late in the afternoon and I know the exact spot!"

"*Bon,* we have outsmarted these devils for now, yet continue fishing for our dinner, *mon fils.*" Then Baudouin's line jerked with a fish.

After a day of writing and listening to Benoit's version of the Merlin legend, we reached the riverbanks close to the hamlet of Pont-de-Vaux.

"*Mon père,* beach the barge near that outcropping of rocks," Benoit said, pointing toward a big face-shaped rock, which partially hid a small cave entrance.

Just as the barge slid on the beach, Baudouin leaped over the side and landed near the entrance and we disembarked to load our food supplies. Quickly we finished and continued on.

"Lyon lies fifteen leagues from here. We'll have to dock the barge before we merge into the river Rhône. There is a portage at the hamlet of Thoissey. If we reach it before dawn, the darkness will help us navigate unseen. There's a mill near there, which is accessible for grain making. In addition, we can use the packhorses to pull the barge through the shallow canal and not disturb the villagers. I'll leave a toll fee with the miller after paying him for our horse feed."

A more confident tone sounded in Rémy's voice after telling us of our next destination.

We reached Thoissey right before dawn broke. Without a sound, we hurried to disembark with the horses, right before the barge entered the canal. After the horses pulled the boat through, we loaded them, the sacks of oats, and milled grain without seeing a villager, other than the miller. Once on the other side of the canal, the swift current grabbed the barge's hull and pulled us toward Lyon.

That evening we arrive at the outskirts of Lyon. The candlelit homes and businesses seemed to go on forever. Rémy said the town sat between the converging waters of the Saône and Rhône.

"We'll stop before passing the town," he said. "The currents are quite treacherous, and my barge might break up on the boulders at night. I have a plan we can use to trick the men who are stalking us," my wily bargeman stated. "I have another barge similar to mine docked not far from here, we can use it as a decoy."

"How will that fool our pursuers?" I asked. Then I observed a twinkle of delight in Rémy's eyes.

"We'll construct some straw-stuffed lookalikes and have Baudouin hide inside the barge to steer it."

"Where will he sail?" I inquired, not seeing the logic in his plan.

"There is a small river upstream on the Rhône, which flows into it as it comes down from the Alps. At the source of this stream is a hamlet, where Baudouin and I know the village blacksmith. There he can dock the decoy, ride overland, and then meet us farther downstream on the Rhône. After docking, he knows a secret shortcut trail, known just to us. Our killers are bound to lose their way. This gives us extra time to stay ahead of their evil plans and arrive early at Arles."

"I now understand."

Everything progressed as planned with Baudouin tiptoeing from our barge to the decoy docked at another hidden cove. Now, darkness covered the river, and this made our ruse easier to accomplish, even with the light of a half moon and a clear autumn sky. I followed Baudouin along with Rémy and his other *fils* to the decoy barge.

"Lord Robert, bring those hay bales from the back of the barge. Benoit, you cut some of that old canvas into human shapes. Baudouin, you take the cut lumber and nail together some scarecrow frames," Rémy said.

"How do we know if this will trick them?"

"It has fooled numerous river pirates in the past. We are experienced in making these fake dummy men."

"Who is the skinny one standing in the stern?" I asked.

"It is you," Rémy chuckled.

To my amusement, he even duplicated the horses, further giving the phony barge more authenticity.

He left right before dawn, while we stayed back in the hidden cove, giving him ample time to lure our tormentors.

Lyon came into view about midday, followed with the roar of rushing water. That's when Rémy started shouting to Benoit and me.

"Lord de Borron, grab the poles and use them to push against the boulders. Benoit, draw down the sail and then secure the cargo!" He struggled with his hands to steady the tiller.

The barge's bow popped into the air, followed with downward *swooshes* into the swirling water, almost knocking me overboard. I jumped up, grabbed one of the poles as a lance, and started fighting with each approaching large jagged rock. The barge continued to pick up speed along with my fear of crashing on the rocks. The bottom of the hull kept making a *thumping* sound each time the bow rose and then fell forward. The barge appeared to skate on a thin layer of water and each *swooshing* sound found us propelling over a small waterfall. My knuckles turned white and began to ache from gripping the poles. In front of me, I saw our patched hull spew forth a broad spray of water. The nailed board popped loose and flew toward my head. I tried to duck, but the nail-covered plank hit my forehead. Both silence and darkness invaded my mind.

CHAPTER VI

Southern Gaul
Montpellier Fortress

The next thing I remember came from Rémy's voice.

"Lord Robert, are you hurt?" I now lay in ankle-deep water.

"You were knocked out for a while."

"*Non*, I'm not hurt, but are we sinking?" I asked. My lips tasted drops of salty red blood.

"I must repair the hull first before I can repair you," Rémy screamed above the roar of the falls. Small star-size spots appeared before my eyes then total darkness once again. I regained consciousness a second time.

"Rémy, where will Baudouin meet us next?" I mumbled as Benoit sat me on a wooden box.

"I patched your forehead with needle and thread," Benoit stated. "He'll meet us at Roussillon if God wills it. We have a storage location outside of Roussillon. We'll have to wait for him to catch up. I expect him in the late evening. During this time, an attack could happen, yet if the decoy barge works, we'll continue down the

Rhône and pick up some more speed at night. During that time, the currents will remain calm. We'll exercise and feed the horses once we pass Vienne. Until then relax and continue your writing. The clear skies and sunny day will brighten all our spirits."

"What about your barge?" I asked.

"I used three boards and double the nails to repair the break this time. *Dieu* protected you, for you didn't drown when you blacked out. You fell backward into the hull's water."

Rémy spoke correctly about me not drowning, and I needed to relax.

The river shimmered with what seemed many dancing diamonds as the sun bore its rays across the water. On the bank to my right, came the quacking of feeding ducks near the river's edge. After dipping their bills in the water, a V-shaped formation of other ducks coming from the north landed and started feeding. It appeared near Saint Michael's feast day, for the shoreline trees displayed a tinge of yellow forming near their tops.

After passing the town of Vienne, we docked, unloaded the horses, fed them, and gave each some much-needed exercise. Later, we loaded them. The swift current and steady wind pulled us toward Roussillon. We arrived there about daybreak and faced a glutinous cloud of fog, which made our visibility almost nonexistent.

"Rémy . . . can you see where to dock?" I asked with a whisper. He nodded his head *oui* and eased his straight index finger to his lips for me to say no more. The dense fog seemed to capture each little sound, creating an intense sensation of apprehension as we came close to the shore. The nearer the barge approached the invisible bank, the more my eyes and ears strained to see or hear movement above the lapping of water against the bow.

With an unexpected *thud,* the barge struck the sticky mud of the riverbank and stopped. As we finished securing the barge, Benoit, with ease, slipped an armed crossbow into my arms. We hunkered behind the gunwales, pointing our crossbows toward the rolling wall of fog, with each of our heads turning back and forth to see any movement. After what seemed an eternity, Rémy's quiet voice spoke.

"I think we are safe for now; besides the fog is lifting," he said as he pointed toward the middle of the river. "You can now see the opposite riverbank. Let's break our fast and afterward, Benoit will lay some traps to alert us of any intruders."

After a short time, Benoit returned.

"I wonder what's taking Baudouin so long; he's never been this late before."

Just as Rémy finished his last word, there came several *clanking* sounds from deep in the fog-shrouded woods, followed by thumping horse hooves.

Then a voice penetrated the dense moving white sheet.

"*Père*, please don't shoot!" Baudouin cried out.

"Sweet Marie and Joseph, you're safe, *mon fils*. We almost killed you. Don't do that again to an old man, *mon coeur* isn't as young as yours."

There, standing on the bank, stood an apparition of a saddled horse and rider. Baudouin dismounted and approached the barge. At once, I grabbed the gangplank and swung it over the side. After boarding, he gave us a report on how well our deception worked.

"You now have lost killers, who are on their way to the Alps." His beard and stomach then bounced with a laugh. "It will take many days for them to backtrack and try to find our whereabouts. By this time, you'll have arrived at the Templar fortress at Montpellier."

Several days ensued without any sign of our stalkers. Each uneventful stop with the horses gave us a slight sense of relaxation.

After passing Roussillon, the villages and hamlets grew bigger and more frequent as we drew closer to the sea. Not just white flying seagulls indicated such, but the ubiquitous presence of ancient Roman ruins. Our barge now traveled a well-navigated and ageless trade route through the southern interior of Gaul. This became apparent after passing Avignon's large stone quay and surrounding fortress walls. The red, blue, and green-colored sails of the many barges and galleys lined the numerous docks of the quay. The river became crowded with the tight maneuvering of each vessel, making it difficult for Rémy to steer. Several times he shook his fist at each ship that came too close.

One league from Arles and my final destination, Rémy began giving me some instruction and advice.

"Lord de Borron, we'll reach Arles this afternoon. I suggest you stay with us at a local inn for the night."

"*Non*, I need to arrive at Montpellier as soon as possible. How many leagues from Arles to the commandery?"

"It's about thirteen leagues along the safer and longer coastline. I beg you to reconsider and stay at the inn. Yet if you are so resolute, please consider using the coastal route tonight."

His words made a bee-buzzing sound with no meaning, leaving his advice useless. Hell, my family might die, and I dared any earthly person to delay me from seeing the commander.

"How many extra days to travel the coastal route?"

"Two to three days, *mon ami*, but let me send Benoit with you; he knows the shortcuts. Besides, he can keep you company with his stories about the prophet Merlin."

Rémy's kind offer and record-making time eased my mind for me to agree to his suggestion.

"*Oui,* your proposal sounds agreeable to my travel plans and *merci beaucoup* for your wise counsel. Benoit, shall we leave, once docked?"

"Lord de Borron, let's leave as soon as we secure the barge at Arles. We have enough daylight to travel at least two leagues before nightfall."

We reached Arles with its ruined Roman bridges, amphitheater, and walls interspersed among the small wattle and daub houses. A stone built *église* and its steeple overshadowed the town. What a contrast in architecture; if the ancient Roman Empire hadn't taxed and spent so much of the people's money, these old buildings might now serve a useful purpose. My thoughts reminded me how a great and powerful civilization declined because of foolish spending.

Arles's docks overflowed with what seemed colorful bunched ducks, as each barge and ship tried to find an empty slip. Rémy knew of an empty secluded spot on the lee side of the town, where few boats docked. There we anchored the barge and unloaded the horses. I paid his fee, a bonus, and tied several of the supply animals to my steed and Benoit's horse. Both Rémy and Baudouin hugged me *au revoir*, with Rémy giving me some parting words.

"I hope you discover what the warrior-*moine* commander desires of you, *mon ami*. It appears God has commanded both of you to seek out His divine plan. Beware, Lord Robert, I am told that the closer a man moves toward our Creator, the more the devil desires his soul. Always protect your back, for the evil one backstabs. He uses doubt and despair as tools in his wicked workshop. Journey in peace, Lord de Borron. Your honor and determination are *bon* examples for all men."

The wise bargeman bowed and said *au revoir* as I mounted my horse to leave, knowing his travel wisdom and experience stood behind me.

The ride along the salt marshes advanced with a pleasant salty sea breeze blowing in my face. My thoughts of fear for my family were my main distractions, along with the constant sounds of the shrieking and chirping seagulls and large-winged pink birds with long curved narrow necks. As the late afternoon progressed, from the west came a small bank of dark clouds. The winds grew stronger as the clouds neared, and my nose experienced the first droplets of rain.

"Lord de Borron, let's ride inland for a bit. There's an overhanging outcrop of rocks we can use as shelter and keep dry for the night."

We reached the overhanging rocks just as the storm pelted us full force, along with bolts of lightning. We camped for the night.

I didn't obtain much sleep during the thunderous night. The next morning, Benoit revealed our next destination.

"I estimate we're about seven leagues from the village of Saintes-Maries-de-la-Mer. If the weather clears today, we'll reach there late this afternoon."

Once mounted, the rain stopped, and we galloped our way to Saintes-Maries-de-la-Mer. We made up lost time traveling across the flat, tall grass plains. I saw a profusion of wildlife in all directions as I observed galloping herds of wild horse, bulls with long-pointed horns, teeming birds with narrow-sharpened beaks, and strange waterfowl with long skinny legs. Shimmering brackish estuaries sur-rounded us on all sides, making any threat of ambush impossible.

As Benoit promised, we reached Saintes-Maries-de-la-Mer late in the afternoon, stopping just to eat supper on the outskirts of the village. In the distance, on a rise of land facing the sea, stood a small Romanesque-designed *église* for worship.

"The villagers call Notre-Dame-de-Ratis the 'women of the boat.' I call it the 'Maries of the sea.' Two Maries accompanied Marie Mag-dalene to the resurrection tomb. Miriam Salome, Marie Jacobe, and the locals say they shipwrecked here after fleeing from Jerusalem. Also, a dark-skinned servant girl accompanied them. They called her Sarah. The locals named her Sainte Sarah."

Without any explanation, my ears caught a distant whisper on a sea breeze that didn't carry the crashing sound of waves.

"Remember, *mon ami*, Robert," it stated. "You'll come to know them," spoke a soft voice.

"It's her!" I exclaimed.

"Did you say something to me, Lord de Borron?" Benoit asked.

"It's the woman's voice from the Vézelay *église* that I told you about. She just spoke to me. Didn't you just hear her, *mon ami*?"

"*Non*, Lord Robert, but maybe she just speaks to you."

We stopped near a large pool of water writhing with a multitude of silvery fish feasting on some unknown long-legged water insects and camped for the night.

"Benoit, let me stand the first watch, my eyelids aren't heavy. Besides we're so close to the fortress and the anticipation of what the warrior-*moine* might say will keep me awake."

"*Oui*, your angst will keep you alert and prevent our stalkers from surprising us. Let me finish my dried venison and *vin* and af-terward I will rest, then take your watch." He handed me the skin of *vin* after taking several large gulps.

The cool red liquid slid down my throat and at once relaxed the knotted muscles in my neck. The crackling campfire drew me into its bluish-colored flames, causing my mind to ask itself a mul-titude of questions about what the warrior-*moine* might reveal. This mindless game continued for some time. That's when the sound of a twig snapping drew my eyes and ears toward a dark sightless spot, forcing my hand to reach for the pommel of my sword. Then another snapping wooden sound followed that compelled me to rise and unsheathe my sword.

My fingers constricted around my sword's hilt to ready myself for the intruders. Several *thumping* sounds came rushing toward me. Had they found us after these several days? My empty hand eased down into one of my knee-high boots and pulled out a dagger. Stepping backward and out of the light of the campfire, my feet crept toward the sack of crossbows. The *thumping* sounds grew closer but came from two separate directions. At once, I hollered at Benoit to wake up.

"Benoit, we're under attack, grab some crossbows!" I hollered. He jumped up, ran toward me with the sack of crossbows. Then he pulled two of them out and turned his head in several directions to identify the attackers' whereabouts. Oddly, I heard no further sounds of movement. Two dark shapes approached near the camp's edge. Each black image crept closer to the firelight until two sets of dark glistening eyes appeared, reflecting the campfire.

"Lord de Borron, our attackers are just two wild horses and nothing more." He gave me a slight grin. "They smelled our food and used our campfire to guide them to a quick meal. It's a blessing these wild horses want us to feed them; typically, they shy away from strangers. Now, I have two new horses to help us with our barge business, but my *père* will have to train them. They are so hungry, they will let anybody feed them." He gave each horse a handful of small apples and while they ate them, he slipped rope harnesses over their foreheads.

"Please, forgive my stupidity for not knowing horses stood in front of me," I said. "My nerves have deceived me since arriving at Vézelay."

"No need to apologize; it's now an excellent opportunity to leave. Dawn isn't too far off and besides, your early arrival will let you see Montpellier before dark."

"*Oui*, you're right and the jocularity falls on me." This seemed to lighten my anxious mood. We broke camp as the rising sun sliced through some dark, narrow red-streaked clouds.

It drizzled with rain most of the day, and the countryside changed to rolling hills with scattered outcroppings of giant rocks. We reached Montpellier late in the day, as Benoit said. My eyes caught the sight of two large hillocks separating the town. On each summit rose a *château* and *église* with wattle and daub houses blanketing both hillsides.

"In the *château* reigns *Seigneur* Guillaume the eighth, *seigneur* and master of Montpellier," Benoit said, pointing in the direction of the square-towered fortress. "The Templar commandery *château* isn't too much farther, just over this next hill." He spurred his horse to trot faster.

My *coeur* raced with mixed emotions in meeting the commander. I wondered what he might divulge as we crested the hill to see another rocky summit. A black and gray-colored fortress covered the entire flattened hilltop.

"Here's where we part company, *mon ami*." My emotions became quite gloomy to see him leave.

"Let me pay you a bonus for the peril I have caused you."

"*Non*, Lord de Borron, you've paid *mon père* his bonus. There isn't any need to pay me too."

"I insist, Benoit. If nothing else, you have revealed valuable information to me about the prophet Merlin and his *mère's* confessor and scribe, Blaise. Do with these coins as you desire, you deserve them. Your *père* has raised an excellent *fils* and I know he's quite proud." I took the coins and slipped them into his saddlebag, then turned to see his face display a dimpled grin. "

Au revoir, Benoit. If God wills it, we'll meet again." We both embraced, with each of us reluctant to release our hugs. He pulled away first, then stuck one foot in his stirrup and mounted to leave.

"Don't forget, Lord Robert, what Merlin said. 'Always pay attention to the darker side of mankind, for your kind heart can deceive you.'"

Benoit spurred his steed and led his newfound equines, along with his supply horses, and disappeared into the valley's approaching fog.

The fortress ahead appeared as a giant stony-toothed leviathan opening its mouth to swallow me. The relief and excitement of reaching my destination now vanished, replaced with the dread of what I might hear. A black-mantled guard, standing along the embrasure saw me approach and shouted for me to identify myself. I said my name and he directed me across the drawbridge and through a raised spiked-tipped portcullis. The guard then met me at the end of a bent passageway and pointed toward a postern gate that led to a high-towered square keep.

"See that small gate, enter there and it leads to a long stone corridor. Follow it until it stops; there wait for him." He then scurried back to the stone stairs from whence he came. He didn't mention the *chevalier's* name, and I couldn't obtain an answer. For he trotted back into the interior of the *château* and disappeared.

CHAPTER VII

Flickering flames emanating from rusty iron torch holders lined my passageway. They gave the labyrinth of stone walls the effect of movement, which deceived my mind enough to upset my sense of balance. Without warning, a disembodied voice from a dark side passage caused me to reach for my sword.

"Lord de Borron." A tall man with sun-darkened swarthy skin spoke as he stepped out of the shadows. He appeared middle age, dressed in a worn white surcoat emblazoned with a large red-splayed cross. A hefty broadsword swung at his side, with a garnet-colored cross embedded in its hilt. His dark flashing eyes seemed to penetrate my thoughts, and he seemed uneasy as he looked over his shoulder before he again spoke.

"It's our custom to offer you hospitality and welcome you to our commandery, but I have little time. Before I can divulge the secrets, which brought you here, you must agree to several absolute conditions."

"Why must I agree to your demands and conditions?"

"Danger might visit your family, and that's all I can say, for now. Please trust me."

"Who threatens my family? You haven't yet earned my confidence and you're a total stranger to me."

"There isn't much time, so listen with care. It concerns a sinister cardinal within the Roman Curia who wishes you and your family harm. You're speaking to a Poor Fellow-Soldier of Christ and a man sworn to do God's will. Please, Lord de Borron, have faith in me, I have little time to discuss."

How did this man know of a threat to my family? I declined to decide with little information. Is this a possible trap?

"Did you send a man to fetch me?" I wondered if the stranger standing before me had written the note.

"*Oui.* He never returned. I presumed something dire happened to him."

"Your ominous note concerning my family forced me to come here. Your sergeant gave up his life to carry out your orders. I provided him a decent burial and said a psalm over his body." We both crossed ourselves and said a quick prayer. "Do you know who killed him?"

"Time doesn't allow me to say right now, but your immediate reassurance will help me, and you must agree to listen to me in all matters."

Reluctantly, I nodded my acceptance.

"You won't come out of your cell any time during your visit. Evil plans afoot surround us, which you don't comprehend, and I need your unconditional agreement."

"*Oui,* you have my acceptance, because this concerns my family and their safety; however, to whom am I speaking?"

"I am known as *Frère* Gilbért."

With some reservations, my mind made the decision to follow the warrior-*moine* to my unseen abode. We passed several musty stone corridors, before stopping in front of a large oak door with a pattée-shaped cross burned into the wood. The door matched the design in my vision at Vézelay. A shiver darted down my spine.

"For your comfort, there's wine, cheese, and fruit to sustain you during your stay. However, under no circumstances open this door or come out of your room unless I or my squire come for you. None of the other *frères* knows what you're about to see," he said with raised eyebrows.

A resonant *clank* distracted my attention as the *frère's* large key turned a squeaking lock, admitting me inside. The shadow-lit room held just a straw-filled mattress and a table with two candles. I observed a single window in the shape of a small cross similar to the one on the warrior-*moine's* tunic. On the table in the corner, lay a large leather-bound book.

"*Mon ami*, I'll return in two days to unlock your cell. You must finish reading this holy book during that time." He pointed at the gem-covered leather-bound book. "I trust you will memorize, copy it, so to protect it for future generations. The holy relic, my sources say, will disappear in a fortnight or less. Three days ago, a vision came to me of a female voice revealing the book's destruction. In addition, she spoke your name and your next destination. In anticipation of your visit, I set aside this small room for you to scrutinize the book's contents. Just I know who you are."

I walked over to the book for a closer look, then glanced back at the *frère*.

"Before I leave," he continued, "you must swear an oath to our Lord and Savior not to divulge its contents until the right time. Your heart and soul will tell you when this gospel will enlighten our uncertain world. This secret belongs to us and us alone."

"*Oui*, I swear before my Lord and Savior," the words spilled from my lips.

Frère Gilbért edged toward the door to leave.

"We'll meet again soon and I bid you *adieu*. God be with you, for your spiritual life will have a powerful new meaning I suspect after reading this book."

The large oak door closed, and he locked it with a creaking sound. My several days of anticipated confinement left me with an uneasiness that squeezed my chest each time the task jumped into my mind.

This room exuded a silence, that of a tomb, until a bird started chirping in the distance, followed with gusts of whispering wind blowing through the narrow cross-shaped opening. My ears drew me to the whistling wind and the distant bird, with my body sensing another person in my room. The repetitive breezes blew the candle flames, causing them to appear dancing with their wicks. This further drew my attention back to the sparkling gem-stone-covered book.

Before committing myself to read and copy this mysterious book, I took in my surroundings. On the ceiling above the book, I saw a sizable stone-carved dove peering down with radiating lines coming from its head. The immense carving covered most of the ceiling and embedded itself in an arch high above this ancient book. Without thinking and with an irresistible urge, my fingers reached for the jewel-encrusted codex. Its allure and unknown contents caused my hands to tremble as they grasped the thick binding, making it difficult to open and reveal its secrets.

I began the ancient tome on the first page, my eyes focused on large detailed letters written in a heavy-styled script. Along with the letters, I spied two ornate illustrations of a large cup or goblet with wine spilling down its sides and a spear tipped with blood. Below both renderings, I observed the words "Grand Saint Graal."

I gasped. Were my eyes deceiving me? Many narratives in the past spoke of the alleged authenticity of the Last Supper cup and the spear that pierced Jesus the Christ's side. Surely, it's a mistake, I thought. Although many spoke of the legends, including my story of Merlin about the "Cup of Christ." The factual evidence of these sacred relics appeared as a mist in nature. Disappearing when the warm sun's rays arrived in the morning. Why me for the chosen one in this copying task?

How foolish to think such a thought? Perhaps he'd mistaken me for another, worthier individual. Nevertheless, here I sat, the sole person in the room. Maybe after reading the book, my mind might discover a hoax or at least another interesting, but fanciful tale. However, if real documents, an enormous responsibility would rest on my shoulders. Were they wide enough or strong enough to accept this yoke?

The mysterious book lured me closer to the many musty-smelling parchment pages, compelling me to read its contents. Yet, the indecipherable words left me perplexed. "Aha!" I exclaimed. The strange language prevented me from taking on this heavy burden. Several parts I recognized were written in Latin. The story began with the Roman date *Anno Domini* XXXIII, in the Holy City of Jerusalem. The first couple of lines I translated but proceeding any further was impossible.

Bearing a sense of both regret and relief, my fingertips edged the book closed, and I let the smell of the fruity wine entice my hunger. The clay *vin* carafe brimmed with ruby-red liquid and the pungent-smelling cheeses spilled over the plate. I didn't realize the intensity of my hunger until all the cheese and most of the wine had disappeared.

Sitting there, alone in the sparse cell, let me reflect on what the warrior-*moine* had divulged, but he told me little about the threat to my family. I knew I wasn't the man to undertake this charge. Yet, the visions the *moine* and I had scared me. Were the forces of our Lord using us both? How did one know with certainty?

My refreshments had left me full and sleep beckoned, causing me to drift off into a light slumber, but still aware of the increasing sound of the wind. Now, it's a dream overtaking me as whispering words came to my ears. Each gust of wind spoke soft, clear sentences. To my amazement, the voice sounded identical to the one I heard in the sanctuary at Vézelay. As the wind continued to increase, the voice strengthened. I jumped up, shook my head, and realized this isn't a dream.

In the corner of my cell, a swirling white orb formed before my unbelieving eyes. The ball of light took on a human shape, creating a young woman dressed in ancient red-colored clothes. She moved toward me, not striding, but gliding across the floor. Her face radiated a golden white light of unbearable brightness. With both hands cupped and raising them to cover my eyes the room grew brighter and my nose filled with a pleasant rose fragrance. Squinting with an occasional peek between my fingers, her starlight-surrounding form drew closer. At once, fear stabbed into me that permanent blindness might overtake me. I knew as a writer, sightlessness wouldn't just remove my vision, but also my soul to write. At once, a prayer rolled off my lips. Then the astral female form began to speak.

"Robert de Borron, you're wondering if I am the same voice from your vision at the church in Vézelay. *Oui* indeed, my spirit now speaks to you. In addition, you doubt you're the one charged with reading and memorizing the *Sangraal* book. Again, I must answer, *oui*. Right now, your mind tells you that you're not worthy to complete the quest our Savior asks of you. He knows your reputation as a master of words; all of Gaul acknowledges your talents. The journey you're facing requires someone with not just writing experience, but also a man of great faith. You are that man, Robert. Right now, you cannot see how to accomplish this holy task because you have no knowledge of the languages written in this book.

"My visit here this evening will explain how you'll achieve our God's plan. Tonight, my Lord will bless you with certain powers to read and memorize this holy book. These powers will pierce your soul just as the Holy Spirit became one with the first saintly *abbas* of our Church. As Peter spoke in tongues at the Pentecost to different nations, your mind will interpret several ancient languages written about our Lord and His disciples."

Her nimbus grew brighter just as she stopped speaking. My mind failed to comprehend the miracles transpiring before me as I buried my head in my arms. She had read my mind, knowing my hopes and fears. Whom might I tell or say nothing about the spirit before me? Most people would think I had lost my mind, yet one person would understand about the apparition, *Frère* Gilbért. Once more, the undulating lights of her form began to speak.

"After our Lord's death and resurrection, there came forth one disciple charged with our Lord's burial and the book of *lé Sangraal*. In the next several days, you will see his ministry revealed in this singular book, there on your table. You're the chosen one to read, re-member, and write with the speed of his life that took place long ago. The powers of darkness will soon destroy this sacred book. Therefore, waste no time in reading and copying its holy contents, for evil lurks quick and silent.

"There are those who want to expand their selfish interests and evil motives. These men will try to prevent you from speaking of these written events. Your life will come under the sword at times; hereafter, travel with caution.

"I implore you to keep these written events in your heart always and not just in your mind, for they explain in detail the life and holy words of our Lord. You'll need the words inside this book to assist you in your quest. Read these words with care, for they have many clues to help you."

"What quest? I came here for answers and not a quest. I fear for my family's safety and now I am asked to copy an ancient text which I can't read."

"My holy intercession will grant you great writing abilities of memorization, translation, and speed with a quill. Your quest doesn't end here. It is now just the beginning. Many new lands lay ahead for you to discover. I must depart now and leave you to your ministry. You have little time left to protect the words of our Holy Lord and his forgotten disciple."

"What will the clues tell me, and who are you?" I asked. "You never said your name."

"I am called Miriam of Magdala, but some have named me the Apostle of Apostles."

She spoke her last words as her image disappeared from the small room. Once again, I crossed myself and pinched both my arms. The sainte, Marie-Magdalene, just appeared to me and spoke to a mere mortal man. The whole event seemed incredulous, and without warning shivers crawled down my spine. Then I glanced at my arms and saw a tender red bruise swelling from one of my pinched arms.

Repeating its mysterious allure, the holy book drew me back to the shadowy lit table. This time, all the before indecipherable words I now knew. Still, my ignorance needed more light, but somehow, I knew that would soon change.

As I read, the full impact of what I read hit me. These were the words of Saint Joseph de Arimathea. Here lay the lost gospel that few people knew existed. The canonical gospels mentioned little about this saint. After our Lord's burial, the author's life disappeared with time. My eyes focused on each word, revealing his account of my Lord's life in Joseph's own handwriting. He had written it the omniscient style of the canonical Gospel writers.

It humbled me for this precious miraculous opportunity, but where would his words lead and what new epiphanies would Jesus the Christ say? His beginning paragraph stated that his written ministry began in the thirty-third year of our Lord and Savior.

PART TWO

Passover

CHAPTER VIII

Jerusalem City
A Week before Passover
Jewish Year 3793
Anno Domini 33

As Yoseph traveled the streets of *Yerushalayim*, he wiped off a thick layer of dust from his clothing, which resulted from the jostling crowds who crammed the city for *Pesach*. He anticipated an appearance of upcoming events, yet his skin shivered with an unknown foreboding. The street merchants' voices buzzed of a great *maishiach* to arrive, who would reveal great spiritual revelations. The dust hung in a hazy brown cloud over the city marketplace, drying his throat as he neared home.

Slowly, he approached a large two-story building and a vacant side street; without warning several large clay roof tiles crashed down as he entered the street, projecting their shattering shards in all directions. At once, he looked up and saw a shadowy outline of a man jumping across the rooftops. With *El Shaddai* intervention, none of the tiles struck him. Another moment faster in his approach and the tiles would have killed him or somebody else?

He struggled to his courtyard door and then unlocked it. Upon entering, he met his daughter, Yosa.

"*Abba,* I am happy to see you. I hope business didn't wear you out."

"No, my daughter, but some falling roof tiles almost killed me, and the dust from the market square has left my throat parched."

"Did the broken tile hurt you?" A forehead wrinkle of concern formed on her face.

"No, I'm just a little shaken, as you can see from my trembling hands."

"Let me fetch you some wine to soothe your nerves and dry mouth. *Abba,* please sit here on this bench, and I'll return soon."

The quiet of the courtyard garden comforted him after the cacophony of *Yerushalayim's* streets. She returned a short time later, holding a large goblet replete with dark ruby-colored wine.

"Have you heard the news about my cousin, Yeshua? When will he arrive in *Yerushalayim?*"

"Yes, my dear, I have heard the news. The gossip of his impending arrival travels faster than a Roman courier."

Yoseph's daughter conducted herself quite mature for her age of sixteen summers, but her dark brown eyes bespoke her youthful innocence. Her excitement concerning her cousin further jangled his nerves.

"Yosa, I hope you aren't disappointed if he doesn't come to visit us. Yeshua and his followers are always confronted with special requests."

He knew his forthright comments would open a clay container of difficult questions, which he would have to answer.

"What do these people request of my cousin?"

"There are many unusual stories about my great-nephew Yeshua. I have heard others say he can heal people of their afflictions. In addition, the marketplace gossip says he's a great prophet. I haven't spoken to him in several summers, but from what I remember, he displayed great concern for humanity. His religious knowledge coupled with great wisdom exceeded most scholars. His *amma,* my niece Miriam, didn't understand him sometimes as he grew up in

Nazareth. His knowledge far exceeded his age, yet his *abba* tried to train him to become a carpenter and mason, but he never took well to that trade. As you know, Miriam lost her husband when Yeshua entered his thirteenth summer. His brothers and sisters tried to help the family stay together."

"Don't forget, Yoseph, you helped them too!" Enygeus, Yoseph's younger sister said, as she entered the courtyard holding a flagon of wine. "You need to share all your worthy deeds with your daughter. What other family stories have you told her?"

"Just about Yeshua, Miriam, and Yoseph ben David," he answered to his outspoken sister.

"Yoseph of Arimathea, you know you helped them with money after his *abba* died. Moreover, have you heard the *Yerushalayim* gossip about Yeshua? They claim he brought a dead man back to life and healed many people. His behavior sounds delusional, which Miriam has had to endure. You are more than generous to them these many past summers, but don't you think it's about time you focused on your daughter and our immediate family?"

No one ever said Enygeus didn't speak her mind. His sister had the correct point, yet he knew in his heart of Miriam's hardships living in the remote Galilean countryside. He looked at how well-dressed his sister and daughter appeared compared to Miriam's family. Without a doubt, in his mind and heart, he had done the right thing for Yeshua and his family.

"My dear sister, while there's truth in what you say, I have plenty to share. You and your husband, Hebron, are wealthy; my daughter and son lack nothing. Please, don't lose sight to help others, either with food and shelter or, more important, with our hearts. You know this distinguishes us in our faith from the Romans and their deities."

"I guess you are right, Yoseph. It seems we both know how to speak our minds. It's quite evident why the Sanhedrin say you're quite outspoken for the poor. And we have the same blood, don't we, brother?"

Her waggish comment gave them a big laugh. As always, Enygeus's humor helped ease the tension during the uncertain times of Roman rule.

Yoseph turned to his daughter. "Yosa, have you heard from Alein Yosephe? Will he arrive in time for our Seder dinner?"

"I haven't heard from Alein in about two *Shabbats*. The last time he wrote to me, business matters at the port of Caesarea kept him away, negotiating tin mine contracts." She poured him another cup of wine. "*Abba*, please share some information about the family business with me. I know it isn't appropriate for a woman to understand business matters, yet I am still interested."

"You must forgive my oversight. Let me provide you a brief explanation of what your brother's business entails. The metal comes from Gaul and the Isle of the Celts. It is then shaped for both the Romans and our people into making plates, bowls, and cups. *El Shaddai* has blessed our vast fortune and this family. But enough about business! Did Alein Yosephe give us an arrival date?"

"He said he would send a courier to let us know in advance. I am expecting the arrival of his messenger at any time."

"Glory be to *El Shaddai*, then he's coming," Yoseph said. "It's expensive to hire a courier and this guarantees his arrive for *Pesach*."

He knew his son quite well. Their family came first and business second. He conveyed excellent merchant skills, but the laws of Moshe superseded them.

It hadn't been easy raising both Yosa and Alein after his wife's death. He'd married late in life and *El Shaddai* had blessed him with two wonderful children. At that time, he still maintained the responsibility of Miriam and her family. Also, he traveled on business for months at a time making it more difficult for his wife and family. Alein and Yeshua had the same number of birth summers; together as small boys they visited each other and became close cousins.

"Yoseph, there's a courier at the front gate!" Enygeus announced.

Yoseph rose from his seat, strolled toward the courtyard entrance to greet the messenger. In the doorway stood a young man who looked exhausted from his travels, with sweat and desert sand caked in his hair. His clothing bore several brown-encrusted sweat stains on his chest.

"Young man, you look tired. Please come into the courtyard and have some refreshment."

"Are you Master Yoseph of Arimathea?" At Yoseph's nod, the young man continued. "I am called Shimon ben David, and your son sent me with this message."

"Thank you, Shimon. Now, please, come into the courtyard and my sister will pour you a cup of wine."

The young man handed him the parchment letter, and Yoseph broke their family wax seal with his fingers. They then gathered around the bubbling courtyard fountain to hear what his son had written. He began to read aloud for all to hear.

> *Dearest abba, I will arrive soon before Pesach. I hope all of you are well. My business will conclude today, and I'll arrive in Yerushalayim within two sunsets. Tell Yosa I have a special gift for her when I arrive. In addition, here in Caesarea, all the people are talking about my cousin and his anticipated grand entrance into Yerushalayim. Perhaps you can tell me more when I see you next.*
> *Your devoted son, Alein Yosephe.*

After Yoseph finished the letter, Yosa spoke first. "*Abba*, where will Yeshua stay during *Pesach*? Can I visit him there?"

"The bazaar gossipers say he's staying with one of his followers named Yohanan Marcus. They believe Yohanan Marcus lives in a large house with upper rooms used for spiritual gatherings. It's somewhere near the Temple. However, I am afraid for you to visit this house. Though my nephew preaches peace, a few of his friends are Zealots. Some of his followers are Gentiles and tax collectors, yet the high priest Caiaphas will have them followed during *Pesach*. As you know, Caiaphas wields tremendous power over all aspects of life in *Yerushalayim*."

"But *abba*, you're part of the Sanhedrin and have considerable influence in *Yerushalayim*."

"That's true, but Caiaphas displays his ruthlessness when provoked and rumors from the bazaars say that Yeshua comes to overthrow the Romans. I know this isn't true, nevertheless, we can expect trouble. I'll try to arrange a visit through Miriam, hoping he will come with her when he arrives."

"Thank you, *abba*. I hope he visits, for I have many questions for him."

Making his daughter happy gratified him. Seeing happiness in others gave him great pleasure, but most of all satisfying his daughter's happiness gave him deep delight. She reminded Yoseph of her deceased *amma*, which comforted him. This meant he needed to minimize the risks for her and his family.

"Yoseph, do you know when Yeshua will arrive?" inquired Enygeus.

"At the beginning of the week of *Pesach*." The excitement in seeing his niece and nephew came with possible danger for them in *Yerushalayim*. He forced his mind not to dwell on problems and worry about things before they happened.

Turning to the young messenger, he offered him the use of their bathing quarters before he returned to Caesarea, which the young man declined and then thanked Yoseph for the wine. He said he must return to help Yoseph's son with his final business. They said goodbye, thanked him for the reliable news, and wished him well. At once, he departed.

After the messenger left, Yoseph watched Yosa enter their living quarters to obtain some food. Enygeus stayed behind, her raised eyes, indicating she wanted to speak to him in private.

"Yoseph, I believe you're creating some risk in what you promise Yosa. Please think of her safety when you arrange this family gathering. I don't trust Caiaphas and his family, for they stole their wealth, but you've earned yours with an honest heart, my dear brother. I know power and position have stolen him away from the teaching of Moshe and Eliyah. Just look at the moneychangers, merchants, and vendors he has inside the Temple grounds.

"In addition, Caiaphas acts and thinks similar to a sly fox stalking his prey and holds sway over the Sanhedrin. Most of the members will agree with whatever he says. Everyone knows he has spies everywhere. Yoseph, please arrange this meeting somewhere else besides our home. Perhaps your friend Nicodemus might help to arrange such a meeting?" It wasn't often that Enygeus allowed others to sense her fear, but her words revealed such.

"Yes, that's possible, but why place others in danger? Our nephew and his *amma* are our late brother's daughter and Yeshua is his grandson. If our brother, Yoachim lived today and our circumstances reversed, he would bring us into his house without any questions. Enygeus, you know in your heart that's so."

"You are right, my brother. How selfish of me to place your friend Nicodemus in danger. Maybe Hebron can help you arrange this meeting. His business dealings aren't as well-known as yours in the community."

"I agree with that idea, but will he approve?"

"He won't object. Remember, my brother, he knew Yoseph ben David many years ago when young Yeshua taught in the Temple. After Hebron and I betrothed each other, Yoseph ben David built many pieces of furniture for us. Hebron always had great respect for Yoseph and Miriam. Let me depart and speak to him. Did you say they're staying with a man named Yohanan Marcus?"

"That's the latest information I know from the marketplace, but let me speak with Nicodemus. He stays abreast of the latest information. Tell Hebron to wait until the next watch to speak to Nicodemus. I'll return soon. Let's hope we'll obtain the information needed. Tell Yosa I will eat later and return as soon as possible."

Leaving the courtyard garden, Yoseph returned to the dusty *Yerushalayim* streets. The packed throngs reminded him of a crowded Roman circus stadium, making it hard to navigate late in the afternoon. Animals and carts blocked intersecting streets as he tried to reach the house of Nicodemus. What he dreaded most about this festive holy week came from the smells of all the different animals.

The pungent aromas of manure and human sweat forced him to cover his nose with his shawl and those odors didn't dissipate until he saw Nicodemus's house. His home butted up against the Temple wall yet was still secluded from the street. One had to stroll down several small alleyways before reaching a dark alcove entrance to his home.

As he approached the main entryway, he heard a shuffling noise behind him. At once, Yoseph turned to seek out the source of the sound. He observed a shadow that vanished behind another building. Sensing uneasiness, he decided to slink along the building walls before announcing his presence. After circling the neighboring buildings once again, he spied the main entrance to Nicodemus's house. This time, he didn't hear or see anything suspicious. Just as he started to knock on the door, it opened and Nicodemus yanked Yoseph into his house. His clenched white teeth stood out amid his gray beard and swarthy skin.

"Yoseph, let me shut the door at once. I viewed your arrival from an upper room window, which allowed me to see your approach. You used wise judgment in circling the house before announcing your presence. Let me close the door and we can speak in private."

Yoseph followed him into the dark interior of his home, where they sat down in a room that had many scrolls lying about on shelves and tables. Sitting on the table he observed a lone lamp radiating a dim sputtering flame.

"Yoseph, I know somebody is following me and I suspect also you!"

"What causes you to think this?"

"I think you heard or observed something before approaching my entryway? I believe Caiaphas planted a spy there."

"Do you have any information to prove that?"

"I don't have any explicit evidence that we can verify. My sole piece of information came from a man named Yohanan Marcus."

Once again, this name came up. How strange, Yoseph thought, that his friend knew this name too. Why and how did this Yohanan Marcus know where Caiaphas's spies were located? What motives and reasons might the head of the Sanhedrin have in spying on both of them? Visiting his old friend at this time gave him an opportunity. He knew his friend Nicodemus always gathered information beneficial to Yoseph's family.

"It seems I am in luck. I came here for information about Yohanan Marcus. Please tell me all you know; my visit here concerns this man."

Before Nicodemus spoke, he gathered his thoughts in a moment of silence, revealing an unusual tremor in his hands. Yoseph pretended not to notice.

"I am sure you have heard that your nephew will arrive at the beginning of *Pesach* week?"

"Yes, it's no secret; most of *Yerushalayim* knows this about Passover. It's my primary reason for visiting you. Now speak and tell me what you know, for my daughter and son are excited about his visit. They want to see Miriam and Yeshua while they're in *Yerushalayim*. I hope you can work with Hebron, my brother-in-law, to arrange a meeting. Because you aren't a part of my family, not many questions will arise."

"You want me to arrange a meeting with Yeshua during *Pesach* week?"

"Yes, if at all possible. My sister Enygeus suggested that both you and Hebron work together to arrange such a meeting place without indicating apparent ties to me. She thought it best that I stay out of these arrangements. I had to agree with her. My daughter Yosa wants to see my niece and her cousin. Therefore, my concerns aren't for me, but for her. Still, I desire to speak to Yeshua and his *amma* in a secluded place if possible. I am sure the many seasons have brought changes in them. The rumors and gossip I have heard the previous summers say he's a great teacher.

"My son Alein Yosephe has traveled to the borders of *Yehudah*, Samaria, and Galilee and even to the Isle of the Celts this past spring and summer on business. During this time, he reported many stories to me concerning Yeshua. I can trust you, my friend, so please listen with care what these stories will reveal.

"He said Yeshua has brought the dead back to life. I know it seems impossible, but both he and those in our bazaars have said so. Alein Yosephe revealed the dead man's name. He goes by the name Lazarus of Bethany and numerous witnesses saw him come out of his tomb four days after his death. My son spoke to some of the witnesses in person and they told him how a rabbi from Galilee called forth Lazarus from his tomb. He then tottered forth in his death shroud and called out the name of Yeshua."

"That I heard too. Also, there's a rumor of a young girl from the house of Yarius. Her *abba,* a leader in the synagogue, pleaded with Yeshua to see his daughter. As they approached the house, his relatives announced her death. Yeshua told the man to believe in him and fear not, for he commanded the little girl to awaken, rise up, and see her parents, to which she did to the amazement of all present.

"The last account, which I haven't told anybody until now, came to me two summers ago. He and Miriam, your niece traveled to a wedding at Cana. The wedding had more guests than the family expected, causing the wine jars to empty too soon. To save the bride's family from embarrassment, Miriam implored Yeshua to help refill the large amphorae. He then instructed several young boys to fill the jars with drinking water. One of Yeshua's followers desiring water dipped his cup into the pot and tasted the red wine. This incredible act of Yeshua, the party declared a miracle and all who saw this spread the story throughout the village of Cana."

The nervousness, which Yoseph detected earlier in Nicodemus, didn't improve as he continued to speak. His hands trembled and his bushy dark eyebrows took on a noticeable scowl. It appeared he wouldn't honor his meeting request, for he began pulling at his gray beard, followed with silence.

"Yoseph, my friend, I have a confession for you to hear. Your nephew and I have already spoken. You mentioned the miracle at Bethany with his friend, Lazarus. Several days later, I disguised myself so people wouldn't know me as a ruling member of the Sanhedrin. I feared some of our fellow members might accuse me of heresy if recognized. I traveled at night to visit him at the home of Lazarus. Days before the death of Lazarus, I had a dream about it as if I witnessed this event. A radiant light emanated from Yeshua's head as he prayed to *El Shaddai* and Lazarus emerged from his tomb speaking your nephew's name.

"The next morning upon awakening, my mind had an unquenchable thirst for answers. This thirst became an obsession for more knowledge. To my surprise a couple of days later, I heard from several Pharisees about this miracle at Bethany. After questioning them in length, they thought it some sort of magic trick raising Lazarus from the dead. They knew your nephew and Lazarus were close friends. Each of them chastised your nephew in person about breaking the laws while practicing medicine on the *Shabbat*. He rebuked them, saying they must follow the spirit of the law, not the letter of the law. Yeshua also said that the people came under too many laws, which harshly burdened them. He further stated that they need to help the poor and hungry and not sit there in their homes.

"I am sorry to say your nephew didn't win any converts of these two Pharisees and someday soon they'll bring trouble to him and his followers."

"Do I know these men?"

"Yoseph, do you remember Uzziah and Zephaniah? Both of them are sly and close to Caiaphas."

"Yes, I know them." Yoseph sighed. "Nicodemus, are you saying you won't arrange a meeting with Yeshua because of the danger? If you say no, it won't disappoint me."

"If you had asked me that question before I met Yeshua, I would now say no. There's much involved in planning such a secret meeting; however, I think the spiritual reward will outweigh the risk."

Nicodemus paused, silent in thought before he spoke again.

"Yoseph, when did you speak to him last?"

"Maybe two summers. Why do you ask?"

"I don't believe you'll recognize him."

"Why make that statement? Has he disfigured himself?"

"No, he hasn't, but something strange happened at our secret meeting in Lazarus's home. I noticed several unusual events. Our meeting started late at night and I observed only one lit oil lamp. We sat in a small dark room away from the main living quarters. As he began to speak, the room took on an unexplainable brilliance. Streaming lights emanated from all corners of the room and calmness came over my entire body.

"His dark eyes seemed to read my thoughts before I spoke. His voice exuded a soothing smoothness that filled me with happiness. We must have conversed for one full watch, with me asking about his miracles and the Kingdom of *El Shaddai*. I questioned him about performing his supernatural deeds. He told me that no one can see the Kingdom of *El Shaddai* unless he seeks a new birth.

"How can an old man be born again? I asked him. How can one enter his *amma*'s womb a second time? This didn't make any sense.

"Yeshua puzzled me with his statements, but I think I know what he meant. Yeshua spoke of those people born of water and spirit, who will enter the Kingdom of *El Shaddai*. 'No one has entered Heaven except the One who came from Heaven—the Son of Man.'

"He then spoke of Moshe lifting up the snake in the desert. Therefore, he said, 'the Son of Man will lift himself up.' The last thing he said before I left, stunned me. 'Whoever believes in the Son of Man won't perish but have eternal life. *El Shaddai* didn't send his only Son into the world to condemn it, but to save the world through him.'

"Yoseph, don't you see, he's the foretold *Maishiach*!"

This left Yoseph numb with disbelief. "How . . . can you speak of such things? It's . . . blasphemous to think of this."

Nicodemus knew his friend wouldn't understand, but he too still didn't comprehend all of what Yeshua told him. "My intentions aren't to speak blasphemy, but to tell you what I have heard and observed. You may draw your own conclusions."

"Why haven't you spoken to me before of this secret meeting?"

"Some unknown person followed me that night after my meeting with Yeshua, and I didn't want you involved."

Yoseph knew his true friend wanted to protect him. But he knew he must tell him some of his own secrets.

"Yes, many years ago I remember, Miriam spoke of strange events surrounding the birth of my nephew. She spoke of three men from Persia visiting Yeshua as a young baby. They brought gifts to honor him as their Savior. Can you imagine, Magi from foreign countries believing my nephew the foretold Savior!

"Miriam mentioned one other event that might lead you to believe Yeshua a *kodesh* man. I remember her telling of a virtuous and devout man named Simeon. *El Shaddai* spoke to him through the *Kodesh* Spirit that he wouldn't die before he saw the *Maishiach*. They saw Simeon praying at the Temple when Miriam and Yoseph brought baby Yeshua there for the blessing. When he saw Yeshua, Simeon knew at once that his eyes recognized the *Maishiach* foretold to him. He told Miriam that her child would instigate the rise and fall of many in *Yisrael*. Simeon further prophesized to her that a sword of pain would pierce her heart and soul as the result of bearing this child.

"Miriam never spoke at length about any other holy events or prophecies. Yet, another strange occurrence happened to Yeshua and me. We had sailed to the Isle of the Celts called Albion, where I witnessed Yeshua healing one of the Celts. At the time, it appeared a miracle, but later I told myself it seemed a coincidence and forgot about it over time."

"So even with these restored memories, you still don't believe he's the foretold *Maishiach*?"

"I am not sure what to think anymore. Perhaps things will become clearer if I am able to meet with him in *Yerushalayim*."

"Then it's decided. You have my help to arrange a meeting. I believe Yeshua's future life bodes trouble, yet his followers are increasing each day. Your nephew poses a significant threat to many men of power, but I believe the most dangerous is within his own following."

Yoseph's mind still raced with questions, but their future reunion place stuck foremost in his thoughts. "Do you have any suggestions for a safe place for our meeting?"

"Before we decide where, we need to determine when. Most of his followers will arrive in *Yerushalayim* several days before *Pesach*. The people of *Yerushalayim* will attend Yeshua's arrival; however, many now hope for a warrior-king *Maishiach*. We must wait until after his entrance through the Golden Gate before we plan on meeting at your house."

"It's too dangerous to meet at my house," Yoseph replied.

"Then listen to my second plan before you say anything, Yoseph. My words are logical in what I am about to say. Most of his followers will stay at the home of Yohanan Marcus the next day. Have Hebron come to my house at dusk, and we'll leave to see Yeshua's friend, Yohanan Marcus, later in the evening. If he agrees, we will escort Yeshua and his *amma* to your house in the dark of the night. Knowing where all Caiaphas's spies are lurking, we can avoid these streets and use caution to deliver him unseen to your house. My messenger Saul will arrive and inform you when we're coming."

At once, an ideal location leaped into Yoseph's mind. "Wait! I have a better meeting place. Do you know my garden at Gethsemane, on the Mount of Olives?"

"Yes, I am familiar with the garden."

"My olive garden contains a secluded cave and the heavy-laden flowering olive trees will conceal our presence. We'll arrange the meeting close to the cave. I'll prepare the garden spot, while you and Hebron arrange it with Yeshua and Miriam. What do you think of my idea?"

"I think it's an excellent plan. With my informants knowing where Caiaphas's spies are hiding, this will keep the meeting safe from prying eyes. Let's have a cup of wine to toast our forthcoming event, my friend."

As they raised their cups, a sigh of relief came over Yoseph that their plans sought to protect all of his family during the reunion.

"Yoseph, when you leave my house, I want you to travel a different way home. Caiaphas knows of our close friendship. Also, he has announced that the Roman prefect, Pontius Pilate, will march his Tenth Legion into *Yerushalayim* during the week of *Pesach* and use them, if needed, to crush any riots or demonstrations that might occur. Moreover, I hear that the tetrarch, Herod Antipas, will travel from Galilee and arrive here tomorrow. Therefore, we need to display caution at all times, starting with tonight. Please, follow me to my back door and then hurry home."

As Yoseph rose from his chair, an exhale of tension came forth from his lungs, yet their reunion plans still left him with some concerns. He knew the Roman governor, Pontius Pilate, Herod Antipas, and Caiaphas would all congregate in *Yerushalayim* the same week. This meant trouble for all of them.

He thanked Nicodemus, said goodbye, and then left. Evening shadows had already formed as Yoseph exited the back door. His return home, through the streets of *Yerushalayim*, caused no consternation and he arrived at his house just at sunset. Yosa greeted him upon entering the courtyard and gave Yoseph a hearty embrace.

"*Abba*, Aunt Enygeus told me that you visited the house of Nicodemus. She said that you seek a meeting with Uncle Hebron, Nicodemus, and my cousin. Is that correct?"

"Yes, but we must show vigilance, for there are men who wish him and our family great harm." He hoped his warning would deter her from forcing this meeting, but it didn't work. Yosa's beguiling stubbornness came from her dear departed *amma*.

"I can't wait to see them again. I don't remember the last time we met. It seems to me that this meeting *El Shaddai* has ordained."

"Uncle Hebron will see to the meeting particulars with Nicodemus and the reunion at my olive presses in the garden of Gethsemane. First, your Uncle Hebron and Nicodemus will travel to a house of a man named Marcus. Yeshua and Miriam will lodge there in Marcus's house along with your cousin's followers. A young man named Saul, a student of Nicodemus, will arrive at our house to let us know they have approached the cave. Our meeting will start sometime during *Pesach* week. Until then, keep watching for your brother and tell no one of our meeting."

"I promise, *abba*, not to tell anybody about this gathering."

At once, her face generated a flushed broad grin, which thrilled him. "My dear child, will you bring my supper to my room? My eyelids are quite heavy and sleep beckons."

"Yes, *abba*, please rest. I won't disturb you when I deliver your food."

Yoseph strolled through his courtyard, past the gurgling fountain and entered the front entrance to their family living quarters. At once, his servants lit all the house oil lamps, giving Yoseph's home a brilliant yellow celestial appearance, brighter and more ethereal than usual.

His sleeping quarters had several lamps already lit. They appeared brighter for some unknown reason. Each corner displayed lights radiating from spots not lit from the oil lamps. How odd, he thought, in a day filled with strange events. The mind can produce mysterious things when it wants, he reasoned. As he drifted off to sleep, he thought about what Nicodemus said concerning the strange lights in Lazarus's home and he wondered if these were the same.

CHAPTER IX

The next morning arrived too soon; as a result, he stumbled out of bed. In the distance, he heard the clatter of the servants preparing the morning meal. He looked down at himself and saw his wrinkled robes from last night. With haste, he grabbed his tunic, washed his face in the cold water of the washbowl, and combed his long beard. At the foot of his bed, the servants had laid a fresh robe and shawl for him to wear.

After changing, his sister and Hebron met him in the courtyard as they approached the entranceway for the morning meal.

"Yoseph, I trust you slept well?" Hebron asked

"Quite well, thank you."

A farsighted thinker of a man, Hebron knew of both calamitous and excellent crop years in their vineyards. His height just fit through the entranceway and his massive frame resembled an ox. His face produced a prominent nose, yet it fit his large head quite well. His short beard glistened with palm oil and smelled of perfume. Hebron excelled as a merchant too and handled Yoseph's olive oil interests with intense shrewdness.

"Yosa has told me about your meeting with Nicodemus yesterday. I think your reunion plans are excellent. I accept the challenge to help Nicodemus arrange our meeting and I look forward to seeing Yeshua. I know many summers have passed since I last spoke with him and Miriam. He differed from his brother Yáakov; he always exuded a mysterious presence, yet quite kind to anyone and everyone, including strangers. He projected a vulnerability about him that made me always want to protect him. However, when I think back to his earlier summers, he seemed to not show fear of man or beast."

This secret challenge and meeting reassured Yoseph's trust in Hebron with such a great responsibility.

"When Yosa spoke earlier this morning of your friend Nicodemus, she said he mentioned a man named Yohanan Marcus. Why does that name sound familiar to me?"

"He's a distant relative of Yonath Annas, *abba* to the wife of Caiaphas," Yoseph answered. Yoseph hoped Hebron wouldn't change his mind after hearing this new information. What matter of men did his nephew garner? His doubts started creeping back into his mind along with fear for the safety of his family. Was Yohanan Marcus a spy for Caiaphas? Yoseph didn't know.

"Hebron, maintain your vigilance whenever you leave the house. Scrutinize every passageway and shadow that you see. Fear not for me, but exercise your caution for the sake of Yosa and Enygeus."

"You know I will protect our family with my life."

Hebron's considerable-sized right hand reached across his blue tunic belt and grabbed an ornately carved ivory-handled dagger. His size and determination frightened many men, Roman or otherwise.

"I have complete faith in you, Hebron, but there are many factions at work here we must face."

"There's no evil over which we can't triumph. Our resolute family comes from a line of warriors reaching back to the time of Yoshua."

Yosa rushed toward us with excitement on her dimpled cheeks.

"*Abba*, Alein Yosephe has arrived. Come and greet him. Uncle Hebron, come too. He wants to see you and Aunt Enygeus!"

They ran toward the front of the courtyard where Yoseph embraced his son. He hadn't noticed until now, but the sides of Alein Yosephe's hair were streaked with gray, making Yoseph sense his own advancing summers. After their greeting, Alein embraced Hebron, Enygeus, and Yosa. He then handed his sister a detailed carved chest made of tin. The lid and sides displayed garnets and small-inscribed cups or bowls on their surfaces.

"Look what Alein brought me! Isn't it gorgeous, *abba*?"

"Yes, my dear. I can see you're excited and your brother's extravagant gift for you shows his love. Now, Yosa, fetch some food and drink for your brother, for he has journeyed far with thirst. Alein, come, sit down and tell us about your trip home and all the gossip in Caesarea."

"The road home didn't excite me, but the news in Caesarea did."

"What stirring news?"

"It's about our cousin coming to *Yerushalayim* during the *Pesach*. The rumors say many followers are coming with him and they now call him their *Maishiach,* which our prophet Isaiah foretold. I concluded my business beforehand in Caesarea, permitting me to reach home and wait for his arrival. I am hopeful we can meet our cousin while he's in *Yerushalayim*. So, *abba*, what news do you have of Yeshua?"

"Your Uncle Hebron will arrange a meeting for the latter part of this week, with the help of my friend Nicodemus. In helping us, Nicodemus might bring harm to himself. Especially with the questionable character of your cousin's followers, with their past troubles with the authorities. The marketplace rumors say there are Zealots among his disciples. Nevertheless, we are his family and obligated to see him, regardless of the danger.

"We are arranging a reunion at our olive presses on the Mount of Olives. The olive trees are just now flowering, and we have few workmen there. Do you know the cave located in a grove of olive trees that your Uncle Hebron uses to produce olive oil? The cave and trees are quite secluded, which will hide our reunion."

"What risks are you speaking of?"

"Alein, Nicodemus has informed me this week will pose a threat for our family. The street merchants tout he's a warrior king coming to overthrow the Roman governor, Pontius Pilate, and will bring

Zealots with him. Your Uncle Hebron and I know this isn't true, but it takes little for the city to revolt, no matter who starts it. Alein, we need to practice discretion for the next several days."

"I agree with your plan, *abba*; however, will my cousin consent to meet in secret at the Mount of Olives?"

"I don't know, but your Uncle Hebron will secure it for Yeshua and his *amma*."

"*Abba*, I hope you don't mind if we discontinue our discussion for now. I am famished and ready to devour the food you brought."

After the meal, Yoseph enjoyed sitting down and talking with his son, especially since Alein's absence in dealing with their tin mines in the Celtic Isles. Discussing business with him took Yoseph's worries away. The financial interest in his tin mines greatly helped their profits, yet Yoseph's curiosity about the Celts didn't come from their mines, but from the Celtic people. Their warlike race perplexed him, yet they excelled as artisan metal workers. Also, their mysterious priests, about whom they knew little, seemed peaceful.

"Alein, how are our Celtic partners doing with our tin metal business?"

"They are coming along quite well." He bit into a juicy pomegranate. "The tribe's new war king, Arviragus, praises his people's mining efforts. He presented me with this ornate metal box that you see here which I've brought back as a gift for Yosa. It is his way of thanking us for our excellent trade relations. King Arviragus told me his chief priest inscribed the intricate design. The design symbolizes one greater than King Arviragus or his priests. King Arviragus said it would help protect our family until we entered through the veil. He further stated his priest revealed to him that an object of great importance would lay in this box. An object he said would benefit mankind for all eternity."

"What an unusual story. You must thank King Arviragus for his mysterious ornate gift on your next visit to his kingdom. I know Yosa will cherish this chest even more after hearing its history."

"Oh, *abba*, their king said something else. He wants to meet you. Also, there's a place in his kingdom he thinks you must see. His people call it the 'Isle of Mist.' He said there isn't anything similar to it in his entire realm. One day, he said it will become the most sacred place in his kingdom and his Druid priests told him a holy man will reside there. He hopes you will come to visit him and thereafter travel to this unique place."

"How can I resist such an attractive invitation? I say we plan a trip after the festival of First Fruits. What do you think, Alein?"

"I see no problem with this time. King Arviragus desires our wines and we will have an enormous crop of grapes, which we can use for trade. I will start planning our trip after *Shavuot*."

Yosa entered the courtyard. "*Abba*, what have you and Alein been discussing?"

"Nothing of importance, but your brother did tell me the story about the gift he brought you."

"Will you share the story with me, Alein?"

"Better yet, Yosa, I'll tell you the meaning of my gift. It's a gift for you and our family to cherish. A great king of the Celtic Isles said his priest told him its future contents would protect our family and save mankind for all eternity!"

"I see just an exquisite box with nothing in it. How can an ornate box and its empty contents protect humanity and us for all eternity? All I notice are small intricate-carved cups or bowls on the sides. And see, there are strange symbols, which appear as twisted ropes or snakes."

"The king told me the designs speak of eternity. His priests seldom use written words. They communicate with designs, symbols, and the priests, or Druids as he called them, memorize the Celt's history. Older priests pass this knowledge on to younger priests whose training starts in childhood. They have female priests too!" Yosa's eyes lit up with this information. "I knew you would enjoy hearing that. Their powers are just as great."

"*Abba*, didn't you travel to the Celtic Isles with Yeshua when you started your mining business?"

"Yes, I did." Yoseph thought of their journey long ago. "Twenty summers ago, I sailed most of the time on business. My niece Miriam asked me to escort her son to the Celtic Isles with me. Only your *amma* and Miriam knew of this trip. Yeshua was thirteen summers in age. Miriam's husband Yoseph ben David died that spring. Yeshua needed an *abba* figure and Miriam asked me to look after him.

"The fair weather made the sea voyage uneventful; however, the one thing that stands out the most came from a strange comment Yeshua made as we landed. He told me as we traveled through the woods, 'to whom much is given, much will be asked in return.' I asked him what his statement meant, but he gave no explanation; however, he said, 'In due course, all will be revealed,' and then he said no more." Yoseph's cryptic explanation encouraged Enygeus to ask a question.

"Yoseph, please tell me more about his childhood? I was just a young girl of fifteen summers and still living in Arimathea."

"As a young child, maybe six or seven summers, Yeshua differed from most children his age. Yeshua's intelligence was far greater than most scholars. He loved his *abba* and learned the trade that he practiced. At first, he excelled in the carpentry and masonry trade, but he didn't continue. After Yoseph ben David died, his demeanor changed, and he became introspective and more interested in spiritual matters. When looking into his eyes, he always gave me a sense of peace that left me flummoxed. Sometimes it seemed he saw into the depths of my soul.

"His persona exuded peace and kindness; I never saw him become upset or anxious. Also, he took an interest in those who had extraordinary needs . . . secular or spiritual. My business interests kept me away from home for numerous summers. It left me with angst in leaving Miriam and Yeshua many months at a time. That's when your Uncle Hebron helped me and visited them some years after my voyages to the Celtic Isles. To my knowledge, he never spoke of hearing or seeing anything unusual about your cousin. There isn't much more that I can tell you. If you have any other questions, you'll have to ask your Uncle Hebron."

"Did someone call me?" Yoseph's brother-in-law asked as he joined the gathering. He carried a welcome tray of pomegranates.

"Yes, Hebron, I did, and Enygeus wants to know about the time you spent in the town of Nazareth with Miriam and Yeshua."

"Hebron, you have told me little about the young boy Yeshua," Enygeus stated.

"Several years after his *abba* died, he preached as a rabbi. He studied and prayed every day. His brother and sisters said he traveled to many faraway places, then he returned and spent many hours preaching to the learned men of the synagogue. Numerous times, he prayed alone or at other times speak to crowds about *El Shaddai*. I have heard that his *abba* learned the masonry trade while they lived in Egypt when Yeshua was a baby."

"I didn't know they lived in Egypt," Enygeus said.

"I do remember some unknown messenger told them to leave our country for their safety. Baby Yeshua and his *amma* and *abba* traveled a considerable distance to move his family out of harm's way."

"Miriam did mention something to me about their flight to Egypt, I do recall. She told me three Magi from Persia came to visit baby Yeshua. These wise men presented Yeshua with valuable gifts to honor his birth. Their celestial maps had predicted a great king would come forth, born under a massive star. Yoseph took Miriam and Yeshua to Egypt using the Magi's gifts for expenses. I don't know what else I can tell you about them. Many summers have elapsed since their last visit. I guess we'll have all our questions answered when we have our family meeting."

"I am sorry that we have to end our conversation." Yoseph interrupted. "Hebron and I have pressing business to conduct today, and we need your assistance, Alein. It's time for us to start making arrangements for our meeting with Yeshua."

CHAPTER X

L eaving the eating area, Yoseph, Alein, and Hebron proceeded out of the courtyard into the busy street. The tight squeeze of visiting *Pesach* pilgrims made walking difficult.

Each year during spring, they visited the olive presses at Gethsemane to begin the growing season. This made it easy for them to use this time and place as the site for their secret family gathering. Yoseph believed the darkness, the dense olive trees, and their seasonal activities would hide their reunion and not create alarm among the workers or anyone else.

It typically took a full league's travel from Yoseph's home to their olive garden, but he knew a shorter way. His eyes focused on the mount in the distance as they trudged a steady pace up the inclined stone steps through the heart of the city. He and Alein rested on a large rock before going forth to meet the workmen. A cool breeze blew out of the valley that helped dry the sweat from their brows. Yoseph didn't see Hebron, thinking he might have continued on while they rested. Yoseph gazed to his far right and there stood Hebron, staring at the valley floor.

As they drew closer, Hebron didn't appear winded or dripping with sweat as the rest of them. He seemed stronger after their strenuous climb. His face held a placid expression as he still peered at the valley below.

"Yoseph, did you know the prophets say this Valley of *Yehoshaphat* will one day become the . . . judgment place of both the living and the dead?" His voice cracked as he continued glaring across the valley. His brother-in-law didn't show his sorrow or emotion often, they were as solid as the Temple stone walls.

"Yes, I've heard that prophecy told before, but what made you speak of this now?"

"Yes, Uncle Hebron," inquired Alein Yosephe. "Why did you recollect it at this time? You have often looked from this hill before."

"I don't know, Alein. Something came over me, maybe a premonition. I heard a stranger's voice speaking to me about many deaths in the future and the blood that would flow. I can't explain it, but let's not dwell on this now, yet see to our work here."

Hebron didn't answer any further questions, but the gaze in his eyes scared Yoseph. He turned, motioned for them to follow while taking long strides, reaching the top first.

Their workmen smiled to see them as they approached the entrance to the small cave. All along the path, blankets of white blooms dragged down the olive tree branches. An abundance of flowers covered each limb leaving no exposed wood, thus indicating a rich harvest.

At once, Yoseph's brow cooled on entering the cave as they ambled farther into the passageway. Their workers had lit torches along the walls that led to the central chamber. On closer inspection, the wood on their olive presses had weathered well.

"Hebron, how long will it take before the presses start producing?"

"We'll begin production two weeks after *Pesach*."

"Alein, have you made arrangements with the Roman merchants in Gaul to buy our olive oil?"

"Yes, *abba*, they're most anxious to receive the oil, for the Iberian farmers had a severe drought last year, creating a shortage this year. The Roman Army in Gaul has requested all the olive oil we can supply them. Also, they want some of our tin products. This year, I forecast our family will make an excellent profit."

"Let me speak to the workmen about the presses. With luck, they won't suspect anything about our activities here," Hebron said.

"We come here every year at this time and perform the same activities. Yet, not much happens in *Yerushalayim* without people knowing about it," Yoseph added.

"You're right, but our workmen respect your good pay and my authority, and both will stop idle gossip. Anyway, Aaron, our overseer can keep a secret. I'll ask him to guard the grounds when our family arrives. In addition, he knows how to use a sword."

"I appreciate your reassurance, Hebron. Don't let me interfere with your business with Aaron."

Hebron strolled toward the workers congregating near the olive trees. Each man embraced him with smiles on their faces. So far, it appeared their visit hadn't aroused suspicion. A short time later, after concluding his business, Hebron joined them as he ambled down the mount.

As they descended the path to the valley below, Yoseph heard a rumbling sound from the east. At first, it sounded similar to thunder, then he spied an advancing Roman legion. Yoseph's heartbeats surged with fear as they marched down the valley road, heading straight toward the Antonia Fortress. The afternoon sun's rays bounced off the legion's helmets and spears, causing the three of them to shield their eyes. The army's movements caused a steady thumping sound from their sandals, similar to a fast-approaching thunderstorm. Out in front of the wide dusty column of soldiers, several men carried red and gold-colored standards. One man held a metal eagle on a wooden staff with a banner underneath; on it, Yoseph saw the Roman letters, SPQR. Their metal idols most offended him, which contradicted his faith.

"Damn them!" Yoseph cursed

Several legionnaires carried golden curved horns that they blew a cacophony of sounds with every few steps. Hebron pointed to two men; one of them marched ahead on foot. This soldier carried a bundle of rods with an ax blade embedded on top. The bundle of rods bore the office of the *procurator* of Rome. The other man rode on horseback and wore a Roman-style toga with a garland of greenery perched on the top of his head.

"Look, *abba*, it's Pontius Pilate."

"Yes, I know. It's best we avoid him, I've been told."

As the legion moved closer to where they stood, Yoseph saw Pontius Pilate gazing at them through the drifting brown dust cloud created by his soldiers. Yoseph stood some distance up the side of the mount, but their path intersected the road on which the legion marched. The tumult of the numerous soldiers hitting against their shields, scabbards striking metal-pleated skirts and the ever-present shrill of their long-curved horns gave the Roman Army the appearance of a noisy giant tortoise lumbering its way along the valley road.

As Yoseph raised his hand to cover his eyes from the dust and glare, the *procurator's* posture reminded Yoseph of someone he'd met many years ago in the northern reaches of Britannia. He raised his hand to acknowledge their presence. Here rode the son of Marcus Pilate. Yoseph's hand reached into his cloak and touched the ring given to him many summers ago.

It took a while for the legion to pass, as they made their way toward the road. The rumble of the soldiers continued to echo throughout the valley, even after they disappeared.

"*Abba*, it appears Pontius Pilate thought you saluted him."

"I'm sure it gave that appearance. I just raised my hand to protect my eyes from the sun's glare shining off their helmets. The prefect doesn't know we're Jews, and we know a Jew would never salute a Roman Gentile. Anyway, we must hurry, for our meal awaits."

As they retraced their steps back across the Kidron Valley, the dust from the Roman Army hung low in the air, causing their eyes to tear.

Would the Romans ever leave their city? Yoseph saw many reminders of their presence around *Yerushalayim*. What would their ancestors now say about their lands occupied with these foul heathens?

The sun cut its way downward through the rooftops as they arrived back home. His daughter greeted them with a smile as they entered the courtyard.

"*Abba*, do you have great news for me? Did you arrange for our place to meet with Yeshua and Miriam?"

"Yes, my dear, that's correct."

"Nicodemus's messenger delivered this to you after you left. He said to read it as soon as you returned."

The folded paper bore an unknown red seal covering the back side of the note. The embossed wax seal displayed a fish symbol enclosing a sword in its center. Yoseph didn't recall Nicodemus using this symbol before to seal his notes. He made a mental note to ask him about this symbol the next time he saw him.

He read the missive's contents to himself. It told him what they had just seen. The Prefect Pontius Pilate's arrival with his tenth legion of soldiers, and again begged Yoseph to use caution with their plan. Nicodemus wanted Yoseph to visit him tonight for further details.

"*Abba*, what does Nicodemus say in his note?" Yosa asked.

"Just about *Pesach* and the arrival of Yeshua and Miriam." Yoseph didn't want to divulge Nicodemus's caution about Pilate to his daughter. He tucked the letter into his tunic just as Enygeus entered the courtyard and announced the evening repast. They sat down on recliners to partake of their bountiful meal, but Yoseph wasn't hungry. Enygeus poured the wine into each of their goblets. He said the *Birkat ha-mazon* and then she began asking questions about the reunion.

"Have you completed the arrangements? Will we see Yeshua and Miriam soon?"

"Yes, in fact, we'll see them late in the evening, tomorrow, from what Nicodemus said in his note. Yeshua and his followers will arrive at the Golden Gate tomorrow morning. This will grant us an opportunity to see him and his *amma* from afar before meeting them in person."

"Do you anticipate any trouble during his arrival, *abba*?" Yosa asked.

"No, Yosa, he's a man of peace and won't incite the crowd or his followers." However, Yoseph knew that potential riots might break out even if Yeshua didn't arrive in *Yerushalayim* for some reason.

The women strolled to their bedchambers, leaving Alein, Hebron, and Yoseph to discuss the events to come. Forthright Yoseph mentioned his impending visit to see Nicodemus.

"Tonight, I don't want you to travel alone to Nicodemus's house," Hebron said. "Let me accompany you, for two people are better prepared to deal with any threat they might encounter. After all, you said Nicodemus thought somebody followed you on your last visit, and I suspect Caiaphas has hired additional spies to watch us. He'll find any excuse to confiscate our wealth."

Yoseph glanced down and saw Hebron touch the dagger hidden in his cloak. His gesture helped reassure him that if anyone tried to harm either of them, dire consequences would result from their actions.

"I appreciate your concern; nevertheless, I must do this alone. You need to stay here tonight and protect the most important things in my life, my family. Spies are harmless; they just gather information and won't harm me."

"I will honor your wishes, but don't forget you are a rich man here in *Yerushalayim* and, therefore, a desirable target," countered Hebron.

He knew Hebron thought Yoseph underestimated his adversaries. "You're an excellent person to rely on, Hebron, and I think of you as my brother. However, I must handle this myself. If trouble follows me, I don't want anyone else involved.

"Alein, I would appreciate it if you would stay at our home tonight in your old room. Listen close to what I am about to ask of you." Yoseph took a deep breath and continued. "If something does happen to me, gather your sister, Aunt Enygeus, Uncle Hebron, and travel to my old hometown of Arimathea. Nobody outside our family knows the exact location of the cave you played in as a child."

"But, *abba*," Alein interrupted, "nothing will happen to you. You're an influential man here in *Yerushalayim*."

"That's correct, Alein, but supposed accidents can happen and go unnoticed during *Pesach*."

Alein looked as if he wanted to argue with him yet said nothing and respected his request. At this point, Yoseph took his leave and said goodbye to them. "I shall return before the moon rises."

At once, his stomach clenched and a quiet inner voice said, "Yoseph, don't risk your life tonight."

CHAPTER XI

oseph strolled through his courtyard to the front door, touched the *mezuzah* post to strengthen his faith, and stepped out onto the street. The cobblestone passageways weren't as crowded as during daylight. He passed many strangers, speaking unfamiliar languages, who weren't fortunate enough to find sleeping quarters during their pilgrimage. Instead, they rested in doorways of any entrance. The trip to Nicodemus's house produced different smells at night than during the day. His nose detected no pungent camel dung. In its place floated the sooty smells of lit olive oil lamps. Each home thrilled him with a sense of pride to see his people cleaning and preparing for *Pesach*.

Close to his destination, he heard the faint sound of movement behind him. The rustle of small bushes and the swish of the closed street vendor's tent flaps caused Yoseph to pause and listen. When he stopped, the sounds stopped, causing him consternation. Against his better judgment, his feet moved forward with a shuffle. As he turned down a side street, the unknown sounds became louder and then identifiable as soft footsteps. Each footfall became more hurried as it thumped against the stones of the street.

Nicodemus's house appeared just ahead and with luck he would arrive at the entrance before his phantom stalker reached him. The moonlight helped guide Yoseph to his friend's welcoming entryway. As he approached the doorway, he saw a man sleeping beside the entrance. He moved closer to knock on the door. At once the stranger bolted from his sleeping position brandishing a large forearm-length dagger aimed at Yoseph's stomach.

In a raspy voice, the attacker spoke. "Yeshua will cause your downfall," then he lunged at Yoseph.

Yoseph dodged the stabbing thrust of the glowing blade and then without warning somebody hit him from behind, causing him to fall forward and slide on the dew-covered cobblestones. Though out of breath and knocked down, it didn't prevent Yoseph from scissoring his legs to trip his first assailant. Before he reached a standing position, the second man didn't follow-up on his attack but lunged toward the first man with his dagger. The larger man didn't intimidate the smaller combatant. The bear-shaped man held the advantage in size; however, the smaller man moved quicker. At once, the smaller man screamed out in pain, broke free, and fled into the night. Then he heard a familiar voice. "Yoseph, are you, all right?" Hebron removed his hooded scarf so Yoseph could recognize him.

"Yes, I am. I thought you stayed with Yosa and Enygeus."

"I know I defied your wishes, but a voice told me to follow you, so I asked Alein to guard our household tonight."

Both relief and disappointment came over Yoseph, yet Hebron had just saved his life. "I can't say I am sorry you decided to defy my wishes."

The door swung open, revealing a yellow stream of light. Nicodemus at once motioned for them to enter. "Yoseph, are you all right?"

Yoseph nodded.

"I can't believe someone wanted to kill you and moreover, in front of my house!" Nicodemus exclaimed.

"By the protection of Hebron and *El Shaddai*, the attempt on my life failed. I didn't plan for Hebron to follow me. I told him to stay with Yosa and Enygeus, but my persistent brother-in-law took matters into his own hands. Hebron and Nicodemus, did either one of you recognize the attacker?"

"No, but I am certain I can identify him if I see him again." Hebron smiled at Yoseph. "That little coward will carry a reminder of mine from our brawl tonight. I twisted the dagger away from me and into his flesh. The dagger-man will bear a permanent scar on his arm."

"Glory be to *El Shaddai*!" Nicodemus exclaimed. "Let us celebrate Hebron's intervention with some wine."

With a slight limp, Yoseph hobbled his way into their host's study. Nicodemus excused himself and then reappeared a short time later bearing three cups of wine. Despite Yoseph's outward appearance of calm, fear for his family gnawed inside him.

"Nicodemus, please hand me one of those cups of wine to help my composure."

"Me too," Hebron said, and he gulped down his first cup.

"My friends, do you think our impending meeting with Yeshua has something to do with this terrible deed?" Nicodemus asked.

Hebron answered first. "It's someone who has gained knowledge of our plans and doesn't want them to come to fruition. The attempt tried to scare us; however, the person didn't realize to whom they faced. Yoseph, you didn't become a successful merchant bullied by fear these many summers. You, Nicodemus, his shrewd friend, move in high places and can accomplish much to permit our family gathering to succeed."

"Whom do you suspect, Yoseph?" Nicodemus further inquired.

"I have been followed before, but this is the first recognizable attempt on my life. I don't have any specific evidence at this point, but from what I have heard and seen, it mimics Caiaphas's machinations."

"It's quite apparent that at least one person knows of our discretionary plans," replied Nicodemus.

"Though there's one other possibility; maybe it's one of Yeshua's followers? However, what would they benefit from keeping us apart? What about the man called Yohanan Marcus? After all, he's related to the wife of Caiaphas."

"No, I don't believe he attacked you," Nicodemus replied. "To my knowledge, Yohanan Marcus has distanced himself from Annas and his son-in-law, Caiaphas. Many of my credible sources in the marketplace say it as fact. Someone who wants you dead hired this killer. What do you think, Hebron?"

"Yes, that's true, however, silver can tempt any man to murder. I know some of Yeshua's supporters are quite fanatical about him over-throwing the Romans and they might not think well of our family's business dealings with Rome."

"Yes, even the most passionate followers of Yeshua might suc-cumb to temptation. There's an old saying of one of the prophets, 'The closer you are to *El Shaddai,* the more the evil one will tempt your soul,'" Nicodemus stated.

"What have I said or done to the Sanhedrin that would bring down the wrath of Caiaphas?" Yoseph asked of Nicodemus.

"I am not sure at this point, but there are two possibilities that might arise to want you out of the way of the Sanhedrin. Your lucrative tin mine trade, I see as one motive. The Romans at this moment haven't conquered all of Britannia and taking over your tin mines, with an ex-cellent financial arrangement between Pontius Pilate and Caiaphas, will show Rome their prestige and power. The second motive could include the high priest's religious power base. Yeshua chastised the Sadducees for their beliefs, and Caiaphas knows you're his uncle. Caiaphas fears Yeshua will overthrow him and become the high priest or king. Here are your two simple, but compelling reasons."

Yoseph contemplated these ideas. Had the Sanhedrin involved themselves in a murderous cabal with Caiaphas? Did Yoseph have a naïve perception of the politics coming from the remaining mem-bers of the Sanhedrin? Yet, he agreed with Nicodemus. Had the web of politics, power, and greed overcome them?

"I don't want to agree with you, but you're right. I see no other reasons at this time. We must use vigilance about everything we do in the next few days. Also, before you leave, there's something I want to ask. I noticed a strange design on the seal of the missive you sent to my home. You know how curious I am about unusual symbols. Can you explain what the fish symbolizes on your seal?"

"Yeshua inspired me to have the ring seal made after our last pri-vate meeting. He said by teaching his disciples the way to their salvation, they would, in turn, become 'fishers of men' and his followers would become as plentiful as the fish in the seas. Thus, his righteous news for humankind's salvation would spread throughout the Mediterranean. The sword represents *El Shaddai's* constant protection for us from evil. To me, the sword represents our baptism under combat, and I pray to Heaven, *Adonai* uses his sword for our protection."

Nicodemus's excitement gave Yoseph the shivers. After all, what had happened this night, his telling Yoseph of Yeshua's powerful words and the meaning of his ring, helped strengthened his resolve. Yeshua's words also reminded him why he came here.

"Did Yeshua agree to meet us tomorrow night?"

"Yes, it's arranged. Let's hope our joyous time with him will leave us with pleasant memories instead of danger and intrigue. Our greatest potential for harm will occur on the trip to and from the Gethsemane cave. Hebron will make sure of everybody's safety. However, Yoseph, I will ask you one more time. Are you sure you don't want to postpone this gathering?"

"No, I am sure we're doing the right thing in pursuing our plans. Also, I sense he'll reveal something of most importance. He could divulge part of his divine plan. I don't know, yet there's now something unforeseen pulling me toward our meeting."

"Then I won't delay you and Hebron any longer. I know your family expects your return soon. Again, my friend, your life will change after seeing your nephew tomorrow night." He turned to leave the room. "Please wait while I find two of my oil lanterns to guide you through the dark streets."

Once again, Yoseph started worrying about their late arrival and his family's concern. A short time later, Nicodemus returned with several well-lit oil lanterns for their journey home. The smell of burning olive oil instilled a sense of calm in him as they bid farewell to his friend.

"May *El Shaddai* accompany you, my friends, until we meet tomorrow night."

They entered the dark, narrow streets to face whatever dangers awaited them. Having the oil lanterns to shine on the alleys and doorways gave them a small measure of protection. A rising full moon gave Yoseph and Hebron additional light to see the streets ahead. Ever watchful, Hebron stayed a short distance behind him as they moved along the shadow-covered stone-paved streets, searching for anyone who might approach. They arrived home about midnight to a dark house except for one lit oil lamp in Yoseph's room. He stumbled onto his bed, unable to sleep as he considered the attempt on his life and the faceless dagger-man.

After tossing and turning with a sore hip and apprehension, sleep came to him sometime before a lone cock crowed. Still exhausted, he stiffened his resolve to not let any person or persons stand in his way. However, some of his uneasiness vanished, knowing another day approached *Pesach* and solving some of his questions about Yeshua's past. He washed his face, trimmed his beard, and limped toward his clothes. Every muscle and bone in Yoseph's body ached from last night's attack. Slowly completing this task, he joined Hebron, who sat by himself eating some dates.

"Oh, Yoseph, did you rest well? I see you have a limp."

"No, I had too much on my mind last night, and, yes, I am sore over my entire body. Last night's attack and wondering who attacked me, left me restless."

"Sleep didn't happen for both of us last night. Nevertheless, it's too late to second-guess your decision. We'll see it through and prepare to meet any danger."

"I believe in what Nicodemus said. His plausible explanation about using Yeshua and his followers as an excuse to implicate me makes sense. If the attack on my life had failed, which it did, this still leaves me with a possible conviction of heresy or treason. If it had succeeded, they would then defame my reputation and steal all our wealth and possessions. It's a nasty predicament, which means we must stand strong at all times. Yet, my resolve tells me not to fear this and dire family matters. I haven't spoken to Enygeus, Yosa, or Alein Yosephe concerning last night's attack, but I have no problem with telling Alein." His words stopped as Yosa and Enygeus came into the eating room.

"*Abba*, I heard you tell Uncle Hebron you had no problem telling Alein about some matter. Is there a problem seeing Yeshua when he arrives in *Yerushalayim* this morning?"

"No, my dear, it just concerns business matters."

Yosa's blue samite dress enhanced her smooth curves of womanhood: the little girl had vanished. Her delicate features and quick smile mimicked Yoseph's late wife. He remembered Yosa's excitement as a small child when he would return from his trips to the tin mines. Her now-grownup grin reaffirmed his vigilance in keeping her safe during tonight's meeting.

"We need to leave soon, for I hear Yeshua will arrive before the sun rises over the Antonia Fortress," Yoseph announced. "Hurry, fetch your brother, Yosa, so we can finish our breakfast and depart. We'll leave for the Golden Gate entrance and there await his arrival. Not far from the gate, stands a small market booth; from there we can observe unseen."

"Yoseph, you look haggard," his sister stated. The tone of her voice led him to believe she knew what happened last night.

"It's nothing at all. I didn't sleep well after arriving from Nicodemus's house. The anticipation of seeing Miriam and Yeshua caused it. Why don't you see what delays Yosa and Alein Yoseph?"

After she left, he turned to Hebron. "I hope to tell Alein what happened last night and the danger we might face today. So, try to keep Yosa and Enygeus occupied on our way to the Golden Gate entrance. The noise from the crowd will keep them from overhearing our conversation. Tomorrow, I'll have Alein Yosephe travel to Arimathea and prepare a retreat for any troubles that might befall us this week. He will transport some food and hide some silver there to prepare for the worst." As Yoseph finished his conversation with Hebron, both his son and daughter returned to the room chattering about something.

"Why are both of you dawdling?"

"My fastidious sister's hair combing delayed us," Alein Yosephe replied.

"Well, both of you sit down and have some food before we leave. You'll need your energy for all of today's events." As he observed his son and daughter eating, he kept thinking how fortunate he was to be blessed with two healthy children and the means to feed them.

"*Abba*, can we leave soon?" Yosa asked.

"Yes, but not before we say our *Birkat ha-mazon* blessing together." Then came the unison sound of giving thanks to *Adonai* for their food

"Now, Yosa, follow us to the Golden Gate. Though, let's hurry to obtain a secluded spot to observe Yeshua's entry into *Yerushalayim*. Your Uncle Hebron and I know a place near the entrance with an unobstructed view and not crowded with people."

The five of them moved through the courtyard to the stone entranceway of their home. Yoseph touched the *mezuzah* post, closed the heavy door behind them, and then locked it as they entered the street. There they merged with a large number of people traveling the streets for *Pesach* and to see Yeshua's arrival. The crowd moved as a human river of bodies flowing over the cobblestone streets. The humming sound of voices increased as they approached the Temple, as did the dust and dirt.

Yosa and Enygeus drew their veils around their faces to keep out the dust. The morning sky cracked with pink-streaked light browns as the dust drifted upward, stirred by the feet of many pilgrims. Yoseph's eyes began to tear as they traveled through the faint dusty light of morning. Drawing closer to the Temple Mount, he detected a low murmur from the crowd chanting inaudible words. Just then, it occurred to him to discuss his plans with Alein Yosephe. He touched his shoulder and told him to slow down, while Hebron sped up to stay in front of the women.

"Alein, fall back a little, so we can talk in private. I need to tell you something important."

Having his attention, he informed him of the events from last night and their escape plan. "Alein, the attacker escaped, but he left with a dagger gash on his arm by your Uncle Hebron. Your sister and aunt don't know about the attempt on my life and let us keep it a secret. Promise me you will do as I ask?"

Alein Yosephe nodded his assent.

"If something happens to me . . ."

"*Abba*, don't say that!"

"You must listen. After last night, anything might happen. In the event that something does befall me, please see to it that our family leaves at once for Arimathea. Prepare today the food and the silver. Arimathea will hide all of you quite well."

"But *abba*, why would anybody want to harm you?"

"There's not enough time to explain right now, I'll do that later. Alein, in the meantime, see to your aunt and sister while your Uncle Hebron and I keep a look out for trouble."

By now, they had arrived at their destination, close to the Golden Gate entrance. The crowd now surged its way toward the main entrance road. Hebron and Yoseph fell back a short distance from Yosa, Enygeus, and Alein while discussing tonight's meeting. Yoseph noticed Hebron staring at a young man darting in and out of the alleyways between buildings and then he stopped and stared in their direction.

"Yoseph, there's a man following us. He looks similar in stature to the dagger-man."

"Is that the man we fought with last night? Even from this distance, I can see his arm, it's covered."

"Let's wait at the next side street and confront him." After which, he reached for his concealed short sword.

As they ducked into a small side street, the man drew closer and raised his arm to block the sun. His sleeve slipped down revealing a narrow red slash from his wrist to his elbow. Yoseph's heart started racing. At last, he would have some answers, ease his fears about his family, and exact revenge for the previous night's attack.

After darting past two buildings, they ran into a dark passageway and saw the stranger looking the other way. At Hebron's nod, they grabbed the man's arms, held on tight, and threw him on the cobblestones. At last, they had their attacker.

CHAPTER XII

He seemed taller than his attacker. However, the man winced when they grabbed his left arm and his eyes grew enormous as Yoseph twisted it further while escorting him to a side street.

Right away, Hebron examined his scar.

"Who are you and why follow us?" Yoseph demanded.

"Yes, and speak your name," Hebron insisted.

"I mean you no harm, but I want to speak to you, Master Yoseph. A messenger came to my house and said you long to meet my rabbi and teacher."

"How do you know who I am?"

"I found where you lived and followed you and your family. Your son and daughter favor my master, Yeshua, and his *amma*. I must admit I had difficulty following you in this crowd."

Hebron shouted his displeasure while still gripping the man's arm. "Enough of your lies! Tell us your rightful name."

"I am called Yohanan Marcus and I am an acolyte for my rabbi." Yoseph glanced at Hebron and gave a sigh of relief, but still noticed Hebron's narrowed eyes.

"How do we know you are telling us the truth? I put that cut on your arm," Hebron insisted.

"Nicodemus sent the messenger who brought this missive to me. I know that both of you are a member of the Sanhedrin and are close friends."

"I have no apologies for knocking you down," Yoseph said, "for someone attempted to kill me last night. My family accompanied me today, and I suspect all strangers with unusual behavior. I hope we didn't hurt you. However, we acted out of desperation."

"Do you have more substantial proof you're telling the truth?" Hebron demanded as he released his grip but didn't loosen his sword hand. Yohanan Marcus's left hand then eased toward his cloak. He reached inside his tunic and pulled out a small scroll, which he handed to Yoseph. The scroll had a broken wax seal, which displayed a fish with a sword design embedded in it.

"Master Yoseph, please forgive me for not coming forward in delivering my message to you. I sensed somebody following me, which made me cautious. Of course, I had no idea about the attempt on your life. When my rabbi and I meet this afternoon, I'll inform him of the dangers you experienced."

"Your master's name and reputation have preceded him the last several years and I now understand he's a rabbi."

"Yes, his disciples call him a scholar. I have heard him teach and I have faith in his beliefs. Yeshua's preaching abilities differ from any others I've known. His wisdom and kindness have no bounds. Some of his disciples profess he's the *Maishiach* foretold by the Prophet Zechariah."

"You speak blasphemy, young man! My nephew exudes kindness and intelligence, but the *Maishiach*? I think not." At that point, in their conversation, the crowd roared louder. Yoseph and Hebron came out of the alleyway prompted by the crowd's yelling.

Alein Yosephe raced toward them, shouting, "I see him, *abba*! Yosa and Enygeus want you to come right away." His joy became subdued when he spied the young man standing next to Yoseph. "Who are you and why are you speaking to my *abba*?"

"Let me introduce Yohanan Marcus to you." Yoseph gestured to the man. "He travels with Yeshua as an acolyte. He delivered this message for me from Nicodemus." Yoseph turned back to Yohanan

Marcus. "I assume you'll help us tonight when we meet my nephew and his *amma*? The rumors say that Yeshua lodges with you this Holy Week. Is this correct?"

"Yes, you're accurate on both questions. I see it as a great privilege to have Rabbi Yeshua to stay with my family during this sacred time."

"Forgive me, Yohanan, for my suspicious manner," Alein Yosephe apologized. "Somebody tried to take my *abba*'s life last night and I feared the worst when I saw both my uncle and *abba* holding you."

Another loud roar came from the crowd, causing them to twist their heads toward the Golden Gate. Just a short distance from where they stood, Yoseph observed the backs of Yosa and Enygeus as they positioned themselves above the dense crowd of spectators. Both had moved closer to the raised open-air market tent located next to the gate entrance.

"Come, Yohanan Marcus, join us while we wait at the gate for Yeshua and his retinue." Accepting his invitation, Yohanan Marcus hurried with them to the predetermined vantage point to meet Yoseph's sister and daughter.

The crowd began to shout, "Zechariah foretold, Zechariah foretold, Zechariah foretold." Palm branches, held as a sign of honor, waved in the air as the shouts increased. Standing not more than one building from the Golden Gate opening, they had an excellent view of the forthcoming procession.

At once, Yoseph spied the ears of a donkey coming through the gate entrance. A tremendous rumble of voices came forth from the crowd with shouts of, "Hosanna, Hosanna, Hosanna." Then Yeshua entered on the back of a donkey, with its small colt trotting close behind. Here rode a man without the young boyish face Yoseph once remembered. Yeshua had a royal demeanor, but without its usual imperial arrogance. Though not large in stature, he exuded a quiet power far greater than that of earthly kings.

Yeshua's bearing reflected a wisdom observed in those who have lived many years, accompanied with peace and kindness. His large round, dark eyes seemed to draw each person in the crowd to fixate on his face. His long dark brown hair curled out from the sides of his shawl and a full beard covered his face that gave him the appearance of a rabbi. He presented himself as an ancient prophet to whom earthly property and vanity didn't possess him.

Rays of the morning sun rose over the entrance gate, bathing Yeshua with a glow that radiated from his head in all directions. Were his eyes deceiving him, Yoseph thought, as the radiance still followed him as he passed into the shadows of the buildings? Despite what he noticed, his nephew, he had known since his birth, now enraptured him.

"My rabbi never fails to capture the attention of the people wherever he travels. He has the same effect on me as he does on everyone here," Yohanan Marcus commented.

Now the members of Yoseph's family joined in with the crowd, shouting, "Hosanna, Hosanna," as the crowds pushed forward into this mass of humanity. Individuals started laying their blue, green, and yellow-colored cloaks on the ground in front of Yeshua's donkey, creating a colorful road of cloth. The large gathering of people waved their palms and then threw them down causing a fresh breeze to sweep through the air.

"*Abba, abba*," Yosa came scurrying to him out of the packed crowd. "Did you see my cousin's grand entrance?"

"Yes, and quite inspiring. I am glad we witnessed this memorable event." He saw the curiosity in her eyes as she approached his new companion. "Yosa, let me introduce you to one of Yeshua's followers. Yohanan Marcus, please meet my daughter Yosa. She's quite anxious to see your rabbi."

"I am quite pleased to meet you, Yosa, and everyone must have an opportunity to experience the joy I have had as one of his followers. When in his presence, he produces a powerful change in the lives of those who have had this privilege. Indeed, I am honored to assist in your family gathering tonight." Yoseph saw Yohanan's dark eyes glisten with admiration speaking about his rabboni.

"Master Yoseph, I must depart now and meet with my teacher and hear his lesson at my home. I'll see you tonight. For now, *shalom*."

Yosa's round face grinned with excitement as she considered the events they had scheduled. His message from Nicodemus had set their meeting plan in motion. Yet tonight, he wouldn't just see his nephew, but he would see a religious man whom many thought the foretold *Maishiach*. It seemed incredulous to him that Yeshua, the son of his niece, would have the divine knowledge imparted by *El Shaddai*. The more this thought spun around in his head, the more vexed he became.

CHAPTER XIII

Yohanan Marcus disappeared into the large crowd as the masses followed Yeshua's procession. The dust in the air coated Yoseph and his family's throats as they headed toward their home, leaving gritty tastes in their mouths. The trip back became an arduous task as they pushed their way through the mass of *Pesach* celebrants. As they proceeded, Yoseph noticed that Hebron's shifting brown eyes squinted to see each person who approached Yoseph.

"I can't wait until we arrive back home," Hebron said in a whisper.

"I agree with you and long to see our *mezuzah* post." Both he and Hebron knew large crowds posed a greater threat to their safety. One close bump by a stranger and a dagger thrust could end his life and he wouldn't know who did it.

Although he saw no one suspicious, Yoseph had a strong sense that somebody lurked behind them.

Once seeing his red-tiled roof, a sense of relief came over Yoseph. Without delay, Hebron took out a metal key from his sash belt, pushed it into the padlock of their large iron gate, and unlocked it. Afterward, he locked the gate behind them. This unusual act drew both Yosa and Enygeus to inquire about locking it late in the morning.

"*Abba*, why did Uncle Hebron lock our entrance?" Yosa inquired.

"He's preparing for tonight's visit to Gethsemane and thought it best to secure our house, as there are many strangers in *Yerushalayim*."

"But *abba*, it's almost midday. Why this part of the day?"

"My daughter, there's an entire Roman legion at the Antonia Fortress, and they're expecting trouble. The Roman *procurator* leads them, and he doesn't tolerate any political disorder. We must embrace vigilance for the next several days."

"I guess you're right, but what about our meeting with Yeshua? Do you think it's too dangerous?"

"No, we have secret plans arranged for us to travel through the streets tonight. At the appropriate hour, Nicodemus's messenger will arrive to signal the time to leave. We'll depart in different groups at different intervals. One group will travel by way of the Golden Gate; the other group will journey by way of the Antonian Gate. One trip will take longer than the other; this group will start first. This will allow us to meet at about the same time at Gethsemane. My overseer, whom I trust, has set up a banquet for us to share with Yeshua, Miriam, and a few of his disciples. Nicodemus will arrive first. So why don't we refresh ourselves, eat our meal, and obtain some rest before our visit tonight? I know you have many questions for your cousin and his *amma*. I'll see you soon after we clean up."

Proceeding to his quarters, Yoseph washed his face, hands, and had his servant prepare a foot-washing bowl. After his ablutions, he draped a clean shawl over his head and proceeded toward his noonday meal.

"*Abba*, I am too excited to eat much now." Yosa paced around the table. "Besides, *Pesach* has forced me to fast. And I'll have something to eat tonight."

"Of course, you will, but supper will come late. Therefore, eat now and give yourself sufficient energy for the long trip ahead." Yosa reclined at the table.

"Yeshua and Miriam will travel by way of Yohanan Marcus's house and will wait for us. Hebron, that reminds me. Do we have sufficient torches and lanterns for all of us to travel tonight?"

"Yes, they're ready and also are the servants with the food. I sent the wine ewers this morning along with flat loaves of bread, meats, and honey cakes."

In Yoseph's mind, he still questioned the risk of meeting his now rabbi nephew and his followers. He gazed into his wine cup, contemplating this.

"Yoseph, I see you are occupied with other thoughts," Hebron inquired. "Is something troubling you?"

"No, just the same old doubts." He changed the course of the conversation and then thought about the small swords Hebron had gathered for their protection. Yoseph prayed to himself that they wouldn't have to use their weapons.

"So, have the servants prepared everything for tonight's visit?" he asked, knowing he sounded repetitious.

"Yes, I've told you that. Now we wait for Nicodemus's messenger."

Hebron's self-assurance gave him some confidence that tonight's supper he'd enjoy. At last, his nerves relaxed enough to think about taking a short nap before their late-night visit.

"Look for me in my sleeping quarters if you need me, but first let's say our *Birkat ha-mazon* food blessing." After which, Yoseph ambled to his sleeping room and fell onto his bed.

The sun crept behind the next-door house as he lay on his bed. A cool breeze blew through his open window from the courtyard. The sound of a cooing dove lulled him into a light slumber. A short while later, a commanding voice aroused him from his semiconscious state. Its words emanated from a bedroom corner.

"Yoseph of Arimathea!"

One corner of his sleeping room erupted with blue-tinged shafts of light, surrounding a man-shaped apparition in a long white tunic. He radiated such intensity that it threw off sparks. His appearance exuded an overwhelming smell of rose petals, further giving Yoseph a sense of euphoria. He then glided toward him, causing his euphoria to change to apprehension.

"I am the cup bearer called Gabriel and *El Shaddai*, our *Abba* has sent me with a message of great importance. It involves you and your nephew, Yeshua. Listen with care to what I have to say."

As the celestial spirit moved closer, his words registered quite well to Yoseph's ears, he heard fine, yet to his horror, his burning lips stuck together, and he couldn't speak.

"The next three days will reveal a turning point, not in just your life and your family's life, but the entire world. You will hear the words of *El Shaddai* spoken through his only Son. Don't turn away from anything your nephew asks of you, for his words come from the Kingdom of Heaven. Your *Adonai* requests you to write down everything you see and hear the next few days. In addition, you're to keep a record of all things your future destiny beholds.

"You'll face many evils," his booming voice announced. "Beware, Yoseph, for there are many obstacles on your future path. Hurry now and meet your nephew, and listen to all his *kodesh* words."

At once, the blue-tinged light dissipated as the wraith stopped speaking and disappeared. He left nothing behind to indicate his bizarre visit, or was it a fitful dream? No, it appeared not a dream, for Yoseph's fingers touched his opened eyes. He tried to cry out, but no sound came out of his throat.

He lay there for a few moments attempting to collect his thoughts and struggled to speak again. Without notice, his voice issued forth a garbled sound in summoning his servant.

"Is there anything wrong, Master Yoseph? You sound ill."

"No, just a bad dream and nothing more. Thank you for rushing so fast. Please, bring me some wine for my dry mouth."

At once, he left, as Yoseph sat there pondering the words of the apparition. Why had this angelic spirit appeared to him? Why him? He wasn't worthy enough to serve his *Adonai*.

His servant trotted back with his wine. "Is there anything else I can do for you, Master Yoseph?"

"Oh, yes, have Hebron come to my quarters."

After his servant had departed, Yoseph removed writing material from a chest that held his personal effects. What prevented him from writing down these strange events of the last several days? Nothing, by journaling them he might relieve his distress. Perhaps in organizing the words, he might make some sense out of the past few days.

His merchant experience had taught him not to overlook important written details . . . however, the spirit's dire warnings amounted to more than any ordinary business transactions. After all, he had warned him, in the next three days Yoseph would face great evil and intrigue.

As his writing hand positioned pen to paper, a realization struck him. His spiritual beliefs would change. What additional revelation might he hear over the next several days? Hebron entered his sleeping quarters and distracted his innermost thoughts, but his new euphoria still possessed him. Unexpectantly, his mind started seeing a dark pit devouring the warm golden light in his head.

"Yoseph, you sent for me?"

"Yes, Hebron, I did. I have to share something with you, though you might find it difficult to believe. I'm not even sure myself it happened." Yoseph's heart started racing in anticipation of explaining himself and his mind stalled in trying to take his thoughts and give them to his tongue.

"Sometime . . . after the noonday meal, something strange occurred as either a dream or a hallucination, I am not positive of which, yet it seemed quite real." Yoseph swallowed a deep breath before continuing. "An apparition appeared in my room and portended that evil would surround Yeshua for the next several days. The *malach* spirit further said I must listen to Yeshua and do what he asks. Also, the *malach* told me *El Shaddai* would speak through his Son in the next three days. This angelic spirit's abstruse statement left me confused and I think his warning doesn't bode well for our family. What do you say?"

"I am just as perplexed as you are, but it appears you and our family are about to become involved with Yeshua's dangerous ministry. If a *kodesh malach* indeed commanded you, our destinies will intertwine with Yeshua's fate. I hope Yeshua will reveal his plans for us during our supper. If not, I expect a tasteful feast and a chance to spend some time with him and his *amma*."

"Of course, you are right. Until we meet with Yeshua, this wraith's ambiguous warning means nothing. However, please don't mention to the others what I have said. I don't want them to think I am losing my mind."

Indeed, Yoseph feared this most of all. Yet, maybe the strain on his nerves the last few days and the attempt on his life caused this dream.

"At this point, there's nothing we can ascertain from the *kodesh* messenger now, and we must see to our trip to the olive gardens. Hebron, will you notify the servants we are ready to leave? By now, the pitch torches are ready to carry. As soon as I'm ready, I will meet you at the courtyard gate. The messenger will soon arrive."

"Remember, Yoseph, we must not fear, for we have the power of *El Shaddai* with our family." Hebron exited.

He left Yoseph alone with his thoughts and gave him some reassurance, yet he knew Hebron too carried an enormous responsibility on his shoulders tonight.

They met in the courtyard and waited for Nicodemus's student to arrive with the message to leave.

"*Abba*, how do I look?" Yosa said, twirling her shawl.

"You look gorgeous, as usual, yet the earrings and ankle bracelets look familiar. Did I buy them for you?"

"Don't you remember? They belonged to *amma*."

"Yes, my child, I now recall. I am sorry I forgot." A tear came to his eyes as he gave her a tight embrace.

"*Abba*, don't cry. I don't want to sadden you tonight."

A blue veil covered her small nose and full lips, but not her dark flashing eyes. Her youthful image reminded Yoseph of his young wife many *Pesachs* ago. "But you are right. Now isn't the time for tears. There are more important things for us to do."

As his sister entered the courtyard, there came a knock on the door. "That's Nicodemus's messenger with news about our trip." He opened the heavy wooden door and there stood a young man.

"Master Yoseph, my teacher Nicodemus sent me to tell you to prepare to leave at once. I am Saul of Tarsus, Nicodemus's pupil, and he swore me to secrecy, though I don't know why."

"How did you recognize me?" Yoseph inquired of Nicodemus's pupil.

"Master Nicodemus spoke of your membership in the Sanhedrin, and I saw your medallion of office around your neck."

"Come in, young Saul, and have a refreshing drink for your trouble."

"No, I can't stay. Master Nicodemus has other tasks for me. He gave me strict instruction not to dawdle."

"Nicodemus has trained you well in both observation and obedience, and I won't detain you any longer. May you live in the spirit of Eliyah."

The young man left Yoseph's courtyard door and disappeared into the shadows of the surrounding buildings.

Their torches burned with a bright yellow-orange flame as they left through the large front gate of their courtyard with Alein Yosephe leading the way. Hebron, in back, padlocked the gate as they headed down the dark, narrow streets of *Yerushalayim*. Both Enygeus and Yosa moved close to Yoseph, at his sides. How fortunate, he thought, that the side streets displayed few people as they traveled in a different direction during this time.

The narrow passageways maintained their silence as they crept along the sides of each building. The sole noise came from the jingling of Yosa's ankle bracelets as she strolled near him, holding tight to his arm. The dark alleyways glowed with their numerous lanterns and torches making giant shadows dance across the sides of the houses. Two of his servants carried fresh, prepared food that emanated the honey-sweet smell of dates. Occasionally, the servants' torches emitted popping and hissing sounds from the sticky tar that kept Yoseph in an anxious state.

They had traveled just about half a league before they split up. The first juncture came near the Temple and on the same side as the Antonia Fortress.

"Listen, Yosa, we must split up for our safety. You and your aunt must leave with Alein Yosephe. The servants, Hebron, and I will travel another path. Your brother knows the way and what to do if there's trouble. Here's a small sword to carry in your shawl just in case there's a problem. I will follow a short time later by another path."

As they moved apart, Yoseph's mind filled with worry and apprehension. Most of his family strode down another street and melded into the dark night. However, the jingle sound of Yosa's ankle bracelets continued long after she disappeared from sight. His heart beat as fast as a drum each time they came to a doorway entrance and saw a dark shadow crouching at the threshold.

CHAPTER XIV

A sense of relief came over him when their lanterns revealed nothing more than a large clay pot.

They stopped for a short period, resting, before setting off in another direction. The passageway they chose came close to the Temple wall leading them toward Gethsemane. At one of the several Temple gates, they encountered a guard patrolling the entrance.

"Halt, who goes there?" he ordered.

"It's Yoseph of Arimathea, a member of the Sanhedrin."

"Come closer," he demanded. Yoseph ambled near him holding his torch close to his face.

"Members of the Sanhedrin have a badge of office. I command you to show it if you indeed have one." Yoseph reached into his tunic and pulled out his medallion of office.

"What's your business, Master Yoseph?"

"We're on our way to some much-needed repairs to my presses on the Mount of Olives. I don't want the *Pesach* celebration to delay production of the olive oil that I am preparing to send to Iberia. These men are assisting me."

"You may pass, but beware. During *Pesach,* there are thieves hiding in the streets to attack visiting pilgrims."

"Thank you for the warning, but we have brought protection of our own." Each of them reached at their sides to show the hilts of their swords.

Quickly, the guard jumped back and motioned them on and then marched back to his post. They continued in the direction of the Valley of *Yehoshaphat* as the moon rose above the horizon, providing them with extra light. This caused additional shadows to appear on the street passageways. Yoseph's mind still raced with imaginary human figures that disappeared when they shone their torches over the many house entryways. They stopped several times when they heard approaching voices or saw actual people sleeping in doorways and then changed direction.

As they rounded one side of the Mount of Olives, he observed several fires ahead near the cave. A slight breeze blew across the valley floor and helped cool Yoseph's sweaty face. In the darkness, he heard the quiet murmur of voices coming from the fires.

"Yoseph, I am continuing ahead to check for any problems," Hebron whispered.

"I'll wait here until you come back and tell us to proceed." Soon, the wind started howling just as Hebron came back to tell them to come and join the others at the campfire.

"Yoseph, let's go. We're still waiting on Yosa, Enygeus, and Alein Yosephe to arrive. Our foreman, Yoel, said he saw their torches and lanterns ascending from the valley floor not more than a quarter of a league away."

Yoseph crept toward the campfire and saw the outlines of two women and five men warming themselves. His foreman approached and spoke. "Master Yoseph, come join us at the campfire. I hope you're pleased with the evening meal."

"Oh, Yoel, I am sure you have done well; you always follow my wishes." The man smiled as they followed him to the campfire.

Near the fire, Yoseph noticed a small boy of about three summers in age dash out from behind a woman he didn't recognize. The boy

stared at him as he approached. Then his nephew and his *amma* rose
to greet him.

"Welcome, Yeshua bar Yoseph, to our feast. It has been quite a
while since I saw you and your *amma*. Miriam, my kind princess of
Galilee and niece, has *El Shaddai* looked after you?"

"He has, Uncle Yoseph." Miriam gave him a soft kiss on his
cheek. Afterward, Yeshua embraced both Hebron and Yoseph.
Yoseph noticed that Yeshua wore his prayer shawl covering his head
along with a phylactery on his forehead. Next to him, he observed
a woman of about twenty-five summers with the little boy clinging
to her long red robe. Her large round brown eyes, long lashes, and
shiny shoulder-length dark brown hair gave her an unsurpassed
beauty. Her eyes blazed in the firelight.

"Uncle Yoseph, let me introduce to you Miriam of Magdala. Behind
me stands Yudas Iscariot and Philip of Bethsaida. Yohanan bar Zebedee
stands next to *amma*, and I believe you know Yohanan Marcus. For many
days, we have looked forward to visiting with you, Uncle Hebron, and
Aunt Enygeus. Uncle Yoseph, didn't you bring my cousins Yosa and Alein
Yosephe?" Yeshua's eyes searched into the dark distance.

"Nicodemus waits for them and they will arrive at any moment.
We took separate ways for reasons that I'll explain later."

Just then, Yoseph heard the rustling of bushes to his right, alert-
ing his faithful servant to at once use his lantern and seek the source.
Yosa rushed out of the darkness toward him, with bracelets jingling,
eyes sparkling, followed by Enygeus and then Alein. Nicodemus
followed, looking over his shoulder with his lantern held high.

"*Abba*, are we late?" Yosa gasped, trying to catch her breath.

"No, my child."

Yoseph experienced relief to see them unharmed.

Yosa approached Yoseph's nephew first and they embraced. The
greetings were repeated by the rest of Yoseph's family.

As Alein and Yeshua stood side by side in the firelight, he noticed
their clothes differed. Yeshua wore plain white clothes, reflecting a
mason's son, while Alein Yosephe wore rainbow-colored clothes,
reflecting a rich merchant's son.

Yeshua appeared lean, but not from sickness. His beard seemed fuller than Alein's, yet not as long as a prophet or a desert Essene. Yeshua wasn't tall in stature, but his presence seemed omnipotent. When Yeshua spoke, he seemed to know what Yoseph thought before he replied. His dark auburn-colored hair, covered with his rabbi shawl, revealed a white toothy smile that drew everybody to him.

His hands were quite dark from the sun, but exhibited no coarseness in them, no evidence of a son of a carpenter or a mason. Yet, on his right hand appeared a birthmark in the shape of a white dove. How odd, Yoseph hadn't remembered seeing this mark until now. He displayed a sense of calm and his workers sensed the same serene presence. The one exception came from a man named Yudas Iscariot. He seemed quite nervous while circling the campfire numerous times as they stood still. Yudas never made eye contact with Hebron or Yoseph but held his head down.

After Alein Yosephe had stopped speaking to his cousin, both Yeshua and his follower, Miriam of Magdala, approached Yoseph.

"Uncle Yoseph, Miriam and I desire to say something to you in secret."

"Fine, Yeshua. What about using the coolness of the cave where my olive presses are located? Is this satisfactory?"

"Yes, but please ask Yosa to amuse the young boy while we're in the cave."

"Let me ask Yosa and excuse myself from our gathering." As Yoseph approached the fire, he saw Yosa entertaining the young boy with a small carved-shaped wooden camel.

"Yosa, my dear, please watch this young one while I guide Yeshua and Miriam of Magdala on a tour of the olive presses."

"Of course, *abba*. Look, he's already quite happy playing with his toy."

His pretense didn't seem to arouse suspicion or curiosity as they moved toward the cave.

"Nicodemus, I need to use your lantern. I'll return it soon."

As they traveled down the small path to the cave, Yoseph noticed that between the small rocks were hawthorn shrubs covered with white and pink flowers. They seemed to glow with an ivory color when the lantern light revealed them.

They traveled for a short distance without saying a word to one another, Yoseph wondering why Yeshua and the woman from Magdala wanted to speak to him in private. As they approached the cave entrance, the conversation started, first with Miriam of Magdala. She took the red veil away from her mouth and began to speak. He noticed her lips were full and wide before she began to speak.

"Master Yoseph, your nephew and his *amma* have spoken much praise of you and the kindness you have shown them over the years."

"I have always loved them." He glanced at his nephew with pride.

Miriam of Magdala continued speaking concerning him and his help for Yeshua and Miriam of Nazareth. She seemed to know everything about him. Her round face and dark eyes held Yoseph's attention as she spoke with clarity. Her maturity and wisdom far exceeded her age, and he learned she came from an old merchant family. During the course of the conversation, she kept looking at Yeshua for approval about what she said. It didn't resemble the kind of support or assurance a wife would seek from her husband, but that of a student from her teacher.

"Yeshua has shown me the 'way' and I have become a far better person," she stated. "In the past, your nephew did help my troubled soul. All I once cared about was business and not helping others in need. I worshipped idols of gold and silver."

It appeared Yeshua's mentoring had played some significant role in her life. After a short period of silence, she continued speaking.

"Master Yoseph, I'll now have your nephew, my teacher, explain what he asks of you. Nevertheless, before he does, one last thought; thank you for allowing me to forthrightly speak with you."

Yeshua nodded to Miriam with a smile of approval.

"Yoseph, my beloved uncle, once again it's great to see you and my *amma* appreciates the same. Unknown to *amma,* I planned to visit you before she received your supper invitation. However, I am here to ask not a boon for me, but from my Holy *Abba.*"

Why did he say this? He knew Yoseph, Yeshua's *abba* practiced his faith as an upright man, but he wasn't a sanctified parent. What *Kodesh Abba* was he referring to? No, he's not telling him his *abba* was spiritual. Yoseph's hands reached for the cool stone wall of the cave, to steady his body from swooning. An appeal from the *Kodesh Abba*, this didn't make sense. Why would their *Kodesh Abba* need Yoseph?

"It involves Zechariah, the young boy child we left with Yosa. He is now an orphaned child of Yohanan the Baptizer. As his cousin, Yohanan wanted me to see after his son if something happened to him. For reasons I can't now explain, raising him myself is impossible. Soon you'll understand why. Until that time, I know his destiny isn't with the 'Sons of Light' and the Qumran community. He's destined to travel with you, as I did many summers ago to the Isle of Britannia. I see in his future the start of a line of kings ruling that isle. You, Uncle Yoseph, are the sole person I can trust with his welfare."

The spirit Gabriel's prophecy just became true. Yeshua's revelation unnerved Yoseph. Once again, he steadied himself against the cool damp sides of the cave.

"Yeshua, I already have a family, and this young boy doesn't know me. I am afraid he won't want to live with my family and me. Besides, he needs the loving care of somebody younger. I am now older than when you and I traveled to the Isle of Britannia."

"Uncle Yoseph, to whom much has been given, much will be asked in return. You and the Baptizer's son will forge many links in the chain of mankind's future. The 'way' will pass from me to you and then to Zechariah. Yoseph, my dearest uncle, you will become a 'fisher of men' and carry the *Kodesh Abba's* Heaven-sent commandments and my love to the land of Albion. My days are short, but my *Abba's* wishes will appear in a vessel to the lost tribes and the Gentiles."

To Yoseph's surprise and consternation, Yeshua's arcane philosophy and prophesying were far beyond his grasp and understanding. Although he didn't understand all the cryptic references he made to him, his prophecy seemed infallible. Especially, the Baptizer's son and Yoseph traveling to Britannia.

"What will cause me to return to the Isle of Britannia?" Yoseph asked.

"Uncle Yoseph, *Yerushalayim* will cease to exist as we now know it. The secular world will vanish in a fiery storm, yet a new *Yerushalayim* will rise."

"Is this what you said to Nicodemus about 'born again'?"

"Yes, my uncle. We must first sacrifice the physical body and material world before we can see a second birth. Right now, will you raise the Baptizer's son? For your family will start on a spiritual journey in the next few days."

Miriam of Magdala's gaze fixated on Yeshua's mouth with keen interest. The look in her eyes and smile reflected her admiration, satisfaction, and love for her teacher. In her silence, she stood quite close to his nephew as they spoke in the cool cave air. Yeshua often glanced at her, but the look on his face reflected that of someone respecting her counsel. His constant smile at her seemed to glow against his dark beard. However, Yoseph noticed he addressed her face to face, distinct from their custom of a third-party male speaking for a woman in public. He wondered briefly if she were indeed his wife.

"Yeshua, I understand your uncle has concerns about raising a young child," Miriam stated. "He fears his age and the responsibility of helping to provide for his family would overburden him in his later years."

Yeshua replied to her concern with the authority of a prophet. "Our *El Shaddai* will provide for you, Yoseph, in the coming summers. What you will accomplish and sacrifice will help mankind for all eternity. Many revelations will come in due time, Yoseph. You and Miriam must trust me with all your hearts and souls."

However, at this point in their discourse, Yoseph's apprehensions disappeared. All at once, a loving concern surged in him, which left his heart content, as if Zechariah were one of his own children.

"Yeshua bar Yoseph, I will accept this young boy into my household as you request. It's your loving concern for this young child that has changed my heart. Will he leave with us tonight?"

"Not tonight, but soon. Besides, Uncle Yoseph, my cousin Yosa has already shown her kindness toward the young child. My confidence tells me he'll return that love and give you his loyalty."

Cautious thoughts returned to Yoseph about what he had just decided. His misgivings must have shown on his face as Yeshua gazed into his eyes.

"Uncle Yoseph, do you have anything else to discuss with me?"

"Yes, now that I have another soul under my care, I must confide in you about an attempt on my life the other night. A stranger attacked me on the way to the house of my friend, Nicodemus. Your Uncle Hebron disobeyed my wishes but saved my life. Upon approaching Nicodemus's house, a man who appeared to be sleeping near his entrance attacked me. Hebron caught the dagger-man by surprise and both men fought with daggers before Hebron cut the other man's arm and he fled. The mystery man received a deep gash on his left arm. In addition, a young man followed me this morning, while our family viewed you from afar, as you entered *Yerushalayim*. When we confronted him, he informed us that you had sent him. I didn't believe him at first, especially because he had a bandage on his left arm and thought him the man who attacked me."

"Yes, you were followed by Yohanan Marcus. His family has housed us in their home during the *Pesach* week. He sought you out at my command. He isn't the man who attacked you, as you well know. Yohanan Marcus has the heart of a lion but wouldn't hurt a flea. He injured his arm helping us prepare for the Seder celebration when a heavy wooden table fell against his forearm.

"Yoseph, there are many events in motion that will change your life and the lives of your family. I know that in the coming days there's a great danger for you. Listen with care to what I am about to say. You must come to the Seder dinner at the home of Yohanan Marcus in three sunsets. Come with Uncle Hebron, Nicodemus, and your immediate family."

Yeshua's last statement left Yoseph anxious. Why did his nephew want him at the Seder dinner?

Miriam's eyes expressed the same sense of composure as Yeshua as she looked at Yoseph. Between the two of them, they kept pushing Yoseph's doubts and apprehensions away with a strong sense of their calmness.

"Dearest nephew and Miriam, we need to return to the others and eat our meal. We'll converse later." Now he knew what Yeshua expected of him. As they ended their secret visit, Yoseph's doubts and fears had vanished at his nephew's words and the warm, luminous glow radiated from him. Indeed, his words came from the *Kodesh Abba* that meant his nephew possessed closeness to *El Shaddai*! Were the rumors true? Did the ancient prophets predict him as the one true *Maishiach*?

CHAPTER XV

They left the cave and strolled into the refreshing night air. The wind continued to blow as they traveled back to the campfire. The many olive tree branches made a light *crackling* sound as the wind swayed them back and forth.

Yeshua walked ahead on the path and Yoseph followed Miriam from behind. She gave forth a light *clinking* from her wrist and ankle bracelets as she ambled down the narrow path that created a certain cadence in her stride. Her hands displayed numerous jewel-encrusted rings bearing precious and semiprecious stones that were befitting a woman of wealth, reflecting her financial independence. She presented herself as an extraordinary woman in her intellect, charity, and spiritual devotion. As they walked along the path, their light conversation revealed she contributed to their common fund and sold some of her jewelry when their funds ran low.

As they drew closer to the campfire, Yoseph heard Yosa's sweet voice singing the *Hallel* festival song as they approached the fire, with Miriam of Nazareth joining in with her soothing voice. The young boy of the Baptizer started dancing with Yosa as she held his small hand. At once, Yoseph's heart overflowed with happiness and his voice filled with laughter.

The campfire glowed with a blue-orange color as they sang and ate the many dishes of food that lay on the ground. The wine never ended, and it helped all there to appear at ease. The sole exception came from the Iscariot man called Yudas. His glowing firelit eyes fixated on Yoseph after he sat down.

Right after the songs ended, a man by the name of Philip, one of his nephew's followers, approached him.

"Master Yoseph, our teacher Yeshua has spoken much about your travels to many distant lands. I must confess that I haven't journeyed any farther than *Yerushalayim* from my village. If you have time, may I ask you to reveal something of your adventures?"

Yoseph noticed the man's intense eyes. He judged his age at close to thirty summers. His beard and hair were a dark red color that glistened from the campfire flames. Both his grin and contagious laughter infected their group. He became quite interested in the Isle of Britannia, the Druid men and women priests of the oak forests, and their strange rituals. The Celtic tin miners interested him too. He conveyed a great thirst for knowledge.

"Is it true, Master Yoseph, that there are human . . . sacrifices on the isle you visited? I have heard tell of this from seafarers when they visit the port of Sidon." Philip didn't appear educated in a formal sense, yet self-taught and had an excellent memory.

"No, Philip, I haven't heard or seen this in my travels to Britannia. However, I have observed their priests and they are quite skilled in languages of Greek and Latin. There's no distinction of who's eligible for priesthood. A king's son or daughter, or a poor huntsman's child may join."

"I have never heard of such things."

"Countless years are devoted to becoming a priest and their creature comforts are few, which are in stark contrast to our priests, who have an abundance of material possessions. It's mandatory for novice young priests to attend school many years, thus sacrificing both their childhood and young adulthood. The senior Druid priests teach their culture, history, and significant local events to their initiates to memorize. Philip, you need to speak to my son Alein Yosephe about the priests of the oak forest. He can tell you more details than I can."

"Thank you, Master Yoseph. I appreciate you discussing your adventures with me. My *rabboni* has praised you and what you have learned from traveling to different cultures. I am seeking an understanding of all our *Abba's* people and hoping it will render me a better person and help me teach tolerance to others."

As young Philip departed from the fire to seek out Alein Yosephe, Yoseph realized he seemed quite sincere in his questions with a longing for understanding and tolerance. It appeared his nephew had chosen wisely a pious young postulate to join his diverse group of followers.

As the night slipped away, the food continued, always replenished by Yoseph's servants to all guests and relatives. Praise be to *El Shaddai,* he prayed, thanking Him for the evening that they hadn't faced the threat of danger. The evening festivities continued to fill all his guests with happiness. Once again, the sole exception came from the Iscariot man, who gave Yoseph several nervous glances. His daughter's singing voice held them captive while Alein Yosephe accompanied her on his kinnor. Both his children chanted the psalms, which made his eyes tear while his guests remained silent; however, they eventually joined in chanting with his son and daughter. The night air reverberated with many joyous voices and Yoseph wished this evening wouldn't end.

After they had finished singing, Yeshua rose to speak. Miriam of Magdala sat at one side of his feet and Yoseph's niece Miriam hugged the other side. An unexplained silence commenced on the mount as Yeshua's voice penetrated throughout the olive grove.

"*El Shaddai,* our *Abba.* In times when we are defeated and all things seem to trouble us, always remember the history of our people who have borne the burden of much suffering. Moreover, as we look to that memory, let us respond greater to the joy of your grace. You have called on me, your Son to create reparations for our sins and those of countless others. *Omein.*"

A bright *kabod* then glowed above Yeshua's head that came over his body. Curiosity and shocked faces manifested from the crowd. His reference as the Son of their Creator, Yoseph didn't want to hear. It sounded like blasphemy.

But as he spoke, his liquid brown eyes landed on Yoseph as he told them about the coming days ahead. Yoseph could only stare at him, wondering if his great-nephew was indeed capable of blasphemy. The servants arrived with more food and broke Yoseph's gaze. Once again, many conversations began as they gathered around a common pot of food.

"Uncle Yoseph," his nephew spoke above the crowd, "tell me about events taking place in the council of elders."

"The council fears the Roman Army and Pontius Pilate. They are afraid his legions will set off an insurrection and prevent our freedom to worship. And also jeopardize our delicate trade relations. The council fears the presence of volatile fanatics in the city and the surrounding countryside. They also fear for their authority. We desire peace; however, I worry for our people and our culture's demise by the actions of a few malcontents. Alein Yosephe and I have traveled throughout the Roman Empire. Most people in *Yerushalayim* and *Yehudah* have no concept of what power the Romans can inflict on us, either in taxes or physical control."

With Yoseph's final words, he noticed Yudas's red-flushed face contorting with anger, yet he said nothing. *Here's a dangerous man,* he thought.

After slight pauses in the conversation, his servants refilled their empty cups with pomegranate wine. He knew the copious amounts of wine would continue the gaiety of the evening.

"Master Yoseph," Yudas called out, "you speak of the Roman Empire and know what harm it can execute on so-called malcontents. Have you not forgotten what our great leader, Yudas Maccabeus, and his followers did to our Greek ruler?"

"I am quite familiar with what he did against the Seleucidian rulers," Yoseph retorted. "We're speaking about an empire with many different people who compose its society. There are also numerous trade alliances and tremendous wealth at stake."

"Yes, Master Yoseph, you have a selfish motive in dealing with the Roman dogs. You sell them lead and tin, and you obtain your wealth by their authorization. From what you say, they might, without difficulty, prevent you from trading in these commodities and transfer that license to someone else."

"Yes, that's true, but I have local dealers who trade in my other commodities. I am not just dependent on the Romans."

"My heart tells me there's a different way to overthrow suppressor rulers," Yeshua interceded. "The Roman Empire grew on greed and fear. It expects the same in return from its enemies. The Romans know no other way to conduct themselves in their conquests. My *Abba* has told me a man's words are powerful weapons to conquer adversaries. The loving of mankind and understanding your fellow man are far more powerful than five Roman legions. Many of our brothers and sisters in the past have used these loving tenets.

"Uncle Yoseph, can your written words command men to action? What I mean by this are the words of kindness and respect. 'People of the law' must obey and respect our holy *El Shaddai's* words. We say kind words to our wives and they in return provide us love and respect. Our *ammas* speak and write kind words to their sons and daughters and receive love and respect in return.

"My ministry seeks out those who can speak of kindness, serve others, and act compassionately to their neighbors. Sometimes it's difficult for some of my followers to embrace their enemies, but we must demonstrate this to show future generations.

"Many future scribes and men of wisdom will write of our past and the many sacrifices we gave for our brothers and sisters. Kingdoms, nations, and tribes will rise and fall in my name, the 'Son of Man.'"

Yoseph froze as his nephew finished his last words. Yeshua's face and head now radiated a moving rainbow of colors, which caused those gathered to shield their eyes. A long silence ensued among their group, brimmed with stunned opened mouths.

"My beloved nephew, what a profound observation and statement. You speak of a new covenant for us and other nations. Words and kindness are powerful weapons against your repressors, but your ministry will need many more followers to spread your logos. In addition, the perseverance of a new faith and belief can try the resolve of most mortal men and women."

"Yet, I disagree, Master Yoseph," Yudas Iscariot interjected. "We must protect our master's teaching with a sword. The Roman dogs know this, and they definitely know how to persevere. I say we attack them in a guileful manner and kill their officers first, thus striking at the snake's head."

The words uttered by Yudas Iscariot weren't the ones Yoseph wanted to hear. And he observed Yeshua's dismay with Yudas's contentious reply. Right then, he decided to change the direction of their conversation and started conversing with Yeshua's female novice.

"Miriam of Magdala, how many people have joined you from Galilee?"

"My master has drawn twelve male followers from his home region. They come from many backgrounds. We have additional women too. We have a tax collector for Rome, a Roman centurion, a Samarian woman, and several fishermen. I owned many properties near Galilee and lost sight of what my spiritual life entailed. Money and wealth consumed my days and left me troubled with many demon masters. Your beloved nephew has shown me his 'way' and rid me of these evil monsters controlling my thoughts. Galilee has become a far better place since our rabbi has started his ministry. His followers have relinquished many material things to help spread his word. We hope to accomplish the same in *Yehudah*."

A sudden noise distracted them from Miriam of Magdala's discourse, followed by footsteps and rustling bushes coming from the path that led to their campfire. At once, Hebron jumped up to investigate, as did Alein. Hebron clutched his sword hilt as he ran down the path. "Who goes there?"

Then came a faint reply. "I come to speak to my teacher."

Yeshua stood up and then strolled toward Alein and Hebron. Yoseph didn't hear what Yeshua said, but soon they ambled toward the fire.

"Come, meet Shimon bar Yona, also known as 'our rock' and one of my faithful followers. He fears for his life and travels alone at night. At dawn today, Yohanan Marcus told him about this gathering, Uncle Yoseph."

"Please, join us at the fire and have some food." Yoseph gestured to their new guest.

The man sat down next to Yudas and acknowledged him. Yoseph introduced him to all the members of their retinue, and his servant poured the stranger a cup of wine. He appeared about thirty summers in age and had a close-cut beard. One sandal on his foot displayed a broken strap, and his left arm displayed a scabbed-over nasty scar; part of it disappeared under a dirty bandage. Yoseph began to wonder how many more suspects might brandish similar scars like his nefarious attacker.

Yohanan Marcus came over to where Yoseph sat and hunkered down beside him. "Master Yoseph, I appreciate the hospitality you have furnished us tonight. Our rabbi told us to expect an excellent supper with superb wine."

"Yohanan Marcus, let me see your arm."

He pulled up his sleeve that revealed no bandage, only a scabbed scar on his arm.

"Due to my *amma,* it's healing. Speaking of my *amma,* she and my rabbi have asked me to remind you about our Seder dinner in two nights. Your nephew and I insist that you and your family attend."

"Yes, please expect us. Yeshua has already requested my presence."

Yoseph stood and looked around at those gathered. "Well, it's quite late, my friends, and we have some distance to travel. Yeshua bar Yoseph, you and your *amma* are more than welcome to stay with us tonight." He knew that most of the inns and homes were full during *Pesach.*

"We appreciate the offer, Uncle Yoseph, but our plans have changed. Yohanan Marcus knows we won't stay at his house tonight. I promised Miriam of Magdala's brother we would stay with him and his sister Martha. Bethany isn't far, but maybe we can break the fast with you before dawn. We'll go to the morning worship at the

Temple and hope you can accompany us. We'll arrive before dawn at your home. The huge crowds at the Temple will let us blend in with the rest of the pilgrims."

"We'll expect you there, Yeshua, and hope you can break the fast with us. Yosa still has many questions to ask you about your ministry."

"Then it is decided, I will meet you at your home before dawn!"

They stood up, hugged each other, and watched as Yeshua's followers disappeared into the darkness. Yeshua accompanied by Miriam of Magdala and a sleepy Zechariah were the last to leave the star-filled night.

Then Yoseph and the others gathered the cups and bowls and gave them to his servant and overseer to store in the cave.

"Yoel, leave them in the cave for tonight. You can bring them home tomorrow. It's late. We must depart now. Please, Hebron and Alein Yosephe, douse the fires and gather the torches and lanterns. Let me say something to Nicodemus before we depart."

Nicodemus had just grabbed his lantern as Yoseph approached. "Nicodemus, meet me at my house before sunrise. It's important that I speak to you about what Yeshua has told me."

"Yoseph, expect me there before the first cock crows. I am anxious to hear what you have to say. Have a pleasant night, Yoseph."

They traveled back home their separate routes, with Yoseph's alert brother-in-law leading their group with his dark searching eyes, and a large hand holding a firm grip on the hilt of his sword. It appeared to Yoseph the webs of their potential adversaries had now increased even more.

They arrived exhausted at the front entrance of their home. Yoseph stopped and held the lantern to watch for Alein Yosephe, Enygeus, and Yosa's arrival. Right away, Hebron entered the large iron key into the lock and let the servants enter first. He then relocked it and stood guard with Yoseph at the front of the door. A short time later, Yoseph saw torches and lanterns coming down the long narrow street. The flickering lights caused their shadows to form different heights. The closer they moved toward them, the longer their shadows stretched against the side of the building.

"Hebron, at last, they're here. We can stop worrying about their safety and praise *El Shaddai* for an uneventful night. It's now safe for you to unlock the gate and hurry everybody in for some much-needed rest."

Hebron unlocked it just as a phantom figure jumped out of a side doorway of a home a short distance away and rushed toward the forthcoming party of torches. Yoseph heard a scream and recognized that it came from Yosa. His heart seemed to leap out of his chest with fear, and bile rose from his stomach as Hebron ran first toward the group. Hebron drew his sword, ready to inflict a mortal blow, but the attacker bolted from Alein Yosephe and fled down a side passageway. At once, Hebron, Alein, and Yoseph raced toward the attacker, but Yoseph stopped, realizing he must return to the women and protect them from other potential attackers.

Alein Yosephe continued the chase. Yoseph watched him racing some distance with the flames from his torch creating dancing shadows until he disappeared down a narrow alleyway. Was this a trap? Were there other attackers waiting to ambush them or the women? Yoseph feared for Hebron and Alein Yosephe's lives. Yet, they were strong men and capable of protecting themselves.

He hurried to the others to let them inside the gate.

CHAPTER XVI

nygeus grabbed Yoseph's arm, her body trembling and her hands shaking and then embraced him. His anger increased tenfold seeing the fear in her face.

"Yoseph, why did that man attack us? Did you recognize him?"

"Maybe it's a robber. Enygeus, you and Yosa stay close to the gate."

He didn't know what to tell her and he didn't have time to think of an explanation. Yoseph hadn't been forthcoming about the other attack and now didn't seem the time to explain. He hustled them to the gate. "Hurry inside at once for your safety! Hide if necessary and don't come out until I tell you!" His fingertips touched the *mezuzah* post and he said a prayer before they disappeared into the dark shadows of the courtyard. His arm muscles tightened to brace himself from further attackers. He stood in front of the iron bars of the gate, straining his eyes in all directions, but he just saw darkness.

He estimated it was near the end of the third watch before he observed torches approaching from the same direction that Hebron and Alein Yosephe had run. Also, he heard low murmuring voices, but not the faces or number of individuals.

As they approached, Yoseph spotted Hebron's sword reflecting the light off the torches. Still moving closer, he distinguished a face among the others that he didn't recognize. Was this the man responsible for all the attacks?

Hebron spoke first. "Yoseph, look what we have here. We just caught this villain responsible for the attack. He's lucky we decided to keep him alive. What do you want me to do with him?"

"*Abba,*" Alein spoke up, "let's question this man and find out what he'll tell us. We need to know if somebody sent him. Uncle Hebron, do we still have the use of the cellar room behind your quarters?"

"Yes, and I am confident once we force him down there, we'll obtain some answers."

All Yoseph's pent-up emotions surfaced, causing him to grab the man's throat. "Why are you trying to kill me and threaten my family? Are there more of you bastards?" His grip further tightened, forcing the faceless attacker to utter unrecognizable gasping sounds.

Alein grabbed his wrist. "*Abba,* stop, we won't obtain any answers if you strangle him!"

"You're right, my son, I need to keep my anger under control."

The three of them led their captive through the courtyard toward the back gate. There, leaning against the courtyard wall, a small cellar door led down into the ground. Yoseph proceeded with his ring of keys to unlock the door. After unlocking it, he sent two of their servants down with torches to light the way.

The man's tied head-covered scarf prevented him from distinguishing any specific facial features, but some things were obvious. He wore custom-made sandals, this he did see, in addition to the expensive golden brocade clothes he wore, which indicated a servant and generous master. He bore a small stocky build and it took both Hebron and Alein Yosephe to restrain the man. When he refused to enter the cellar of his own free will, a violent struggle ensued as they tried to force him down the dank stone steps. Hebron tripped his legs, causing him to fall down the steps.

The attacker uttered a slight moan before stumbling to his feet. The cellar appeared smaller than Yoseph remembered, seeming more of a burial crypt than a cellar. Hebron found a rope in the far corner and used his sword to cut a section of it to tie the man's hands and feet. The man cursed and spat on him as Yoseph tied his feet. Yoseph sent one of his servants to fetch some strips of cloth from his quarters to gag the man. The attacker now belonged to them as a vulnerable hostage and not a threat to his family.

His servant raced back with a cloth, and while Alein Yosephe held the man's head, Yoseph tied a gag around his foul mouth. The man gave them a defiant squint as he stared at them from behind the gag.

Hebron informed the captive, "I'll remove the gag once you provide a satisfactory nod to the questions asked. Otherwise, the gag and ropes stay. Do you understand what we're saying?"

Hebron pointed his sword at the man's throat to reinforce his demands and the young man at once nodded his head in affirmation. Yoseph picked up the torch to obtain a better look at the attacker's face and right away, a large bug-eyed expression of fear came across the man. He edged the burning flame toward his eyes; for his head flinched, after which he groaned with fear.

"Now, are you ready to answer some questions?" Hebron asked. To which the young man nodded an affirmative. "If you tell us a lie or fail to answer our questions, my brother-in-law will warm things up for you. Do you understand the seriousness of this matter?" Again, the young man nodded. Hebron gave Yoseph a sly wink indicating they'd found fire his secret fear.

"Now that we have an understanding, we can proceed," Hebron stated as he removed the gag. Yoseph took over the questioning right away.

"What's your name?" Yoseph asked.

The man replied, "Yáakov."

"What house or town do you belong?"

"I am from the town of Shiloh."

"Is there more than one of you?"

"No!"

"Why did you attack my family?" Yoseph moved his torch closer to the prisoner's face.

"I hoped to see Yeshua ben Yoseph."

"Why did you want to see him?"

"It doesn't concern me at all, but my master."

Alein stepped forward. "Tell me your master's name, Yáakov of Shiloh."

A long silence ensued. Hebron's sword pushed farther into his neck, yet it didn't provide the proper incentive. "I can't say because of death threats if I tell anybody," stated Yáakov.

"Maybe we need to shed some more light on this young man to help him loosen his tongue," Hebron said, pointing at Yoseph's torch.

As Yoseph's torch drew closer to the attacker's face, sweat began rolling down his forehead, causing the smell of fear to waft from his body. The cellar's dank smell did nothing to diffuse this odor. His body began to sway as he tried to dodge the approaching flame. Several hot tar pieces from the torch dropped on his bare neck, causing him to scream out in pain.

"No, please, don't burn me!" Yáakov begged. "I'll tell you who sent me, but please remove the flame, now! Herod Antipas sent me."

Yoseph moved the torch away as he requested, but Hebron still kept the point of his sword at Yáakov's throat. Hebron resumed the questioning. "Why would Herod Antipas want us followed and harmed?"

"I meant you no harm. My instructions were to follow you and find out more about the rabbi from Galilee. They told me his *amma's* lineal family house and yours were the same, Master Yoseph."

"I suspect you were doing more than just following us," Hebron stated, as his hand eased the point of his sword farther into Yáakov's neck, causing a trickle of blood to form.

"Two nights ago, somebody attacked me!" Yoseph shouted. "Were you the one who tried to kill me on my way to visit a friend?"

"No! I haven't seen any of you before! I am just a servant in the palace of Tetrarch Herod Antipas residing at Macherus. When I inquired with the Temple guards, they gave me directions to your home. I followed you, Master Yoseph, hoping you would arrange a meeting with your nephew. Those were the instructions told to me by my master."

"Why did you jump out of the doorway and scare my sister and aunt?" Alein Yosephe asked.

"I saw the big man with his sword rush toward me and I tried to escape, but the other man ran faster than me!"

"I am going to examine your arms, Yáakov," Yoseph stated. Nevertheless, to his chagrin, Yáakov's arms didn't show any dagger marks, just minor bruises from the capture. Once again, another night with no answers, yet more questions. His attacker still remained unknown. Why did Herod Antipas want to meet his nephew, and why go to the trouble of having one of his servants spy on his family?

"Yáakov, why would Herod Antipas want to meet my nephew?" Yoseph demanded.

"Master Yoseph, I don't know."

"I have several personal body servants and they know more than I do about what goes on in my household. Therefore, your answer won't suffice. Maybe we can reach an accord on what Herod Antipas desires of my nephew. I'll have my friend remove his sword from your throat and let you speak your mind."

"Master Yoseph, please untie my feet, for they are numb."

"If you tell us some believable answers I will, if not I'll stiffen the rope and my brother-in-law's sword will press even harder into your throat. Is that understood, Yáakov of Shiloh?"

"Yes, Master Yoseph, but I fear Herod Antipas will execute me for telling his real motives."

"Just three people will know how you respond, Yáakov," Yoseph assured him. "My son, my brother-in-law, and I won't say anything. No one else will hear what you have to say." At his nod, the servants left the cellar. "Please continue, Yáakov."

"My master wants forgiveness for the slaying of Yohanan the Baptizer. The Tetrarch's wife and stepdaughter tricked him into executing the Baptizer. If your nephew can act as the prophesized *Maishiach*, only he can grant absolution. My master wants me to speak to your nephew and set up a time to meet in his palace here in *Yerushalayim*. I have heard Yohanan the Baptizer knew your nephew, possibly his cousin. Is it true, Master Yoseph?"

"Yes, however, how am I to know this isn't a trap? The tetrarch and Herodias aren't trustworthy. Everyone in *Yerushalayim* knows the actual power in his realm rests in her hands. Neither one of them knows fairness, nor how do I know you're unwitting bait for a trap. Herod Antipas imprisoned Yohanan for telling the truth about your master's wife. Then he beheaded the man for no crime whatsoever."

"I can't deny what you say, but I have an official document in my tunic pledging no harm will come to the prophet." His words appeared sincere; however, truth in *Yerushalayim* changed often and Yoseph knew that Tetrarch Herod Antipas habitually lied.

"I'll discuss this with my brother-in-law. We'll return soon. Alein Yosephe, can you handle the prisoner alone while we figure out what to do with him?"

"Yes, *abba*, leave the torch and grab the lantern. I might have to use the pitch torch."

Yoseph and Hebron proceeded up the stone steps into the fresh night air. The sky sparkled with stars; that gave the dark night a milky color and gave him some relief from the confines of the cellar.

"Hebron, do you believe what this man says? Can we trust Herod Antipas?"

"No, Yoseph, I think it's a trap for several reasons. Herod Antipas wants a favor from Rome and will use it to garner power to become a client king ruling over all our people, akin to his ruthless *abba*. Yáakov could know about this plan or Herod Antipas has duped him into thinking his master has worthy intentions. Herod Antipas comes from a bloodline of tyrants to our people. I say we send him back from whence he came and tell him our nephew has left *Yerushalayim*. Did not Yeshua speak of leaving for Bethany?"

"You're right on all your reasons, Hebron. Let's release him at once, but with a warning."

"Let me tell him of the warning, Yoseph," Hebron replied with a sly grin on his face. From a man the size of Hebron, with his tall bear-like shape, intimidation conveyed meaning. They both proceeded back down the steps where Alein Yosephe held their prisoner.

"My nephew can't meet Herod Antipas," Yoseph stated. "He just left *Yerushalayim*. You need to return and tell this to your master."

"But Master Yoseph, I can't. He knows the rabbi's followers are here in *Yerushalayim* for the *Pesach*. Besides, Tetrarch Herod Antipas and his retinue have arrived today and now reside in the royal palace. Even if I leave, more will appear to follow your nephew."

"If this does happen, then this doesn't concern either one of us. You can go back to Herod Antipas and deliver the information you know. Let others pursue this matter. Do you understand?"

"Yes, Master Yoseph, I understand."

"Alein, release our prisoner and let him trek back to his master," Hebron stated with his booming voice. "I don't want to see you again in our presence or things will become hotter the next time."

The man froze with fear when hot pitch dropped on his face. He emitted another loud scream of "yes" and they escorted him up the steps and released him back into the night. Afterward, they gathered in the courtyard to discuss what would come of this affair. Yoseph sent the servants to reassure Yosa and Enygeus they were fine.

The courtyard fountain exuded a quiet gurgling sound as they gathered around and the sole chirp came from a distant nightingale singing for its mate.

"Yoseph, I still suspect Herod Antipas wants to trap Yeshua."

Alein Yosephe nodded his agreement. "I see a trap and I fear for all our safety. Let's not forget about the Baptizer's son. Herod Antipas's wife, Herodias, wants the young Zechariah dead and she has spies too. He's a constant reminder of his *abba*."

"Yes, I agree with both of you, for I have already devised a plan. Don't you remember, I spoke of it earlier. All of you must retreat to Arimathea if something happens to me. Alein, you and Yosa played there in the cave when you were both small."

"Yes, *abba*, *amma* didn't want us playing near the cave because of wild animals."

"Your Uncle Hebron and I have stocked that cave with wine ewers, bread, olive oil, and dates. There are silver shekels in a small chest buried beneath the wine. Close up our house, leaving just a few servants. Don't fetch anything else. Move as fast as you can. If I should disappear, you both must swear before *El Shaddai* to do as I say here tonight. No matter what happens to me, I will try to meet you there as soon as possible."

"But *abba*, why do you speak such? I've said before, nothing will happen to you. It's Yeshua whom Herod Antipas wants. You must not say such things!"

"Listen, both of you, prepare to leave in case the tetrarch sends his soldiers to torture me to find Yeshua. He might hold me for ransom to force Yeshua to come to his palace. Hebron, my loyal brother-in-law, please do as I ask. Sometimes you let your heart do your thinking for my protection. I am appreciative of your loyalty but promise to heed my request."

"I promise to do as you wish," Hebron said with a forlorn look in his big brown eyes. "None of us wants to believe we're at risk, yet we must prepare for action if necessary."

Yoseph slammed his fist on the table to reinforce his point.

Alein Yosephe clenched his fist. "I will do it because you ask me, *abba,* but I prefer you not speak this way. If you're in danger, we're all at risk, and we'll bring forth the necessary steps to protect our 'entire' family."

"I appreciate your forthright manner, my son, but you aren't listening to what I've said. Let me explain it this way. Alein, do you remember the one summer we were at Arimathea and you were trying to hunt some quail?"

"Yes, *abba*, I remember."

"What happened to the mother bird and her chicks?"

"She used herself as a decoy and feigned injury."

"What ensued next, Alein?"

"I chased her some distance until you stopped me and didn't want me to kill her because of her chicks."

"Did we ever find the chicks, my son?"

"No, *abba*, now I see your point, please forgive me for my shortsightedness."

"You both must pledge before *El Shaddai* to do as I have asked. Do you hereafter swear to carry out my wishes?"

"Yes, we do swear," came the halfhearted reply from both men.

"Well, gentlemen, let's retire, for tomorrow will bring many things."

Yoseph strolled to his room, washed his face, then blew out his oil lamps and fell fast asleep. That's when the nightmares started.

CHAPTER XVII

oseph's nightmares were over, as he vaulted straight from his bed. His recollections seemed real. He remembered sitting inside four stone walls while imprisoned without light or food, with his frantic pounding fists attempting to escape. Then things changed and his body stood inside some kind of sailing vessel, leaking water in the midst of a great storm. The sinking sensation appeared real and a lump of doom had swelled in his throat.

His nightclothes were wet; however, not from water, but from his sweat. Looking around, he saw his room, not a sinking ship or a tomb. Yet, was this an omen? However, each dream seemed meaningless, or were they? A fitful dream wouldn't help him with his day.

Additional emotional support arrived in the form of his friend Nicodemus as he entered Yoseph's courtyard. Maybe he could help him interpret his nightmares. One of his servants led him toward the fountain.

"Ah, Nicodemus. Please, come and join me in breaking the fast. It has been a long night and I must tell you what transpired."

As they strolled through the courtyard, Yoseph gave Nicodemus a summary of events that took place since he last saw him. He had no qualms about sharing what Yeshua had said to him but

hesitated from revealing the events from his frightening dreams last night. He might think it's silly nonsense. Yoseph hoped he might perhaps shed some light on the conversation in the cave and their spy from Herod Antipas.

"I didn't know, though like you I thought Miriam of Magdala bore this son too. I haven't heard anything until now that Yohanan the Baptizer possessed a child. It sounds as though you made a commitment, yet I am still not sure of your new responsibilities."

"How does one say no to Yeshua? Knowing my age would render me a poor candidate, it did not matter; somehow, my nephew convinced me that the boy entailed part of his future and mine. His plan appeared to extend beyond this world that we now know."

"Indeed, how does one say no to such a mysterious *kodesh* man? Did he reveal anything else?" Nicodemus raised a bushy eyebrow.

"He said he wanted me to sail with the young boy to the Isle of Britannia, as he enjoyed with me many summers ago. There the Baptizer's son would start a line of kings to rule over that isle. Does any of this sound sensible to you?"

"Yoseph, you left a splendid impression on Yeshua as a young boy, now he wants the same for Zechariah. He knows you're a kind and wise man, willing to help this orphaned child to have the joys he experienced under your tutelage. This speaks much of your character and trust that he sees in you. Yes, some of what you have said sounds sensible, yet some of it's quite puzzling. After all, the Baptizer and Yeshua were once a close family. Moreover, it perplexes me how the Baptizer's son will start a line of new kings in far-off Britannia."

"Yeshua talked in mysterious statements. One about him leaving *Yerushalayim* to go live with his *abba*, but his *abba* died long ago! He didn't say where but said in due time he'd tell us."

"When will you receive the young boy?" Nicodemus asked, pulling on his long gray beard.

"He didn't say and gave me no date but said soon. He also told me I would become a 'fisher of men' too, as he stated to you. I am still trying to fathom his perplexing requests and comments. Although I don't understand everything my nephew says to me, yet he speaks with the authority coming from *El Shaddai*. Therefore, I trust in what he asks."

"Yoseph, you are sapient in trusting your faith and fate to your nephew. I see a most persuasive holy man, as you well know, who has made a great impression on all who have heard him speak and the miracles he has performed. You already know my faith and admiration for your nephew."

"Nicodemus, it's quite comforting to me that we both see the same things in Yeshua."

"So now you have caught the eye of the nefarious Tetrarch Herod Antipas. That doesn't bode well for you, Yoseph. However, the logical assumption I see is that he wants to use you to capture Yeshua."

"I agree and don't forget the Baptizer's son. Hebron and Alein Yosephe concur. I am just a fly in his web to trap both of us."

"I don't believe Herod Antipas alone instigated this matter. This too smells of the evil machinations of Herodias, Herod Antipas's wife. She doesn't want anything or anyone in the way of her husband's ambitions, which are indeed hers."

"But why now, Nicodemus?" He hoped his friend might give him a logical explanation for all these things. Yoseph knew his distraught emotions kept him from seeing the many webs of intrigue surrounding him.

"Yoseph, perhaps some nourishment will inspire us to develop plausible explanations." Nicodemus reached for the salver and grabbed several dates, then popped them into his mouth, after which he peeled several pomegranates before he continued. He momentarily paused and became tacit. Afterward, he handed Yoseph one of the pomegranates.

"Yoseph, I don't think your nephew has divulged all the facts to you. Didn't you see the mysterious glowing *kabod* around his head or the stillness of the night when he spoke to the gathering? How does he do this?"

"Yes, I saw the yellow glow and heard the stillness, but I thought my eyes deceived me from the campfire reflections. Though, his presence radiates a great intellectual light and renders stillness in both man and animal."

"Everyone in attendance experienced the same sensations as you. The masses revere Yeshua and the powerful fear him. Yet, there's no middle ground of thought about your nephew. As for your spy, I think both Herod Antipas and his wife want you, the Baptizer's son, and Yeshua out of the way. He and Caiaphas might charge you with treason against Rome. All of us are guilty by association and that includes me. It wouldn't bother them to have all of us murdered or imprisoned. I suspect they both desire to steal your wealthy mining interests. This would increase their power base in *Yehudah*."

Yoseph didn't want to hear this. Also, it gave him further consternation, along with a sense of impending doom. Just then, he heard a distant cock crowing and the beginning light of the morning beamed into his courtyard. As he and Nicodemus continued speaking, one of his servants hurried toward them.

"Master Yoseph, there are three men at our front door. The holy one, your nephew, requests your presence this morning."

"Let them in and then bring more food. I know they're hungry and we can break the fast together."

The servant left at once and then returned a short time later with more food and their guests. Yohanan Marcus and a young man Yoseph hadn't met before accompanied Yeshua. The stranger looked about sixteen or seventeen summers of age and he noticed his dark brown eyes gazed at everything in his view. His face appeared smooth and showed no sign of a beard. He had a swarthy outdoors complexion and the build of a narrow wooden post, though not from hunger. The long hair on his head shone with scattered streaks of auburn color, bleached from many days traveling in the sun.

"I must say I enjoyed the feast that you and Nicodemus prepared for my companions last night," Yeshua said. "You are both most gracious men of *El Shaddai*." He embraced Nicodemus for his kindness and then introduced his unknown follower.

"Meet my beloved friend and disciple, Yohanan bar Zebedee. He keeps an accurate account of our travels and ministry. He makes an excellent scribe, and his writings are quite accurate and thorough.

Yohanan Marcus helps tutor him in his writing. He and I are quite close to each other as I think you and Nicodemus are."

The young man held a large leather pouch with a strap slung over his shoulder. Yohanan embraced Nicodemus and Yoseph, as did Yohanan Marcus.

As they moved to where the food lay, Hebron and Alein Yosephe entered the sitting area. After completing the introductions again, they sat down to eat their dates and pomegranates. Yoseph noticed Yohanan bar Zebedee writing on a tablet he'd just pulled out of his leather satchel. He left his food uneaten and began to write while they conversed. Yoseph's curiosity conquered the best of him.

"Yohanan bar Zebedee, may I inquire what you're writing?"

"Master Yoseph, I keep a diary of my life and events with my master and teacher. I hope I don't appear rude and inconsiderate of your hospitality. I want to have a record of the kindness you have shown to me and to others."

He thanked Yohanan for his comments and realized for the first time his nephew didn't surround himself with benighted followers from Galilee. All of them worshiped Yeshua, thirsted for knowledge, and had an innate sense of spiritual understanding.

"Yeshua, I spoke to Nicodemus before your arrival, about our conversation last night at the Gethsemane cave. He's my closest friend and we often share our thoughts. I just conveyed to him the frightful event that took place last night when we arrived home."

"Tell me more," Yeshua's eyes encouraged him to continue.

"When we arrived home, an intruder jumped out of the shadows. His appearance caused great alarm to Yosa and Enygeus and I feared he might have an accomplice. The man ran away, but later Hebron and Alein Yosephe captured him."

"And what information did you uncover from your captured intruder? Did he tell you the fox, Herod Antipas, sent him?"

"How did you know?"

Yeshua didn't answer, instead smiled his enigmatic smile and changed the subject.

"It gladdens my heart that you have a friend and confidant

in Nicodemus. He knows your soul and loves you, as I do. The future holds many things for you, great trials and triumphs. Men need loving friends in times of trouble. Also, Uncle Yoseph, I know young Zechariah and Miriam of Magdala will depend on you and Nicodemus in the future. My *Abba* and heart have told me I've chosen the right persons to carry on my legacy to others."

Finding the right words to respond to Yeshua's comments made it difficult for both Yoseph and Nicodemus, so they said nothing.

"I have another request to ask both of you. Would you each accompany me to see the high priest, Caiaphas? I think it's time I confronted him."

"Yeshua, I don't think this is a good idea," Hebron replied. Yoseph saw his son's eye grow wider.

"I agree with Uncle Hebron. Caiaphas might see this as an opportunity to arrest you."

Nicodemus nodded at Yeshua's request, yet Yoseph noticed Nicodemus's hand started to tremble as he spoke.

"Rabbi, Caiaphas reacts as a Sadducee and doesn't show the wisdom of an Essene- trained rabbi. He values power and material things of this world and Caiaphas's influence dominates the Sanhedrin. I fear he won't listen to any of us."

"I agree, Nicodemus," Yeshua stated. "But he lets others defile my *Abba's* house and I must speak to him about this and show him the error of his ways."

Yeshua's voice grew louder about the Temple defilement and both his hands clenched.

"Let's leave at once, Uncle Yoseph." He jumped up from his seat. Yeshua requested Alein Yosephe and Hebron to accompany him on their mission.

Yoseph told his servant Demetrius that Nicodemus, Hebron, Alein Yosephe, and he were to leave right away and to tell Yosa and Enygeus of their departure. They left the front entrance as the sun started moving above the red-tiled rooftops and entered the narrow streets that buzzed with activity. The narrow passageways forced the huge swarms of people to shuffle their feet the closer they advanced

toward the Temple Mount. The *Pesach* week had created an outpour-
ing of worshippers who were climbing the numerous huge steps to
the Temple.

From a distance, it appeared as if a multitude of bees were
climbing the side of a giant honeycomb. As they approached closer
to the mount, the enormous mass of people made it difficult to
breathe, leaving them gasping for air. The seven of them proceeded
with the other pilgrims snaking their way along the narrow streets of
Yerushalayim. After some time, they reached the major walkways and
arches of the Temple Mount, allowing them to fan out to the various
entrance steps. The morning heat burned desert hot, yet the higher
the steps they climbed, a slight breeze cooled their faces.

Reaching the next landing, there were ritual baths to cleanse
themselves. The final landing displayed one last set of ritual *mikveh*
bath pools to become clean before entering the Temple grounds.

"Uncle Yoseph, we must stop here and prepare ourselves for the
Temple," Yeshua said, "and keep our *Abba's* house clean in both body
and spirit." Quickly, they disrobed and dipped their bodies into the
cool water. Yeshua began a prayer as they immersed themselves in
the stone bath.

"Our *Abba*, who art in Heaven, hallowed be thy name . . ."

Just as Yeshua began his prayer, two priests started blowing their
shofars. The din from the horns kept Yoseph from hearing the rest of
his prayer. After they had finished dressing, Yohanan handed Yeshua
two tefillins. He ritualistically tied one of the small wooden boxes to
his head and the other to his left forearm. Each Torah scripture-filled
box had the letters *Shin* written on them and the knots were in the
shape of the letters *dalet* and *yud,* representing the name of *Shaddai.*
Yeshua covered his head with his *tallit* shawl, said a prayer, and
then they ambled toward the center of the Temple grounds. As they
approached the Temple doors, the heat became unbearable and more
humid. Many rug pallets and tables defined their pathway.

The moneychangers seemed closer to the Temple entrance than
Yoseph last remembered, with countless small wooden cages of
sacrificial white doves sold to the pilgrims for their holy oblations.

Numerous scales weighed the foreign silver coins; then they traded them for Temple coins used in purchasing the doves. The cacophony of the crowd grew even louder from the noise of bartering and the coins hitting the scales. Everywhere he looked, coins were stored in baskets. Some of the larger baskets were replete with coins, giving the Temple grounds the appearance of a shopping bazaar, rather than a holy site. It appeared things were out of hand, during the days before *Pesach*, with double and triple exchange rates shouted by the money merchants.

Hebron looked at Yoseph and shook his head as did Alein Yosephe. Yoseph feared to see Yeshua's reaction, but he looked around and didn't see him.

The number of people in the crowd swelled in size, pressing against his chest, making it difficult to exhale as they approached the Temple doors. Without warning, there came a sudden outburst of commotion, and Yoseph heard Yeshua's authoritative voice rise above the noise of protest. Then he saw tables overturned and coins scattered everywhere. Loose coins covered their sandals, causing them to stumble with each step. To Yoseph's astonishment, when he looked up, he spied Yeshua upending tables and shouting at the moneychangers.

"You have made my *Abba's* house into a den of thieves." His right hand tightly gripped two knotted ropes ready to lash out at the next merchant within his reach. Each moneychanger shouted his protest, only to see Yeshua's wrath with his *hum*-sounding rope whipping through the air. Yohanan Marcus and Yohanan bar Zebedee were pushing people away from Yeshua, acting as his bodyguards. Some in the crowd remained vexed and silent. Others were shouting, "He's the *Maishiach*, who has come from Nazareth." The moneychangers were the most vehement in their protests and started forming a mob to seize Yeshua.

Hebron looked at Yoseph.

"Yoseph, what shall I do?"

"Hebron, you and Alein Yosephe move close to Yohanan and Yohanan Marcus. We might have to race for the exits." Yoseph noticed

Hebron's hand slowly reaching for his sword, as if to use it, but Yoseph grabbed the hilt to keep him from brandishing the weapon.

Yeshua still repeated about defiling his *Abba's* house as Yoseph approached behind him. He continued his outbursts with his whip. Never before had Yoseph seen his face and his typically serene countenance contorted. This whiplashing Yeshua left the moneychangers' eyes rolling white with fear. He didn't appear the same person Yoseph had known the last thirty-three summers. Just as the moneychangers were closing in on them, Yoseph heard the sound of a large *shofar* horn. The massive Temple doors rumbled opened and out stepped Caiaphas and his retinue. The sun's morning rays radiated Caiaphas's multicolored jeweled breastplate of authority, causing the mob to suddenly stop and gape. The Temple guards rushed out from all directions with their metallic shields and armor *clanking*.

Several from the moneychanger crowd shouted to arrest the Nazarene, but the larger segment of the crowd drowned them out with repeated shouts of *"Maishiach."* Their words continued to resound until it became a chant. The *shofars* blew once again, signaling the Temple guards to move closer with their sharp-tipped pointed spears. The crowds quickly pushed Yohanan, Yohanan Marcus, Alein Yosephe, Nicodemus, Yeshua, and Yoseph closer to the Temple entrance steps.

Caiaphas stood at the top of the steps, surrounded by scribes, priests of lesser stature, and Caiaphas's *abba*-in-law, Annas, the former high priest. Many of these men Yoseph knew quite well. Caiaphas began to speak, and the crowd ceased shouting.

"Nazarene, why do you disrupt the Temple during *Pesach*? Can't you see the moneychangers serve the needs of the people and our Temple?"

A deathly silence came across the crowd. A few of the beaten moneychangers began to shout in agreement with Caiaphas's question. At once, a sudden wind picked up.

"High priest," Yeshua said, "you and your brethren have defiled my *Abba's* house. You can't allow money to rule over *His* Temple! This house lodges one master, *El Shaddai."*

The wind grew louder as did Yeshua's voice. Yoseph saw Caiaphas glance at him as Yeshua began to speak again.

"This isn't a house of profit, but one of salvation."

"So, Nazarene," inquired Caiaphas, "you don't want us to exchange coins with idols for our Temple shekels."

"The high priest can render unto Caesar what is Caesar's and render unto my *Abba* what belongs to him, yet you can't serve two masters!" He then turned and proceeded from the Temple entrance.

Yohanan Marcus and Yohanan bar Zebedee quickly followed him, pushing through the crowd as he started to exit the Temple grounds. At once, the mass of the people divided as if Moshe had parted the sea, with Yeshua hurrying toward the outer courtyard steps to leave. Strangely, no one touched him or tried to grab him as he withdrew. Shortly thereafter, the three men disappeared. At once, the doves mysteriously escaped from their cages and flew ahead of Yeshua, after which they flew straight up into the clear blue sky. Yoseph observed that the paschal lambs for some unexplained reason had their ropes untied and bleated as they followed the three men. The many faces were open-mouthed at these sudden events. Even the moneychangers were powerless to render a collective protest.

Alein Yosephe, Hebron, Nicodemus, and Yoseph were also in awe of what they saw and heard.

"Yoseph, Yeshua has become a holy prophet and blessed by *El Shaddai*."

"I agree, Nicodemus."

"So do I," Hebron replied. Alein Yosephe didn't speak, but tears were trickling down his cheeks.

Caiaphas looked down at the four of them with his broad nose and an evil squinting glare aimed at them. He stepped closer to speak. "Yoseph and Nicodemus, I hope both of you aren't part of this protest. As responsible members of the Sanhedrin, each of you must set a proper example for the praying masses. Yoseph, I know your Nazarene nephew means trouble, and I expect you to stop him from disrupting our people. The mandatory tax we owe to the Roman occupiers comes from the profit we earn off the exchanged coins. This goes to pacify our Roman governor, Pontius Pilate. In any event, you don't want heathen images on coins to pollute our Temple offering, do you, Yoseph?"

"Caiaphas, I have no objection for the exchange of Roman denarius for Temple shekels and a fair tax paid to our occupiers. However, I agree with my nephew, this isn't the place for these business transactions. Our *Kodesh* Temple and the *Pesach* must remain quiet for praying, contemplation, and remembrance. These money transactions belong in the bazaars away from our Holy Temple. I hope whatever profit the Temple earns, after paying the Roman tax, goes to the poor and the Temple upkeep."

"You need not lecture me on our *Kodesh* Temple," thundered Caiaphas. "I am the high priest and I answer only to *El Shaddai*." He then directed his sharp tongue toward Yoseph's friend.

"Nicodemus, I thought you had better sense than to consort with zealots and thieves."

"Caiaphas, you misjudge the young Nazarene," replied Nicodemus. "He presents himself as a gentle prophet, and I have seen the miracles he has performed. Yeshua ministers to the sick and weak of mind. The people love him as the long foretold *Maishiach*."

"Both of you believe this?" Caiaphas now displayed a crimson face. "You two espouse blasphemy, and you both know it so! Am I now to believe two learned men of the Sanhedrin have become Zealots?"

"No," they both replied. They were now in his arrow sights. His last question caused Hebron to push closer in front of Yoseph as if to confront Caiaphas face to face. Yoseph's hand touched Hebron's shoulder to restrain his forward movement.

"High Priest Caiaphas," Yoseph stated, "we came here at the request of my nephew and his followers to embrace our family fellowship and visit with my good friend Nicodemus during this holy week. Yeshua's intentions are noble and his passion shows the seriousness of the matter. I know you don't disagree about keeping the Temple sacred, however, every man must honor what site King Solomon chose for our *El Shaddai*."

Caiaphas gave an affirming, but pinch-faced nod, turned with Annas, the priests, the scribes, and disappeared behind the closing metal Temple doors. Quickly, Yoseph gazed around to see the crowd's reaction, but the courtyard remained empty, except a few moneychangers. Most of the crowd had followed his nephew after he'd left.

They then proceeded to leave for the midday meal. As they crossed the empty Temple grounds, several remaining moneychangers cursed their names.

"There go the new tax collectors who steal money from our pockets and food from our babies' mouths," shouted one disgruntled man.

"*Abba*," Alein Yosephe turned to speak. "I am proud of you and your bravery to stand up against Caiaphas. Yet, I fear it didn't endear any of us with the high priest, especially Yeshua. Now it appears we've added another person of power to fear. Furthermore, my heart and mind tell me that our fate now belongs with Yeshua's perils. We must initiate the free will we still have and prepare ourselves for the dangers to come." Although his eyes drooped with sadness, his voice held firm.

Hebron spoke up, "Alein Yosephe, I agree. It's time to initiate your *abba's* plan. When we arrive home, I will have the servants prepare some clothing for our trip to Arimathea. It will have the appearance of a business journey to Albion after *Pesach* and to thank King Arviragus for his expensive gift."

"What about Enygeus and Yosa?" inquired Alein Yosephe.

"We can say we want them to accompany us to the port of Yoppa and send us off with their blessings. After we are on the road, we can tell them the truth. The less we say, the less other people will know."

"What about Yeshua and Miriam's safety?" Alein Yosephe inquired.

"I'll see to their safety," Yoseph assured him. "I know several people who will help hide him and his followers. And my dear friend, Nicodemus, I worry about your safety too."

"Don't worry about me, Yoseph. Hebron will furnish me a map of your secret hiding place. I will find my way there and look forward to the cooler climate in Britannia. Anyway, it's best we journey our separate ways in the event something happens."

Yeshua had disappeared into the massive crowds along with his followers. The central passageway from the Temple didn't branch off for some distance, and Yoseph knew they weren't too far behind Yeshua and his retinue. Yoseph did hear loud noises as they turned one corner, but it was only a large caravan of braying camels beginning its journey out of *Yerushalayim*.

"Nicodemus," Yoseph asked, "where has Yeshua gone? He has vanished from sight."

"Yeshua will appear when he's ready. We have observed some unusual behavior from him today. I think it's correct to say there's much going on with Yeshua that we don't know about and can't explain. He has furnished us with just a few clues to some monumental events yet to materialize. Yoseph, to think of one's nephew as the next *Maishiach* I can't imagine. But until he tells us more information, there's nothing we can do, but continue with our faith in him and move forward with your planned preparations."

Nicodemus's summation kept him focused, not to overreact and to stay openminded. *El Shaddai* had made Yeshua an instrument of some kind of immense plan. However, from where he stood the past several days, the future held only danger. His safety didn't concern him, yet he feared for his family.

As they reached the other side of the camel caravan, Yoseph observed Yohanan Marcus ahead of them some distance. He appeared to have Yohanan bar Zebedee's writing satchel over his shoulder. Alein Yosephe ran ahead and stopped him. As they caught up to where he stood, a century of Roman soldiers came marching down the narrow passageway. Each man held a shield in one hand and a whip in the other. The soldiers were acting as a vanguard, clearing the way for what appeared Herod Antipas's enclosed litter. Yoseph noticed the tetrarch's carriage and his slave bearers trotting at a rapid pace, with the soldiers whipping anybody who dawdled. They ducked into a side passageway just before the entourage came their way.

CHAPTER XVIII

The entourage encountered screams, curses, and shaking fists by the crowd of people. The irate mobs gave little distinction between the Roman soldiers and Herod Antipas in displaying their anger. One older bystander stumbled and fell as the litter bearers approached. He gave out a loud cry of pain, which attracted Hebron's attention. The litter bearers and Roman guards didn't let his cry of pain deter their way, for they continued marching over his legs. At once, Hebron ran to the carriage and banged on it to stop.

A voice inside called for the entourage to halt. Hebron pulled the gray-haired man into the passageway where they stood. The curtains of the carriage parted and revealed Herod Antipas and Herodias. Herod's wife looked older than Yoseph would have imagined. There were several small gold coin ornaments hanging from the top of her red veil and her face oozed a thick layer of powder with her eyelids coated with a dark purple color. Added, to her outlandish appearance, her lips displayed a black-red color, with the intent of trying to enhance their narrow size. Her heavy use of face paint gave her the appearance of a prostitute or a high-level courtesan. Herodias's false-colored face twisted as she berated the gray-haired man while glancing at Hebron, Yohanan Marcus, and Yoseph.

"Is this man with you?" she demanded.

"This man fell as your litter bearers approached," Hebron responded. "Can't you see the blood on his leg? Also, it shouldn't matter who his companions are."

His brother-in-law now faced the second and third most powerful persons in *Yehudah*. Here sat the evil woman responsible for beheading the *kodesh* prophet, Yohanan the Baptizer. Hebron's dauntless courage impressed Yoseph, but he feared for his life.

"You're an insolent man and you didn't address me as 'Your Highness.' Tell me your name."

"They call me Hebron."

Providentially, Nicodemus interrupted both and gave his name, and displayed his Sanhedrin-chained medallion. Stooping forward, he looked into the carriage and voiced his reassurance as her hand examined the medal. He explained he would punish the gray-haired man and Hebron himself. The surrounding crowd held its breath on what Herodias would say next. Yoseph gave thanks to *El Shaddai* for his friend who at once had displayed his courage too to save Hebron and the injured man.

With a whisper, Yoseph heard a centurion speaking to Herod Antipas, who then demanded, "Who's this man who has stepped forward?" Nicodemus reached into his robe once again and pulled out his Sanhedrin medallion on its long brass chain. Then Herod whispered something into Herodias's ear, causing her pinched face to flush red with anger. The tetrarch motioned to the Roman centurion and the litter bearers, and then the carriage rose. As the litter commenced to move, Herodias gave a parting shout to Hebron, Nicodemus, and the gray-haired man.

"Counselor Nicodemus, see to it these men are dealt with. Nothing will ever stand in the way of my husband's business!" The Roman guards proceeded at once, marching down the stone street with the huge crowds swallowing them once more.

The gray-haired stranger fell at the feet of Nicodemus, begging for mercy. "Noble counselor, please don't throw me in prison. Have mercy on me."

"You need not beg for mercy. I won't have you jailed. We were just helping you in a time of need." The man smiled, with tears trickling down his cheeks. At once, he kissed Nicodemus's robe and feet, showing his gratitude. "Don't give me all the credit in helping you. This strong-spirited man named Hebron first came to your aid."

The man turned to Hebron and repeated his show of homage. "I am your servant, Master Hebron. I have nothing, but any errands within my physical strength I'll do for both of you."

"Hebron, this dear man can show his gratitude by coming home to join us for our midday meal," Yoseph said. "Then we'll decide how he can help us."

The man's eyes grew large. "May *El Shaddai* shine his light of kindness down on your family," he stated.

He still hopped, which forced them to stroll slower to accommodate his injury.

"Please, tell me your name?" Yoseph inquired.

"I am Shimon from Cyrene."

"Shimon of Cyrene, an inner voice tells me you'll help my family in the days ahead."

"Thank you, Master Yoseph, for taking me with you. I have traveled far and need food."

It appeared the heat of the day had distorted Yoseph's mind, for why did he say this to a stranger?

The hot sun raced overhead. Perspiration dripped off Yoseph's forehead as they climbed the last hill before nearing home. All Yoseph's thoughts fixated on a cool cup of water as they entered the front gate. He touched the *mezuzah* post, kissed his fingertips, and gave thanks they had returned home without harm.

Several servants started scurrying back and forth once they saw the additional guests. Yoseph's group approached several common craters set aside for the washing of their feet. The rose-scented herbal soap calmed Yoseph after the morning upheaval at the Temple and the confrontation with the tetrarch's wife.

Yosa and Enygeus carried trays of food for the midday meal as their guests entered the courtyard. The aroma of spicy cinnamon dates greeted them. Yoseph introduced Shimon of Cyrene and started relaying the incident that caused his injuries. Enygeus and Yosa both frowned as he spoke of their confrontations, but right away he saw to the comfort of their injured companion.

Their midday meal was laid near the courtyard fountain with several salvers prepared with honey, dates, salted almonds, and large pomegranates. Other plates held olives, lamb stew, and salted fish. Surrounding the fountain ledge were flagons, filled with water and wine. All of the people reclined on rugs near the courtyard fountain, with several large pillows arranged for Shimon's comfort. The sound of running water, flowing from the fountain, instilled a peaceful sensation in Yoseph's mind after the events earlier in the day, though apprehension still gnawed at his stomach. Why had Yeshua disappeared after leaving the temple?

"Yohanan Marcus, what happened to Yeshua and Yohanan bar Zebedee? We were following close behind you, and then they vanished from our sight!"

"My master and Yohanan were separated from me in the crowd also, but I knew where they were going. They traveled into the desert to pray."

"I have worried about Yeshua's possible arrest by Caiaphas's guards, and I fear for your safety too."

"I am grateful for your concern, but don't fret for me. As I mentioned yesterday, my home belongs to my second *abba*, for my first *abba* died at my infancy. It's located close to the Temple. I planned to go there when you caught me. My sister and I live in one of the upper rooms."

"We spoke of this the other day when we first met, but Yeshua and I still request your presence at our Seder dinner. Yohanan and his brother are attending, along with Philip. In addition, nine other of my rabbi's male disciples are coming to dinner. I hope that you, Alein Yosephe, Nicodemus, and Hebron will still come. I think you know Yeshua expects you and the rest of your family at our repast. My Seder dinner will reciprocate for your hospitality here today. Besides, I think my master will instruct everyone about some new teachings tomorrow night."

"Your rabbi shows wisdom and scholarship well beyond his years," Nicodemus said. "I've spoken to him in private once before at the home of a man named Lazarus. He spoke of a philosophy that I didn't quite understand, especially his parable of being born a second time. This confused me at first, but after some thought, I think I grasped his nascent faith and philosophy. Do you know if the Essenes taught him those beliefs from the time he spent with them?"

"Master Nicodemus, Yohanan told me he taught among the Essene students and conversed with his fellow teachers. The Essenes think he's Eliyah sent back by *El Shaddai* to warn us of the Roman destruction of our Temple and the scattering of our people. The Essenes say our Temple leaders are fools; they corrupt and defile *El Shaddai's* house. From what you saw today, my master shares this belief. I haven't seen him become this furious since I've known him. He's a peaceful man. Yet, Yohanan knows he isn't Eliyah sent to our people. Master Yoseph, you have known my rabbi as a young child. Please, tell me about him those many summers ago?"

"Yeshua's behavior appeared unusual from the beginning of his childhood. It became more noticeable to me at the beginning of his manhood. As a young man, he spoke in the Temple to the priest and scribes and they were amazed at his knowledge of Moshe's law. About the age of thirteen summers, he came to live with me after Yoseph ben David died. He traveled with Alein Yosephe, Hebron and me to the isle the Romans call Britannia. There he helped me with my tin mine business. He quickly adapted to learning the local languages and the Celtic people often visited our camp to converse with him. In addition, Yeshua has always had a certain charisma that drew people to him.

"I remember one incident while we were traveling in Britannia. It quite astonished me then, but so many summers have passed, and I didn't recognize the long-term importance of it. Forgive me the length of this story, yet I want you to know all the details. We were traveling to a nearby tin mine and a small village located a short distance from the mine. As we approached the village, we heard moaning and crying coming from the center of some mud hut dwellings and spied a crowd of people standing over a young woman lying on the ground. Her face appeared white as a burial shroud and her chest didn't move. A white-haired woman, who looked like her *amma*, stood wailing with raised arms over the body. Also, several small children were crying with little, clinging hands grasping their *amma's* lifeless body. They spoke the language of the Silures tribes, and it made it difficult for me to understand, yet from what I surmised, the young woman had fallen from a high point near the tin mines. Right away, young Yeshua knew what they were saying, knelt down, and then placed a hand on her swollen head. He said a prayer in their language, which amazed me, and when he had finished, the young woman started breathing.

"All the crowd's mouths gaped open and they didn't speak a word as Yeshua continued to hold her head. After a short time, the young woman's eyes began to flutter. At once, the villagers gave out a gasp of wonder; the older woman grabbed his hands and started kissing them. He helped the young woman to her feet, and the older woman started screaming with happiness. She smiled and embraced both Yeshua and her daughter. Next, the village crowd started cheering with tremolo voices and then every person embraced Yeshua and me. Just then, the wind started blowing and a bright orange sun came out from behind the clouds, casting its golden rays upon everyone present.

"Taking all these events as a miraculous sign, the villagers motioned for us to accompany them. I had difficulty in comprehending their language, but it seemed safe to follow, because Yeshua knew what they were saying. We had passed several huts before we turned in a right direction. Standing in front of us were three, white-robed, hooded people. Each displayed a small golden sickle tucked into their white, knotted-roped belts. One man appeared older than the others, for he wore a long white beard. Each sleeve of his robe revealed golden-colored intertwined serpent designs sewn into the sleeves. He held a long dark-colored wooden staff with a mysterious bearded head carved on its top. The other two didn't have any designs on their sleeves. One of the three appeared as a young woman, yet their hoods covered their eyes. The crowd behind us stilled at once and bowed their heads toward them as we approached.

"Yeshua rushed toward them before I had a chance to approach the three. My nephew seemed to know them, but I didn't know how. He started speaking to them in Greek, and they replied. Yeshua called the older man Finstan, who knew Yeshua from a sight he had seen in the stars. He explained to Yeshua that his image came to him in a human-shaped cloud passing in the night sky. I heard them telling Yeshua that they came from an oak forest a short distance from the village. They belonged to a group called the Servants of the Truth. Each said they had a vision of one of the villagers in distress and came right away from their oak grove. The older man stated they rushed to give aid to the woman in their vision. He further said, halfway to the village, he sensed the danger had subsided.

"Finstan then introduced his two companions. He called the young man Finn and the young woman Morrigan. Yeshua reciprocated in kind and then they came forward and embraced us. The villagers were further awestruck by the acceptance of their priests with our newfound friends while still exuberant over Yeshua's miracle. They bowed their heads to both Yeshua and me as we squeezed through the crowd. The group led us to a straw-thatched, roofed hut where a swift prepared feast had begun. There were nine of us there, including the young woman and her *amma* who stood stirring a sizable black cauldron.

"To my surprise, the interior appeared larger than its outward appearance, yet dimly lit. There were several tables, chairs, and a large central fireplace containing a black cauldron, with its contents hissing and gurgling as it boiled. The young woman offered us chairs in which to sit as the *amma* of the young woman came to Yeshua and again kissed his hands. She spoke to Finstan about something and gestured to Yeshua and me, motioning toward a large flagon. We accepted their hospitality and motioned back our agreement. With great care, she poured a golden liquid from a pitcher into nine cups.

"We began to drink the smooth, honey-tasting liquid as I gazed at the gray smoke twisting and turning its way from the open fireplace into a round hole in the roof. The smoke, smelling of cooked meat, spiraled from the bubbling black cauldron. My thoughts were with my cup and the meaty smell when Yeshua started speaking to Finstan. Yeshua stated he knew the old man held a venerated position in his tribe. Finstan stated that seventy-five summers ago, his birth occurred during the season of Samhain, as he called it.

"After we finished our drinks, the older woman served us out of the large cauldron with an arm's-length ladle that spooned the meal into our wooden bowls. The young woman, whom Yeshua had saved, and her *amma* were more than generous with our portions as they dished out the stew. Each gave us helpings of deer meat at their expense, with a smaller portion for themselves. After we had completed our meal, Yeshua and the old man discussed many issues. All four of them spoke in Greek, making it easy for me to follow their conversations. Their subjects touched on Greek philosophy and various religious faiths of which I knew little.

"It seemed odd to me that my nephew, just a boy, had such a great depth of knowledge. His *abba* knew the masonry and carpenter trade and was proficient but knew little about the different religions and philosophies. I sat and observed in wonder as young Yeshua and the older man discussed many esoteric topics, which I didn't comprehend. Quite often, the old man would stop and elucidate to his two young apprentices, then resume the conversation with my nephew. Many smiles, laughter, and enthusiastic discussions came over my nephew those many summers ago in speaking to the venerated old priest.

"As we prepared to leave, the last thing I remembered came from a prophecy the old man said. He told young Yeshua that many in this world would perish in my nephew's name, yet even stranger was his next prediction. Finstan said that mankind wouldn't perish in his namesake but live for eternity if they believed in his teachings. What he said didn't seem to upset Yeshua or cause him to ask questions. Yet, he nodded in agreement as if he knew what Finstan meant.

"We left the village a short time later, after finishing my business with the men of the tin mines. This miracle the people in *Yudah* don't know about. Why did I just remember this now? I thought most people wouldn't believe me and forgot about this episode in Yeshua's life. Not until recently did I remember it with Yeshua's recent succession of miracles."

"Master Yoseph, your travels and experiences with my teacher, have strengthened my faith in his accomplishments for our fellow man. Yohanan, Philip, Shimon, and Miriam of Magdala are his inner circle of students, and I know they'll enjoy hearing what you have just said. They're more than faithful followers, though Yeshua treats Miriam as an exceptional student; however, all of them know a secret knowledge taught by my rabbi. I am still learning from both Yohanan and Yeshua. Yohanan keeps a journal on his healings, ministry, and hidden knowledge our rabbi imparts to us. I, myself, write in my journal Yeshua's everyday events.

"Please, pardon me, I must now leave, and I have enjoyed your hospitality and revealing conversation. Furthermore, Master Nicodemus, I thank you for saving us from the clutches of Herodias. We might have faced arrest and not be sitting here enjoying an excellent discourse about my teacher. Again, I thank you.

"Shimon of Cyrene, I hope your leg mends soon and you can help Master Yoseph and his family."

Yohanan Marcus stood, embraced everybody, and bid a fond farewell as Yoseph escorted him to the front gate of the courtyard. He turned to say farewell but instead spoke of his original request.

"Master Yoseph, Yeshua insists you come to my house tomorrow night. I know he needs your support in a quite an important matter. Please come tomorrow evening; you can locate my house near the east gate. Follow the steps to the upper rooms."

The young man left with his writing bag slung over his shoulder and disappeared into one of the many side streets of *Yerushalayim.* Yoseph strolled back to the fountain area to finish his meal, at the same time, somewhat vexed. Why the persistence of this Seder dinner at Yohanan Marcus's house? What does his nephew now want of him? As Yoseph sat down near the fountain, his servant poured some more wine into his goblet. Nicodemus's large brown eyes had a questioning look as he sipped the sweet liquid.

"You look as though you have much on your mind, Yoseph. Although, with everything I have seen and heard today, I am not surprised; yet what does this all mean?"

"I don't have a definitive answer to your question, but at this point it's conjecture on my part. There are numerous disjointed thoughts buzzing around in my head and none of them make sense. The attacks, the remembrances, the Temple upheaval, and his insistence of us at Yohanan Marcus's Seder dinner have left me bewildered. You know as much about what Yeshua asks as I do. Have you any further thoughts on this matter as it now stands?"

"It's impossible for me to read Yeshua's mind, but my thoughts are just suppositions. I have heard just secondhand information. His disciple, Philip, divulged some information to me in the olive grove last night. He said Yohanan told him their master would reveal a *brit chadashah,* a special covenant and hidden knowledge to all of his disciples. He didn't explain in detail but said it would affect every man and woman throughout the known world. Philip further stated that you're a big part of Yeshua's new covenant. That's all Philip knew, which leads me to believe if you want answers to your questions, you must visit him."

"You're right, my friend. Discussion between us will solve nothing. To know Yeshua's intent, I can't say. I must yield to his request not knowing what the future will reveal. I don't worry about myself, but my family and friends." Right away, a shiver of doom came over Yoseph, but he knew it concerned his family. Hebron commented first, on what he'd just heard.

"Yoseph, we're a close family and have good friends and *El Shaddai* has strengthened us to confront any issue or danger we might encounter. Even the treachery of Caiaphas and Annas can't stop our faith in one another."

"I agree with Uncle Hebron," Alein Yosephe concurred. "My cousin has said we must trust *El Shaddai's* judgment. In addition, as a family, we have considerable influence with the Romans and the Sanhedrin, but there's something I must reveal. I have in place two readied ships docked at a secret location. They're three leagues from Yoppa in a secluded cove. There's enough room to board thirty people and supplies for thirty days at sea. Both ships have four men on retainer to guard them and the location. It will take a day's journey by camel from Arimathea. I see this as augmenting our contingency plan to escape to Arimathea and leaving there if necessary. Hopefully, we won't have to use them."

"Yoseph, I must say your son thinks ahead," Nicodemus stated.

Yoseph appreciated Nicodemus's praise of Alein and wondered why they were now at this dangerous point in their lives that dictated such an elaborate escape plan.

"Yoseph," Hebron touched his arm. "Who will travel with you tomorrow night?"

"I hope you and Nicodemus can journey with me. His house isn't too far from the east gate of the Temple, but some distance from our home. The Seder starts right after sunset and will be held in an upper room of his home. He mentioned this to me at our front gate."

"Will he have ample room for the three of us?" Nicodemus inquired.

"According to Yohanan Marcus, he has room for thirty people, and he wants Yosa and Enygeus to attend."

"We must carry swords tomorrow night." As always, Hebron put their safety first and spoke in a forthright manner about a safe travel plan.

"Hebron, to take our weapons to Yohanan Marcus's Seder dinner might offend his hospitality." Yoseph shook his head. "Besides, my nephew preaches peace to his followers and carries no weapon."

"Part of what you say could be correct, yet, Yoseph, some of his followers are well-armed. They're always ready to protect their great teacher, yet Yeshua isn't afraid of death, but the thought of treachery and what it can do to our family worries me. Yoseph, I insist you and Nicodemus protect yourselves. Some threatening event has occurred every night in our recent travels. If our host and his guests see that we have weapons, we can offer our apologies and give an explanation. Our risks are far greater now since the attempts to kill you."

"In protecting us, I must acquiesce to your wisdom and judgment, Hebron. We'll go armed to the Seder dinner tomorrow night and worry about the consequences later."

Right away, Yoseph's intuition spoke to him and said, "Beware, Yoseph," yet said no more, which left him frustrated with many questions. What next evil event would befall them?

CHAPTER XIX

blood-red sun sank lower on the horizon and the heat increased as they finished their late midday meal. Yoseph returned to his quarters, longing for a fresh breeze while perspiration rolled off his forehead as he sat down to contemplate today's events. Unexpectedly, a gust of wind blew through his doorway that cooled his wet face and beard.

At this point in the day, he didn't know whether to pray, cry, or pound his fists on his table, about the events that had occurred in the past few days. He must have spent some time in contemplation because the sun started casting its long dark shadow into his room. His nature wouldn't let him just sit and do nothing. Lamenting his past troubled days wouldn't suffice. Then an inner voice reminded him of what Yohanan Marcus said earlier, about how he and the disciple Yohanan were recording the events of their rabbi, Yeshua. His words reaffirmed what the apparition Gabriel called him to do for his sanity, his family, and his beloved nephew. By writing them in a journal, this would provide him an opportunity to leave a permanent record for his family. Also, it would clarify the motives for Yeshua's strange behavior and reveal the identity of the man or men trying to kill him.

He reached for a drawer handle, opened it, grabbed some parchment paper, and started writing. To his amazement, his hand seemed guided by some omnipotent force. The events during the last three or four days seemed to magically appear on each page of the scrolls.

He stopped writing at nightfall, due more to the lack of lighting rather than exhaustion. Rising from his writing desk, he had a sincere sense of accomplishment and euphoria.

The servants scurried about, lighting the oil lamps in all the rooms. His sister's voice encouraged them to hurry, followed by the pleasant voice of Yosa calling him to the evening meal.

"*Abba*, what have you been doing in your room this afternoon? You seem much rested, *abba*, after your long day. Please tell me about what happened in the Temple today with my cousin and his followers. Please, *abba*, spare no details."

"All right, my daughter, but these events I am about to speak of are confusing, with no explanation for me to give. Also, I hate to say, some aren't pleasant and even mention future danger for us, including Yeshua."

He told her everything: the near riot with the moneychangers, the Temple guards, Caiaphas, Herodias, and what Yohanan Marcus and Yohanan the writer said. Her placid-faced stare showed a serious interest in each detail and she never grimaced or frowned. He now saw a mature woman, yet most notably, a rock of understanding in their family and above all to him. She now volunteered to carry some of his burdens and always listen to him. Her demeanor and thoughtful words reminded him of her *amma*. *Adonai* had blessed him twice with two women in his life with the understanding and tolerance to listen to him. *Oh, Adonai, if something happened to Yosa, I couldn't go on.* He thenceforth silently prayed for Yosa's divine protection.

"*Abba*, will Miriam of Magdala attend the Seder dinner with Yeshua?"

"Yes, my dear, I expect her there, for your cousin respects her greatly as his disciple. Why do you ask?"

"The other night, when we were at Gethsemane, she asked me to accompany her. Due to all the trouble afterward, I forgot to tell you. She's imparting some of her unique knowledge to me, which my cousin has communicated to her. She honored me when she said you and I would become disciples of Yeshua and travel to many lands. What lands did she mean, *abba*?"

"I don't know yet where these lands are. What else did she discuss with you in the garden?"

"Tomorrow night, she said that Yeshua would tell us more."

"How odd. Yohanan Marcus made similar statements earlier this afternoon to me. My dear, I don't want you to travel tomorrow night. Your Uncle Hebron, Nicodemus, and I will journey with swords and daggers. We must trust your Uncle Hebron's keen senses and foresight in these matters, even though I don't approve. You need to stay here with Alein Yosephe." He took a deep breath before continuing. "Your brother's plans are to leave for Arimathea with you and your aunt if trouble develops."

"Is it necessary for us to leave?" She frowned. "Oh, *abba,* are things indeed that dangerous for us that we must leave home?"

"Yes, my daughter, for great danger hangs over our heads. All of us are threatened, and I take full responsibility to do anything necessary for our protection. Under lesser circumstances, we would stand and fight; however, this evil opponent has many dangerous tentacles. Yosa, if I thought any of you would fall in harm's way or worse . . . I don't want to think about it."

Yosa reached for him and they embraced, then her breath caught, and tears trickled down her cheeks. "*Abba,* you must know that you're as important to us as we are to you. Please promise me you won't risk your safety and that you'll plan to join us if we are forced to leave."

"I will do as required. However, you have my promise not to conduct myself in a perilous manner. After all, seeing you at your wedding and seeing my future grandchildren will remind me to practice caution." They released their embrace.

"I am quite proud you're my *abba* and teaching me when to stand up for the truth and also the meaning of discretion. I love you with all my heart and soul."

They held hands for a moment, but her eyes stared in deep thought about something.

"Let's not dwell on this matter anymore. We'll discuss Yohanan Marcus's Seder dinner for tomorrow night," Yoseph said.

"*Abba*, Miriam of Magdala told me I must attend the Seder dinner for several reasons. She said the young son of the Baptizer asked for me. Also, she said I would supervise him and journey to other lands to tell of the teachings of Yeshua."

It amazed him to see his daughter refocus her thoughts and emotions back to the forthcoming Seder and Miriam from Magdala. Her determination and forthright behavior flummoxed him with her new single purpose.

"Are you intending on becoming his surrogate *amma?*" Yoseph inquired as he pulled on his beard.

"Yes, *abba*, the poor little soul's *amma* died in childbirth and several different people cared for him after the Baptizer's execution. She knew that our family's love might help him. Also, Miriam prophesied that his children would start a line of kings lasting two thousand summers or more! His future and his children's future will become our responsibility to help him fulfill his destiny. *Abba*, please let me guide his future kingship."

"Yes, my daughter, but you take on a great responsibility for this child. I know you've already received him into your heart, yet he's no more than a baby and knows little of his *abba* before Herod Antipas beheaded him. The Baptizer lived in a cave and roamed the desert preaching his philosophy. That's not leading a normal life for a young child."

"I know, *abba*. Miriam told me such. I trust her nascent wisdom and student devotion to my cousin. Miriam wants to include me in my cousin's ministry, and he has no objections. Miriam demonstrates respectable leadership as a teacher, and all the women listen to her, even some of the men. Just the teacher and wisdom seeker for me and the young Baptizer's son."

"How can I argue when you have presented such a strong case in your favor? Nicodemus and I needed your persuasiveness when we have confronted the Sanhedrin to argue a legal point. Yet, please contemplate becoming a disciple of Yeshua. If later, you agree or change your mind, I will offer you my full support whatever you decide."

"Thank you, *abba*, for your encouragement. It's quite important to me."

Yosa's pleasurable smile gave his heart great comfort. However, his mind had other questions that needed answers.

"Did Miriam say where Zechariah's kingdom would encompass?"

"No, she didn't say, but said *El Shaddai* would lead the way."

He added her response to the many other unanswered questions he'd heard over the last several days.

"One other thing I insist of you, Yosa. Promise me at the first sign of danger, after implementing our plan, you'll travel with haste and depart this treacherous land."

"Yes, *abba*, but I must take the Baptizer's son with me when I leave." Her insistence, concerning Zechariah, showed him her high resolve and now the boy's fate became theirs.

"I am a rich man and wouldn't abandon the little soul. Giving either our time or money to the less fortunate distinguishes us from most Gentiles. Well, now our plans are complete. In the event we need to leave *Yerushalayim* right away, I can now rest assured that all of you know what to do."

"I am glad, *abba*, and again I love you with all my heart. If you tell me to leave because of danger, I will do as you say. I hope and pray there isn't any trouble for his safety. His young innocence and the terrible trials he has experienced makes his security my top priority."

"Already you seek to protect him as any loving *amma* and that shows *El Shaddai* has already blessed you."

"*Abba*, don't worry. Our trials will work out."

"My dear child, your reassurance strengthens me. Oh, if your *amma* could see you today, her heart would soar." Once again, she hugged him and started crying.

Their evening meal began with the wine blessing, followed by light conversation, with Enygeus asking a few questions about the Temple confrontation, which Hebron assured her nothing would come from it. This seemed to ease her concerns.

His sister and he differed in personality; she didn't obsess about advancing problems. Her scope of worry concerned the immediate day itself. However, he always filled his obsessive mind with both today and tomorrow's concerns. After completing their repast, each of them decided to retire and regain their strength and senses for tomorrow.

Yoseph proceeded down the stone walkway to his room, while listening to the night birds chirping in the trees. The raucous birds changed his mind about sleep, and he decided to write some more about his recent experiences. He entered his shadowy lit room and asked a servant to bring some additional oil lamps. Sitting down on his chair, all the stressful memories and events started coalescing in his mind.

Once again, to his astonishment, the written words flowed out of his quill pen with incredible speed, as if time didn't exist. The next thing he knew two of his oil lamps began sputtering and then ran out of oil. The room darkened, now forcing him to stop, with just one burning oil lamp left to see to wash his face, beard, and feet before changing into his nightclothes. Once his ablutions were complete, he ambled to his bed, hoping for some sound sleep. At once, the soft bed relaxed his back, but Yoseph's thoughts jumped like gazelles with fear and trepidation, making sleep fruitless. In the past, his mind and demeanor exuded that of a confident business-man, but the terror of the last few days had left him unsettled with bizarre and unexplainable events.

A cold night breeze blew in through his courtyard window and extinguished his last remaining oil lamp. Yoseph's mind then calmed down, leaving him drowsy thoughts. He lay there some time listening to the wind's soft whispering before he fell into a semi-sleep state. Then came a distance voice. At first, it seemed similar to Yosa's voice, but he soon realized he heard a Galilean accent from a female voice. The voice he thought he knew, yet his groggy memory prevented such. Then his mind awakened . . . he recognized the voice of Miriam of Magdala!

She said in a soft whisper, "Yoseph of Arimathea, I will depend on you and you will depend on me for *Adonai's* sake."

In a clear warning, she spoke, "Beware of Caiaphas he isn't one of *El Shaddai's* chosen people. He hasn't any soul and won't see salvation. Yoseph, watch, for you'll become a lowly fly in mankind's spiderweb of injustices."

"Miriam! Is that you?" he asked not knowing if she stood there in the dark shadows of his bedchamber. Yet, he didn't see her, and the voice seemed inside his head

At once, the whispering words ceased, and he raised straight up in his bed. Yoseph's eyes strained in the darkness for her dark image, yet he still observed nothing. Was this a nightmare or a premonition? His heart pounded and he wiped the cold sweat from his brow. He prayed to stop anymore fitful dreams.

The rest of the night remained uneventful and he arose some rested. With reverence, he positioned his prayer shawl and said his *shakharit* prayers, thanking *El Shaddai* for answering his late-night request.

As he looked out of his courtyard window, the morning sun weaved its way through the gathering clouds. He noticed a large knot of slate-gray, storm-colored clouds and judged the storm would reach *Yerushalayim* soon. All the many seasons of traveling by sea made him keenly aware of weather and distances, giving Yoseph the confidence to anticipate coming storms and initiate the appropriate action. He laughed at himself, thinking he was a better judge of events at sea than events on dry land.

His self-deprecating humor vanished when he heard his daughter's voice as Yoseph left his room. "*Abba,* come and eat with us and break the fast." Yosa looked disheveled, yet she saw his distress too.

"*Abba,* didn't you rest well last night?"

"No, I didn't, Yosa. The wind kept me awake." He lied to his daughter, not wanting to alarm her. "You also look like you slept little."

"That is true. I shall tell you about it."

She and Yoseph sat down on the pillows with the rest of the family who were already breaking their fast. The anise cakes gave off a sweet, honey-smelling aroma as Yoseph brought one to his mouth. The servant then filled his cup from his flagon of goat's milk.

It tasted doubly sweet as he washed down his cake with the sweet flavored milk.

"A strange dream came over last night as I slept," Yosa said. "At least it seemed a dream yet appeared real with a disembodied voice speaking to me."

"Was it an intruder hiding in your room?" Yoseph asked.

"No, not an intruder, and to my surprise, I recognized the voice as that of Miriam of Magdala speaking to me in a whispering voice. However, I did notice a faint light shining in the corner of my room. Her voice seemed to originate there. She told of a premonition about us, *abba*. She warned me that Caiaphas would destroy our family's way of life."

"I don't know what to say about your premonition, Yosa," Enygeus said, "yet numerous strange things have transpired in the last few days. I see this as a warning of some close impending danger. These portents demand circumspection in our activities."

What might Yoseph add to Miriam of Magdala's warning? Nothing, yet he hesitated whether to divulge the same warning he'd heard or wait to hear how the rest of his family would respond.

"I agree with Enygeus, Yoseph," Hebron said. "We have seen many puzzling signs by *Adonai* in the last several days and it seems evil and danger have become our constant companions. I am not saying that Yeshua has brought this danger with him. I don't trust his disciples, the Iscariot man in particular. Caiaphas isn't the sole potential danger we now face. Yeshua's disciple, Yudas Iscariot, will further lash out his anger and hatred toward us. I can't trust him, and my sources say he speaks to both Caiaphas and Herodias. We know the Tetrarch Herod Antipas poses less of a danger than his nefarious wife, who displays evil all the time. We know that Yohanan the Baptizer, a *kodesh* prophet, spoke the truth and lost his head for speaking the words of *El Shaddai*. Now a poor innocent child has no *abba* because of her corrupt ways."

"Let's never forget the memory of Yohanan the Baptizer and his sacrifice," Yosa stated.

"We don't know anything yet, but my intuition tells me what we'll hear tonight could cast our fate for many years to come," Alein

Yosephe said. "Caution and preparation will protect us, and we need to listen with care tonight to what our cousin tells us."

"I am relieved we have a plan in place for us to leave *Yerushalayim* if necessary and journey to Arimathea. Then from there, if needed, to the waiting ships I have hired. If separated, for whatever reason or length of time, each of us will wait in Arimathea for the other family members to arrive. We must stay together at all costs. Our faith and determination won't stop us working together." Alein Yosephe looked into each of their eyes and sought out their affirmation. They swore before *El Shaddai* and then prayed for His guidance.

A long silent period ensued as they raised their hands to *Adonai*. After their prayer, they embraced one another, then sat back down in silent contemplation, and continued their meal.

Yoseph ate two more anise cakes and drank some additional goat's milk as Yosa started a conversation with her brother. Yoseph pondered what would unfold today. *How odd*, he thought, not having any emotion of apprehension as he observed the sun rising through the gathering clouds. Unlike his sister, he knew he must think ahead about each future event as it became known, which helped with his confidence, despite all the premonitions and dire chatter. Right away, his thoughts left him when a quiet voice called from the outside gate.

"Yoseph, it's me, Nicodemus."

Yoseph noticed he said a prayer as he passed the *mezuzah* on his way into the courtyard. "Yohanan Marcus has sent me a note this morning." His dark animated eyes betrayed his usual cool demeanor. He pulled a small parchment from his long black cloak and handed it to Yoseph to read. It contained both Greek and Hebrew words with additional Roman numerals. *How strange*, he thought, *a note with mixed letters and numbers*. Reading further, he recognized the code called Gematria.

The first line said, "Beware Nicodemus and Yoseph! Caiaphas will try to set a trap for you tonight. You must use cunning and stealth on your visit to my house." The note ended with his blessing and praise to *El Shaddai* for a safe trip to his home.

Yoseph translated the note for Hebron, Yosa, and Alein Yoseph, to whom he shared its meaning. They looked at him for a response after he had decoded the parchment. His daughter spoke first.

"*Abba,* does this mean we're not leaving?"

"No, my daughter, but prepare yourself to have your strength and faith tested tonight and tomorrow. We must maintain our resolve in the coming days ahead. I know *El Shaddai* will ask us to pay back what He has blessed us with as a family. My nephew and his followers are risking their lives to see us and so are we. Yeshua will speak about his knowledge and burdens with us tonight. We must place ourselves in the hands of *El Shaddai,* accepting the future He grants us."

Forthwith, Yosa summoned the servants to find clothes for them to travel in, and Hebron left to see after their swords. At once, a sudden flurry of activity started. Enygeus entered the courtyard, saw the shuffle, and heard the noise from their many sandals. Yoseph handed her the note, and Nicodemus summarized what it said and why they were departing in different directions. When he glanced over his shoulder, he saw a contorted expression on his sister's face as she dropped the small scroll, embraced Nicodemus, and started crying. However, their departure wasn't as an unassuming ill-prepared family, but one with weapons to thwart any threat to their safety. If the plans of *El Shaddai* destined them to include weapons, so be it. It wasn't the first time their people had to arm themselves for protection and maybe not the last in the future to come.

CHAPTER XX

The *Pesach* week had reached its climax as the sun sank behind the approaching slate-gray storm clouds. The din from the streets and passageways had started penetrating Yoseph's quiet courtyard. The sound of voices and shuffling feet grew greater than the previous day when they'd traveled to the Temple. There came a steady buzzing hum of conversations originating from thousands of people, each traveling from different countries and the surrounding villages for the climax of the *Pesach* celebration. Yoseph knew his nephew moved among this crowd and he prayed for his safety.

Nicodemus followed him to the underground storage area of his home, wherein the corner sat Hebron and Alein Yosephe sharpening their swords. The sharpening stones, with their grinding metallic sounds raised the hair on the back of Yoseph's neck. Hebron glanced up as they approached.

"Yoseph, I found some excellent sharpening stones. I saw them the other night when we had Herod's lackey down here. When we're finished, these swords will hold off anyone trying to harm us." Then he cleaved a small log with his sword. Nicodemus and Yoseph jumped back from the sudden blow.

He and Nicodemus left Alein Yosephe and Hebron to finish their work. As they hurried toward the interior of his house, Yosa, Enygeus, and his servants placed their disguise clothes near the fountain. They weren't a wealthy person's clothes that wouldn't draw attention to them on the way to the Seder or leaving *Yerushalayim*.

"Our servants are letting us use some of their clothing," Yosa said. "I think there's something here to fit each of us; so we can move through the streets undetected. No one looking for our family will expect us to be traveling about dressed as servants. What do you think, *abba*?"

"You have chosen well, Yosa. Dressing us as servants is a superb idea to cloak ourselves. Quite kind of the servants to let us use their clothing for the evening."

Yoseph left, entered his sleeping quarters, changed into his new clothes, after which he left to meet the others in the courtyard for their eventual departure. As they gathered, Hebron handed him his sword. The burnished finish gave Yoseph a strong sense of confidence to combat any foe, dispelling any thoughts of his nonviolent existence. With care, he stuck the short sword behind his waistband against his back. The grip of the hilt seemed comfortable to hold, yet the flat blade's sharpness gave him an odd sense of calmness.

Nicodemus appeared nervous, for his hands shook as he placed his sword in his waistband. His frown revealed his discomfort, most likely because of the clothes he wore. He displayed colors of light gray with a red hat and shawl making him appear as a wine merchant, rather than a scholar. The women looked plain in dress except for Yosa, who wore her *amma's* earrings and ankle bracelets. Yoseph suggested, to look the part of a servant, she might want to leave them at home. He told them they would split up and go separate routes for their protection, once on the streets.

The already lit lanterns allowed them to leave at once. They scurried through the courtyard until they reached the *mezuzah* post. Here Yoseph stopped, touched it, said a prayer for their safety, kissed his fingers, and then they entered the street. By now, the crowds had dwindled significantly from the late afternoon hour. They entered the stone-paved alleyway, hearing their sandals make a light rhythmic *thumping* sound as they hurried toward Yohanan Marcus's home.

His instructions indicated he lived almost a half a league from their home on the west side of the Temple. He told them to look for Yohanan Marcus's servant carrying a large red-colored ewer filled with water going back and forth from a well, and then follow him. Their group parted a short time later and proceeded their separate ways as planned. Alein Yosephe, Enygeus, Yosa, and Shimon of Cyrene limping, ambled toward the shorter route. As they disappeared between the darkness of the houses, Yoseph said a prayer for their safety. Hebron, Nicodemus, and Yoseph journeyed by a more circuitous route.

The cool night air and a full moon guided them, while displaying strings of dark clouds that approached fast from the west. The fast-moving black clouds permitted some darkness, making it difficult for anyone to recognize them.

They traveled about a third of a league when Yoseph spotted a crowd of people standing near a camel caravan, resting for the night. They were next to a local clothing merchant's shop he knew quite well. As they approached, the camels continued to bray, but not from their approach. Something else seemed to disturb these animals. Then, still approaching closer, Yoseph saw fear in the camel's rolling eyes. Yoseph's party crept toward the merchant shop. Out of the shop's entrance doorway, a small man approached carrying a single torch, which lit his face. However, Yoseph couldn't recognize him because a dark-colored scarf covered most of it. Two other men followed close behind. Yoseph saw his companions reach for their weapons, as he too gripped the hilt of his sword, but then he heard his name.

"Is that you, Yoseph of Arimathea, and your big brother-in-law, Hebron? Your clothes don't match your names."

"Eli, my friend and business associate," Yoseph announced to the others. His old friend's voice gave him great relief, as they slid their swords back into their sash belts. "Eli, it's pleasant to see you again." Both Eli and Yoseph were the most successful businessmen in *Yerushalayim*. Not just did he have one of the largest camel herds, but also a thriving cloth business. He had helped Alein Yosephe and him in many business adventures.

"Come in and partake of my hospitality. I know you are thirsty for refreshment."

"Yes, we can stay a short while." The three of them entered Eli's living quarters, still having some time before the Seder and not wanting to deny his offer of hospitality. They sat down on large, blue-colored pillows while Eli asked for his servants to bring them pomegranate wine and dates.

"Let me introduce my family to you. These are my sons. The big one we call Eliyah; he acquired his considerable size from my wife's brother. The other one we call Isaiah and you can see he resembles me in my younger days." A tidal wave of pride came forth from his smiling, dark glistening beard, followed with his booming voice as he finished introducing his sons.

"They have made me proud in how they understand my camels. Our herd has increased tenfold since they were young boys. Yoseph, my friend, why are you traveling tonight? Isn't your family having a Seder dinner? I came outside to help calm my camels, which I am sure all of you noticed. They've brayed most of the day. I don't know the cause of their uneasiness. Anyway, why are you lurking in the alleyways tonight?" he said, while staring at Yoseph's unusual mode of dress.

Yoseph hesitated in replying to his question, but his inner thoughts told him to answer in a truthful manner. Eli and Yoseph were old trusted business associates, but he feared to put him in danger. He had to respond before he detected something amiss.

"Eli, we're visiting a friend's house for a *Pesach* celebration. He lives on the other side of the Temple. Maybe you have heard his name? He's called Yohanan Marcus."

"No, I haven't. Is he part Roman, using Marcus as his name?"

"I don't know, but his *amma* comes from the tribe of Benjamin."

"Yoseph, earlier my son Eliyah told me what he thought was causing our camels' strange behavior. Eliyah, tell these men what you told me."

"*Abba*, they know something terrible will happen soon. They have a far greater ability than we do to sense impending danger and can see it coming in their mind's eye. We must say extra prayers tonight and tomorrow asking *Adonai* for his protection the next several days."

"My son has been right each time in reading our camels' fears. Yoseph, please use caution and ask *Adonai* for his protection in your prayers."

"Thank you, my friend, and also to Eliyah for conveying to us your concerns."

Both Hebron and Yoseph glanced at each other, knowing that the thin veil of the future had opened and the warning had manifested itself in Eli's camels.

Yoseph noticed Eli staring at Nicodemus, fixating on his Sanhedrin badge of office. "I see your friend belongs to the Sanhedrin council too. I don't believe I know you."

"I am Nicodemus of *Yerushalayim*."

"Welcome to my humble home, Nicodemus of *Yerushalayim*. I am honored for you to visit my sons and me. I am Eli, the proprietor of this shop and, as I said earlier, the owner of the camels you hear braying outside. Yoseph, I am wondering why two great men from the Sanhedrin are dressed in Gentile clothes? Also, why are both of you traveling to a *Pesach* celebration that's not at your home? Is it possible you don't want people to recognize you?"

How much information must he tell Eli and his sons? Until now, his family members and Nicodemus were the sole people he trusted, yet again an inner voice told Yoseph otherwise. He remembered a time several years ago he overpaid Eli for some material he'd purchased. Before dawn the next morning, Eli returned his overpayment while apologizing that he didn't catch the error sooner. Yes, he and his sons were trustworthy, but should Yoseph reveal to him all the dangers that had occurred to his family? After a slight hesitation, he warned them beforehand what he was about to say might affect Eli and his sons associating with them. Yet, it didn't matter to Eli or his sons. Yoseph didn't leave out any details to Eli, as his two sons tilted their heads to listen.

Their conversation turned to the troubling events of the day and the possible reasons for all the unrest. Isaiah proceeded to tell them he saw a Galilean man with a curved dagger protruding from his waistband accompanying several members of the Sanhedrin and the Temple priests. They were scurrying toward the high priest's quarters near the Temple about dusk. Also, he didn't know the names of Sanhedrin members who were with them.

Yoseph didn't want to hear this, yet it hardened his resolve to still see his nephew even more and warn him of impending danger, regardless of the risk involved.

"Nicodemus, who do you think they were?" he again asked.

"I say two of them were Caiaphas and Annas."

"But I don't understand why they would escort a Galilean. The people in *Yerushalayim* know Caiaphas has a low opinion of anybody from Galilee."

"Yoseph, isn't Yeshua from Galilee?" Eli asked with questioning eyes.

"Yes, Eli, you're correct. Yeshua and my family are spending *Pesach* supper with his followers."

"Isn't he the same itinerant rabbi mentioned in the marketplace?"

Yoseph hesitated to respond to Eli's question, but he already knew his answer. Eli deserved the truth and his heart further told him to confide in Eli this night.

"Yes, they call him Yeshua ben Yoseph and many follow his teachings. He came from my late brother Yoachim's family. Miriam is my niece."

"I am sorry to say, Yoseph; I think we both know why Caiaphas became involved with the Galilean. Caiaphas wants power alone and your nephew challenges his power. The greed part involves you!"

"What do you mean?" Yoseph replied, knowing all too well the correct answer.

"Yoseph, your tin contracts with the Romans are quite valuable. He might implicate you as one of Yeshua's zealots, have the Romans hand over your contracts, and confiscate your property. He would eliminate a threat to his power and gain wealth with one swift stroke. Now that we know the source of your danger, Yoseph, you must use more caution tonight. My camels' fears are your fears; as my son has already said, they know far more than we humans acknowledge as their masters. However, tonight they're your lifeline. If you sense imminent danger after your visit with your nephew, please send for me. My camels are at your disposal. They're as fast as falcons flying in the desert sky and will travel anywhere without tiring."

"Thank you for your offer, Eli. I am indebted to your hospitality and excellent insight. May *El Shaddai* bless you and your sons. Eli, not every day am I am blessed with another friend such as you."

"Yoseph, you're a righteous and honest man. Not just in business, but for mankind's sake. Your entire family conveys respect in *Yehudah* and the powers of evil and envy seek out your family and friends."

As they left Eli's home, Yoseph sensed a greater confidence. Eli's welcomed insight made him even more circumspect. Also, his offer of his camels for transportation away from harm eased his angst. Eli's deep friendship now protected them, comparable to a fortress. They said their goodbyes and advanced on their way to Yeshua's Seder supper.

Close to Yohanan Marcus's house, a centurion and his men stopped them. Under his torch light, the small centurion displayed a large scar that traveled across the bridge of his nose to the dark side of his face. His silver helmet with its red horsehair insignia made him look taller in stature. He spoke first to Nicodemus in his Roman tongue. Nicodemus at once replied, already versed in the Roman language. He showed the centurion his Sanhedrin medallion and motioned for Yoseph to do the same. Nicodemus spoke at length and made several hand gestures, indicating they were traveling toward the Temple. The centurions kept glancing at their swords as Nicodemus continued to talk. Was he to arrest them and stop Yoseph from fulfilling his nephew's wishes? A prayer came to his lips, asking *Adonai* to prevent this from happening. Then the guard motioned them on, to Yoseph's amazement. Indeed, *Adonai* had answered his prayer.

PART THREE

The Fortress

CHAPTER XXI

Montpellier Fortress and Priory
Anno Domini 1190

From the corridor came a light knock on the door of my small cell, interrupting my deep thoughts on the precious book of Saint Joseph of Arimathea.

"It's Gilbért," whispered the voice. "Lord Robert, I need to speak to you right now." I slowly cracked the door open and saw a dark face in the shadows of the stone corridor.

"Please come in, Gilbért," I said, thinking two days hadn't yet elapsed. Gilbért crept forward, pushing his body into the room.

"Robert de Borron, you must finish *lé Sangraal* book as soon as possible. The seneschal . . . suspects something." His exterior appearance didn't appear shaken. In the candlelight of the room, I noticed a large red scar extending across his cheek and temple. Those features weren't visible the first time I saw him, because of the dim light and his hooded mantle. Yet, how did he receive that wound?

Frère Gilbért's large bear-shaped body displayed the muscular build of a warrior *chevalier;* however, quite noticeable, I glanced at his large log-shaped sword arm. I didn't have to wonder what happened to his enemy who disfigured him. My mind leaped with numerous questions about this warrior-*moine*, the secrets of this great holy book, and the urgency to destroy it. Yet, was this the proper time to ask him numerous questions? However, my inner voice urged me to demand some explanations.

"*Frère* Gilbért, why the urgency for me reading your book?"

"Lord Robert, there's little time left to tell you, but I just heard our Holy *Père* ordered the new seneschal to confiscate it."

"Why does our Holy *Père* want this sacred book delivered to him?"

Gilbért's cool demeanor changed as he began pacing in my small cell. His voice quivered as he offered me an explanation.

"For some reason, this book concerns some in my community of faith. Numerous fellow *chevaliers* and *frères* have died protecting this sacred book in the Levant. When I left Jerusalem, I took the *Sangraal* book and hid it at the Abbey of Clairvaux, believing no one would seek it there. The Cistercian order of monks protected it for several years. The Holy *Père* heard of its whereabouts and asked me to transfer it to our Montpellier Priory."

"How long do I have to finish the *Sangraal* book before they destroy it or use it for nefarious purposes?"

"I overheard our seneschal say soon. He has to deliver it to Rome and the papal legate will arrive any day to oversee the Holy *Père's* orders.

"My Lord de Borron, what does the book say? Our order never determined the meaning of the words."

I knew what had just transpired in this room wouldn't surprise him, so I answered.

"I am sure it wouldn't amaze you to hear about the strange abilities of this holy book. Perhaps it's the reason you hid it these many years, waiting for the right person and now the urgent time to reveal its secrets. But I will answer your question. Joseph of Arimathea is the uncle to our Lord and Savior. His words speak about his nephew and Jesus's few days before his crucifixion.

"It isn't just the holy words holding me in awe, but the strange happenings in this small room. I am having the same experiences of spirits that Saint Yoseph of Arimathea encountered in his chronicles. And do you know about the sacred cup of Christ?" I waited for Gilbért's response, yet he gave none. Was it now time to hand over the precious *Sangraal* book? I hadn't completed all my miraculous memorization, its cryptic translation, and the continued speed of copying the ancient tome. He listened with much interest, with me explaining what Marie Magdalene had foretold. The warrior *chevalier* seemed pleased with what he had heard while thinking me not insane.

My eyes moved away from the *moine's* gaze, drawing me back to the ornate designed holy book, causing me to wonder what the many remaining pages would reveal. A sense of angst and doubt struck the bottom of my stomach. What will happen if I can't finish this book in time? An enormous sense of responsibility began to overwhelm me as I considered the great task ahead.

"*Frère* Gilbért, why don't you just hide this holy book again? We both know how sacred these words are."

"It's too late. As I mention, numerous people know its location and that I hid it once before." A small smirk came across his face as he continued. "However, there were no promises made about not copying *lé Sangraal* words. We have to convey its message to those virtuous men who will later follow us. Many in my order have heard about your way with words, and along with my vision, it prompted me to seek your services. You're the right man to assist us in our great works ahead."

A big part of me always rose to a writing challenge. However, my mind fell into a giant whirlpool of unanswered questions as I took a deep breath.

"We have much discord among our order concerning what the future holds for this holy book. Many *chevaliers* agree with me and think this book must stay with our order. We're the sole religious order capable of protecting it with our warrior-*moines*. The *Sangraal* book or now its completed copy must remain with us for future generations of Christendom. We, the Poor Fellow-Soldiers of Christ, are destined as the true guardians of this book."

His final words sealed my fate but still left me with several unanswered questions. This quest before us transcended our lives.

Definitely, future generations needed to read the holy book's words, either in the form of the original book or a copy. I knew what I faced, yet still worried for my family's safety.

"I am quite honored by your faith in me to copy this most precious codex. *Frère* Gilbért, don't fear. I won't sleep until I finish it and dedicate myself to the preservation of the holy words contained within its covers. Our Lord, Jesus the Christ, has given me special spiritual powers to memorize this entire book before it's taken away." As I announced this, his sad demeanor changed, and a slight grin came over his scarred face.

"You came here not knowing what responsibilities or dangers you would face. I admire your tireless energy in reading these sacred words and agreeing to copy them. I'll dedicate my life to protecting you and the words you write. *Merci beaucoup*, Lord de Borron, may our Savior and Sainte-Marie-Magdalene bless you and protect you." As he turned to leave, his stained white mantle blew in the breeze of the opened door and the red pattée cross on his chest seemed to glow a fiery red. His polished sword hilt glistened, which gave his whole demeanor an ethereal look. This image had transformed him into something more than the warrior-*moine* that I saw earlier. Had he become a warrior angel, to protect people in times of danger? *Frère* Gilbért and his sword gave me a sense of confidence and trust.

"*Seigneur* Robert, prepare to leave when you hear the cock crow. Pray that it's not sooner."

He closed the heavy oak door and then, with much celerity, used his key to lock it. Loneliness and worry about my family now surrounded me, but I sensed solace in what further the *Sangraal* book might reveal. I sat down to memorize what Saint Yoseph of Arimathea would disclose. What will become of Saint Joseph's destiny and will he survive after the resurrection tomb? Anxious thoughts overcame me to find out what he'd written. Now I would become the new chronicler Joseph had once been to his generation.

I sat there focused on reading the ancient book and didn't realize that the dawn's ray had entered my cell. I thanked my God and

Savior for blessing me in the completion of my sacred task. It seemed but a short time ago the Templar *moine*, Gilbért, stood in my small room. Reading this holy book had possessed me, causing me to lose track of time. Then without warning, in the distance, I heard the faint sound of a cock crowing from the bailey portion of the *château*. At the same time, the smell of cooking smoke began wafting through the cross-shaped openings. *Frère* Gilbért de Érail would knock on my door at any moment and fetch this precious book away. Now began the task of organizing the holy words into a new book. This I could complete at my own château. I closed the thick leather cover and rubbed my fingertips over the many precious jewels embedded in its coverings. As I knew the book's fate, a sense of sadness came over me.

My apprehension grew as I waited for the knock on the large oak door. What further dire information would come from my warrior-*moine* informant? The precious codex had left me with an incomplete story about Saint Yoseph of Arimathea. This encouraged me to pray for guidance, hoping the book would stay at the monastery. I crossed myself after finishing my prayers, then came the dreaded knock I didn't want to hear. I gripped the book with both hands and would refuse to give it up, despite what the warrior-*moine* had told me. With hesitation, I partially opened the door, *Frère* Gilbért pushed through it and came into my cell.

"Lord Robert, are you finished memorizing the sacred book?"

"*Oui*, but I don't want to give it up."

"We are both leaving soon. The papal legate wants me to present the *Sangraal* book before Prime. We have little time to prepare to leave for New Castile and Toledo. I'll have my squire lead you to the stables. He calls himself Hughes and you must listen with care to his instructions. I'll meet you at the stables at the beginning of the divine office of Terce. Lord Robert de Borron, look for me with the tolling of the bells. Again, prepare yourself to leave. I don't know how long the audience with the legate will last, but he won't interfere with Terce, look for me then."

A numb sensation surrounded my body that things were taking place with such rapidity. *Frère Chevalier* Gilbért de Érail had surprised me and I had no idea why we were leaving for the province of New Castile and the city of Toledo. I thought maybe one of his sergeants or lesser *chevaliers* would accompany me back to *mon château* at Borron. Instead, my opposite new path seemed a forced direction! At once, I needed time to write and say *au revoir* to my *soeur* and send a separate letter to my *épouse*, Marie. Many reoccurring doubts flashed back and forth in my mind. After all, just two days ago, I met him.

"*Chevalier* Gilbért, why am I following you to such a distant land? What if I don't want to go? I must return to my family."

"Lord de Borron, I don't have time to explain. All I can tell you, before the holy office of Prime, a coded message came to me from Toledo. The note said there's another possible set of *Sangraal* parchments. Please excuse me, I must leave at once. Trust your faith in our Lord, Jesus the Christ, who will protect us." Then with much reluctance, I handed him the precious tome, while quite surprised to hear of possible additional parchments.

"If the other set exists, I think you would enjoy translating it, yet there's danger associated with it, which we have already faced. However, if you prefer to return home, it won't disappoint me, but I would understand. Lord Robert, don't ignore the divine gifts of translating and memorizing these holy words; not many mortal men receive this opportunity."

Frère Gilbért waited in silence and scrutinized my face. The warrior-*moine* seemed to read my thoughts. A lifetime opportunity now faced me. I, Lord Robert de Borron, elected to seek out additional holy words written by Saint Joseph de Arimathea? Without speaking, I nodded, shook his hand, and started gathering my parchments.

"It quite pleases me that you have chosen to join us. My squire will arrive soon. Please excuse me, for I am late."

Gilbért opened the door and then disappeared into the drafty, dark corridor while clutching the holy *Sangraal* book. A short time later, came another knock on my door.

"I am Hughes de Montbard, squire to Commander Gilbért de Érail," a voice whispered. "I am here to guide you to the stables as my commander ordered. It's imperative we leave right now."

I blew out the candles, crossed myself before the wooden crucifix, opened the door, and left my home of the last several days. Hughes de Montbard's hairless face gave him the appearance of a lad of sixteen years, but he possessed a stocky, muscular build. He seemed quite agile as he scurried in front of me holding a flaming torch. We proceeded in a different direction from the one I first entered the *château*. I noticed numerous spiderwebs along the seldom-used passage that ran perpendicular to the fortress wall. This dark passageway had a dank wet smell, with some relief coming from the acrid smelling torches. However, the torch smoke didn't alleviate the ever-present odor of mold. After several moments, we came to a large set of wooden double doors with two large iron rings. Hughes pulled on one of the rings that opened one side of the doors. This led into another stone passageway much narrower than the one whence we came. We had traveled a short distance when he approached an odd-looking round pulley mechanism with a rope.

"Lord de Borron, can you help me with this rope? There's a large stone block for us to pull up before we enter the stable grounds."

"*Oui*, Squire Hughes." I positioned myself to help.

As we pulled the large stone block, folding wooden stairs appeared in front of us and a beam of light came through an opening in the wooden ceiling. I surmised this was a secret passageway to the stables. When the straw fell on my head and I smelled the pungent aroma of horse manure, this confirmed it.

Young Hughes placed his torch in the iron receptacle, and we proceeded up the steps. The young squire reached for a long wooden handle alongside one of the stalls and the trap door closed shut.

The size of the stables measured that of a small *château*. There were three large barns, all interconnected that gave the appearance of never-ending. I estimated at least three hundred horses. None of the animals seemed nervous or concerned with our sudden presence.

"Squire Hughes, why are there such a large number of horses here? There're not enough *chevaliers* in this *château* to ride them."

"*Oui,* my lord, you are correct. Half of these horses are traveling to the Levant. Most of them were bred here and in Iberia, with more superior bloodlines than you would see in the finer breeding stables."

I observed one white horse that didn't appear recognizable to any type of horse I'd known. His legs were thin, yet he exuded a large barrel-shaped chest. He had a slender face and his hindquarters were muscular, presenting a powerful stature. Upon approaching him, his long front legs reared up and he emitted a noisy whinnying sound. Disinclined, I stood there but didn't move any farther, while keeping a safe distance between us.

The other horses in the adjacent stalls displayed a reddish-brown color, with some white blazes on their foreheads. I noticed each one of them stood high at their withers, with hindquarters that were broad and muscular. Each had large oval-shaped eyes that were quite expressive and stared at our slightest move

"What kind of horses are these? I have never seen anything similar in my travels."

"They came from the Moors, who brought them from the African continent. They are called *Banat er Rih* in the Saracens tongue. It means 'daughters of the wind.' Commander Gilbért told me the Saracens ride just the mares into battle. They breed them for speed and control by an ancient wandering tribe in the Levant. I think they're called Bedouins. For over a thousand years, they have perfected their horses. When you ride one, you'll see they're the fastest horses ridden by our *chevaliers*. I, myself, have ridden them and they have no faster equal."

"What about this other big fellow here with his uplifted hooves?"

"He's what we call Andalusian, and they're bred in the southern part of Iberia. Their physical characteristics are great strength and speed. A chain-mailed Templar *chevalier* and Andalusian horse can fight as a battering ram. They can gallop to the enemy with celerity and not tire under the heavy weight of weapons and rider.

"This horse belongs to our commander, Gilbért de Érail. I must saddle him as soon as possible so we can leave at the beginning of Terce. I have already prepared your horse to ride. She's the black one, two stalls down. She's fast and swift to ride. You can call her Fatima."

His fellow *frères* had trained the young man well in horsemanship, I thought. The horses around him sensed his familiar presence and their large dark eyes followed him everywhere he moved.

"Who taught you the skills to work with horses?"

"The man right behind you," he said with a grin.

I hadn't heard anybody behind me. The hair on my neck quickly rose. I turned and saw a tall swarthy-faced man. I jumped back and reached for my sword. The man displayed a dark shiny-trimmed beard, with his head covered in a black-colored silk material. At his side, I observed a long-curved sword and also a wide-curved jeweled scabbarded dagger tucked into his large cloth waistband.

"Who is this?" I shouted to Squire Hughes while grasping the hilt of my sword.

"Lord Robert, meet Muhammad Nur Adin. He oversees our stables and is my mentor. He knows more about horses than any Templar *chevalier*."

Nur Adin greeted me with a strange bow, which I didn't know how to reply. *Is this a challenge*? I quickly surmised.

"Lord de Borron, please reciprocate. Do it right away, or he will think you don't trust him," young Hughes said.

At once, I replied to the greeting but wondered in my mind if I must trust him. This man was a Saracen and my enemy. He'd just frightened me with his silent movements as if he'd dropped from the ceiling.

"Muhammad will accompany us on our journey to Toledo or as he calls it *Tolati-tola*. He's a Saracen from the Holy Land and a *bon ami* of Commander Gilbért. My commander says he will help protect us."

The Saracen appeared as agile as a cat as he proceeded saddling the horses we needed. His green and black clothing had a regal bearing, as if he were royalty in his native land.

After the Saracen departed out of voice range, I asked Squire Hughes a vexing question. "Why do you have an enemy of Christendom here in Montpellier?" Both anger and curiosity had welled up inside me at the same time.

"Lord de Borron, Muhammad once ruled as a prince in his native land. A rival tribe killed his entire family. My commander, Gilbért de Érail, saved his life. However, Muhammad's *épouse, père,* and *mère* were all stabbed to death. The tribe raped his *épouse* before they murdered her and then stole his land. He has pledged his allegiance to our commander and hopes someday to avenge their deaths.

"In the Levant, his kingdom once had many horses and he sold them to both Christians and his fellow countrymen. I have learned many things about horses from him and value Muhammad as a teacher and *bon ami.*"

I cast my gaze farther down the stables and observed the horses' eyes follow Muhammad as he spoke to them. He approached each and mouthed into their ears while calming several large horses that kicked their stalls. Afterward, he leaped bareback on a large stallion, then whispered into its ear. Muhammad and horse rode back and forth as one. *Here appears a true centaur,* I thought.

Just then, the chapel bells started ringing for Terce; now I had to leave with Gilbért de Érail. Muhammad led out from their stalls several tied Andalusians loaded with supplies and weapons. The Saracen attached several quivers of arrows to them along with extra swords. There were two Arabian mares with empty saddles. That left me wondering why they had missing riders. This totaled five saddled horses. Were their more Templar riders to accompany us?

Chanting sounds had just started in the chapel when Gilbért de Érail entered through the same passageway from whence we had just arrived. He carried two crossbows and a small pouch of quarrels.

He motioned for Squire Hughes to come forward, at which time he handed the young man his crossbows. Squire Hughes then secured them to the horses. Once again, the trapdoor swung open, revealing two other Templar men climbing up the steps. Both wore aketon shirts covered with chain hauberks, and their surcoats were a different color than the one their commander wore. Instead of white, their surcoats were black with the same red pattée cross placed over their hearts on their cloaks. They appeared similar in dress to young Hughes's robes, but more worn with use. The men were stocky, and their faces were darker from constant exposure to the sun.

"Lord de Borron, let me introduce my men who have come from the Levant. To my left stands Sergeant Guy de Béziers and to my right is Sergeant Jacque de Hoult. Both men have served me well for ten years and each speaks the Saracen tongue. They have lived at one of our fortresses in the Levant for numerous years until they came south to Jerusalem and joined me. Both are indispensable when it comes to knowing the Saracen culture."

Commander de Érail jumped on his horse and the two men gave me a brief cordial nod, followed by them darting to their horses. Quite impressed by their efficiency of movement, my mind told me these men were lifetime soldiers and their lives depended on leaving at a moment's notice. I gathered my thoughts and voiced a request of the commander.

"Commander Gilbért de Érail, would you let me write a quick letter to my *épouse* and my *soeur*? I wouldn't want them to think something tragic has befallen me."

"Make it fast," came his brusque reply. "While we are packing, utilize this time to write your letters."

I had brought a small leather pouch of writing materials with me upon arriving at the priory. I spied a storage chest four stalls down from where I stood. This would work to write my thoughts with speed. At once, I ran to the empty stall and started writing. Yet, I didn't have enough time to express all my loving thoughts to my *épouse* and my *soeur*. I didn't write our destination city's name, but that we were traveling on a holy quest and I would return in several months. I mentioned the Templar commander's name in my letter too, but no specific details of our quest. I asked my *épouse* and my *soeur* to light candles for me and say a prayer daily until I returned.

Also writing to both, saying I would miss them, with extra words of *amour* to my *épouse*.

"Lord de Borron, we must leave at once," young Squire Hughes said.

"Let me seal these two letters before we depart."

I reached into my writing pouch for some soft sealing wax, then I placed a dollop of the heated red wax on each letter. Taking my ring, with the Borron family coat of arms engraved on its surface, I pressed it into the sticky sealing wax on the folded pages.

"Squire Hughes, will one of your trusted *frères* deliver these letters to my family at *Château* Montbéliard?" I inquired.

"*Chevalier* Bernard St. Clair will deliver them with the utmost speed and confidentiality. He's another member of our holy order whom my commander trusts with his life. I'll see that he receives them before we leave. I expect *Chevalier* Bernard to leave the chapel at any moment and I will meet him near the keep."

The young squire grabbed my precious missives and ran toward the keep entrance. The Saracen, Muhammad, motioned with his hand, signaling Commander Gilbért de Érail to leave, and we mounted our horses, except for the young squire. To our consternation, the horses started whinnying as we left the stables. Muhammad began whispering to them and they quieted at once, as we trotted out into the mist-filled bailey. The damp fog air caused moisture to trickle down our leather saddles and bridles, forcing me to pull my cloak tight around my chest and then wiggle my hands into a pair of chain mail gauntlets.

Out of the mist-filled morning appeared a wraith-shrouded image of young Hughes, whose horse trotted toward our party. He didn't speak a word as we started our journey. The sole sound I detected came from the light thumping of our horses' hooves against the ground. As we reached the first portcullis, Commander Gilbért de Érail gave a hand signal to the sergeant on sentry duty, whereupon it creaked upward. We proceeded down a stone-covered pathway that led to the main gate. Again, Commander Gilbért de Érail signaled another sentry who raised the final portcullis.

Two additional sergeants came forward and raised a massive

cut timber, which secured the main entrance doors. We crossed the drawbridge and the hooves of our horses emitted a thundering sound, as we spurred them faster across the wooden structure. At that moment, I sensed we were leaving the *château* under questionable circumstances.

CHAPTER XXII

We traveled some distance before the sun, positioned high overhead burned off the fog. The Saracen gave a hand signal to stop at a nearby stream and we dismounted to water our horses. My attention focused on numerous small birds that were drinking from the rocky gurgling stream as we approached.

"There are extra wineskins we must fill with water before we leave," Commander Gilbért de Érail said as he led his horse to the stream. "Our journey ahead will see dry plains, many hills, and a dearth of streams and rivers with drinkable water. The heat will become quite warm before we arrive at the Cathar inhabited mountains."

The commander strolled a short distance away from his men and called to me. I placed the water-filled wineskins on my horse before joining him. Who were or what were the Cathars? I'd never heard the name before. "We need to talk, Commander."

"*Oui*, Lord de Borron, I have an unusual request to ask you. I would prefer you wear one of our mantles and surcoats, which will create less suspicion on our mission. People don't question Templar *chevaliers* traveling these many pilgrim roads, but if a noble lord from Burgundy travels, they'll become suspicious and might steal your purse. One of our goals isn't to draw attention to ourselves.

190

Henceforth, it's better if you blended in with the rest of us. Young Hughes has an extra *chevalier's* surcoat and mantle in his horse bags. Please change your clothes now, while our horses are being watered."

His request made sense, but at the same time, more doubts filled my mind. Now came the proper time to see if he would answer some of my questions. It seemed odd dressing in a white surcoat, mantle, and coif of chain mail, which made me think I had another identity.

"Who are we urgently hiding from and why?" I asked. "You gave the book to the Holy Father's legate. I don't understand the need for us to leave the *château* priory in such a hurry. Also, why are we traveling to Toledo on such little information?" I wondered if his lack of information was part of my test of loyalty. His contorted brow and the lack of his quick response reflected in him not having his men question his authority.

"I am sorry . . . I haven't told you more details, but, Lord de Borron, I didn't have time, as you well know. Our Grand Master knew of you as a gifted poet, writer, and swordsman. We realized you were the man for the task of recording the information we found at our Holy Temple in Jerusalem. It's my belief that there are two other sets of *Sangraal* parchments. One you have already read, the second set could be hidden in Toledo, and the third I don't know where or even if it exists. I am convinced Saint Joseph of Arimathea wrote all three codices near or after our Lord and Savior, Jesus the Christ's crucifixion. Also, I believe he continued writing his own life's account after the crucifixion and resurrection.

"The people of Languedoc tell the legend about Saint Joseph traveling from the Holy Land to Marseille and from there they don't say where he ended his mortal days. To my Grand Master, I have sworn with my life to protect the sacred words written by Saint Joseph of Arimathea and at the right time reveal his holy words. The legate will report to Rome with the book you have read, and I think he suspects some subterfuge on my part. In secret, our Grand Master approves what you and I are doing to preserve any future parchments, but he believes certain men in the Roman Curia will want you arrested or your family harmed. Many trials lie ahead to

find these legendary documents, but I have full faith in our Lord
God that we'll accomplish this quest to His greater glory."

We crossed ourselves and said "Amen" when Commander de
Érail finished his account.

"I am grateful you have such trust in me and my abilities." I wasn't
yet sure if his compliment and explanation would bolster my courage.

I kept thinking of the possible martyrs who died over the years
to protect these precious codices. My reluctance vanished some and
my religious concerns about the quest's challenges left me giddy now
for adventure.

We completed filling our waterskins and broke fast. After eating
our meal, Muhammad took out a small red and buff-colored rug from
his horse bag. The carpet revealed a quite curious geometric design
woven into its wool fabric. The rug's design appeared as an arch or door
entrance. In a moment of silence, he knelt down and appeared praying,
yet I didn't recognize his words. The horses, however, watched their
master pray and bow several times on his rug. Without delay, he finished his prayers, rolled his rug up, and placed it in his horse bag. With
a quick leap, he mounted his horse and conversed with Commander de
Érail, who afterward translated for me. "The Saracen will scout the road
ahead and we must leave at once." Commander de Érail nodded his
approval and then motioned for him to depart, to which Muhammad
spurred his horse and galloped away.

After Muhammad left, Commander Gilbért said something to
Sergeant Jacque de Hoult that I failed to hear and right away all the
Templars fell to their knees. The young squire, Hughes de Montbard,
motioned for me to do the same.

"Lord Robert de Borron," said squire Hughes. "It's time to do
our holy office of Sext. We must pray and say at least thirteen *Pater
Nosters* before we leave."

Commander de Érail led us in prayer and we recited our thirteen
Pater Nosters in a military cadence. Upon completion, we crossed
ourselves and jumped on our horses to leave.

We traveled across lands not familiar in my travels. Our small
band followed south near the coast toward Béziers and the sight of

seagulls flapping their wings against the azure sky.

About midafternoon, we noticed a lone rider and his dust cloud racing down from a rise.

"I think it's Muhammad!" exclaimed Commander Gilbért de Érail.

"Guy, hand me my spyglass, so I can confirm our visual sighting." What a strange-looking instrument or weapon he put to his eye. I hadn't seen anything comparable to this apparatus that Sergeant de Hoult handed to his commander.

"Yes, indeed I see our Saracen *ami*, Muhammad," replied Commander de Érail.

"How does he know at this distance it's Muhammad Nur Adin?" I inquired of Sergeant Jacque de Hoult. "Our commander uses a spyglass that Muhammad brought back from the Outremer. This round-looking instrument causes objects to come closer and appear larger."

To my eyes, the rider appeared as a small swift animal. As the Saracen raced closer, my eyes, at last, saw the white sweat on his horse's withers. Muhammad's horse raced across the long bottom ravine at an unbelievable speed.

Commander de Érail galloped out to greet Muhammad Nur Adin and then stopped to have a verbal exchange. Afterward, they turned their horses, and then they raced back with even greater speed toward us. The commander shouted. "Cut some long tree branches and gather blankets!" What a strange request, yet the urgency in his voice caused me to reach for my blanket.

Sergeant Guy de Béziers took several large blankets out of his horse bag, attached some ropes to his saddle, and placed the rope-looped blanket over his horse's hindquarters. The blankets fell to the ground as Sergeant Jacque de Hoult placed heavy rocks on each. As both the commander and Muhammad returned, the sergeants had completed their work. Right away, Muhammad spurred his horse to the nearest tree. With several strokes of his curved sword, he felled two large lower limbs dense with leaves.

All their strange movements were puzzling. However, sensing danger heading our way, this prompted me to shout. "What danger confronts us?"

"Muhammad with his own spyglass observed twenty unknown *chevalier* riders rushing toward us one league back," the commander replied. "I suspect they want you, Lord Robert, for your holy skills and knowledge. We must hide our trail at once, for Muhammad has discovered their tracks and saw them after scouting our rear. The trail ahead is clear, and it appears a local *chevalier* leads them; he knows the rough trails in this part of Languedoc. The other *chevaliers* are carrying what appears a cardinal's standard. Also, Muhammad said we ought to double back a third of a league to a small hidden cave. We can assemble camp there tonight and rest our horses. I want us to ride single file to the cave and Sergeants Guy and Jacque will ride two abreast behind us to cover our horse tracks. Muhammad will destroy any remaining tracks we miss, along with his own, as we ride on some flat rocks just before entering the cave. It will appear as if we had vanished."

Things were transpiring fast as I fell into a single file behind the commander with our horses moving at a quick trot in military fashion. The blankets and tree limbs accomplished their purpose, for as I looked back our tracks vanished right before my eyes. It appeared these men were experienced in deception and their commander had trained them well.

We'd traveled about a third of a league and encountered some rock cliffs and rocky ravines. Our horses entered a large gorge, and I observed many twists and turns as we traveled on the snake-curved ravine trail. Then we raced in the direction of the forthcoming cardinal's *chevaliers* and rode just a short distance. Both Templar sergeants perused our previous trail for horse hoofprints. Once again, the tree limbs and leaves destroyed any remaining trail we'd left behind. After some sweaty palm moments, the Saracen led us to a narrow crack opening, topped with overhanging cliffs. It seemed impossible for man or horse to enter, but to my surprise and relief our horses just fit.

However, to my dismay, my horse refused to enter the narrow, jagged opening. Several times she reared up and gave out a desperate high-pitched whinnying cry. At once, my stomach tensed.

"Lord Robert, hurry and enter now!" shouted Commander Gilbért. "They'll arrive soon. Spur your horse," he commanded.

Muhammad's long arm grabbed her bit, pulled her head toward him, gazed into her eyes, and whispered some words into her ear. To my amazement, she tucked her head down and shimmied through the narrow opening.

The path into the interior of the cave led to a sudden incline where a cool breeze brushed my face. The farther we penetrated this cavernous hiding place, the cooler it became. The path then declined and our horses' *clacking* hooves hesitated. Muhammad and Hughes began speaking to them in soft voices and addressing each by name. This calmed their fears as we proceeded farther until our light faded. Commander de Érail stopped in a small rock chamber that long ago held an underground spring, now dry.

"Lord de Borron, what do you think about our overnight accommodations with its rock pillows?" The Templar commander gave me a slight smile. His wit surprised me, coming at a tense moment.

"*Bon*," I replied. "If you and your men can handle it, so can I. Though I can't say that I have ever slept in a cave before, but this hides us from the evil men pursuing us."

"We'll spend the night here, rest, water our horses, and leave before first light. Don't light any fires. Muhammad will post the first watch. Hughes will maintain the second and I the third. Sergeants Jacque and Guy will prepare a cold supper and see to the horses."

Each member of our party proceeded to their stations and commenced doing their appointed duties. A short time later, we each received a portion of dried venison, a chunk of crusty-seeded bread, and copious amounts of dark red wine served from a large leather pouch. First, before eating our viands, Commander de Érail said a blessing. Indeed, I thought, these were warrior-*moines* and lived the part, not just skilled with a weapon, yet cunning too. In addition, they weren't remiss with their monastic religious responsibilities.

Commander de Érail rose with the bulky brown-colored leather *vin* pouch and raised it overhead to speak.

"My fellow *frères*, we're on a great sacred quest, preordained by our Lord God to protect the memory of our Savior, Jesus the Christ. The glorious *Sangraal* parchments we seek, praying they still exist, will also test our faith and strength. Our band of holy *frères* here tonight won't fail. Using this *vin* and bread as our sworn covenant, we pledge to seal our resolve not to retreat from any enemy, mortal or otherwise."

The five of us raised our swords, with the blades pointed downward, kissed the cross-shaped hilts, and swore before God as we each took a drink of the wine, after which we ate our bread. Thus, this oath sealed our destiny, both theirs and mine. I didn't see turning back now an option and my home in Burgundy seemed just a distant memory.

After our pledge, we each strolled back to our respective posts. My butt hurt from riding all day, yet the sunlit cave coaxed me into writing further. Sitting on a large damp rock, I continued my written chronicle from the holy *Sangraal* of Joseph's experiences about Jesus and himself. The writing and remembering were effortless as my words flowed onto the vellum.

However, I had a nagging question about the identity of this unnamed cardinal and his reasons for sending men after us. Was he the papal legate, to whom Commander Gilbért gave the original codex? Yet, my mind told me he wouldn't answer all my questions from what little he'd already divulged.

Receding daylight, lack of sleep, and tiredness were now my enemies. A night of silence reigned outside, and it appeared we'd avoided our pursuers, which calmed my gurgling stomach. Sleep, at last, overtook my writing, causing me to fall into a restful slumber.

After what seemed a short time of sleep, young Hughes poked me with the hilt of his sword. He had one finger pointed in front of his lips, warning me not to speak while slipping my sword into my palm as we crept on our stomachs toward the entrance of the cave. Drawing nearer, my ears heard the *clopping* of horse hooves on the rocky path next to us. I remained quiet as a stone, but the closer the clopping hooves, the louder my heart beat. Each beat sounded as a pounding drum while thinking our pursuers might hear it. Despite the chilliness of the cave, sweat formed on my palm as I gripped the pommel tighter.

From my lookout point, all the cardinal's men appeared as dark moving phantoms. As they came closer, their torches revealed more than a dozen secular *chevaliers* and one guide or leader who pointed toward the path ahead. A great helm covered his head. I prayed the hidden cave entrance prevented them from seeing us, yet their leader continued pointing in the direction of the overhanging cliffs. Would he lead his men to investigate and see the narrow opening? Our concealed entrance gave us some defense because we were outnumbered.

The *chevaliers* carried numerous banned crossbows slung across their saddles that I knew our chain mail wouldn't protect. Quickly, I surmised the men were from the Toulouse region, for the scout displayed the ball knob-shaped tips affixed to the cross of Toulouse on his shield. After several discussions between the leader of the *chevaliers* and his men, they spurred their horses and left. We viewed with some relief as they passed out of sight. Yet, still hearing their horses' hooves make their *clacking* sounds down the path.

"I assumed they are gone?" I continued to peer into the dark.

"*Oui,* it appears they've left the area. Come, we must inform Commander Gilbért de Érail."

The commander listened as Hughes gave an account of what transpired outside the cave. Muhammad overheard too, as Jacque de Hoult translated for his benefit.

By now, the moon had perched itself high in the night sky and I knew my slumber wouldn't happen. This left me with a small dilemma, no writing or sleep. I sat near the entrance of the cave and gazed toward a full moon above me. Commander de Érail joined me as he relieved Muhammad from his post.

"Were you afraid, Lord Robert?"

"*Non,* and I am still here and haven't any intentions of leaving. I made a commitment to you and to the *Sangraal* parchments and I intend to live up to it. Besides, the writing pen isn't the sole item I can handle. My brother-in-law will tell you about my sword abilities."

"*Oui,* I already know. In my investigation of you, your battle skills were one of the many compelling points in choosing you. Yet, are you prepared to kill many of these men if confronted?"

"*Oui*," I lied. I hadn't killed anybody but only wounded several men and many yielded to my sword.

"You see what odds we're now facing as we continue our quest, yet sometimes words are deadlier than the sharpest sword. You're superior at both, *mon ami*." Commander Gilbért smiled.

"Lord de Borron, why don't you resume your sleep and rest for tomorrow's journey? I can stay awake unattended."

"I can't sleep or write. Commander, what do these men want from us and what about the cardinal who sent them?"

"I don't want to scare you, but these men want to kill us because we are protecting you and your spiritual gifts. The Roman Curia and Cardinal Folquet, along with his men, want to annihilate us, but don't you worry. *Mes frères* have fought against greater odds. The way I see it, the five of us against the cardinal's fourteen are even odds.

"You might not have noticed, but each of my men show scars from the many battles they fought in the Levant. I have seen things and done things most mortal men wouldn't believe. God has granted me a rare gift, for He has told me through prayer about my preordained destiny. It's my fate in life to protect the *Sangraal* parchments. Our Lord God has given me certain visions, which you also have. Fear not, Lord de Borron, no harm will come to you, yet Lord de Borron, henceforth, keep your sword buckled to your belt. I always trust my judgment and faith. Now prepare yourself, for we'll leave here before daybreak. The full moon will give us sufficient vision to leave and stay ahead of the cardinal's *chevaliers*. My men and I know these trails and paths by rote even without a full moon. We won't see these men again tonight, for they have camped."

I said my good night and returned to the spot I had slept. Now, I had a name of who caused us to flee Montpellier and wanted to capture me and kill my protectors. Gilbért de Érail's reassurance sounded well, but my faith in him still faltered with my apprehensions of facing the entire Roman Curia and an evil cardinal. His boastful wit, though, surprised me, but he didn't exhibit overconfidence, for his facial battle scars told me otherwise. For several years,

I had heard rumors and stories sung by my fellow troubadours about an unknown *chevalier* and his fighting prowess.

Without knowing it, I fell asleep again and then was awakened a second time by Jacque de Hoult. He wanted me to jump on my horse and leave. The ivory-colored moon had reached its zenith in the sky as we left the narrow crack in the rock facing. We trotted down the dark path and reached the main trail. Muhammad cantered his horse out ahead to scout for any unusual movement. His black steed passed in and out of the shadows from the full moon and, at last, disappeared into the distant cliffs. The trail ahead presented nothing but the cool night air, with one noise coming from the steady *clip-clop* of our horse's hooves and the second from crickets. Their constant chirping produced a rhythmic haunting sound that seemed to say, "Turn back." I ignored their imagined warnings and continued following my fellow companions.

After we'd journeyed several leagues, the sun rose between the pink-fingered clouds. The moon appeared low on the horizon but was waning in its brilliance. We had traveled some distance into the hills when out of a grove of oak trees appeared Muhammad. His dark horse dripped with lather and wheezed heavily, indicating his horse had raced from a great distance. He approached Commander de Érail, spoke quite fast in his native tongue, and used several hand gyrations to indicate what he had seen. Commander de Érail listened with one ear bent and came back to me to explain. I hoped his return didn't mean more trouble for us.

"Lord de Borron, Muhammad has told me the camp of the cardinal's *chevaliers* lies three leagues behind us and this will allow us sufficient time to reach Carcassonne before they do. We'll arrive about midday in Carcassonne, where one hundred fellow *frères* reside. The cardinal's men won't travel to the town fortress. If they do, we could even hold off Saladin Joseph's great army with just one hundred of my Poor Fellow-Soldiers of Christ."

Once again, Commander de Érail's wit came forth. After translating his words for Muhammad, the Saracen laughed with sweat shaking off his jet-black beard. Until now, I hadn't seen any indication that Muhammad Nur Adin had a sense of humor. I assumed his past troubled life gave him little reason to laugh.

We stopped a short distance near a river to break our fast and pray. Commander de Érail reached into his saddlebag and pulled out a strange-looking metal cross. Rust had formed on its steel surface from many years of use and the weathered cross displayed a pat-tée-shaped design, with a fitchée end that he drove into the ground. His makeshift altar was now readied for morning Prime.

We said the morning office with psalms and *Pater Nosters,* while Muhammad took his prayer rug, hurried a short distance to face east, and prayed. After our prayers, we ate our food, which consisted of a simpler fare than the previous night, with just bread, olives, and *vin,* diluted with water from the nearby river. Our stay here ended quickly and we traveled to a nearby ford and crossed the river. We rode but a short distance when I heard the soft *tinkling* sound of small bells that came from a dark forest. The farther our horses trotted, the louder the sound. The bell sounds came from a bent path in front of us and I heard the faint shuffling of sandals approaching. Were these the cardinal's *chevaliers*? If they were, my mind now readied itself for the ensuing battle.

"Commander Gilbért, are these the cardinal's men?" I whispered. He didn't say anything but raised a straight finger to his lips. As we rode closer, ten men revealed themselves wearing hoods, each bore cloth wrappings across their nose, mouth, and chin. *What a frightening sight,* I thought. The lead man stopped ringing his small set of bells when he saw us approach.

The dreadful-looking man in front raised his hand to greet us and started speaking in a muffled voice. When I looked closer at the man, to my horror he had just a palm and no fingers on his right hand. His other hand, which held his small bells on a stick, had cloth bandages around it. My mind didn't want to comprehend what these bandages meant. The other nine men had similar afflictions and stared with bewildering eyes seeking mercy. Right away, my hands began to shake the reins of my horse. These poor men bore the most dreaded misfortune that beset mankind: leprosy. I sat just four-horse lengths from the man speaking to us with nine other lepers behind him! I started to turn my steed around, but Muhammad grabbed hold of my reins and stopped me. That's when my horse sensed my overwhelming fear, for she started champing at her bit and reared up on her hind legs. Muhammad shouted some words to her in his native tongue and at once, my horse stopped rearing. I wished Muhammad's words would calm me as quickly as he did my horse, even if I didn't understand him.

Commander de Érail began to respond to these men after the first man finished speaking. "Dear pilgrims," Commander de Érail responded, "it appears you have come from afar and are thirsty and hungry. Our order calls me Gilbért de Érail, commander of the Templar Priory at Montpellier, and we wish you no harm. Let's help refresh you and your friends, giving you the strength for your long journey ahead."

"I'm pleased to see you, Commander de Érail, and *merci beaucoup* for your generous offer. We have few travelers stop and share their food with us. I am called Godfroi de Mountauban and my fellow travelers were once *chevaliers* in the Levant. Our Saracen captor held us for ransom, but our disease had progressed too far for them to hold us any longer. We languished in their *oubliettes* for ten years; just a short time ago, they released us because of our sores and the grotesque features you see on our faces. Now, neither our fellow *chevaliers* nor our families claim us. We are the living dead. We ask nothing from you, sir *chevalier*, but a blessing that we will reach Santiago de Compostela. I hear tell there're miracle cures there for poor lepers."

"We, the Poor Fellow-Soldiers of Christ, are obligated by our Lord and Savior to offer you our hospitality and share the food we have," Commander de Érail said. He then motioned for Sergeant Guy to hand them some of our viands. It amazed me the commander's men weren't scared to help these horrible-looking wretches. Why did these men risk all to help these strangers?

Commander de Érail reached into his saddlebag and plucked out what looked similar to a silver coin, but the object didn't shine.

He rode over to the man, reached down, and placed the coin into his palm.

"Godfroi de Mountauban, convey this token to the nearest Templar commandery close to Santiago de Compostela, and they will exchange it for silver. My *frères* there will furnish you additional food and supplies for your pilgrimage. Also, I will write you a letter of protection. Henceforth, no harm will come to you and your fellow pilgrims."

Commander de Érail motioned for me to come forward, which caused my throat to become dry. I wondered what he wanted from me, as my horse ambled toward the man in front. To my anguish, up close he appeared more hideous in appearance. Some unknown glistening- encrusted substance grew on one of his eyes and the other eye didn't exist. I said a silent prayer to God, hoping my encounter with this man wouldn't last long.

"Lord de Borron, might I have some of your parchment paper and a writing pen?" Commander de Érail said with the authority of a soldier of Christ.

My hands still trembled as I reached into my saddlebag to obtain my writing satchel, while almost dropping my clay inkwell and writing paper as I passed them to him. He started writing at once, which surprised me. Church clerics had told me about the Templar *chevaliers*' fighting prowess but said they lacked literacy.

He wrote quite fast as his thoughts transferred to the parchment. When finished, he asked me for some soft sealing wax. I handed him the red wax, which he poured with ease onto the missive, then blew it dry, clenched his fist, and affixed his ring to the soft wax. He handed it to Godfroi, prayed, then crossed himself, and bid the men *adieu*. As he turned his horse to leave, Godfroi spoke one last time.

"Commander de Érail, *merci beaucoup* for your kindness and may you and your men have the blessed Holy Savior and Lord Jesus the Christ watch over all of you."

What he said next made chills crawl across my arms and raised the hair on the back of my neck.

"Dear *frères* of Christ, your quest you seek, God will partially fulfill it in the city of Toledo. There, look for what you seek in the earth. Others who come after you will carry on the knowledge you've found in the holy parchments. Your lives and deeds will influence mankind for centuries to come."

With his last prophetic statement, the lepers turned to continue on their journey southwestward in the direction of the Santiago cathedral. We observed their shuffling movements until they came to a fork in the road and disappeared into some woods. Yet, their bells jingled long after the forest swallowed them. We rode some distance not saying a word to one another before Commander de Érail broke the silence.

"I knew of Godfroi de Mountauban. His great bravery as a *chevalier* preceded him before he took 'the cross.' The troubadours in this region still sing of his bravery and exploits. His *chevaliers* fought alongside our holy *frères* to help protect the 'true cross.'"

"Commander, why weren't you afraid . . . of his afflictions?" I asked, no longer holding my anxiety.

"We learned from the Saracen doctors, you don't receive leprosy by initial close contact. Their advanced medical knowledge has taught us so. We have much to learn from them. The ten years of prison confinement caused their condition. You can rest easy, Lord de Borron, you won't contract their ailment."

"*Merci* for imparting this knowledge to me. Your experience and information have eased my fears, but how did he know that we are searching for the *Sangraal* parchment?"

"I don't know the answer to your question. He and his family have lived in this region for hundreds of years. The rumors say they're keepers of many ancient secrets and can see into the future and know the ancient past. Perhaps that's how he came about his information."

Interesting words, I thought, but not a reasonable explanation. I hoped Godfroi's prophetic words would stay a secret. It appeared too many people already knew of our quest.

The rest of the day stayed uneventful, and we camped at sundown in a wooded grove of oak trees, with the promise of arriving at Carcassonne the following day. The sky remained clear and sufficient daylight let me do some writing. Passages from the holy book were still fresh in my mind that needed copying. I feared something might happen to me at any time. My death and the unfinished writing of this holy book heavily weighed on my mind. Torn between not seeing my family again and not completing my spiritual duty caused a tightness in my chest. Sainte-Marie-Magdalene had done her part to help me remember what Saint Joseph of Arimathea wrote and where his first book ended. I had written maybe ten parchments before we were ready to pray for the office of Complines. After we said our *Pater Nosters*, we consumed our remaining food, not worrying about conserving it. Just one league down the road, the commandery at Carcassonne lay over the next several ridges.

After I finished eating, my mind leaped with thoughts of Saint Joseph's written words that kept me from sleeping. In the moonlit oak grove, I still couldn't believe the incredulous events the last several days, as I sat there with the echoed words of Saint Joseph. The trees still held their leaves, as a strong cool breeze tugged at their stems, which reminded me of winter's approach. We now faced the season of autumn with its hot days and cool nights. Later, our evening grew cooler and the wind howled as it picked up speed. A cold chill caused me to shiver, forcing me to search for a blanket from my saddlebags. The thin Templar mantle disguise didn't break the cold wind from penetrating my body. After retrieving it, I wrapped the blanket around my shoulders, gulped another drink of wine, and fell asleep.

The next morning, a cold wind brushed my cheeks, yet the nickering of the horses awakened me. My horse had come to me after getting loose and started licking my face, further arousing me from a cold sleep. Already the sun had begun casting its shadows among the oak trees as I ran to the supply horses, gathered some oats, and readied her feed. Fatima's eyes became quite large as she nuzzled my hand to coax the oat sack into her mouth. I draped the small bag over her fuzzy ears and tied it to her head as she chomped into the oat-filled sack with vigor. I helped Sergeant de Hoult saddle her and afterward placed a waterproof satchel of my writings in the saddlebags.

I stuck one foot into the stirrups to mount my horse as Sergeant de Hoult removed her feedbag. Then we exited our small encampment without breaking our fast as the sun's warm rays touched my face. The commander had decided to forestall eating; letting us arrive in Carcassonne by afternoon. This became an easy decision for him because we were out of food. After exiting the oak grove, the shadows disappeared, and the sun's rays started warming my cold chain mail.

We had traveled just a short while when we saw a strange sight. There, next to an oak grove, appeared several ancient stone circles. The stones themselves were twice the height of a man and placed in the perfect shape of a circle. My curiosity questioned their origin. Each stone dolmen had slash marks in a vertical fashion, which, to my surprise, I didn't recognize. Did my spiritual powers just comprehend our Lord's writing and the ancient saints?

"Commander de Érail, what are these stone markers?" I asked

"Lord de Borron, these are called *menhirs* and were once used by the ancient Druid priests. I suspect they were constructed years before our Lord and Savior. The local folks believe malevolent spirits possess this place. The Druids used these stones for meetings and worship places. Look there at the *ogham* symbols carved on this one!" He reached his hand to touch the chiseled marks. "It's quite obvious Caesar failed to destroy these monuments in his conquest of Gaul."

We passed the stones at a slow walk, letting us examine them in detail. I observed one of the stones had a crucifix cut into it. Either the Druid priests converted to Christianity or some local *moines* had chiseled their mark on this rock. For some unknown reason, I didn't want to leave this mysterious place. After much urging, Commander de Érail insisted I leave the Druid priest writing stones and we continued down a small wooded path.

The sun burned hot as we approached the outskirts of Carcassonne. We had to ford a river before approaching the fortified town. The river current roared fast as we attempted to traverse it on our horses. The cold water cooled my hot aching legs. Without warning, my horse started to falter. She stumbled with rolling eyes of fear and with her high-pitched whinnying, my Saracen horse reared and then slipped. She fell backward into the rushing water, my feet caught in the stirrups. At that moment, the undertow pulled both of us underwater and swept us downstream.

At last, I broke free and tried to swim away, but the weight of my chain mail held me down and the current sucked me farther into the rushing maelstrom. My lungs burned with pain from lack of air, as the cold water entered my nose. Then I realized I might die from drowning and began to pray to God. My heart ached for my family and the fear of the *Sangraal* quest endings for me. Still, I had the presence of mind to thank my Lord and Savior for all the *bon* men I had met and His sacred words. After my brief prayer, everything became dark as I lost consciousness.

CHAPTER XXIII

The Land of the Cathars

Occitania

Fall

Anno Domini 1190

The sudden taste of bile and regurgitated water gushed out my mouth as Muhammad pressed hard on my chest.

"I see you are back with the living world, Lord de Borron," Commander de Érail said. "You can thank Muhammad for saving your life. He fished you out of the bottom of the river and brought you back with the 'breath of life.'"

As I sat there trying to clear my head, I crossed myself and said a prayer. Afterward, I pondered the words called the 'breath of life.' Muhammad's life-saving experience had humbled me, especially because I didn't trust the Saracen prince from our first meeting. Would he have saved me if he knew of my prejudice toward him?

"Commander, please tell Muhammad how grateful I am to him, as he risked his life for me, yet I don't speak his native tongue. Would you please translate for me letting him know my appreciation?"

He surprised me when he replied, "*Non.*"

"But, Commander, I don't understand his language."

"Sometimes it isn't the language that you need to know, but how it's spoken from the heart. Offer Muhammad your thanks of appreciation, he will understand."

Commander Gilbért's prediction came true, for the words flowed from my heart as I expressed my gratitude to my new *ami*. A grin came over his glistening bushy black beard, causing him to expose a full set of white teeth. He replied with his bow of acceptance and said, "*Rasul, salaam alaikum.*"

"What did he say?" I inquired of Commander Gilbért.

"He said you are an exceptional person, who his God, Allah, has smiled upon you in our quest. You're similar to an ancient prophet or religious leader. Take his words as praise, for it isn't commonplace that Muhammad bestows this honor to a nonbeliever of his faith."

His praise and confidence didn't strengthen me, quite the contrary. Here I stood, just a wet mortal man, and right now confused and dazed. I further expressed my gratitude to my Saracen *ami* by bowing my head several times, yet I suspected he knew the meaning of all my words. Why the secrecy? However, my question remained for another time.

With some effort, I staggered to my feet to dry myself off, but my chain mail and clothes squished with water. With the assistance of Squire Hughes, we removed my white-hooded mantle, followed by my white surcoat, and placed both pieces of clothing on one of the supply horses to dry.

After removing some of my outer garments, I realized I didn't see my horse. I feared she hadn't survived, and then a knot formed in my stomach. In addition, my stomach further constricted, knowing that two of us riding together would slow our quest efforts.

"What happened to my horse?" I asked as I regained some sensibility.

"She stands on the riverbank," replied Commander de Érail. "After Muhammad dragged you out of the river, Sergeant Jacque rescued your horse. In addition, it appears you didn't lose any of your weapons or saddlebags. Both of you were lucky and blessed in many ways. Fatima stands behind that grove of trees at the top of the riverbank. See those sycamore trees to your left? She's behind the largest group."

Squinting into the sunlight, I saw her faint outline. Again, with Squire Hughes's help, I stumbled up the bridle path and reached my horse. Her legs trembled from fear and a muffled whinnying sound came from deep down in her chest. After rubbing her ears and stroking her neck, she calmed, allowing me to reach into my saddlebags. With shaking hands, I said a silent prayer and pulled back both leather straps to check the parchments for damage.

However, before leaving our last encampment, I had prepared my parchments and wedged all my writing materials in a waterproof leather bag. Though, my frantic urge remained to check them for damage.

"Commander de Érail, let me check my saddlebags for any damage to the *Sangraal* parchments before we proceed."

The sheepskin coverings were soaked with water. A lump formed in my throat, and I said another prayer before unbuttoning the leather bags. The other men slowly gathered around me staring at my hands. Jacque de Hoult bowed his head in prayer and Commander Gilbért moved next to me for a better look. To my great relief, everything inside remained dry. This time I voiced a loud prayer to our Savior, Jesus the Christ, and crossed myself once more. I raised the bag in the air for all to see and shouted, "Glory be to God and Amen!" My companions raised their arms too and shouted the same words, then crossed themselves.

Commander de Érail motioned for us to leave at once; as a result, additional rejoicing didn't ensue. My accident had caused further delays and the commander didn't smile with our God-answered prayers. We jumped on our horses, spurred them hard, and raced toward Carcassonne. After my guilt of delaying them, I hoped the men would understand and not hold me responsible. Yet, they were experienced warrior-*moines* who made few mistakes and timing meant everything to them. Though my accident had sharpened my alertness, giving me some sense of military toughness.

The road to the walled city forced our horses to trudge uphill, yet quickly we reached the outskirts of Carcassonne. In the distance, the afternoon rays reflected off the buff-colored barbican. We reached the gatehouse a short time later. I noticed how fortified the town seemed as we crossed the drawbridge and advanced toward its interior. I counted sixteen exterior guard towers and thirty interior towers, with all of them roof-covered. According to Commander de Érail, the Trencavel families had built the town and fortress over many years. The *château* of the *Comte* Trencavel loomed the largest edifice visible as we continued into the marketplace. As we rode farther into the town, my clothes were now dry, and Squire Hughes gave back my cape and surcoat to wear.

Smells of salty dried meat and fish mingled with the pungent smell of herbs, along with earthy aromas of vegetables and hot baking bread. Was this market day in Carcassonne? The open-air stalls were crowded with people buying the many foods and wares of the local merchants. The fresh yeasty-smelling breads dominated all the other smells in the market. My mouth watered as I thought about purchasing several of the hot loaves, at the same time hearing my stomach growl.

Images from my childhood assailed me as I thought of market day at Borron. However, soon thoughts of my raven-haired *épouse* and my two red-headed *fils* replaced them. My family and I enjoyed market days, which left me with fond memories and longing to see them. We approached the other end of the market stalls, where appeared jugglers, fire-eaters, Romany fortune tellers, and magicians performing various tricks. The draper merchants' stalls were the last we saw before approaching the commandery house and chapel.

The commandery stood attached to *Comte* Bernard de Trencavel's *château*. Commander de Érail told us the *Comte* Bernard had constructed the commandery house and chapel in remembrance of his late *mère*, Marie de Trencavel. The commandery house seemed large, yet not to the extent of the priory at Montpellier. Sentries stood guard at the stone-fortified entrance and greeted our commander with a hardy, "Hail, Commander Gilbért."

Our horses ambled through the main gate, stopping at the bailey section of the commandery, where two young squires ran out to grab our halters. The divine prayer office of Sext had just finished as a stiff-bearing, tall, red-headed man with facial scars stepped out of the chapel. His swagger and markings on his white cowl-covered mantle indicated to me he commanded these Poor Fellow-Soldiers of Christ.

"*Bienvenu,* Gilbért de Érail," the man said. "It's quite pleasant to see you once again. Come and eat with us. As usual, you have arrived just as we are about to eat. Not only are you an excellent fighter, but you still have perfect timing. You and your men are welcome to join us. We have plenty of room in our refectory for visitors. This will provide your fellow *frères* a chance to taste real food. Come, we are having some hot venison, fresh-baked bread, and tasty *vin*. You can introduce me to your new Templar *chevalier* after we eat. We have plenty to speak about, *mon ami.*" The two commanders then gave each other a hardy slapping embrace.

All the commandery *chevaliers* and sergeants were standing in silence, poised at the entranceway to the refectory. Their chaplain led the way, followed by the sergeants, *chevaliers,* and both commanders. We entered in complete silence, leaving the sole sound of shuffling boots in military cadence. After entering with the *chevaliers,* a white-surcoated monk motioned for me to sit at a table closest to the two commanders, who had seated themselves in back of the refectory hall. As I sat down, I spied a large wooden cross, nailed to the front wall over the entrance we had entered. The hall seemed drab, except the red-colored cross. Along one side of the long rows of tables, I observed an elevated pulpit with a fellow chaplain *frère* ready to recite a blessing and psalm. When he started the blessing, we jumped up, bowed our heads, after which we said amen, then crossed ourselves, and sat back down in martial unison.

The numerous young squires ran to serve us food and to my surprise, the salvers had several large pieces of roasted venison stacked quite high. Each flagon contained some dark ruby-colored *vin*, replete to the pitcher's brim. It tasted excellent but was watered down. The fresh yeasty-smelling bread they served last, which once again made my mouth water. It tasted slightly sweet as if made with honey. My ravenous appetite overwhelmed my manners, and I found myself eating the roasted venison and crusty bread with a sloppy zeal I hadn't experienced before. My hunger kept me preoccupied, so I failed to hear all of Psalms sixty-three through sixty-nine. Upon completion of the psalms, fingerbowls came forth and we washed our greasy hands. Afterward, we stood for the benediction and later we crossed ourselves and started marching out the same way we'd entered. Once outside in the bailey, Commander Gilbért's fellow commander approached us. "Commander Gilbért, who's the new Templar *chevalier* we have here?"

"Let's depart to your private quarters, Commander," Commander de Érail responded, "where we can discuss this matter in more detail. There I'll tell you more about him."

We proceeded a short distance and climbed five flights of stone steps. Upon reaching the last fight, the commander of Carcassonne opened a large wooden door with an iron key revealing a carved pattée-shaped cross on the door. His living quarters were more than I had expected for a warrior-*moine*. There were numerous cross-legged chairs, a feather mattress bed, and a large leather chest, placed at the foot of the bed. Also, I observed a small table with various parchments lying on top. On the wall, above his bed, I noticed a strange-shaped amulet hanging from a nail. He had the usual pattée cross above it; however, the amulet below appeared as a small flat golden-shaped hand dangling from a small metal-linked chain. Upon the open palm, I observed a single etched opened eye with unfamiliar symbols surrounding it. At once, my mind begged to know the amulet's meaning and the words engraved in the palm.

"Commander Armound de Polignac, let me introduce you to Lord Robert de Borron. Lord Robert has come all the way from northern Burgundy to help us with our *Sangraal* quest. Lord de Borron's schooling consists of well-versed letters, poetry, music, and he's known also for his sword acumen. Although, I think he prefers the pen to the broadsword. He's traveling with me incognito as a

Templar *chevalier* to thwart any suspicion about what we are doing. Our Grand Master did approve our secret quest."

"Lord Robert de Borron, are you a friend of *Comte* Gautiér de Montbéliard?" Commander Armound de Polignac's searching brown eyes waited for my answer. Before replying, I noticed a large scar on the side of his neck.

"*Oui*, he's both my benefactor and close friend. *Comte* de Montbéliard has encouraged me in my writing and poetry. In addition, he's my *épouse's frère.*"

"You have a great man in your family, Lord Robert. He's both wise and courageous. In the last crusade, I fought many battles with him in the Levant. There's no braver fighter than your brother-in-law, with three exceptions; me, Commander Gilbért, and Guillaume le Marshal."

We laughed and I admitted to myself that I already had a fondness for this commander. After the laughter and jest had ceased, Commander Armound cleared his throat and became serious.

"Gilbért, I heard you ran into some trouble on the road to Carcassonne. Is that accurate?"

"*Oui*, but just a minor inconvenience. Cardinal Folquet, the archbishop of Toulouse's men tried to intercept us. The one thing that infuriates me about the cardinal, he has garnered the Holy *Père's* ear," Commander Gilbért gripped the hilt of his sword. "I suspect Cardinal Folquet thinks there's a second set of *Sangraal* parchments, but I don't know this for a fact, yet my heart tells me there's a second set."

"Have you found any clues, which could tell you another exists?" Commander de Polignac inquired.

"We have found just one set to date. However, Cardinal Folquet used his influence to confiscate it from me."

His trusting friendship with Commander de Polignac caused him to divulge definite information on who wanted to kill us. Yet, why would his men still chase after us for additional parchments, if Commander Gilbért doubted they might exist? This told me that they were probably after me for my miraculous translating skills.

"I asked Lord Robert to translate and memorize it before the papal legate confiscated the book. Lord Robert, so far, has copied numerous pages of our first book from memory. He has assured me of its replica completion before we reach Toledo."

Commander Armound stared at me for a moment and then glanced back to his old *ami*.

"*Frère* Gilbért, how did he memorize all the words and know their meanings?"

"Let me answer that," I insisted. "Sainte-Marie-Magdalene helped me with special spiritual powers she gave me with the help of our Lord, Jesus the Christ. Don't ask me why they chose me. It's something I don't take lightly. My family and my life are at stake here. I am still trying to comprehend this miracle. Several of those spiritual gifts were excellent memory, fast writing ability, and translation of ancient languages. It doesn't make any difference to me if you believe me or not."

"Lord de Borron, I am sure Commander Gilbért has told you the need for these sacred holy parchments and their protection. Yet, paramount are the written truths, knowledge, and ways of our Lord, Jesus the Christ. Any information that reveals new light on the darkest days of our Savior needs protecting. Of course, we have other gospels from the Holy Bible; however, Saint Joseph de Arimathea's newly discovered gospel, I fear has fallen into the wrong hands."

Commander Armound paused and took a deep breath. "I have heard tell of legends that say where the *Sangraal* parchments reside, there lies the Cup of the Last Supper. Each purported parchment, legends say, fits into the puzzle to find the 'Cup of Christ.' *Seigneur* Robert, I know your quest has a much greater cause compared to any army fighting in the Levant. We, the Poor Fellow-Soldiers of Christ are just an instrument or tool for this completion. Your writing pen has a far sharper edge than any sword in existence. That is the significant difference between us. You have a God-blessed talent for understanding many languages. I see Saint Joseph's words penetrating the hearts and minds of the entire human race and upsetting many. I have the utmost faith in Commander Gilbért, and he has the utmost confidence in you. I know you will succeed in your quest."

"Commander Armound, I appreciate your compliments and your faith in me. I pray not to disappoint your order and our Savior."

Looking my way, Commander de Érail asked, "You didn't realize we would face such a persistent adversity when you joined us, did you, *mon ami?*"

How odd, I thought, *he just read my mind, for I surmised the same.*

"*Non,* Commander, I did not. However, I am not a man to back down from danger and I won't start now. I always keep my word and the sacred texts are quite important to me. The words I've copied from Saint Joseph de Arimathea's writings are much holier compared to ordinary sentences on a page. They reveal many new revelations about our Lord, Jesus the Christ, some of them quite unknown to date!" My sudden passion surprised me. Both commanders nodded their heads in agreement, followed with giant grins of approval. My emotions boiled with an untamed zeal.

"Don't doubt my commitment to our quest, for I intend to see it through to its finality and won't hesitate to lay down my pen and brandish my sword to assure our success."

Commander Gilbért glanced at me and spoke. "Well-spoken, Lord Robert. It confirms you are committed to the success of our godly mission. Don't you agree, Armound?"

"*Oui, mon ami,* but enough of this discussion, let me pour each of you another cup of *vin.*"

"*Bon,*" replied Commander Gilbért, holding out his cup as Commander de Polignac poured each of us a brimful of the ruby-colored liquid.

After a quick swallow from his cup, Commander Gilbért started discussing our next overland destination. Some relief came over me in the change of subjects, for I still doubted my abilities to complete this great sacred journey. In particular, the thought of unknown trials ahead tightened my stomach to gut-wrenching proportions. However, at the same time, I sensed the fire of my Lord and Savior's determination burning inside me. I realized these holy *chevaliers* and sergeant *frères* had faced the same angst and physical pain that I now faced. This did give me additional confidence and fortitude, thus, for the moment, deterring my lingering doubts. An inner voice told me that from this day forward, I would call upon my Lord's strength to defeat any devil's doubt that tried to enter my mind.

Commanders Gilbért and Armound were discussing the road conditions to Tarascon as my mind joined them.

"How many leagues to Tarascon?" I inquired.

"Fifteen to twenty leagues," Commander Armound answered.

"It's just another thirty leagues to the Somport Pass and into Navarre. Navarre is less than five days ride, if not delayed by the Cathars. They have a strong presence in the foothill region of the Pyrénées Mountains and their perfects or priests are suspicious of anybody representing the Holy Père. I would advise traveling through these areas at night, *Seigneur* Robert. I might add, their religion differs from ours and the archbishop of Toulouse has unmercifully persecuted them in the past. Our commandery keeps a respectable relationship with these people, and it will stay this way. Don't linger in any of the caves in their regions, for these are secret worship meeting places."

I'd heard many stories about the Cathar faith and Commander Armound's information caused my imagination to anticipate the worst.

"What do the Cathars believe in that differs from our faith?"

"Well, for one, their priests don't eat meat or fat of any kind. This means no milk, eggs, or cheese too. They consume vegetables, some fish, and value all living creatures that procreate. They won't destroy them for food. They don't swear to any oaths and upon death, the Cathar souls can travel through nine transmigrations before they reach Heaven.

"They believe their spirits are sometimes trapped into another human or animals of all sorts and their perfects must give them *consolamentum* at death for them to journey straight to Heaven.

"Also, they believe the Holy *Mère* of God, our beloved Marie, did bear the Son of God. God created Him alone, but He didn't appear in human form, yet divine in all appearance. However, they still believe in the Trinity, but not the Holy Eucharist. They say most of our priests and bishops are corrupt."

"I admit they're some right in this respect. We know the power of the bishops and cardinals and how their greed can permeate the land."

"*Seigneur* de Borron, you can recognize the perfects by their black-hooded robes and long beards, making the Cathar priests similar in appearance to some of our fellow religious orders. They leave us alone and we reciprocate in kind. Once you have fought in the Levant against a true enemy, you're more tolerant of others back home. I hope I've answered all your questions about the Cathars. Now, let's drink another cup of *vin* and discuss your trip to Toledo."

My thoughts pondered what each said as I sipped my cup of *vin*. I knew my ignorance and poor knowledge of the area were apparent, but shame didn't overtake me. These holy men were now my new teachers and left me with the privilege to sit in their presence and listen to these great warriors and their knowledge of mankind. Their swords weren't the sole weapons sharpened by warfare, but also their minds.

"Armound, have any of my men from Toledo sent some current messages to you?"

"*Non*, Gilbért. The last news we received consisted of a warning about the cardinal and his men, which you already know. Yet, my secular sources did mention something, which vexed me. They said to tell you, beware of the 'brethren,' yet I don't know who they are. Do you?"

"I am afraid I not familiar with this brotherhood or brethren, Armound. Do they collaborate with the cardinal's men? Did your source say where this brotherhood originates?"

"*Non*, they didn't. Their last comments were a final warning, telling me these men are dangerous and don't fear for their lives."

"Tell your sources in Toledo we thank them for this warning, and we'll pass this along to my other *frères* after leaving Tarascon."

"Armound, that reminds me. Can your squire show us the way to your provision area? We're in great need of *vin*, water, dried meats, and bread. Also, I need two additional crossbows and some quarrels. We'll leave right after Nones prayer service. This will allow us about six hours of daylight to travel and position us on the outskirts of Tarascon. As you know, the trail through the Pyrénées Mountains starts a short distance from Tarascon."

"*Oui*, you're *bienvenu* to anything we have here at Carcassonne. Also, my latest reports say the mountains have limited amounts of snow. The Somport Pass remains clear, yet too many pilgrims travel it. Gilbért, I do know a seldom-used pass you might know. It starts at Gavarnie. There's a large stone cross on the trail directing you up to the side of the mountain. The path will carry you to the top of Monte Perdido and over to the town of Bielsa and the Cinca river. If you travel it, use caution; this pass becomes quite dangerous with unexpected snowstorms. Otherwise, most people don't know about it."

"*Oui*, I do remember this pass. *Merci beaucoup*, Armound, for reminding me of this trail. I am sure the cardinal's men wouldn't know about this pass, yet they will come here. Somehow, they have knowledge of our destinations and the roads we are traveling. Our Holy *Père's* legate or Cardinal Folquet has alerted his men. My *bon* Saracen *ami*, Muhammad Nur Adin, has helped them lose their way for now."

"Gilbért, you have an excellent tracker and horseman in Nur Adin. I remember several dire events he helped extricate us from in the Levant."

Both men started reminiscing over their past narrow escapes in the Holy Land, when Squire Hughes de Montbard rushed in.

"Commander de Érail, pardon me." The young squire's flashing eyes reflected urgency as he apologized for the interruption. "I have just received word from a fellow *chevalier* returning from Toulouse. He said the cardinal's men are just one day's ride from here, and they're heading toward this commandery. Do you want us to prepare the horses?"

Commander de Érail acknowledged young Hughes's request and rose to leave. Both commanders embraced and wished God's blessing on each other. To my surprise, Commander Armound reached for the wall, removed the golden amulet, and placed it into my palm.

"*Seigneur* de Borron, earlier I saw your curious eyes gazing on this object. I am loaning it to you. The Saracens call it a hamsa, which I found in our Temple grounds. Legends say it came from the time of King Solomon and protects all who possess it. I hope you'll wear it always to safeguard you and all the holy parchments you seek. When you complete your quest, I'll expect its return."

He left me overwhelmed with the offer of this ancient biblical amulet. "Commander de Polignac, *merci beaucoup* for your generosity. I'll keep it on my person at all times until my quest ends and promise its return."

With a slight smile, he embraced me and led all three of us to the provision house. The rest of our fellow *frères* and Muhammad met us there. The house door held a locked large iron padlock, which Commander de Polignac unlocked. There were crossbows, quarrels, and food supplies around each wall. In the center of the room were stacked swords in a peaked fashion. We loaded the supplies onto our destriers. After we finished, the bells for the divine office of Nones rang, so we ambled toward the large chapel, called Saint John the Baptizer. There we prayed, and after a short service, said our final *au revoirs*. "What if the cardinal's men arrive here; what will you tell them?" Commander de Érail asked Commander de Polignac.

"*Mon ami*, nothing. For God's business calls me to another commandery house." He grinned as we mounted our horses to leave Carcassonne. We waved *au revoir* and proceeded back through the streets from whence we'd arrived, yet this time we departed by a different portcullis. We galloped across the drawbridge, then Commander Gilbért gave a final salute to the guard in the barbican and we raced down the open road.

With the cardinal's *chevaliers* one day behind us, I knew we had a hard ride ahead before sundown and encampment. Our fine-bred horses had received some rest, yet I still wondered if they were up to the grueling pace they faced. We followed the Aude river straight south for several leagues before stopping to water the horses and ourselves. With caution, I led my horse to the edge of the river. The current revealed small whitecaps and the banks were steep. Sergeant Jacque helped me with Fatima to ensure she didn't slip and fall into the rapid current. None of us wanted a repeat of what happened to me the last time I traveled near a river. Somewhere unseen, I heard the loud roar of a waterfall, making it difficult to hear one another's voices as we rested. All at once, Sergeant Guy de Béziers started waving to his commander and pointing toward three men on the opposite side of the river. They were moving along a high ridge road at the top of the embankment.

"Cathars, Cathars on the opposite bank!" he shouted over the din of the falls.

The three black-hooded men with long beards looked much as described by Commander de Polignac. At first, the group of priests didn't see us, but all at once the first perfect glanced our way and raised his wooden staff to acknowledge us. They continued on their way along the far ridge and not once did the other two acknowledge our presence. I suspected they reflected some apprehension on their part, because of our military order, yet they strode along at an unhurried pace until out of our sight. As I sat on a large rock, near the river's edge, I ruminated on what I had already seen in this mysterious region called Occitania. This land consisted of many contrasts with strange rocky land formations, peoples, spirits, religions, and unknown languages. I guess the quest for the *Sangraal* parchments would have it no other way.

Without warning, a large stag broke through the brush, distracting my deep contemplation. He ambled down to the waterline to drink and appeared oblivious of our presence. His great thirst for water overcame his need for caution. I sat there staring at him, thinking he and I had much in common. Both of us had a thirst for something, yet not cognizant of the dangers around us. The rest of my fellow compatriots failed to see the animal from where they sat, which allowed me to observe him for a short time until a wind rustled some dried sycamore leaves. He took one last swallow, turned, and trotted back up the hillside, unnoticed by everyone except me.

Young Squire Hughes hurried toward me and then spoke. "Lord de Borron, we must leave to reach Tarascon, and it is quite far before nightfall. Also, the cardinal's *chevaliers* appear to be gaining on us. I hate to interrupt your prayers, but we must leave now."

I hastened to my horse and made sure my bags were secure, after which I leaped upon the saddle, ready for the ride ahead. The pace became furious, with all the horses snorting for breath. Muhammad's high-pitched voice seemed to cause our horses to fly over the dirt road. They traveled faster with each of his firm commands. However, I didn't recognize his words, it had something to do with the word *Allah*. He kept repeating the same chant over and over, screaming, "*Allahu akbar, Allahu akbar*." Muhammad wore a black headscarf, covering his entire face, except a narrow slit for his dark flashing eyes as he galloped by me, whipping his horse, he called *Buraq*, with his reins. He appeared like a man racing out of Hell with the devil himself chasing after him.

The speed of our steeds forced me to crouch much lower on the neck of my horse to stay mounted. Clouds of dust and flying small pebbles from the dry trail stung my face and made it difficult to breathe and see. By now, both of my eyes were tearing, along with a starting cough, which increased with each gallop. We had ridden another three leagues before the pace slowed. The horizon ahead appeared watery and distorted, and I knew that any moment my eyes would swell shut.

When the cloud of dust had dissipated, my stinging eyes saw a large distorted grassy plain, with the Pyrénées Mountains rising through the clouds. I hadn't seen snowcapped hills this large until now, so I wondered if my swollen eyes were deceiving me. We stopped our horses by a small rocky gurgling stream, where we let them drink and rest. I used this momentary time to wash my face in the icy waters. My vision concerned me the most, though, my thirst won out. After slaking my thirst, I reached into my saddlebag and pulled out a small cloth to wipe my face. I soaked it in the cold stream, wrung it out, and applied it to my face and neck. Then I cupped my palms and dipped them into the icy water again to remove the grit from my eyes.

Our horses were dripping white lather from their withers to their hooves. The poor horses appeared fagged, yet Muhammad leaped on his horse and shouted out a command in his native tongue. At once, all the horses stopped drinking, raised their heads, and started pawing the ground with their hooves. Quite exhausted and the last to mount, I left the icy waters of the mountain stream. We proceeded at a steady gallop, but not at the previous speed.

We changed directions and then headed in a more southwesterly course. The Aude river had disappeared, leaving rolling hills and small forests of golden-leafed white birch trees. The closer we approached Tarascon, we saw more forests and steep rolling hills. The cooler air increased and made me shiver as I fixated on the white-capped peaks of each mountaintop. The clouds were indistinguishable from the snowy peaks and the sole noticeable difference came from their movements.

At last, our small band stopped and camped near a cave entrance as the setting sun fell behind some white birch trees, interspersed with evergreen trees. I thought the trees would grant us some protection from the anticipated cold night air. Also, they were of sufficient height and number to hide our presence, including the horses.

Each man advanced to his appointed task of helping to set up our camp, cool down the horses, and prepare the food for our evening meal. Commander de Érail walked over to me as I removed the saddle from my horse.

"Lord de Borron, do you have sufficient daylight left to write about the blessed Saint Joseph and our Savior?"

"First, may I ask a boon from you, Commander de Érail? Is it possible to have a campfire tonight? By firelight, my words will double."

He thought for a moment before replying. "Lord de Borron, you may start writing as soon as we've finished cooling down the horses, but we need to wait on a fire. As you are aware, we aren't just traveling to Toledo, but away from Cardinal Folquet's men. Muhammad rides near and around Tarascon. When he returns at dusk, if there isn't anything suspicious to report, you have my permission to start a fire."

"*Merci beaucoup*, Commander. I pray he will find nothing."

My hunger didn't distract me. I had a driving desire to write more words. Commander de Érail initiated our Vesper prayer office and a short while thereafter our evening meal. My body ached from our hard ride, but my thoughts raced around my mind. It sped with lines from the *Sangraal* book. After a quick meal, I opened my saddlebags for my writing supplies.

Young Squire Hughes assisted me by finding a large flat rock nearby on which to lay my parchments. To my surprise, I had a perfect writing table, and this would help quicken my writing pace. With much care, he arranged all my writing materials nearby. He said he would check with me quite often to see if I needed further assistance. I completed each parchment sheet at a furious rate, and later my companions were amazed at how many completed sheets lay before me.

I wrote until my hands ached, still hoping that Muhammad Nur Adin would return at any time with beneficial news. The cold evening air further exacerbated my pain, making me think I must rest my hand tonight.

All of a sudden, a rustling sound came from a grove of dark evergreen trees. Behind one tree crept a dark figure who didn't say a word as the pine branches still concealed the phantom's face. At once, my warrior-*moine amis* jumped up and drew their swords with the quickness of several cats. Muhammad acknowledged himself by whispering in his Saracen voice, followed by the metallic sound of all our swords sliding back into their scabbards. Commander de Érail and Muhammad spoke.

"Lord de Borron, Muhammad just reported excellent news. He says there isn't any imminent danger that they're following us. The town of Tarascon appears safe and shows no sign of the Cardinal's *chevaliers*. The trail to Gavarnie shows no ambushes too, Muhammad said, but I think it best if we travel it later tonight. Muhammad used coded marks to direct us tonight."

Commander de Érail gave the order to start a fire and said not to travel far from the camp and especially not to enter any caves. Before long, the campfire's roaring red and orange flames glowed against the darkness. The cold winds started blowing through the birch trees, causing their dry leaves to crackle, similar to my many rustling parchments. I knew the fire would temper the cold winds and help me write faster. Squire Hughes followed his commander's orders and started a second fire in quick martial fashion. The precision with which he used his flint box amazed me.

"Hughes, I want to say I appreciate what you have done for me. Your helpful assistance and knowledge will make Commander de Érail quite proud of you as his squire. Soon I know you'll become a great *chevalier* and a Poor Fellow-Soldier of Christ."

"*Merci beaucoup*, Lord de Borron, for letting me help you on our quest for the *Sangraal* parchments. God has made me an instrument for His divine plan. My family, in particular, my much beloved deceased uncle, Saint Bernard de Clairvaux, helped write our monastic rule in furthering our holy order. It's my destiny to help preserve the *Sangraal's* history."

Not until now did I connect his relationship with the great saint. Seeing the spiritual exuberance coming from this young man about his uncle didn't surprise me. No doubt he had inherited his uncle's evangelistic fervor.

By now, young Hughes had stoked the fires to create sufficient warmth. My right hand had rested some and the hot fire relieved me of its stiffness. Once again, I resumed my steady pace of writing and young Hughes de Montbard continued his excellent assistance. The steady crackling of the fire caused me to stop numerous times and stare into its flames. The multiple-colored flames held me in its trance, with blue, orange, and yellow tongues of fire pulling my eyes down toward the bright red-hot embers. Each time, after gazing on the flames, the words flowed faster from my pen without one moment of forgetfulness.

Were my thoughts coming from the red embers? The fire refreshed my memory of what I'd read several days ago. It exhilarated me to dip my quill pen into the black ink well while realizing my Savior had bestowed a precious gift to me. Without logical reason, my hand wrote with a mind of its own. Its movements seemed possessed by some divine power as my eyes stayed fixated on the fire. After a while, my mind appeared to float out of my body as in a dream, yet I heard the movements of the men around me. They were chattering, as the wind whistled, and the horses nickered. Was I awake or not?

The flames continued to intensify in brightness until I saw a small-shaped red chalice forming in the flames. What did the cup mean and why in my vision? My hand stopped writing, as Saint Joseph's words vanished from my mind. In front of me, the cup apparition now seized both my thoughts and focus. It continued to grow bigger from the embers until the chalice reached full size. The glowing red translucent cup must have formed from some knot in the log, I thought, but *non*, I observed its perfect-shaped rim and base. The object stayed translucent as it began to rise out of the flames. The suspended chalice moved to my eye level, remained suspended in front of me for a short moment and then disappeared without a trace. My tired eyes were blurred, I thought, and nothing more.

CHAPTER XXIV

I waited by the fire, hoping the chalice would reappear. I glanced around to see if anyone else in the camp saw the object, but they were now asleep. Muhammad remained hidden, out of sight, away on watch, so I knew he couldn't see the campfire. I hesitated to wake them, certain they would believe it a fitful dream. Nothing in my life seemed normal since my first vision at the church in Vézelay, yet now I must accept what appeared as abnormal behavior in my life as normal.

Young Hughes had fallen asleep with the rest of the *moines*, but he slept the closest to my recent phantasmal event. I woke him with a whisper and asked him if he saw anything before he fell asleep.

"Hughes, did you see anything unusual in nature before you fell asleep?" I had some hope he indeed saw something.

"*Non*, Lord de Borron. All I saw were the stars overhead."

"What about something unusual in our campfire?"

"The fire seems large and warm, but nothing of an unusual nature. What did you see in the fire?"

"Never mind. So sorry to have disturbed your slumber, Squire Hughes, please, forgive me." He acknowledged my apology and fell back to sleep.

226

I placed all my writing materials back into my saddlebags and prepared myself for tonight's ride in several hours. However, before sleeping, I had to relieve myself.

The fire nearest the rest of our men still burned with a hot blue flame. A cautious person by nature, I grabbed a sizeable burning stick to use as a torch, turned, and then ambled toward what appeared a cave entrance. I stopped just a short distance from the camp, stuck my burning torch in the ground, and relieved myself behind a large boulder. To my surprise, I heard a howling wind call my name as it roared through the cave entrance. Curiosity and fear now waged a battle in my mind. Yet the words of Commander Armound de Polignac and Commander Gilbért harkened back to me. They had warned not to trespass into any Cathar caves in this region and said they wouldn't appreciate my intrusion into their sacred sanctuary. However, was this cave one of their worship areas? Without meaning any disrespect, I decided to enter.

A strong wind seemed to pull me into the cave's dark interior, causing my torch to splutter faster. The flames flapped so loudly, it distracted my concentration. To my amazement, there were weather-beaten painted symbols on each side of the cave. Moving closer, I observed the shape of a fish and another shape in the outline of a chalice. Were these symbols a portent not to enter or welcoming signs for me?

I studied the drawing of the chalice, similar in shape to the one I had just seen in the flames of my campfire. It appeared they were holy cryptic designs beckoning me to traipse deeper into the cave and seek out their meaning. Before traveling any farther, I turned, glanced back, and saw a small flicker of light coming from our campfire. Then I realized how far I had wandered from our camp. My inquisitiveness continued to pull at my body. I crept into the rocky, damp, dark interior that nature had carved out during the mountain's formation. Once inside, my torch settled into a steady flame that enabled me to see more than nature working here on these moist rocky walls. My excitement became boundless at what my torch revealed, not just painted and chiseled symbols, but written words. To my further surprise, I recognized the writing. It appeared the same type of script written in the *Sangraal* book at Montpellier.

Yet, most of the writing looked dimly visible, obscured by soot from the many burning flames brought by those who could have worshipped here. The closer I moved my torch to the wall, the more words I translated. One group of words, in particular, said, "Our *Abba*, who art in Heaven, hallowed be thy name . . ." To my astonishment, I recognized our Lord's Prayer! The prayer of our Lord I didn't expect to see, and above all, written in the ancient language and handwriting of Saint Joseph de Arimathea. In addition, why written on a cave wall here in the Pyrénées *Montagnes*? I continued to follow the writing on the walls, deeper into the cave's interior. On the cave floor were many strewn melted candles that caused me to slip on several occasions. This didn't deter me from continuing beyond the cave's cavernous rooms until a sudden flurry of bats pelted my head, which made me stop.

My heart started racing from fright, yet a moment of guilt assailed me too, as I became aware of the importance of this sanctuary. No doubt, the Cathars worshipped here as mentioned by Commander de Polignac. None of this made sense to me. I hadn't intended to desecrate this sacred cave. Yet, an unseen, mysterious force kept pulling me deeper into the cave. "Just one more step and I will stop," I kept repeating to myself, "and no one will know." I raised my torch to inspect the area to my right when I heard a sound.

Then I perceived spoken words muffled by the noise of a drafty wind.

"Bless this man, O Lord."

Once more, my heart hammered in my chest after hearing this strange voice. My sweaty palms slipped at the pommel of my sword as I tried to grip it. The voice continued to come forth from the dark interior of the cave. Ahead of me were two passageways that forked off from the main tunnel. In the area beyond my torchlight, my eyes saw a distant yellow glowing light emanating from the left passageway. Also, the source of the chanting voice. The closer I advanced, the narrower the tunnel became. The eerie voice spoke in an Occitanian dialect; most of the words of his chant I understood.

"I pray for this man. Please lead him to the Kingdom of Heaven and let him fear not."

Oui, a human voice and not my imagination. He repeated the same words many times until I crept closer and saw the dark outline of a man. "Who are you?" I asked, hoping my presence hadn't offended him. When no response came, I continued. "Please, forgive me for entering your sacred sanctuary. I come not to desecrate your sanctuary or harm you. My curiosity drew me to the mysterious carved symbols at the cave entrance."

Two large candles were on each side of him, which lit up a hooded-looking *moine.* Close to his knees, I observed a bronze chalice, which wasn't the same chalice from the fire. This wasn't a floating image, but a solid object. It displayed unrecognizable engraved designs around its rim. The closer I came to him, the more the cup's interior glowed with red and white rays.

By now, I stood over his shoulders and he had yet to acknowledge my presence. After a long period of silence, he turned his head, but his pointed hood concealed his eyes. This prevented me from a clear view of his face in the dark cave. His lips began to move in a faint whisper as he started to speak.

"Wise men are often curious men and, *non,* I am not offended by your presence. I expected you tonight." He turned his head and gazed at the large flames emanating from the cream-colored candles.

"You were expecting me? How did you know? Even I didn't know about this cave!"

"Is this what you seek, pilgrim?" His long bony finger pointed toward the glowing cup. "We are both a part of something far greater than the two of us and yet guided by the same divine spirit."

It troubled me in our quest that others knew of our experiences, but I knew not how. However, here before me stood a Cathar *moine* speaking of the *Sangraal* cup, which seemed incredulous to my mind. The cup appeared similar to the one drawn on the parchment at Montpellier.

"Come this way, *mon ami,*" he said, as he rose, clutching the radiant, glowing cup.

Accepting his invitation, I proceeded forward, holding my torch in my sweaty palm. Ahead of me the passageway continued but bent at a sharp angle to the right of the main tunnel. I followed his muffled voice as it directed me through a narrow opening. After ambling a short distance, the constant glow from the cup gave me a better picture of his stature. The mysterious black-hooded *moine* stood slightly taller than me yet bent at the shoulders and quite thin to the extent of emaciation. It wouldn't have surprised me if I might see a skeleton instead of flesh under his hooded robe.

We entered a large cavern. In front of us stood a murky-lit wooden table with two narrow tapers placed at each end. On the table, he placed the glowing cup between the candles and at once, it changed to a fiery red-orange color. With some trepidation, I approached the blazing chalice to obtain a better look at its surface. Out of fear or reverence, I dared not to grasp the cup, but with squinted eyes stared at its surface for details. The chalice's golden rainbow had diminished some, giving me the opportunity to see the delicately etched rim covered with small identical-shaped fish. Its glowing surface seemed composed of some type of yellow-colored metal. The closer I drew, the cup's spear-shaped rays increased in their intensity. The cave's walls surrounding us took on a glistening pink rose color, accompanied by a rose flower fragrance.

"Pilgrim, don't touch or look inside the cup. You are not ready to receive its holy grace. This is the Cup of Christ," the monk announced, as I stood enthralled by the object. At first, I didn't comprehend his words but focused on the cup's rotating beams of light. At last, his words struck me, forcing me to stagger against the moist glistening cave wall, leaving me to stare at his seemingly unmovable lips.

"Many seek it, but few have seen it. Just those deemed worthy by the Holy One will know its truthful meaning. He has chosen you, as the perfect to uncover what truth this sacred cup will reveal. I am but a messenger, one of several, sent here to guide you on your way. The men you travel with are similar to me, for the Son of Light has cho-sen them to help complete your holy quest. They're the tip of your spear. Stand behind them and doubt not their tenacity. Each man has his own unique gift to furnish in your quest for the truth, Lord de Borron. Look for several more comparable to me who will direct you down the road of truth. The parchments you seek will reveal the source of this holy truth. The words in these parchments are one of your keys to the Kingdom of Heaven. No matter what happens, don't let any man deter you from your quest. I must now leave, but one last warning. Beware of what seems similar to kindness. Heed my warning and search your soul if in doubt."

With his last warning word of "doubt," he stood up to leave. Before he left, his bony hand reached down to pick up the chalice. To my amazement, the cup stopped glowing and became a dull gray color as he tucked it into his robe. Why didn't he give me the chalice? Was this a further challenge to continue my quest? Yes, that was it, an enticement. Slowly, he turned and disappeared into the dark tunnel of the cave. Was I now to search for both the new parchments and the Cup of Christ? For a moment, my voice froze, and so did my movements, yet my mind ached to know how he had obtained the sacred cup. Was this the actual cup at the Last Supper before the crucifixion? Did he possess more knowledge that I needed to complete our quest? Did he know how long it would take to find the alleged *Sangraal* parchments and their locations? Posthaste, I thought I must thank him for the great honor he'd bestowed on me, yet I didn't know his name.

"*Mon ami!*" I finally shouted, "Who are you, and what name may I address you? I want to thank you and pray in your name."

A faint voice came from the darkness, which replied, "A *bon ami*, a *bon ami* in Christ."

Still unable to move my feet, I squatted down above the moist soil of the cave floor and tried to comprehend everything I had seen and heard. Was this a dream and I would wake up next to our cold campfire? By now, my wooden torch had burned out, leaving me with one small lit candle. At last, the sensation came back into my legs and I took the candle from the table and proceeded to exit the cave. My mind struggled with the belief that I saw myself as the chosen one for such an important holy task. Why just a minor lord from Burgundy and not an *abbé* or a bishop? Yet, God did select me as his instrument and why should I question His judgment? I must not fail what God and Saint Joseph de Arimathea have preordained for me. I surmised that everything in my life, up to this point in time, was spiritual lessons. I knew there were more difficult spiritual trials ahead for me, which now included the elusive Cup of Christ and the holy parchments!

CHAPTER XXV

By the time I exited the cave entrance, the wind had subsided and the ink-black night sky held the brilliance of the Milky Way. My path back to the campfire became difficult, while lighting my way with just the candle. I focused on our distant glowing speck of campfire, yet the fire seemed to keep moving a greater distance away as I traveled toward the flames. After a considerable length of time, I arrived. My *amis* were still asleep. I blew out my candle and tried to acquire some sleep. However, my mind flashed with images of the old *moine* and the cave, no matter how hard I tried to fall asleep. I lay there on the cold ground listening to the light snoring of my companions as they were in peaceful slumber.

At last, the central fire burned down to its red-hot embers before I fell asleep. However, I drifted back and forth between sleep and a semiconscious state. In my dream state, I kept seeing the dark-hooded shape of the *moine* priest. His white bony fingers pointed at my face and he tried to speak, but no words were coming out of his mouth. This vision repeated itself numerous times, along with a dark wraith-like image with the word *traitor* written on its forehead. This was followed with glowing chalices, men with knives, and fleeing horses, until, to my shock, the dark, faceless *moine* began to speak.

I gasped in horror as the hooded face reached out to grab my throat. Yet, he didn't complete his task but called my name, "Robert! Lord de Borron! Wake up, you're having a bad dream." Nevertheless, the hand that touched me didn't look the same. This large powerful hand had a vice-like grip; however, his hood still covered his face, but the voice belonged to Commander de Érail. "It's me, Gilbért de Érail, we must leave right now." I praised God that he'd interrupted my fitful dream, as my eyes opened wide and saw both of my hands grasping Commander Gilbért's tunic.

"Commander, please forgive me. I experienced a nightmare and nothing more."

"Don't worry, Lord Robert, these things happen to all of us. I didn't mean to frighten you. You appeared quite disturbed before I shook you. It's time to break camp and mount our horses."

"*Non*, you didn't frighten me. Once again I must apologize."

Dousing my head with one of the skins of water, I prepared to leave. Yet, my angst continued as I rolled up my remaining writing materials and slipped them into my saddlebags. After which, I mounted my horse and followed the rest of my companions. However, the monk's warning vexed me. Was there a traitor in our midst, and who was he?

The rocky and steep road to Gavarnie held high canyon walls that disappeared upward into the dark night sky. The sole things visible were man-size dark evergreen trees growing out of the lower canyon crevices.

Their small manlike silhouettes gave off the appearance of men standing to challenge our entry, and the images raised the hairs on the back of my neck. Right away, a dark moving figure came out from behind a large boulder. Muhammad's horse ambled out first and our Saracen *ami* started whispering to Commander de Érail while we stopped to rest our horses. Jacque de Hoult, who rode next to me, dismounted and drew closer to hear their conversation. After Muhammad had finished his discourse with Commander de Érail, Sergeant de Hoult translated for me.

"Lord de Borron, possible safe news. Muhammad said the road to Gavarnie shows no physical evidence of the cardinal's men, but his senses tell him otherwise. He told our commander he heard much movement by the wildlife, yet it's too early before dawn for the animals to start feeding. He thinks one possible cause of their unexpected movements were several Romany camps up ahead, who just stopped for the night. It isn't unusual to find Romany tribes in this area; however, keep your eyes on the horizon as we ride ahead."

We spurred our horses and trotted down the dark canyon path until we reached a high plateau. There we reached the top of the canyon cliffs. A brisk cold wind engulfed us as we stood there observing the road ahead. I pulled my hood over my head while hoping it would add some warmth to my face. The night sky displayed countless stars salting the horizon as far as we could see.

To our left were the ever-present Pyrénées *Montagnes* with their tops appearing as giant snow-covered crenellations of an everlasting fortress. After about a league of riding, dawn broke behind us, with the extra light helping to quicken our pace to Gavarnie. However, the rising sun provided little warmth on our cold chain-mailed bodies, as the large mountain shadows prevented most of the sun's rays from reaching us.

We continued to travel four or maybe five leagues into a thick-forested valley with a smooth, well-defined trail, thus making it easy for our horses to gallop faster to Gavarnie. Surrounding us were large granite boulders, which stood as silent sentinels as we made our way to the valley floor.

We came to a large clearing and Commander de Érail gave a hand signal to stop. To one side of the trail loomed a large cliff above us with a thundering waterfall, which crashed down upon numerous rocky boulders. A fast-moving river emanated from these rocks, which raced farther down into the valley.

"Lord de Borron," shouted Commander de Érail above the noise of the falls, "I think we'll stop here and break our fast." The night ride and the cave encounter had left me exhausted. I welcomed the respite to stop for a while.

After we had prayed and completed our divine office, I unsaddled my horse while the others did the same. Muhammad and my companions knew their horses came first and fed and watered them before our needs. Afterward, I helped build a fire while Sergeant de Hoult procured a small iron pot from the supply horses. Into the pot, he gathered water from the mountain river and placed it over the fire. He then added some oats from the horse feed, dark berries, and honey. The mixture cooked just a short time before he began serving it to us. Young Squire Hughes gave each of us a wooden spoon with which to eat the thick mixture. It tasted delicious, to my surprise, and having a hot meal would invigorate us for the cold mountain trip ahead.

After my meal, which furnished me some much-needed energy, I started writing again while Squire Hughes and Muhammad attended to the many camp chores. None of the men asked me to participate in our chores, for the warrior-*moines* knew the importance of me duplicating the *Sangraal* book. There never appeared any jealousy or complaining that I didn't participate in their hard work. These well-disciplined men didn't question anything but obeyed what their commander told them, never doubting his judgment.

I sat down at a peaceful spot, and even the roar of the falls didn't distract me from remembering. I had written a goodly amount of words about Saint Joseph and his intended Passover meal with our Lord.

Suddenly, I heard Guy de Béziers shout, "Commander de Érail, look toward the top of the falls!" All of us glanced up.

Upon this ledge, stood a young woman about fifteen years of age with long straw-colored hair that streamed loose down her back. Her skin appeared snow-white in color that matched the chemise she wore. Her arms hung as narrow ropes and her small limb-sized legs gave the young woman an emaciated appearance of starving. She stood there, not acknowledging our presence but appeared frozen in fear. Her head stayed bowed, even after our continued shouts to acquire her attention.

Commander de Érail had obtained his spyglass, focused it on her, and started shouting to us, "I am afraid she'll jump." He too began waving at her, screaming for her name, and begging her not to go any farther. All of us joined with Commander de Érail and yelled his same words. In that brief instant, she leaped from the high ledge into the foaming rocks below.

We frantically looked for a sign of her thin body floating upon the foaming river. It wasn't until she began to drift away that we noticed a scarlet billow of blood trailing behind her.

After the shock had worn off, Squire Hughes and I were the first to dash toward the riverbank. I continued praying as the current swept her frail body along the rocky edge of the bank. Each time Hughes tried to reach her, the swift current pulled her lifeless body from his grasp. Growing out into the river, some tree roots, at last, ensnared her. That's when I ran to her. Without hesitation, I jumped into the cold water and reached for her arm.

"Squire Hughes, help me retrieve her before the swift current carries her beyond our reach!"

"I am coming!" he cried. With our loud responses, all the others of our band ran toward the slippery rocks at the same time. Her frail body continued to bob in the river with the lightness of a small tree branch, as Hughes lifted her shoulders onto the rocky riverbank. With my hands, I grabbed her hips, then picked up her body, which seemed the weight of a wet feather. As both of us reached the upper bank, Sergeant de Hoult, with gentle care, took her small body and placed it on some soft grass. Upon regaining my footing on the dry bank, Sergeant de Béziers wrapped my shoulders with a dry mantle. At once, Muhammad pounced on her body and started his procedure to blow life back into her. He worked fast for some time until he became crimson-colored from exhaustion, yet to no avail would she breathe. Slowly Muhammad rose, bearing a tight-lipped expression on his face, reached his arms to the sky, and said, "*Salaam alaikum.*"

"Commander de Érail, what did Muhammad say?" I inquired.

"He gave his blessing, or *baraka,* Lord Robert. Muhammad asked *Allah* that peace be upon this young woman in her spirit world. It appears *morte* was her young destiny."

The finality of his words caused the taste of bile to rise to my mouth. Young Hughes knelt next to her, crossed himself, and said, "Lord Jesus the Christ have mercy upon her soul, *in nomine Patris, et Filii, et Spiritus Sancti. Amen.*" Gently he removed her golden hair from her eyes, and that's when I saw a tear or two dropping from his cheek onto her pale blue chest. Around her neck, she wore a small chain with an odd-shaped cross. What did the cross mean? Sadly, I wondered what her name was. Were her parents looking for this poor soul? Yet more important, why had she killed herself?

"Commander, you know these people and their customs. What just happened here?" Instead of answering my question at once, he confused me by asking a question of me.

"Have you ever seen this before, Lord Robert?"

"I have heard of those who have surrendered their lives, Commander. However, I haven't been present when they did it. Still, what drove her to such desperation?"

"I can't say for sure, Lord de Borron, yet my suspicions were answered when I saw her leap from the edge of the waterfall. I prayed she would survive, but I knew better. This Cathar girl had put herself in the throngs of death. Once they know they're dying from sickness or tragedy, their perfects, or what we would call priests, administer consolamentum. Their sacerdotal hierarchy absolves them of their sins, and they wait to die. If they don't die at once, they enter into a fasting state called endura, refusing to eat and sometimes committing suicide, which hastens their spirit to Heaven. The fleshy shells of their bodies are an anathema to their faith. They must remain pure after receiving consolamentum and swiftly obtain their celestial kingdom of God."

"So, you already knew what would happen before she jumped?"

"Unfortunately, *oui*, however, seeing her jump still horrified me."

"Why do the Cathars commit this terrible act and not believe it a sin?" I asked. "Why so?"

"As to why she did such, the locals call it the *Pays Cathare* or the Land of the Cathars. They have many different beliefs that differ from our Roman church."

"Do you think she had any relatives living near the falls?" Once more I glanced at the strange-designed gold cross. "The odd-looking cross and necklace look expensive."

"You are correct, Lord Robert, and, *oui,* I suspect there are some relatives of high degree nearby. The height of the falls and its possible vicinity to her home made it quick for her to die. Did you notice the unusual design of the cross?"

"*Oui,* it's a shape I haven't seen until now."

"The Cathar cross shows no crucifixion of our Savior. If you notice, each arm has the same length and the ends have a rounded fishtail design. I am almost certain if you turn the cross over, you will see the outline of a dove etched on its surface."

With reluctance, I reached down and touched the cold chest of the young woman, with my hand shaking the cross as I turned it over. The small area revealed a finely etched dove. I looked up at our leader. "How do you know such details about the Cathars?"

"Commander de Polignac and I have spent numerous years befriending the people in this region. We have lived among them and know some about their obscure religion and legends. We can discuss more of this later, but we need to bury this poor soul."

Commander de Érail picked a small clearing, free from rocks, some distance from the riverbank for us to bury her. Muhammad and Sergeant de Hoult retrieved two shovels from the supply horses and then dug a sufficiently sized grave. I noticed the soil consisted of a sandy loam texture that made their dolorous task quick.

Commander de Érail tenderly lifted her frail body and placed it into the grave. The commander then said a eulogy oration, consisting of eleven *Pater Nosters* and a psalm. After he finished, he crossed himself. We did likewise and the rest of us covered her body, using the shovelfuls of dirt that we'd dug.

I didn't know what to say or do about this poor woman's salvation. The anathema of suicide I didn't agree with, and my faith told me she would go straight to Hell. *Indeed, what a strange and mysterious land*, I thought, as my eyes gazed at the pile of earth contemplating what to say. Then I remembered a verse from Saint John the Evangelist and whispered his words.

"If we travel in the light, as He is in the light, we have fellowship with one another, and the blood of Jesus His Son cleanses us from all sin."

With much sadness, I crossed myself, turned, and with my fellow companions ambled back to the camp. For obvious reasons, we decided to leave right away. Quickly, we saddled our horses, mounted them, and left.

As we rode along, my thoughts kept telling me what an odd land surrounded me, and I wondered if the young girl's suicide meant another omen for us. For the next half a league, no one spoke a word. We were still despondent and vexed about the tragic events.

"Lord de Borron, she and I were about the same age. Why did this young girl die at such a young age?"

"Remember what your commander said, it's a belief held by the Cathars. To them, it isn't a sin but hastens their way to Heaven. I wish I knew a better explanation, but some things defy logic. Remember Hughes, our Lord gave up his mortal life to cast aside the sins of our world. Some things will remain a mystery until the proper teacher comes along."

Young Hughes's face appeared frozen as he rode, contemplating the young woman's death. His usual spirited demeanor had vanished, and I understood his despondent manner, for I too became quite morose. Yet, his lamentations seemed to linger longer than mine.

"Lord de Borron," Hughes said. "I know most daring warriors died in combat before their time. In addition, the aged know their days are few. Each group knows the fate of death hovers over them, but she came from an apparently prosperous family and had little to fear."

I knew he questioned his mortality, which his benighted youth thought never ended. *When we're young, our ignorance shields us*, I thought. The doubts and fears of death don't exist and thoughts of youthful immortality negated them. However, I sensed more than a premature young girl's death, which disturbed me. I knew doubts were attacking my faith, for what reasons I didn't know. The young girl's death pressed on my heart and determination. Something terrible had happened to this young girl, and my intuition told me it wasn't an illness. It said that somebody had forced her to kill herself.

CHAPTER XXVI

Once again, the road ahead became precipitous, narrow, and rocky as our horses ascended into the sharp-peaked *montagnes*. All around were high cliffs on each side of the road. Muhammad kept speaking to his horses in an affectionate voice, as if they were his children. Less than a league, the road began to descend into a valley and a small village edged up the side of one *montagne*.

At first, the village seemed an illusion of floating homes hovering along the *montagne* sides. Upon closer observation, numerous stones and timbers supported each house affixing it to the sloped ground. Most of the homes were one-floor structures and the tallest building consisted of a small single-towered church. At first glance, the village appeared destitute with several houses having collapsed roofs.

"Lord de Borron, we have at last reached Gavarnie!" Commander de Érail shouted. "Now we can rest in some real beds tonight."

Sergeant de Béziers commented, "Hot food and *non* campfire tonight!"

At the moment, even a poor broken-down village excited my fellow comrades.

Commander de Érail laughed at the enthusiasm of his men, and even Muhammad smiled.

"It does my heart well to see my men happy." Our commander looked toward the church. "First, I must see the local priest to help with our accommodations. Hughes, assist Sergeant Guy as he sees to our horses; afterward, join Lord de Borron and me at the *église*."

After dismounting, we ascended a narrow muddy path to the church, while noticing a few local villagers staring at us from their open windows. Some of them waved while others merely frowned. *Such a strange greeting*, I thought.

The parish priest, who came out of his church, looked small in stature, but he displayed a huge grin. His happy smile and raised hands to Heaven indicated he recognized our group.

"*Bienvenu, bienvenu, mon ami*, I am quite pleased to see you, Commander Gilbért de Érail. It has been a long time since your last visit. Come inside, all of you." The priest rounded the six of us up and drew us inside toward the narthex, as a hen would do with her chicks.

"It appears you have brought several newcomers with you this time. Please, come inside and rest; all of you look exhausted."

I wondered if the priest was always this affable with visitors. It appeared he longed for seldom-seen visitors and the sight of his *bon ami*, Commander Gilbért, livened his day.

"*Oui*, indeed, it has been a while," Commander Gilbért replied. "Let me introduce you to Lord Robert de Borron from Burgundy. He just joined our holy order. *Abbé* Jean de St. Gaudens and I go back a long time, and we are close *amis*."

"My pleasure to meet you, *Abbé*. Commander de Érail knows so many excellent *amis*." The priest welcomed me with a hardy embrace and then crossed himself.

"*Dominus vobiscum*, Lord Robert, and what brings you to my humble parish from your distant homeland?"

"*Pax vobiscum* to you, *Abbé* Jean . . ." I hesitated not knowing how to answer his question.

"He's quite modest, and I am sure Lord de Borron wouldn't mind for me to answer your question. He's a noted writer and poet in his province of northern Burgundy and helping our order collect and translate some ancient holy books." Commander de Érail chose his words with care. "We're on our way to Toledo in the province of New Castile. Many months have transpired since I have seen my old commandery at Zaragozza. I know I have much paperwork waiting for me, and my fellow *frères* long to see me.

"*Abbé* Jean, we're in need of refreshment and rest. Is it an imposition upon your village for warm beds and hot food for the night?"

"*Non*, Commander Gilbért, you know you're always *bienvenu* here in Gavarnie. My conscience wouldn't forgive me if I allowed the Poor Fellow-Soldiers of Christ to leave without offering our hospitality. I'll have my young assistant attend to the arrangements at our local inn."

"Pierre," he called to a young boy sweeping the church nave. "Run to the inn and have Renard arrange some rooms for our guests." The young boy nodded and ran barefoot out of the front entrance of the church.

"We receive few visitors to our humble village, and your visit will excite the young boy's speed." The priest smiled. "I expect he will move faster than anything he has done today. I am sure he will arouse the whole village. It isn't every day we have a lord from Burgundy visit us."

"*Abbé*, are you sure the rest of the village thinks the same way as you do?" I asked. "Some of the villagers didn't seem too welcoming and hid as we passed their homes, leaving me perplexed as to why they were afraid of our presence."

"It's not as bad as it appears, Lord de Borron. Seldom has our humble village seen Templar *chevaliers* and a Saracen lord from the Outremer. Furthermore, some of our people are suspicious because they are Cathars. Once they know you won't cause them harm, they'll greet you with more friendship."

A short time later young Pierre returned, motioning for us to proceed. Commander de Érail said *au revoir* to *Abbé* St. Gaudens and thanked him for helping us. He gave the young boy a small silver coin and left a donation for the parish church.

The young boy's eyes widened while admiring his new silver coin. Then I added two more silver coins to his small hand. Instantly, his mouth gaped open and once more he ran outside. I then heard him exclaim to his *amis* and the village people of his newfound wealth.

"Lord de Borron, I don't think my fellow parishioners will hide from you now," *Abbé* St. Gaudens said with a belly laugh.

I reached for my poke that held three gold coins tied to the inside of my tunic and untied the drawstring

"*Abbé*, I wish to donate these three gold coins to your church. The matters of nobility and wealth are worthless unless combined with the power of God. I know you have already blessed us and will pray for our safe journey; however, would you pray for my *épouse* and children? Also, my *soeur* and my departed *mère* and *père*." *Abbé* St. Gaudens's eyes grew larger than young Pierre's when he looked into the small pouch.

"*Oui*, and bless you, Lord de Borron. This will indeed help the needy. What's the name of the loved ones for whom you desire prayers?"

At once, I gave him all their names, which he repeated several times to memorize them. "I expect no prayers for me, but please accept these gifts for the greater glory of our God and His Son, Jesus the Christ."

"*Abbé*, your cooperation and hospitality have pleased my men and me," Commander de Érail gave him a respectful bow.

We finished our *au revoirs*, left the church, and we spied young Pierre, who had perched himself on top of a small stone wall. He saw us come down the steps and shouted at us to follow him. We passed the village fountain, where our horses were drinking and looked back at the village church and saw *Abbé* St. Gaudens still waving *au revoir* with an exuberant smile on his face.

The roads were sticky brown from recent rain and each step almost sucked my boots from my feet. From some distance, I saw a whitewashed inn clinging to the side of a large hill, which amazed me that this large-sized structure remained affixed to the side of the mountain. It grew two stories in structure, and its sides were composed of large timbers and wattle. The smooth daub reflected its recent whitewashed color. The inn rested about a third of a league from the village fountain.

Alongside the inn stood a large stable, sufficient in size to bed our horses for the night. First, we focused on our horses and Muhammad, as usual, told Commander de Érail he wanted to stay with the horses tonight. Likewise, young Hughes desired to attend the horses. Also, he informed his commander this would allow Muhammad a chance to scout around the village. Commander de Érail, pleased with the foresight of his young squire, agreed, and the remaining four of us started to proceed inside the inn. How odd, the extravagant exterior and interior didn't compare to the rest of the village homes. Both the inn and the tavern were brand new, with weighty new trestle tables and ornately carved chairs throughout. I wondered why a poverty-stricken village had such a grandiose inn.

A door opened from a side room and a stocky, narrow-eyed man greeted us. "It's a great honor to have *chevaliers* of the Temple to visit my establishment. They call me Marcel de Tournay, and I am the proprietor of this humble inn. My cook will prepare a meal for your men, Commander de Érail. I hope you enjoy our Pyrénées *Montagnes* food."

"What happened to Renard the innkeeper? We were told he would meet us here," Commander Gilbért asked.

"He's my business partner, and he just left to visit some sick relatives in another village," replied the innkeeper.

"How did you know my name, *Monsieur* de Tournay? I haven't introduced myself." I heard the doubt in Commander de Érail's question. His suspicious questioning and my confusion left me not trusting this man.

"Your excellent reputation has preceded you. Besides, young Pierre described you as the biggest man among your *chevaliers*. Let me direct you to the tables and pour your men some special *vin* from my excellent reserves."

De Tournay's smarmy demeanor didn't bode well for our overnight stay. Even without Commander Gilbért's unusual scowl, I had a bad impression about this man. Nevertheless, the *vin* tasted exceptional and he continued to keep our cups full. A short time later, his cook brought out a large salver of meat and slid it on our table. The meat smelled delicious; it had a slight sweet taste and looked lean. I hadn't savored meat such as this and inquired as to its origin.

"Is this venison, *Monsieur* de Tournay? I haven't tasted meat comparable to this."

"*Non*, it's a wild animal we call an ibex. They're most plentiful in the higher elevations of our *montagnes*. Are you planning on crossing over our lofty *montagnes*?" I glanced at our commander, wondering what to say, but he took the initiative and spoke.

"Proprietor de Tournay, my men are on a journey to a holy site. We need to protect it from robbers and murderers."

"What site might this be?" He then displayed a thin smile, which raised *Monsieur* de Tournay's pink facial scar.

"It doesn't concern you to know our mission," snapped Commander de Érail, his eyes narrowed for emphasis.

"I am sorry for my effrontery. Please forgive me, Commander. I'll let your men eat undisturbed. If you desire anything else, please, don't hesitate to ask. I'll try to fulfill my duties as your humble inn-keeper while you are visiting our fair village. Your sleeping quarters are upstairs and down the hall to the right. *Chevaliers*, I hope you have a pleasant slumber."

De Tournay then left, proceeded to open the door from whence he came, and disappeared into his living quarters.

"That man isn't trustworthy," Sergeant Guy de Béziers said in a hushed voice. Sergeant de Hoult concurred with a nod. They both looked at their commander for his opinion.

"I agree, Sergeant Guy," stated Commander de Érail. "First, de Tournay has a military man's background and knows nothing of innkeeping. *Mon frères,* did you notice his forearms? They were larger than that of an average man. He has brandished a sword and shield often in battle. The scars on his cheek and above his eye are sword scars. Also, I observed a dagger pommel peeking out of his boot, which I'm sure he thought we didn't see.

"Sergeant de Hoult, I want you to speak to the *Abbé* Jean about Marcel de Tournay and the inn. Afterward, report back here and oversee the first watch outside our rooms. I will relieve you when I am rested, and then you can obtain some much-needed rest.

"It appears Marcel could work for the cardinal, but I am still not sure. And if you noticed, I didn't go into much detail about our mission with *Abbé* St. Gaudens. Also, I sense something odd about my old *ami's* demeanor. He was too quiet.

"I didn't mention this before, Lord de Borron, but the cardinal and his *chevaliers* enjoy persecuting the people of this region called Occitania. Cardinal Folquet desires to steal their lands. Cardinal Folquet wants to increase his financial power at the expense of the Cathars' so-called 'heretical faith' by taking their fiefdoms. This is one of several pieces of his power grab. We and the parchments are another evil blackmail tool to help him gain the papacy.

"Don't consume too much *vin* tonight: that will cause us to fall into a deep sleep. Fellow *frères*, stay alert to any unusual noises. Please, pardon me; I must speak to Muhammad and my squire, Hughes."

Commander de Érail jumped up from his unfinished meal and proceeded outside toward the stables. His keen insight had answered several lingering questions that plagued my mind. I now suspected, somehow, that de Tournay indirectly caused the young noblewoman's death at the falls. However, there were several men here, me included, who would consider it an honor to revenge her death. In addition, this would explain the reason for some of the fear gripping the villagers.

The rest of us finished our meal, left the dinner table satiated, and trudged up the wooden steps toward our rooms. Each of my companions strolled to their quarters, as I did the same. My room overlooked the church and the stables. The sound of church bells now pealed in the distance. The large bed had fancy-trimmed lace linens covering the mattress and pillows, and the room air smelled of acrid paint.

On a square oak table stood a large clay pot filled with water, a wooden washing bowl, and several towels. At another table lay a flagon of *vin* and several goblets. In a far corner stood a wooden commode chair and several more linens placed on the arms. The bed tempted me, but the whole place seemed like a trap, prompting me to stay alert. I thought it an excellent time to continue my work on the *Sangraal* book. However, my writing materials were still in my saddlebags. Thus, I proceeded back out of my room into the hallway. Sergeant de Hoult had already returned and posted himself next to the stairway facing the front entrance.

"Where are you going, Lord de Borron?"

"I need to obtain my writing materials. They're in my saddlebags." I descended the creaking wooden steps and he followed me. Commander de Érail stood next to Squire Hughes as I approached the stables.

"I forgot to retrieve my writing material before I retired to my room." I started past them when Commander Gilbért tightly grabbed my arm.

"*Abbé* St. Gaudens has vanished," he said with a whisper. "It's a trap."

I looked around and didn't see Muhammad Nur Adin. "What happened to Muhammad?"

"He has just left to scout the surrounding countryside; however, he'll return later tonight. My military training tells me *Monsieur* de Tournay will warn the cardinal's men of our presence. I gave instructions for Muhammad to observe them if this happens. He's to report later tonight. If hostile visitors show up, I have a battle plan we can instigate. I suspect they will try to kill us while we are asleep. Lord Robert, when you go back to your room, prepare your bed for sleep and stuff your pillows under the sheets. Hopefully, the cardinal's men will think we're sleeping.

"The same goes for you, Squire Hughes, here in the stable. Those of us sleeping in the inn will leave by the upper rear windows and rendezvous in the ravine behind here. It's quite important for everybody to stay awake, henceforth, no more *vin*. Each of us must sharpen our weapons and bear a minimum of two daggers on his person. Squire Hughes, grab the crossbows and hide them in the ravine at once." He turned to go but abruptly stopped.

"I have changed my mind, Squire Hughes. After hiding the crossbows in the ravine, I want you to stay with Lord de Borron. Sergeant de Béziers, you stay here close by the stable tonight and wait for Muhammad. Now, let's all retire to our rooms and prepare for tonight. May God protect us as we face whatever threat comes our way." We then crossed ourselves.

I followed Squire Hughes to the stable for my writing supplies and our precious copied parchments. He took a large cloth bag from a stable stall and crept out the back door, with the intention of hiding the crossbows. After a short while, he returned through the same back door, still carrying a full bag.

"You still have the same full bag?" I inquired.

"I just switched them with some rocks in the back of the stable, hence if Marcel de Tournay did spy on us, he will suspect nothing,"

Commander de Érail led the way while Squire Hughes and I followed with my writing supplies and our precious copied parchments. As we passed in front of the inn, the commander nodded his head toward the front window. Marcel de Tournay's silhouette appeared behind a thin curtain, observing us out of the corner of his window. We entered, looked around, and advanced up the steps, with our boots pounding on the wooden stairway until we reached the long hallway to our rooms. Commander de Érail opened a door and disappeared into the room of Sergeant de Bézier. Squire Hughes followed me into my room, carrying my writing supplies. I grabbed two stools for us to sit on and placed my writing material on the table. After sitting down, I heard my *épouse's* voice in my head. I wondered what she, my *soeur*, and my two *fils* were doing while staying at my brother-in-law's *château* at Montbéliard. A worried look appeared on the young squire's face, as his lips pursed and his forehead wrinkled. Then he spoke to me after I had organized my writing material.

"Lord de Borron, this place exudes evil. Its appearance deceives one's heart and mind. I am scared."

"Fear causes you to react in unknown ways in such times as these," I explained. "A man must confront his fears, but a wiser man knows how to respond to that concern. Look toward Commander Gilbért for your human strength in battle. He senses fear the same as all of us but doesn't cower in his room. *Non*, he prepares for it and helps the rest of us in our preparations. You're fortunate to have such a wise and brave Poor Fellow-Soldier of Christ as a mentor."

"*Merci beaucoup* for your confident words, Lord de Borron. *Oui*, indeed God's words work through you in our holy quest. Well, enough of my ramblings; let's start copying what sacred words our Lord has bestowed on you. Before we start, let me ask one favor of you. Tell me what Lord Jesus said at his Last Supper. I think it will calm my nerves for whatever happens here tonight."

I granted Hughes's humble request. I looked at the young squire and saw a beardless smooth face. Just a short time ago, he had left his *mère's* home. Yet, he acted like a man, for his sake and the sake of the other warrior-*moines*. At this point in our quest, part of my responsibilities encompassed protecting his life, as the same importance as protecting one of *mon fils*. At once, I said a prayer, asking my Lord to bless me with success in my task.

"My writing has progressed to this part, in our Lord and Savior's life. You have shortened the time in assisting me to copy Saint Joseph's sacred words. For which I am grateful and much indebted to you."

My words of gratitude further lifted his spirits as he smiled at me with his large dark brown eyes. I read out loud the many sheets of parchment as I spoke of the Last Supper and what Lord Jesus said. The time passed without delay, and then I heard heavy footsteps moving in the hallway. Then came the slight rustling of Commander de Érail's hauberk as he passed our door, followed by a hush-toned voice spoken to Sergeant de Hoult. I didn't know what he said but did hear several doors shut. That meant we must leave and prepare ourselves for battle. Hughes gathered all my completed parchments, writing supplies, and placed them into my saddlebags. He pulled out a sharp-pointed dagger from his tunic and gave it to me.

"Our commander wanted you to have his best dagger. Also, I took the liberty of sharpening your sword the other night while you were asleep, making it in top fighting condition!"

The hilt of the dagger consisted of unadorned yellow ivory, except the pommel. It had a large flat-faced knob attached, which had the splayed red Templar cross on one side and the obverse side had the outline of the Church of the Holy Sepulchre. The dagger seemed light but consisted of well-finished steel with a thickened portion of the steel originating at the guard.

"Where did he procure this unusual dagger?" I asked. "The knife's design and metal I've not seen before."

"Commander de Érail told me it came from Toledo, at the priory that we'll visit. You must examine his sword blade too, which originated in the Levant, at a city called Damascus. His sword can cleave a small log in the hands of my commander. Woe to the man who crosses swords with Commander de Érail."

With care, I draped on my chain mail coif, checked my aketon, leg chausses, and cinched my sword belt to prepare for our trap. Squire Hughes helped me arrange my bed to fool our impending enemies. I handed him my saddlebag of holy parchments to take to the stable. Finishing our tasks, my fingers extinguished the candles and we then crept to a side window to lower a rope. Young Hughes climbed down the side of the inn without a sound. Then I descended the dew-covered sides of the inn. No moonlight shone and the dark night hid our exit. The next to exit their windows were Commander de Érail and Sergeant de Hoult. As we gathered, each of us used hand signals to communicate.

Commander de Érail continued his hand commands as we skulked between the houses. From there, the three of us took a circuitous route on the side of the hill to arrive at a ravine behind the stables. Each of my *amis* delayed himself before crossing the main road.

At last, I crept across the road and, to my dismay, slipped on a muddy patch of ground. I tried to catch myself but fell down hard. My sword and chain mail gave out a loud metallic *thud* as each collided and echoed throughout the sparse outer village. I feared we had lost the element of surprise. I widened my eyes in the darkness while trying to see if de Tournay and his men were coming. Would my sudden clumsiness instigate our failure?

CHAPTER XXVII

I lay there for a short time hoping I hadn't aroused any suspicion. I visualized at any moment, de Tournay and his men would spring upon us with swords drawn, ready to kill. Yet, to my relief, I heard a dog barking off in the distance with a background of chirping crickets. After a short while, no threat materialized. Still in my crouching position, and with the stealth of a cat, I hugged the ground, listening for danger. The rest of the men had disappeared into the ink-black night. The whitewashed sides of the inn were just visible in the distance to my left. I embraced the moist sides of the unlit houses while praying to see my companions. The last house before the ravine seemed large. I touched its corner and after several cautious steps, I crouched down and listened for any sound. The hope of a responsive voice or signal, rather than foe, tugged at my ears and eyes.

To my chagrin, a large open field faced me, which melted into the darkness. I had forgotten about the large dark field between me and my goal. Delaying any further didn't make sense, as I took a deep breath and stepped out to cross. I raised myself to run, but without warning, a hand clamped over my mouth and a curved dagger pressed on my throat. With instant knotted fear in my throat, I waited for the dagger to end of my life. Just as I reconciled my last moments, Muhammad stepped in front of me. He motioned for me to leave. I ran across the open field, and an instant chill came over me. He could have killed me by mistake. He must have the vision of a cat, I realized, or he would have slit my throat. At last, I reached the ravine, where, to my relief, crouched Commander Gilbért waiting for me. On one side of the commander were several dark moving figures, which I assumed were my other companions.

In a hushed voice, he said, "Lord de Borron, I hope you're a better fighter than a walker. I became worried when I didn't see you behind us. I told Muhammad to keep an eye on your back."

"*Merci beaucoup, mon ami*; I won't slip again."

"I suspect more trouble, for our movements haven't gone unnoticed. Muhammad said there are a total of a dozen men on horseback approaching the Gavarnie road. We are surrounded in all directions, and Muhammad has identified them as the cardinal's men."

Commander Érail's face had melted into a tight set of clenched teeth, as he slid his hand on the pommel of his sword. His eyes stared out into the foggy darkness, making me believe he already saw the *chevaliers* approaching the village.

"I have a plan, which I've shared with the others. When the cardinal's men arrive, as expected, they will attack the inn, thinking we are drunk. Their horse handlers will remain outside. My men will use our crossbows to kill them. It's our job, Lord de Borron, to kill the remaining men when they exit the inn.

"I know the cardinal's men will want to kill our horses after they realize we aren't there, but Muhammad and Squire Hughes will protect them. We are outnumbered, two to one, yet we have the element of surprise. I know you're a tenacious fighter and you're not a quitter, but I don't want you and the parchments captured. If for some reason, this fight doesn't result in our favor, I want you to ride the hell out of this place with any of my men who survive. We'll rendezvous at an odd-shaped stone cross near the mountain pass. It's one-third of a league from here and there's a hidden trail into the *montagnes* by it. Notice which way the group of pelicans point their beaks at the bottom of the cross. They should point right and Commander de Polignac told me we'll see a cabin about one league into the mountains. It's a hidden location known solely by him and me."

I started to object, but Commander de Érail interrupted me.

"It's of utmost importance that you and our holy parchments are protected at all cost. My fellow *frères* and I are God's instruments to see you doing his will. We could lose our lives in this fight, but it's for the greater glory of our God and his Son, Jesus the Christ."

"I will do as you have instructed, Commander," I replied. "I agree with you about this quest and our written holy parchments. You have my word, Commander de Érail, yet I have some reservation. I am not happy at the thought of leaving my fighting companions behind and riding away as a coward."

"It requires a warrior to understand a warrior, *mon ami*, but it's God's will you must do this."

We moved along the ravine and stopped closer to the stable and the inn. Muhammad had melted back into the night, and I sensed his eyes focusing on our backs. Sergeants de Hoult and de Béziers were clutching their crossbows, armed and ready to strike with two more on the ground next to them. We heard young Hughes signal with a chirping sound, indicating his readiness to protect the horses. Commander de Érail and I positioned ourselves next to the stable, as we lay on our stomachs covered by a misty fog blanket.

Some time had passed, while we lay in wait, with both of us chilled by the wet darkness of the night. After what seemed an eternity, candlelight appeared, flickering from a second-story window of the inn. The flame stood still at first, but after a short while, the candle started moving back and forth. There's the signal, I surmised.

A hand touched my shoulder and I saw Commander de Érail pointing to our right. Out of the foggy darkness of the night, I observed the ghostly bobbing of horse heads and twelve men leading them. One man, the point *chevalier*, raised his sword as he led the others. They were void of any markings on their surcoats, yet their saddle blankets had the faint partial outline of the cardinal's white *fleur-de-lis* crest on their corners.

As they approached, the front door of the inn edged open and a dark outline of a man appeared, holding a candle. Commander de Érail had predicted this, for six of the men crept inside and the other six stayed outside with the horses. As the men ascended the stairway, we heard their rapid muffled steps echoing out the front entrance. After a short moment of silence, Commander Gilbért gave his hand signal to attack.

The quarrels flew from our crossbows, giving out a sound similar to six hissing snakes as they advanced on their prey Then six metallic thuds were followed by six groans. We jumped to our feet and ran toward the inn entrance. Commander Gilbért raced ahead of us toward the first wounded man, who had reached down to extract the quarrel from his leg. He glanced up, saw Commander de Érail's raised sword, and reached for his with a look of horror in his eyes. With a single downward stroke of Commander de Érail's blade, his opponent's head came off its body with blood squirting in my face.

Another *chevalier* had a quarrel sticking out of his neck but ran toward me with a dagger in one hand and his sword in the other hand. At once, I raised my sword as I sidestepped his downward stroke and smote his dagger arm, dismembering it from his shoulder. He fell forward, squirting more blood on the path.

We had killed all the horse handlers in less time than it took us to cross the ravine. Yet, in the time it takes two heartbeats, came the clamoring of six of the cardinal's men scurrying down the stairway. By now, their horses had scattered, and we were ready for them. All our daggers were drawn, and the five of us were prepared to finish the fight.

As the first two men ran out the front entrance, Commander de Érail used his dagger to stab each in their throats. The remaining four were more cautious and didn't come out of the front door but came at us from the side windows. All four had their swords drawn and rushed toward us from different directions. Nevertheless, we ran at them and when we collided, there rose up a great *clanging* sound from our blades. My attacker, a tall barrel-shaped man with a definite size advantage, kept trying to push me against the inn. Yet, with faster feet, I anticipated his slower moves, but I slipped on an unseen pool of blood and fell backward. To my horror, the sword in my hand flew skyward as I hit the dirt. My left hand still gripped my dagger, but I didn't rise fast enough as the big *chevalier* approached me ready for his kill.

For a fleeting moment, the fear of doom came over me. He took two steps forward, pointed his sword straight downward at my chest, and he too fell backward. To my surprise, he'd slipped on the same pool of blood. At the same moment, I rolled over and plunged the commander's dagger deep into his chest. I reached for my sword, now steadying myself on drier ground. At this point in our battle, the fight seemed over.

All my fellow *frères* were still standing, and twelve bodies lay on the ground. Right away, I thought we were victorious and ran toward my fellow warriors to celebrate. Then without warning, out of the darkness came two sounds, which I didn't want to hear. My ears heard the horrid hissing sounds of quarrels coming through the dark foggy night air. Then came the hair-raising sound of grinding swords coming from their sheaths. Both ominous sounds were a mistake, I thought, for we had defeated the cardinal's men. Now we were the prey caught in a trap, not the cardinal's men. However, the diabolical cardinal had used some of his own men as bait and hid others in the village houses until nightfall. They had waited until now to spring their trap. This explained the villagers' reluctance to greet us.

Glancing to my right side, I saw Sergeants de Hoult and de Béziers standing next to their commander. One quarrel made a dull thud into the inn next to my head. The next one didn't miss but struck Commander de Érail in his left shoulder. Sergeant de Béziers took a quarrel to his thigh. That followed with several misses, further hitting the inn. Sergeant de Hoult and I ran to our companions' aid, yet to my dismay, out of the darkness appeared twelve more *chevaliers* sprinting toward us.

Their commander shouted to us, demanding our surrender. Showing no pain and with a quarrel sticking out of his shoulder, Commander de Érail replied, "We answer to no man, but our Holy

Père in Rome. Now prepare to meet Saint Michael's judgment!" He raced forward, screaming some indistinguishable psalm while holding a raised sword in one hand and in the other brandishing a large dagger. I followed right alongside him, praying Muhammad Nur Adin would soon join in this one-sided fight.

From the ravine, once more came the hissing sound of crossbow quarrels. Right away, I recited a psalm for courage and deliverance, yet, this time the quarrels sailed toward our adversaries. Three of the cardinal's men were hit and each fell backward. Then, out of the dark, foggy night appeared Muhammad carrying three empty crossbows. He threw the crossbows down and pulled out what he called his *Jambiya* dagger, or judgment knife, from behind his surcoat. At the same time, he raised his large scimitar above his head and ran toward the nine *chevaliers*. He screamed the same words I'd heard him say to the horses. "*Allahu akbar, Allahu akbar.*" Muhammad shouted these words many times, drawing their attention away from us, as he swept through the mass of *chevaliers*. He took on the image of a constant moving human scythe mowing down men instead of wheat.

Part of us ran toward their left flank while Commander de Érail joined Muhammad in the thick of the fighting. Countless sparks emanated from our swords and daggers as their sharp edges clashed, illuminating the black night sky around us. The din of the metal hitting metal made communication difficult. I killed one man with a single blow of my sword, with the impact splitting his helmet in the center, causing spurting scarlet rivulets of blood to flow over his forehead and eyes.

We were now in a fight for our lives, yet I remembered what Gilbért de Érail had told me. I must protect the *Sangraal* words at all cost and further my mission. I had to fulfill my oath to my Holy Lord, Jesus the Christ, and to Commander Gilbért.

At this point, the battle appeared a draw; however, there were still five of the cardinal's men standing and not one of them wounded. Commander Gilbért staggered with a quarrel protruding from his shoulders and another, I hadn't seen until now, in his side, though it appeared superficial. Sergeant de Béziers bore two quarrels in his thigh. Suddenly, Sergeant de Hoult screamed out in pain as an attacker's dagger penetrated his side. The odds were turning against us. A man now stalked me with his cat-like movements. He anticipated my every thrust and parry as he glanced at my feet, I moved closer to our horses. He tried to place himself between the horse stall and me, but, to my relief, young Hughes came up behind him and used his dagger to stab him in his armpit. My opponent then fell forward while glancing off my sword arm before collapsing on the blood-soaked ground. I jumped away from the dead man and rushed to my horse. Yet, before mounting, I turned to see how my companions were doing, and, to my surprise, there were three red pattée-crossed men still standing. Outnumbered four to one, we'd defeated our opponents, but at a high cost.

Commander de Érail's wounds appeared severe as did Sergeants de Béziers and de Hoult. Sergeant de Hoult seemed to have the worst injury. He fell to his knees, pulled out the dagger from his side and collapsed sideways on the ground. Squire Hughes jumped over the stall and ran to help him. To my left, out of the corner of my eye, came a shadowy figure on horseback. Not another *chevalier*, I told myself, but a dark phantom rider coming from behind the stable. His face appeared dark as the inside of a tomb. He held a crossbow in his arms and pointed it in the direction of Squire Hughes then fired the quarrel.

"*Non! Non!*" I screamed as I saw the quarrel find its mark deep in the back of young Hughes. He tried in vain to grab his back, but he fell forward on top of Sergeant de Hoult. This *bâtard* rider turned his horse before me, dropped his crossbow, and raised his sword to strike. The first blow stuck in a timber of the stable stall. He moved closer to my horse and tried to grab its reins. Right away, my horse's front hooves reared up in protest. This left me between my rearing horse and the dark rider's horse and sword. To my surprise, he didn't strike me but sliced my leather saddlebag straps that held our precious documents. Now I recognized the real focus of his objective. When he reached down to retrieve the saddlebag, I saw his face. The familiar narrow grin on his sun-darkened scarred face belonged to

Marcel de Tournay. Then, I grabbed the bag from his lowered hand and clasped it under my arm. He kicked me in the face with his chain mail-covered boot, propelling me backward. I screamed with pain, but to God's greater glory, I had wrenched the saddlebags from his grasp with blood gushing from my nose.

My victory didn't last long. With one quick move, he leaped off his horse and raised his sword, ready to strike a fatal blow. Though the blood from my face obscured my vision and my nose crunched from facial movement, my survival instincts caused me to partially dodge his downward blow. His sword struck the earth first, followed by a blow to my chain mail. Another agonizing pain shot through my left shoulder and chest from his downward stroke. Again, he raised his sword.

"Damn it!" I shouted. "Go to Hell, where you belong, you son-of-a-bitch. You aren't about to rob me from my family and our holy quest." Unexpectedly, I heard two loud *thuds*. De Tournay's rotten-toothed grin vanished as his arm fell to his side dropping his sword. To my relief, de Tournay turned around and placed his boot into the stirrup of his horse. Protruding from his back, I saw a throwing dagger and a small battle-ax embedded in his right shoulder. To my chagrin, the wound didn't appear mortal, for his chain mail and aketon had protected him, thus allowing de Tournay to mount his horse. A short distance away stood Muhammad, poised with his long scimitar ready to strike. De Tournay had had enough, with his reins, he whipped his horse, spurred it in the flanks, and escaped toward the open road.

"You will see Marcel de Tournay once again, you *bâtards* of Sainte-Marie. I most enjoyed the young Cathar girl before you buried her!" he lastly shouted. Marcel de Tournay now turned his horse, spurred it once more, and disappeared into the ink-black night. My clenched teeth told me to go after this evil man and seek retribution, but I needed to see to my comrades' grievous wounds.

Muhammad had saved my life twice, and shame still filled me for earlier doubting this noble Saracen prince's integrity.

CHAPTER XXVIII

Muhammad ran toward me to check my wounds. Instead, I motioned him toward the others. I knew their injuries were far worse than mine. Squire Hughes lay on top of Sergeant Hoult, both moaning with pain. As I looked around, the number of dead enemy *chevaliers* appeared unbelievable. The sick-sweet smell of blood filled my nostrils, causing me to cry out, "*Mére de Dieu!*"

Even though my wounds seemed minor compared to those of my companions, I tried to rise but failed. Each breath I took stabbed my chest with pain. Looking around, I saw the son-of-a-bitch Marcel de Tournay's sword still lying on my chest. I used it as a temporary crutch to help me stand on my feet. As I reached to grasp his sword, I swore aloud, "The next time you see this sword raised, I'll send you to Hell. You *bâtard*, Marcel de Tournay won't rule the day and try to interfere with our quest for the *Sangraal*." Did de Tournay command Cardinal Folquet's *chevaliers*? And now it begged the question of how many *chevaliers* were under the cardinal's control?

With great difficulty, I stood with bone-grinding pain and then limped toward Commander de Érail and Muhammad. They were standing near Sergeant de Hoult, who had managed to sit upright. Muhammad propped Sergeant de Béziers up against the side of the inn, with his hand still clutching the two crossbow quarrels, and whispered something into his ear. With each man, he began to remove the quarrels sticking from their bodies. He broke the iron tip from each quarrel shaft that protruded from Sergeant de Béziers and just the shaft from Commander de Érail. Each of the broken shafts he yanked out, with the men just grimacing.

Afterward, he extracted a pouch from his tunic and poured a white powder into each wound opening. When finished, he moved to the commander and treated his injuries the same way. Was there any end to the knowledge of our Saracen *ami*? Strangely, he neglected to do the same for Squire Hughes. The young man still displayed a deep-shafted quarrel embedded in his back. Muhammad spoke to the commander in a quick high-pitched voice, and I assumed from their animated conservation that young Squire Hughes needed additional medical attention.

After the two men had talked, the commander staggered over to his injured men and had Muhammad help assist him to sit. I too staggered toward them, using Marcel's sword as a crutch to toddle, and then sat down next to Commander Gilbért. However, my breathing forced a grinding sound from my chest with each gulp of air. I tried to ignore it.

"Fellow *frères*," the commander said, "what you did here tonight just begins the great battle we now face. You were quite brave *mon frères* and I know the Holy *Père* would bless you. Look around; these men came here with the evil intent to kill us. Your fearlessness and the divine guidance of our Savior helped to defeat these demon monsters. However, this isn't the end of our trials. We know God has chosen us for this task, hence let us raise our level of cautiousness and redouble our efforts to see too the success of finding the second set of *Sangraal* parchments.

"Muhammad tells me my wound might become mortal, and I must have the broken quarrel tip cut out of my side. However, more important, young Hughes's injury appears more grievous than mine. It's imperative that we transport him to a place that has a hospital to provide the care he needs. The nearest Templar hospital-commandery lies twenty leagues over the mountains in the kingdom of Aragón, but it's not reachable in our current condition and de Tournay knows we'll travel there. Lord de Borron, we must prepare at once to leave this hellhole, yet there are some much-needed duties to perform. I must ask for your assistance with one of the responsibilities, even though you didn't escape the sword of our enemies."

"Commander, don't hesitate to assign any task to me and I'll do it. My wounds are but a scratch compared to my dire wounded companions and yourself. What can I do to hasten our departure from this horrible place?"

"Ah, Lord Robert, you're an asset to our quest and not just in the area of your expertise. You're not a sworn soldier of Christ, but you are a true warrior at heart. I am proud to have you at my side in battle." He paused momentarily to gasp for air, his speech becoming labored. "Now, listen closely to what I have to say. Go to . . . *Abbé* Jean de St. Gaudens and convey my . . . purse." He paused. "I believe *Abbé* de St. Gaudens betrayed us. Not for greed or power, but fear for his parishioners' lives. He knew Marcel de Tournay's men were hiding and holding the villagers as hostages."

To my amazement, Commander Gilbért's statement didn't make any sense. He and *Abbé* Jean were close friends. Why didn't the *abbé* signal to us about the cardinal's hidden men?

"Lord de Borron, come closer and listen to what I am about to say. *Abbé* Jean started to tell me about a trap but feared for his fellow villagers. Upon summoning the boy, Pierre, he knew of the possible slaughter of the children too, if he didn't cooperate. Lord Robert, acquire a dozen men from the village and have them bury the cardinal's *chevaliers*. Tell the village men they came here to kill their fellow Cathar men, women, and children, and we foiled their plan. Also, gather up eight of the *chevaliers'* horses and give them to the burial party. Here, accept my purse," he said with a grimace on his face.

"Don't let *Abbé* Jean de St. Gaudens know we suspect him of betrayal. Lord Robert, what would you do if confronted with the same decision as *Abbé* Jean? Some of our decisions aren't easy to decide and we must torture ourselves to weigh the risks."

I knew Commander Gilbért sympathized with his *ami*, but could I have made the same anguished decision and forgiven *mon ami*?

"Let me retrieve it for you, Commander, for you must rest," I said with some authority. He acquiesced and let me grab the purse from his surcoat.

"Lord de Borron, one other thing." Even with his severe injuries, the commander didn't relinquish from issuing orders. "When you return, help Muhammad with the remaining horses." With an extra gasp of breath, he forced his next words. "I have already instructed him to keep four horses out of the dozen for the transportation of the wounded. He will have eight of them tied together for you to present to *Abbé* Jean. He will explain further upon your return. Leave at once, I fear for young Hughes's life."

Commander de Érail appeared still in charge, for as I limped away, he shouted orders telling his disabled men what they were to do next, even though their injuries deemed otherwise.

Muhammad stood waiting to help me mount my horse. Each of the eight horses had a rope tied to their saddles and halters as he handed me the lead rope. As I swung my leg over the saddle of my horse, I cried out in pain from the grinding broken edges of my rib bones rubbing together.

The moonless night, coupled with low-lying clouds of fog, made it difficult to navigate the eight horses through the muddy roads. My one eye remained swollen shut from the blow of de Tournay's boot and the other almost the same. Halfway to the church, I heard a young boy's voice calling from a side path next to a small house. At first a whisper, yet it grew louder as I stopped.

"It's me, Pierre. Do you remember me from the *église*? You look as if you need some help. Were you in a fight?"

"*Oui*, Pierre, I do remember you. Also, you're right; I fought many men to protect your village. Would you lead my horse to the church?"

"*Oui*, I will help you, sir *chevalier*. Was it those strangers . . . who entered our village several days ago? They threatened to . . . kill us if we said anything to you." Pierre's voice quivered as he replied.

"Can you count, Pierre?"

"*Oui, Abbé* Jean taught me how."

"Tell me how many men arrived several days ago."

"There were twenty-four men on horseback. Twelve left yesterday and twelve stayed behind in different houses throughout the village. Sir *chevalier*, we were quite scared when these men arrived. They forced us to feed them and stable their horses. We'd heard about the Templar fierceness in fighting the Saracens and thought you had captured the dark one and you were now here to take us as prisoners too. Half our villagers are of the Cathar faith and some escaped to hide in the *montagnes*. Your Templar *amis* didn't scare me," he boasted. "The tall one, who's leading you, I knew wouldn't capture us after his donation. *Abbé* Jean then left our church and hid in the woods."

By now, we approached the church. "Young Pierre, please find *Abbé* de St. Gaudens at once."

I didn't consider myself a weak man, yet I refrained from dismounting my horse and announcing to the *abbé* my helpless condition.

"*Oui*," he said. His small legs were a black blur as he ran past the fountain and raced into the woods. *Abbé* Jean emerged a short time later and ran ahead of young Pierre in my direction. A sorrowful fear of recognition replaced his normal pleasant smile, as he saw my battered face.

"Lord de Borron, what has . . . happened to you?" He wheezed from racing from the woods. "Do you need . . . medical aid?" Young Pierre told me a great battle ensued over the attempt to execute our Cathar villagers. I know Cardinal Folquet wants their lands. Is this true about the battle?"

"To answer your first question, *non*, but *merci beaucoup* for your concern. To reply to your second question, *oui*, they tried to kill us, but we foiled their plan to kill the Cathars. We engaged in a great battle on the outskirts of your village. Several days ago, the strangers who came here were *chevaliers* from Toulouse, with the definite purpose to seize the Cathars' land. We were victorious for now and you're safe. However, my companions and I must leave right away, and we need your help. Commander de Érail has instructed me to convey his message and ask for your assistance."

"Of course, I'll do whatever he asks."

"You're to obtain a dozen men and bury the dead in unmarked graves. You and your villagers are to remove all traces of weapons, blood, and the *chevalier's* insignias. Donate these horses to those who need them most. Also, Commander de Érail wanted me to contribute his purse of gold coins to share with the men who will help you with this task." I pitched him the small bag of gold coins, causing another sharp pain to shoot throughout my entire body.

"Have no worries, we'll do it right away. Speaking for our entire poor village, *merci beaucoup* for your protection, and may God bless you and Commander Gilbért de Érail."

Quickly, my vision darkened, and I began to swoon. The *abbé* reached for my pain-racked chest and helped steady me back into my saddle.

"Lord de Borron, are you confident you don't need some medical attention or the other wounded men? Let me ask some of our midwives to look at the injured men and attend to your wounds."

"*Non*, my wounds aren't serious; however, I will pass your concerns on to Commander Gilbért. It's urgent that we leave at once and complete our mission."

He noticed the sticky blood on the pouch that I just pitched to him.

"Is Commander de Érail injured, Lord de Borron?"

"*Oui*, he is."

"Will he die?"

"I don't know, *Abbé*, but I must return to him without delay. One other thing Commander de Érail mentioned. If anybody asks what happened, tell them the *chevaliers* fought with the Warriors of Christ and it took place away from the main village."

I turned my horse to leave and gave a feeble *au revoir* to the *abbé*.

"*Pax vobiscum, mon fils*," he replied.

I then halfheartedly spurred my horse in the direction of my fallen *frères* as I heard *Abbé* Jean say a soft-spoken psalm as my horse ambled toward the outskirts of the village. I recognized the psalm, so I whispered it to myself. "Your hand will find out all your enemies; your right hand will find out those who hate you. You will change them into a fiery furnace when you appear. The Lord will swallow them up in his wrath and fire will consume them."

My horse seemed to creep toward my wounded *frères* while I sensed the need to rush back to my companions. Yet, to my chagrin, each hoofbeat jarred my ribs. The hot blood of combat and my survival instincts had masked the pain. I had suffered wounds before in combat, but this new one had incapacitated me. It appeared I had defended myself well and now earned the fighting respect of the Warriors of Christ. The fact that I'd made it back and forth without falling off my horse seemed impossible.

I approached the bloody carnage, still lingering with the sweet sick smell of blood. I needed help to dismount. Then a shadowy image appeared out of the darkness with his scimitar drawn. Right away, he identified me, and Muhammad resheathed his sword. With his determined movements, he helped steady my horse. Normally, I would have refused his aid. For pride and noble bearing still remained important to me, yet with Muhammad, things were different. To him, I had nothing to prove. My sharp burning dismount caused me to scream out, "God have mercy on me."

Muhammad grabbed my waist, and afterward, with much hesitancy, I placed one boot on the ground. Once again, I howled with pain when his hand held my sword belt. He stopped, said something in his native tongue, and made the hand motion of something breaking. I focused my attention on him as he reached down, picked up a small branch of a birch tree and snapped it in two pieces. Taking one broken end, he pointed it all around my chest. It appeared I'd broken numerous ribs. He cut several more branches and again pointed to my chest. Commander de Érail motioned for me to come near. I used my horse to steady myself as I approached him.

"Lord de Borron, did you convey to *Abbé* Jean my message and donate my gold coin purse?"

"*Oui*, I did, and he now sends men from the village to bury the cardinal's *chevaliers*. I told him to bury them in unmarked graves."

"*Bon*, and also you told him what to say happened here tonight?"

"*Oui*, I gave him all your instructions, after which he said a psalm and a final blessing for us. With God's assistance, the villagers won't have to worry about retribution from the cardinal and that *bâtard* de Tournay."

I noticed Commander de Érail's face had turned white and more blood had saturated his white surcoat. The red pattée cross on his chest had become almost invisible from the ever-increasing bloodstain.

"Commander, I must ask for your forgiveness and apologize to you. I didn't do as you instructed and leave with the sacred parchments when things turned for the worst."

Commander de Érail forced a smile through his pain and replied, "No . . . need for apologies . . . or forgiveness. I know you are a righteous man. You did what you thought best, and I am most grateful. However, we need Muhammad's special medicine and surgery. He can do the surgery once we reach the cabin, but he needs your help."

"*Oui*, I will, but let me try to help Squire Hughes."

"*Oui*, by all means, but . . . follow Muhammad's instructions. He now wants you to help him construct a *traîneau*, a primitive sled, for each of us who are wounded and can't travel on foot or ride."

I nodded and then shuffled over to the squire. Young Hughes's chest barely moved as I approached his almost lifeless body. Tears formed in my eyes as I gazed on his pale-colored face. There lay a young boy, who had fought as a seasoned warrior. Overnight, he became more than a man. My pain refused to let me kneel or bend over to treat the young squire; however, I did hear a gurgling exhale of breath. His paleness far exceeded that of Commander de Érail's, and I detected blood oozing from his mouth. He must have sensed I was there, for he reached up for me. He had an icy touch, and I knew my warm hands would give him some comfort.

"I am sorry I abandoned my post, Lord de Borron, but I feared for my fellow *frère* of Christ."

"You need not apologize, for I understand. We were both doing God's will. Now rest, while I help prepare our transportation." I let go of his hand and moved in the direction of our Saracen *ami*.

Muhammad's hurried pace secured the long birch poles to the saddle knob of Squire Hughes's horse. The poles formed an upside-down V shape behind his horse that had eight crisscross-shaped ropes attached. These ropes formed a cradle over which I placed blankets. Muhammad motioned for me to do the same with a stack of loose birch poles he had trimmed. When I was finished, I prepared our horses to leave.

All the *traîneaus* were completed, and we loaded our companions. We backed the horses up to each wounded *frère* and Muhammad deftly lifted and placed our warrior *amis* onto each blanket-covered *traîneau*. Afterward, with care, Muhammad helped me mount my horse. He then leaped on his saddle. We each grabbed two *traîneau* horses to lead. They, in turn, led the supply horses on a long rope lead.

Nothing but moans permeated the stillness as we rode away from Gavarnie with Muhammad and me the only riders. We were triumphant, but at a great cost. Finding a safe place to nurse our wounded companions in time, prompted me to pray and ask for a miracle. Afterward, I heard the faint clanging of the villagers' shovels.

By name, Muhammad whispered into the ears of his horses as they ambled down the dark mist-filled road.

The road ahead leveled out and Muhammad led the way with his lantern. The path we took had few bumps, which didn't elicit pain on the injured. Although we were moving at a dilatory pace, once again my pain rose to make me swoon in my saddle. I didn't know how long I might stay conscious. Muhammad must have heard my moans, for he stopped our horses and gave me a small vial of white thick liquid to drink.

He said in his Saracen accent, "Opium drink," and indicated to me to swallow its milky contents. He repeated his instructions several times along with his hand gestures to my chest. The liquid had a bitter taste as I drank half of it. At once, my pain subsided, and my strength returned. I handed the remaining liquid back to him and we proceeded on our way.

On the eastern horizon appeared jagged fingers of light, yet large dark clouds obscured most of the sun. The sky glowed with a ruby red color as we approached the *montagne* pass.

In the distance, stood a large cross, and as we drew closer, my uninjured eye saw strange chiseled markings with wedge-shaped arms fanning out from its center. There were three stone-carved men, with one holding a chalice. Was this a clue marker for the additional *Sangraal* parchments? At the base were chiseled-shaped pelicans. I counted thirteen as the commander had said. I saw their beaks all pointed right, which indicated the direction to follow. To my surprise, Muhammad continued forward down the road. Later, some distance from the marker, we doubled back through thick woods and leaf-covered ground. This led to a rocky path some leagues up a hill from the marker. Commander de Érail motioned for me to come closer. He tried to speak, but his lips just moved and then he lost consciousness.

All our men needed immediate rest; with the *montagne* cabin our sole hope to hide, in case Marcel de Tournay returned with more *chevaliers*.

CHAPTER XXIX

Dawn had come, yet the sky turned a slate-gray as we ascended the *montagne* path. After about a quarter of a league, the terrain changed from dense birch trees to evergreens. The weather changed at once, causing a stiff breeze to buffet our faces. Muhammad saw to it that extra blankets covered our wounded companions.

We stopped along the rocky trail to eat and refresh our water sacks at a nearby mountain brook. I checked all our wounded men, including the commander and young Hughes, and they didn't appear any worse.

Suddenly, there came a rustling sound from a copse of evergreen trees. I drew my sword without any pain, as a result of Muhammad's mysterious medication.

Through the evergreen boughs appeared two large dark eyes. My sword hand raised while positioning to strike, when a large animal bolted out of the trees and ran down the path in front of us. Indeed, what a strange-looking creature, similar in shape to an elk, yet its antler or horns were quite long and pointed. It did have the coloration of an elk, though its build and weight appeared smaller. The long straight-tipped horns were its most unusual feature. It appeared as if the beast might fall over at any moment. I surmised this was an ibex. Same as the meat served by the *bâtard* Marcel de Tournay.

Muhammad and I continued up the rocky path with our caravan of wounded Templars and our tied horses. The higher we traveled, the colder the air became. About midday, the snow started falling on the thick stands of spruce trees. The air became eerily still, as if in a burial crypt, and each snowflake appeared to grow larger upon hitting the ground.

The snow made the rocky path slippery. Our horses struggled to maintain their footing and the air became quite thin with the horses' breaths snorting for more air. The previous intense pain in my chest had returned, doubling its pain and leaving me gasping for air. I prayed that the thin air hadn't worsened the medical condition of my wounded companions, but I knew otherwise. As if in response to my thoughts, young Hughes started coughing and moaning with pain as we bounced over several uneven rocks.

Again, we stopped to check his condition. Then Muhammad gave him some painkilling white liquid from his vial. The same painkilling medicine I swallowed much earlier. Young Hughes drank it all, choking some after he swallowed the medicine. I noticed foamy blood coming from his mouth each time he had a wheezing cough. This left me with much angst as my insides ached to arrive at the cabin. Then I heard a moaning sound coming from Commander de Érail and knew he had regained consciousness. Muhammad left the care of the young squire and listened to Commander de Érail issue forth mumbled words. I pulled on my horse's reins to tell Muhammad to speed up our horses. After he had spoken his last words to the horses, we began moving faster. The miracles this man performed with his horses and medicine stupefied me. We were blessed by his presence and I considered him a fellow *frère* in arms.

The winds now roared, and the falling snow started to obscure my vision. Up ahead, a narrow path came in sight, which didn't seem wide enough for our *traîneau* poles to fit. This dangerous path left us with a grave problem. Once any of us started down this narrow ledge, we couldn't turn around.

Muhammad frightened me, for he grabbed the reins of the commander's horse with one hand and with the other used his scimitar to hack away evergreen boughs blocking the way. This exposed a bottomless drop that fell down the entire side of the mountain. Muhammad continued hacking tree limbs and pulling the harness of Commander de Érail's horse, then they disappeared into a white curtain of snow. For the safety of each man, Muhammad dismounted and then with hand signals told me to wait while he led one horse at a time down the icy path. Although it seemed an eternity, after a short while he returned.

All that remained were the horses we'd captured at Gavarnie, which were tied to one another's bridles. They pulled on the lead horse that I held and whinnied with fear. Muhammad untied each one and ambled toward the icy, narrow path. I watched one horse screech above the howl of the wind as it tumbled off the icy path and disappeared into the white miasma below. This horse wasn't one that Muhammad had trained. Muhammad came back a short time later to retrieve my horse that bore Squire Hughes on the *traîneau*. I followed close behind, checking my footing with each step. The path's width would let a horse travel through, but the wind forced each of us to cling to the side of the mountain as we started our descent.

After I had traveled a short distance on the icy rock path, to my dismay, I remembered the fallen horse carried our meager food supplies and blankets. The trail seemed to last forever, and the wind didn't cease. My chain mail froze with ice, and the extra weight made each step almost impossible. Up ahead, I saw the white shadowy outline of several horses. The closer we advanced, the clearer their appearance. My body ached from exhaustion, combat, the thin air, and my injuries beckoned me to lie down and sleep. At this point on the trail, I didn't care whether we reached our destination. Frightened by my thoughts, I realized that my horse, Hughes, and I were becoming casualties of the weather. My inner voice told me not to let my exhausted body and mind contribute to this young man's death. My indefatigable desert horse continued at her steady plodding pace until we reached the others.

The snow had drifted into a large cirque, where the dangerous mountain path ended. Our *traîneau* horses trudged with great difficulty into the many drifts as the air grew colder.

Each *traîneau* appeared as an enormous chunk of ice, creeping to some unknown white-colored destination. We traveled about half a league into the valley when I spied a steaming sky blue-colored lake surrounded by pure white snow.

"*Mon Dieu!*" I exclaimed and at once crossed myself. "Commander de Érail, can you see the steaming lake in front of us?" I shouted in a loud voice.

"*Oui.*"

As we drew closer to the lake, its much-needed heat began to melt the icy grip from my saddle. However, the air around it smelled of rotten eggs. I didn't mind the smell, for the heat from the lake caused my wounded *amis* to stir and weakly gaze toward the warm steam. After a short stay at the lake, the hot steam dislodged the ice from our chain mail, swords, and helms. My hands and feet were now warm, making it difficult for me to leave this lake. After a short time, I noticed Commander Gilbért motioning for me. I saw this a good sign and moved closer toward him. In a hoarse voice, he wanted me to go with Muhammad to hunt for some food. We left the thermal lake and traveled to the opposite bank. With a crossbow, we shot a dozen fat birds, then we returned a short time later with them. Their color matched the snow and its surroundings. They weren't similar to any birds that I remembered, but it didn't matter.

"The locals call them . . . ptarmigans," Commander Gilbért weakly announced. "You'll enjoy eating them in hot soup."

A short time later, we reached the end of the valley and started climbing upward along a wider path. High into the mountain, I saw a small clearing and a log cabin in the middle. "*Mère de Dieu, merci beaucoup!*" I called out in the cold air. Without warning, three large dogs appeared in front of us. More appeared as we neared the cabin and that's when I heard a blood-curdling howl. These were timber wolves and not the farmer's *montagne* dogs. They trotted near the timberline at first, as we stared at each other. A large white-colored lead wolf gave out a long guttural howl and then ten more wolves appeared from the pine trees. The pack totaled a dozen. Our wounded *frères* and the game we had killed drew them to us. Now we confronted another obstacle to reach the cabin.

The light of the day had dwindled to a dark gray, snow-filled sky as we arrived at the cabin. Muhammad jumped off his horse into the thigh-deep snow and handed me the crossbow and several quarrels. I kept watching, while he struggled through the deep snow to reach the cabin door. He returned a short time later with several flaming pitch torches and placed them around the horses. Afterward, he began taking our wounded companions inside as I watched the wolves. He later returned and unhooked the *traîneau* from the saddle knobs and then trudged back inside for more wood to set up protective fires around the horses. With this chore completed, he headed through the deep snow to assist me from my horse. I appreciated he'd kept up my false sense of health for the morale of the other men. He grabbed my arm and sword belt and lowered me into the deep snow. He then returned inside to help our wounded *frères*.

"Damn it," I cursed, as my feet sank in the snow. Then to my torment, I saw the wolves circling closer. I slipped and fell into the snow as I approached the cabin porch steps. My chest pain slowed me from rising, but the wolves were now closer. Hell with the pain, the alternative was obvious. I crawled the remaining distance to the door, watching the pack approach the cabin path.

After entering the cabin, I observed spacious accommodations with one large fireplace that needed attention to warm ourselves and cook the food. Most of my companions were lying on the bare dirt floor next to one another. My pain-racked body bent over to check the chimney flue.

"It's not plugged with debris, and we can start a fire!" At once, I started to remove my gauntlets to use a starter flint, yet my metal gloves stuck tight to my hauberk. With one quick swing against the stone fireplace, my gauntlets released their icy grip. After shuffling around the cabin in search of fire starter material, I spied a small tinderbox with sufficient kindling and straw stuck in an inglenook. As I struggled with pain, I picked out my fire starter supplies from the inglenook and started a small fire in quick order with a small log.

A moment later, Muhammad entered the cabin wearing an ice-encrusted beard. At once, a happy grin came over his face upon seeing the roaring fire. He strode near the fireplace, warmed himself, and then made his way in my direction. He stopped in front of me, stared at my face with his coal-black eyes that held my attention for a moment. At first, I thought he'd speak to me but instead talked to my companions in his native language. Was he testing me or just didn't want to speak in my native tongue? However, either way, he held me at a disadvantage as he spoke in his high-pitched Saracen voice. Shortly thereafter, his grin disappeared.

"Lord de Borron," Commander Gilbért said. "Muhammad says we are in dire need of water." Muhammad motioned for me to grab the bucket sitting in the corner. Instead, I stood there hoping to force him to communicate with me in my language. However, he didn't but proceeded through a series of hand sign motions, which looked similar to cutting food. I started for our door and once again Commander de Érail spoke to me in a low whisper.

"He wants you . . . to fill the wooden barrel in the corner with water, but . . . first go outside with a wooden bucket to pack it with snow. Later, help him prepare the ptarmigans for us to eat. While he's caring for us, he wants you to guard the horses against the wolves and keep the fires burning. Your injuries are severe, but the rest of us have lost more blood."

As I stepped out of the cabin door into a large snowdrift, a mace-hitting wind stung my cheeks. The cold air sucked the warmth of the fireplace from my body and caused my hands to shake as I filled the buckets with snow. I grabbed the few remaining dry blankets from our horses and returned inside. Muhammad had removed the men's wet blankets, and I placed new ones on each man.

Afterward, I trudged back outside to retrieve the ptarmigans and heard the high-pitched whinnying sounds of all our horses. The horse with the ptarmigans had just kicked a large white-colored wolf. The bloody body lay a short distance from his back hooves. With horror, I spied my horse with her front legs raised to stave off an attack by two large wolves. Their eyes glowed fiery red. With their pink gums and snarling teeth exposed, they gave out a low throaty growl. The black wolf saw me first and lunged toward me. I sidestepped his attack and used my heavy oak bucket as a weapon. It came crashing down on his muzzle and forehead with a cracking sound. He emitted a painful *yelp* and retreated. The second wolf backed me against my tethered horse with its four legs crouched to attack. It lunged for my throat just as I rolled under the belly of my horse. She reared on her hind legs, giving the wolf another chance to rip at my throat. Was this my demise, a juicy meal for a pack of wolves?

CHAPTER XXX

I heard the familiar hissing sound of the crossbow. Silent and lethal in the right hands, no man or beast stood a chance of withstanding the lethal power of two crossbow quarrels from finding their marks. This time their target wasn't me, but the dead wolf lying on my bruised body. Muhammad approached me, carrying his crossbow, and then pulled the dead wolf off my chest.

Afterward, he reached down to grab my hand. Pain or no pain, I wanted to stand. I didn't know what had happened to the other wolves until I stared at my surroundings. Red-stained snow and dead wolves littered my view in all directions.

Mon Dieu, without Muhammad's quick actions, my body posed a feast for this bloodthirsty pack. I said a silent prayer, thanking my Savior for this fearless man and his friendship.

"*Merci, mon ami*, I owe you my life once more. How . . . can I ever repay you for what you've done for me?" To my surprise, he replied in my native tongue.

"You are *bienvenu, mon ami, Seigneur* Robert. I am confident if the situation were reversed, you would do the same for me."

I don't know if I was relieved to communicate with him or amazed that he knew my language. Commander Gilbért had only spoken to Muhammad in his native language. I now felt a great sense of relief and surmised he now trusted me.

"We have much to discuss," I replied, "however, let's postpone this for later. Right now, there's much to do and let us not waste time communicating. Yet, rest assured I won't forget this day."

"I have no doubt, Lord Robert. You aren't a man easily fooled, and you have proven this and, *oui*, I agree we can't waste time."

We were fortunate to have sufficient cut firewood on the cabin porch without using our cache inside. As we struggled to step back to the cabin, I thought how odd a pair we made, two *chevalier* warriors, one from northern Burgundy and the other from the Outremer. If my *épouse* saw us now, she wouldn't believe her eyes. Living in a frozen *montagne* cabin, with wounded Soldiers of Christ, and helped by a Saracen, desert prince. Our God does have a sense of humor.

As I stood warming myself, I watched Muhammad prepare each of my companions for medical treatment by gingerly removing their chain mail and aketons. They weren't a pleasant sight to see. Both sergeants were still oozing blood, with inflamed red streaks coming from each puncture marks. Squire Hughes's wound showed the quarrel had penetrated deep into his back and the shaft-feathered end neared his skin. Blood trickled from the corner of his mouth, and he emitted a low moaning sound with each shallow breath.

After a dozen trips outside to obtain snow, the barrel filled with a cold slushy liquid. Muhammad dipped some of the water out of the barrel and poured it into a large black cauldron hanging over the fire.

Taking out my dagger, I started cleaning the birds, finishing each as fast as possible, and afterward, placing them on a spit to cook.

My strength and stamina were on the verge of collapse. Muhammad must have noticed my condition, because he had cut several large sheets of cloth and approached me with their finished narrow strips.

"Lord de Borron, let Muhammad wrap these cloths around your chest," said Commander de Érail. "Your ribs were broken by that son-of-a-bitch de Tournay. Let Muhammad tightly wrap them. At first, it will make it hard to breathe, but this will help the pain, and they'll heal faster. After he's done with you, grab those wooden bowls on the table and help Muhammad prepare soup for all of us. This particular soup will strengthen us after our surgery. Muhammad's doctor skills are excellent, but we are short on medical supplies.

"He'll have to probe me for the broken quarrel tip and prevent any poison from coursing through my body, we have little time . . . do what he says." Commander Gilbért took a deep breath. "You'll have to assist him with the medical procedures and also help raise the men up several times during the day. Otherwise, our lungs will soon fill up with fluid from no movement."

Muhammad stepped toward the commander as though to treat him first, but Commander Gilbért pointed to young Hughes.

"*Non,* not me first. Squire Hughes has greater needs than mine. You must do what you can for the others, and then come back to me last."

Muhammad didn't seem surprised by this order; hence, he motioned for me to assist him in lifting Hughes to a large table used for eating. There we sat him in one of the chairs and covered him with more blankets. Apparently, young Hughes's wound was beyond the Saracen's medical skills. His lack of action left a lump in my throat. Muhammad approached the two sergeants, applied fresh bandages to each, along with several poultices.

Muhammad and I helped the weakened commander to another large table, where we laid him face up to remove the broken quarrel tip.

"Well, it's now time for me, Lord Robert. I apologize for the dire responsibility placed on your shoulders. When we first met, I spoke about you translating and copying Saint Joseph's holy book and nothing more. Yet, here we are, and plans have changed. We have had some setbacks, but our focus hasn't changed. Our sacred quest remains the same. Your faith and leadership skills have sustained us under our current dolorous circumstances. I am much in your debt for this. As soon we're able, we'll mount up and continue our search for the next set of *Sangraal* parchments."

Muhammad gave Commander de Érail some blue liquid to drink, after which his voice grew to but a whisper, with his eyes fluttering several times, causing him to drift out of consciousness. His face appeared as white as the outside snow from the loss of blood as Muhammad prepared to make his first cut. There, lying on the large wooden table sat a small surgical bag. He removed various instruments from it and then placed them in the boiling water of the cauldron. I counted ten surgical tools of different shapes and sizes; however, most of them were strange-looking to me.

With systematic care, he tore and arranged clean bandages on the table next to his medical bag. After he had prepared the bandages, he poured some of the boiling water into one of our buckets. He took some snow from the water barrel and cooled the liquid, afterward proceeded to wash his hands and arms with a strong-smelling soap. He repeated this same process for some time, even to the point his dark skin reddened from the constant scrubbing.

Muhammad poured a red-colored liquid on the commander's chest, rubbing it over his entire upper body. After finishing, he made a small incision in his shoulder. The incision started above where the quarrel had entered. Muhammad reached for a long probing instrument with a set of tongs from the fireplace. Laying it aside, he placed the probe to cool on a clean cloth. When it had cooled, he started probing for the broken quarrel tip.

After a short period, a smile came over his face. He extracted several more instruments from the hot bubbling water, placing them on the table to cool. With delicate precision, he next used a long narrow tool, which appeared similar to the fireplace tongs, except much thinner in size. He stuck the small tong's pointed tips inside Commander de Érail's front shoulder, alongside the probe. Delicately, he removed the tongs after retracting the probe. There, between the bloody tips, glistened the remaining quarrel broken blade. This piece matched the broken tip of the quarrel he had removed at Gavarnie, and his completed procedure drew smiles on both our faces.

The wound exhibited flowing blood in a slow pulsating fashion. However, all at once, the flow ceased, which caused Muhammad's face to drain itself of blood. He put two of his shaking fingers on Commander Gilbért's neck and held them there.

"His heart is failing. Lord Robert, move out of the away."

Muhammad started pressing on the commander's chest and then breathed into his mouth. This procedure continued for some time, followed by an intermittent pause to touch Commander Gilbért's neck. Beads of sweat formed on Muhammad's forehead as his chest pumping increased. I feared that Gilbért was dying and said a prayer. May God keep this holy warrior alive.

CHAPTER XXXI

My prayer was answered, for the blood started flowing again and Commander Gilbért's chest rose upward and continued in its breathing motion.

I tried to help, but Muhammad stopped me before I touched the commander's chest. He told me to use the soap and water before touching Commander de Érail.

While I washed my arms and hands, Muhammad pulled out of the cauldron a curved needle with a long thread attached. I took one of the clean cloths, dried my hands and arms, and with another clean cloth started wiping up the weak stream of blood coming from Commander de Érail's side chest and shoulder. I used several clean towels to stanch the blood as Muhammad started the thread deep inside the wound. As he worked, he poured a moldy-smelling green liquid into the dark wound opening. Blood still trickled out, but to a lesser degree as he completed stitching the outside of his chest. We bandaged the commander. Afterward, Muhammad poured the same green liquid down Gilbért de Érail's throat. Right away, he awoke, with his eyes glazed over, and started coughing. After finishing his coughing spell, he whispered a few words.

"See after Squire Hughes and my men first." After he had finished speaking, our battle-scarred commander drifted back into a semiconscious state. He still worried about his men above all. Muhammad hadn't listened to Commander Gilbért, and his medical procedures saved the commander's life.

Both Muhammad and I set to work and repeated similar surgical procedures on the remaining *frères*. Afterward, he gave the young squire several potions, dressed his wound once again, but didn't remove the quarrel.

After placing Commander de Érail in his chair, I began to swoon with pain and exhaustion. Muhammad rushed to help me sit on the last remaining chair. He took off my shirt, removed the previous bandages that exposed my entire chest to its purple-black color. The lumps on both sides of my ribs had grown to large swollen egg-shaped knots. Muhammad took some hot water from the cauldron and mixed powder into a large bowl. The yellow paste thickened at once, as he lathered it across my chest with meticulous care. After rubbing the paste on my chest, he took some new narrow-sized strips of cloth and started wrapping them around my chest. He did this several times, with each narrow strip pulling a little tighter. When at last he finished, I gasped for air. The bandages also prevented me from bending. However, Commander de Érail knew the results; after the bandages stiffened, the pain subsided.

To my surprise, the broken ribs hadn't affected my appetite, for I consumed two bowls of the ptarmigan soup. After finishing, I grabbed Squire Hughes under his arms and dragged him to a corner near the fireplace, after which I poured him some broth in a wooden bowl. Supporting his head, I held the bowl to his lips and allowed him to drink his fill. This gave him the strength to speak.

"Lord de Borron, please dip me some more delicious broth." His eyes were glassy. "I know this sounds silly, but did we defeat all of the cardinal's men?"

"*Oui*, we did, and we were outnumbered four to one. You were quite brave, *mon ami*. I want to thank you for saving my life and coming to the aid of Sergeant de Hoult. When both of you are better, he wants to thank you himself. Now finish your second bowl of broth; its contents will strengthen you."

Though I was exhausted, I shook the sleep from my head, sat down next to young Hughes, and started giving him the final details of our battle. Sitting close to him, it seemed as if I were back at *Château* Borron telling my oldest *fils* of past events. A smile came across Hughes's face as I looked into his eyes. Then the smile changed to a set of pursed lips.

"My wound prevents me from leaving the safety of the cabin. Yet, I know you can't transport me with the rest of the men. Don't say anything, for I know you will deny it, but I can't ask you to take me any farther."

"There's nothing you can say, which will force me to agree you are a burden," I replied. "Besides, you're an important member aiding these warrior-*moines,* and we need you. Let's not waste your strength worrying about such things; instead, think about your recovery. Also, remember our Heavenly *Père* protects each one of us, and we've made it this far in our holy quest."

"I am grateful for your pleasant words and the kindness you have shown me, Lord de Borron. It's something I shall never forget, whether I am still here on earth or with my Heavenly *Père*. However, I have two . . . requests of you." The young squire's voice now whispered as he spoke, causing me to move closer to his lips.

"Go ahead and ask, Hughes. You know I'll try to grant your requests." Before he continued, he relapsed into an unconscious state. With caution, I straightened his head and checked his breathing moments. His chest still heaved with each breath, yet there were long pauses between inhaling and exhaling. I sat there for a short time making sure he rested fine.

I stood and then stepped outside. The horse fires had dissipated some, but the flames still crackled. I spied a half dozen large and small logs leaning against the cabin that I might use to start the fires roaring once more. The horses welcomed the extra heat, for their legs danced with activity. Muhammad followed me a short time later and brought two buckets of oats, which needed rationing.

After completing the feeding of the horses, Muhammad started chopping some small-size pine trees to erect a large lean-to. The tall poles were quite straight, which helped hasten our chore. We propped them against the roof of our cabin and proceeded to lay pine boughs on them. It took numerous poles to span the width of the roof before we were finished. One side of the lean-to, I laced with short poles and pine boughs. This stopped the prevailing icy winds from entering the area the horses would stay. Muhammad packed snow on the lean-to roof, thus keeping the pine boughs in place from the wind. I finished the rest of the work while Muhammad struggled back in the deep snow to check on our wounded companions. The remaining chopped wood I threw on the bonfires, after which I led the horses to their new shelter.

After I'd finish tethering them, I met Muhammad at the cabin door. He opened it for me, and the cabin's warm air stung my face.

I sat near the hearth, contemplating what to do next with the satisfaction of knowing our recent trials were over. However, we still had the sorrowful task of changing bandages, checking the wounds, and moving my companions around the cabin, keeping their lungs clear. Squire Hughes concerned me the most, as Muhammad and I raised him up, yet his feet and legs just dangled across the floor. His face dripped with sweat over his hot red cheeks and forehead onto his warm chest. Muhammad gave him an extra dose of his green liquid after moving him around the cabin. He became more lucid with each swallow of medicine. On his last trip, before I sat him down, he spoke to me.

"Lord de Borron, I must ask you to finish your book before we leave this cabin. It's quite crucial to me." I noticed how alert his eyes were as he spoke. "Also, tell my beloved commander, if permissible, to invest me as a *chevalier*. If anything happens, I want to die as a *chevalier* in the order of the Poor Fellow-Soldiers of Christ."

"This request I'll ask and recommend to your commander." I held back the tears I sensed forming. "*Merci* for asking me to help carry out your wishes; however, I don't think it will require any discussion. The commander respects you and all you have done while under his command. Also, I will complete our copy and the translation of some of Saint Joseph de Arimathea's words before we leave."

"Since serving as Commander de Érail's squire, my life has changed. He has allowed me to become part of our grand holy quest to keep the forgotten story of our Savior alive. Praise and honor to both . . . of you for protecting this unknown story.

"If my sainted great-uncle saw us now, he would bless our endeavor to proclaim God's glory in his Son's name. What a great honor to travel on this important quest, yet I've contributed little. Tell me, Lord de Borron, have I hindered you in any way?"

"*Non*, what nonsense! Hughes de Montbard, you haven't hindered me in any way and have bestowed on me your strength and determination. Yet note, your courage, kindness, and true loyalty reside in each of us. These attributes represent the Cup of Christ, *mon ami*."

With his shaking hands, young Hughes grabbed my palm and kissed it. Tears trickled down his cheeks, and he spoke once again in a whisper.

"Lord de Borron, please . . . read out loud . . . as you write what Saint Joseph de Arimathea and my Lord and Savior said those many years ago."

"*Oui, mon ami*, I'll recite for you. Now stop speaking and rest, so you can recover your strength."

Young Hughes's dark glistening eyes followed me as I rose to retrieve my writing materials. I kept thinking how much unnecessary pain he'd endured for the preservation of the *Sangraal* parchments. His great physical sacrifice resulted from the evil *bâtards* de Tournay and Cardinal Folquet's machinations. In my mind, I knew the other Templars had sustained grievous injuries, and they were suffering too, even Commander de Érail, but my anger burned over this innocent life as hot as our roaring fire. If young Hughes dies, I would unleash Hell on de Tournay. Saying a silent prayer to myself, I asked my Heavenly *Père* to let me become an instrument of his divine justice and forgive me for seeking revenge.

Later that evening, I washed Hughes's chest, face, hands and brushed his hair. Also, I applied clean bandages over his wound. Muhammad helped me raise him to prepare him for the investiture as a *chevalier* scheduled for the morning. After finishing, we lifted him to a secluded corner of the cabin and sat him down. I recited numerous complete pages, after which I noticed he took his *Pater Noster* beads from his sword belt and proceeded to pray at once.

His chant continued throughout the night, with a steady cadence from his whispering voice. The last thing I heard, before falling asleep, came from the constant droning sound of Hughes's raspy voice. Saying, "Our *Père* who art in Heaven," repeating our Lord's Prayer until I fell asleep.

The next morning, we helped Commander de Érail stand. Muhammad took the commander's left arm and placed it over his own shoulder to steady him. I handed the commander his red pattée cross-pommel sword. Afterward, my arms held Squire Hughes, and then we lowered him to his knees before his leader. Poor Hughes's knees wobbled, forcing me to brace him against my legs. Still, it took both Muhammad and me to hold his upper torso and keep it from swaying back and forth.

"Do you, Hughes de Montbard, promise to relieve and protect widows, the fatherless, the aged, the oppressed, and humankind in misery? Also, do you swear to defend the *église* of God, to propagate the Christian faith in our Lord Jesus the Christ's name? Also, do you promise before God to adopt the vows of poverty, chastity, and obedience under our holy order and its founder, Saint Bernard de Clairvaux? Do you so swear, Hughes de Montbard?"

"*Oui*, I do so swear!" he exclaimed. I marveled at the strength in his reply. Then, in unison, we said Psalm 115, after which Commander de Érail completed the ceremony.

"In the name of *Dieu*, the *Père*, the *Fils*, the Holy Ghost, and our Holy *Père*, Clement III, I, Gilbért de Érail, commander of Provence and chancellor of Iberia and the *royaumes* of Aragón and Catalonia, confer on you the title *chevalier* of our order."

Commander Gilbért raised his sword and dubbed him with the flat side of his blade on each of his shoulders and continued speaking. "Rise, *Chevalier* Hughes de Montbard, you are now a true Soldier of Christ."

Muhammad and I lifted him to a sufficient height that let us drape a long white mantle around his shoulders emblazoned with the Order's red pattée cross. At once, his face beamed with happiness.

I prayed in silence for his recovery yet doubts still clawed at my mind. Would the great-nephew of Saint Bernard de Clairvaux fulfill his Templar vows? Our God and Lord Jesus the Christ knew that answer and not me.

PART FOUR

That Night

CHAPTER XXXII

Jerusalem
Passover Night
Anno Domini 33

e were now free of the centurion guard to continue to Marcus's house and his forthcoming Seder dinner. The current watch was late from the several delays we had incurred. Now I seemed more prepared for what we might face, after meeting with Eli and his sons.

"Nicodemus, what did you say to the young Roman centurion? I didn't expect him to let us pass," Yoseph said.

"I told him we had business at the Temple with the priests tonight. Also, I mentioned the *Pesach* watch had started, and we'd volunteered to help with the sacrifice. That made it easy to explain why we were carrying swords."

"Did he say his name?"

"Why do you ask, Yoseph?"

"I really don't know. Yet, something prompted me to ask."

"He's a centurion by the name of Gaius Cassius Longinus and would patrol this part of *Yerushalayim* for several days."

With much relief, the sound of Gaius Longinus's soldiers marching away abated as they continued on to the house of Yohanan Marcus. After passing several houses with upper rooms, they heard music and singing coming from one orange-colored lit two-story home. A man carrying a large red clay water pitcher entered the front doorway. The melodic musical sounds of a shabbabah flute and stringed kinnor drifted closer as they approached the entrance door. The *plinking* tone of the kinnor reminded Yoseph of another Seder dinner many years ago. In his mind's eye, he saw his wife strumming the strings with her long delicate fingers. Her face always smiled as she played for their celebration.

His dolorous daydream ceased when Hebron's large hand pounded the door knocker. Yoseph's eyes at once drew to the door-knocker itself, as he focused on its odd-looking shape. The knocker consisted of a bronze metal and was cast in the form of a dolphin.

After a short time, came footsteps and then locks unlatching. A young servant girl appeared and welcomed them into a small porch area with several stone benches. The young woman wore a Greek hairstyle with many braids on her head, minus a facial veil. Her hair glistened black and many curled ringlets framed her face. The sweet smell of nard permeated the porch as she began to speak.

"I am called Sophia, and my master welcomes you. The rest of your family and friends are already here."

"I am Yoseph of Arimathea and to my right stands my noble friend, Nicodemus, and to his right, my brother-in-law, Hebron. We are happy to partake of your master's hospitality, but how did you know me?"

"Your daughter described all of you. Please, follow me to the upper rooms," she said with a pleasant voice.

They proceeded up a short flight of stone steps and reached the entrance to a long courtyard. In the center, Yoseph noticed a large ornate three-tiered fountain with many stonefish spouting water into each level. All around the fountain grew blue-flowering hyssop shrubs. Surrounding them were sweet-smelling red-flowered myrtle bushes. At each corner of the courtyard were white five-petaled flowering hawthorn bushes. Dark red bricks covered the paths surrounding this area, with eight open rooms surrounding the sides of the courtyard.

A balcony fronted the upper rooms that streamed the full width of the second story. It overlooked the courtyard below, but from Yoseph's viewpoint, he just saw moving shadows from the rooms. Many voices filtered out from the opened windows as they approached the garden interior stairway to the balcony. About halfway up the stone steps, Yohanan Marcus rushed out on the balcony to greet them and then descended the steps to hug Yoseph.

"I'm pleased to see you, my friends, and I am quite glad you came to visit me and join us. It's an honor to have all of you in my home. Please come, the *Haggadah* will start soon. The rest of your family just arrived, and I see you have met my sister, Sophia. We are quite proud of her, even though she speaks her mind. So far, she and your daughter have already discussed many things." Yohanan Marcus started up the stairs. "Did you have any trouble on your journey here?"

"Nothing to worry about, just a slight delay from an inquiry by a centurion and some soldiers," Yoseph stated. "The centurion saw our swords and became suspicious, but we showed him our Sanhedrin medals and told him we were on the way to the Temple. He didn't detain us after our explanation."

"Excellent. Come, join us. We are quite excited about tonight's dinner. As I mentioned to you the other day, my Master has something important to tell us later." Young Yohanan Marcus motioned for them to follow him.

They entered two large rooms; the first one decorated with palms and set for the Seder dinner. Yoseph smelled a sweet fruity aroma emanating from several large clay ewers filled with wine. In this room sat a long Roman-styled *triclinium* against one of the sizable windows facing the balcony with sufficient pillows for more than a dozen people. In front of the *triclinium* table lay a large red and blue-colored wool rug with various symbols and animal designs. Small bronze cups stood at each place setting for the honored guests.

The place of honor displayed a sizable bronze goblet and a large wooden trencher stacked high with several loaves of unleavened bread. In addition, there were numerous wooden plates with the bitter-smelling herb hyssop cut into small pieces. Yoseph observed several bowls with diced apples and nuts, and a separate small bowl containing salt. Each plate held a small cooked chicken egg. Before them lay a complete Seder dinner and the start of the *Pesach* celebration.

On the floor, at the far right of the table, Yoseph saw one of Yohanan Marcus's servants place a large shining silver *krater*. Next to it stood a narrow oblong-shaped red clay pitcher filled with water. The first room displayed a few lit oil pots scattered around the room. Servants were racing up and down the steps as they entered the second part of the upper rooms.

Many men and women buzzed with conversation. Some of them he knew. Others Yoseph didn't recognize. However, he noticed Yosa speaking to Sophia and his niece Miriam standing next to Miriam of Magdala. To Yoseph's surprise, he saw Salome (wife of Zebedee), Yáakov, and Yudas Didymus, which were Yeshua's half-brothers. He hadn't seen them in several summers. Salome had grown into a tall mature woman and strolled over to speak with his daughter and Sophia. Then he observed Yeshua in deep conversation with Yohanan, the writer. The ceiling and walls glowed from numerous smoky burning torches that made everyone's face visible, with one exception. A man stood back in a dark corner listening to a large man who made little effort to hide a small sword in his tunic. Both men made him a little suspicious by their hidden behavior. Just then Philip motioned for their group to come and join him, thus preventing Yoseph from identifying the two strangers.

"Master Yoseph, I see you have accepted Yohanan Marcus's invitation to join our Seder meal. It pleases me to see you once again. Hebron, how did you convince him to come and join us?"

"He came of his own accord. However, Alein Yosephe and I helped the matter some by providing swords for protection."

"Yes, my brother-in-law maintains our security when it comes to the safety of our family," Yoseph commented.

"Don't forget, *abba*, I played a part too in protecting our family," Alein Yosephe interjected.

"But my *abba's* business calls me away from *Yerushalayim* many months of the year, and I practice my swordsmanship while sailing on ships," Alein added.

"Forgive me, Alein, for not mentioning your contributions. How shortsighted of me."

"I respect your family's caution and concern, Master Yoseph." Philip bowed his head to them. "Would you pardon me for now? I need to help attend to the roasting of the Seder lambs. I will return soon, and we can further our conversation. Please, excuse me."

A short time later, Yohanan Marcus reappeared to join them. "I must ask you to relinquish your swords during our *kodesh* ceremony."

Even though Yoseph knew weapons weren't appropriate for the *Pesach* meal, he suspected the others were concealing their swords and daggers. He prayed that Yohanan Marcus would also gather up their weapons. However, they raised no objections, for their host had extended his hospitality and it bound them to acquiesce to his wishes. As Yoseph glanced at Hebron, he saw a frown as he gave Yohanan Marcus his sword. Ever vigilant, and with just reason, Hebron turned his head to survey the room, looking back at the dark corner with the strangers. Yohanan Marcus left to store their weapons.

"Yoseph, do you recognize the big Galilean in the far dark corner?" Hebron asked. "He still has a sword tucked in his tunic belt."

"I can't see his face in the dark corner."

"Don't you remember? Yeshua called him 'my rock,' the son of Yona! He arrived late at our supper at Gethsemane."

"Now I recognize him, and I am sure Yohanan Marcus will obtain his sword before the Seder starts. Hebron, your stare seems focused on the other man. Why so?"

"Yoseph, don't you see who the big man speaks to?"

The darkness of the corner obscured his face, but the motions of his arms identified him as Yudas Iscariot.

"Hebron, I see your dagger mark," Yoseph whispered, detecting his heart to skip a beat in his chest. "At last, we found our dagger-man!"

"Yes, you're correct, Yoseph. Also, did you notice Yudas the Iscariot carries a concealed dagger in his tunic sleeve?"

Yoseph detected a curved outline of a blade.

"Yoseph, when we leave here tonight, we must travel together."

Both Nicodemus and Yoseph nodded in agreement with his brother-in-law's deduction as Yoseph's stomach tightened like a knotted rope.

Yosa and the other women approached the men. "*Abba*, have you met Sophia?"

"Yes, we did, she let us into the courtyard."

His daughter's presence lessened his fear of the dagger-man. He noticed her dark shiny eyes flashing with enjoyment. She had gathered Sophia, his sister Enygeus, Miriam of Magdala, and their other niece Miriam Salome, born to their brother Yoachim by a later marriage. He judged Yosa and Sophia were the same age, and both exuded the same inquisitive and giddy spirit.

Yoseph's sister, Enygeus, though some younger than Miriam Salome, held to the standards of speaking little in public. Salome's oval-shaped face and slightly tapered nose were some visible under her thin veil. She wore little jewelry, compared to Yosa and Miriam of Magdala. Her dress and shawl were of a simple gray-colored rough wool, reflecting her rural background.

"Uncle Yoseph, what do you think about our new rabbi, Yeshua? He seems to draw crowds wherever he goes."

"I am still trying to reconcile his new vocation. He seems to project an unearthly appearance when he speaks."

Once again, Yoseph focused his attention on Yeshua, who now stood with both Philip and Yohanan the writer. Yohanan had his scribe's satchel slung across his chest and shoulder while holding the strap with his left hand and gesturing with his right. He had forgotten how Yohanan's beardless boyish looks betrayed his older age, yet his flushed face conveyed both seriousness and anger.

He shook his drooped head in disgust and disappointment. Philip stood by, listening with his mouth open. Yoseph observed a small tear rolling down Yohanan's cheek. His nephew then touched

Yohanan's shoulders. Yeshua's full face remained obscured with a prayer shawl covering most of his head, yet a slight yellow glow emanated from the top of his *tallit*-enclosed head. Yoseph had noticed this before but thought it just a sign of his older vision.

After grabbing Yohanan by his elbow, this shimmering *kabod* light surrounded both men; however, not sufficient to brighten the room and attract attention.

He finished speaking to them, and then Yeshua approached the first part of the upper room and stood near the silver *krater*. All of the followers, disciples, and guests moved to follow him.

At once, the crowd became eerily silent, as Yeshua stood behind the *krater* and started pouring gurgling water from the clay pitcher into it. The water splashed against the large silver-colored bowl, making a bell-ringing sound, which for some unknown reason beckoned Yoseph to come forth. Yeshua reached down with his right hand that bore the mysterious birthmark of a white dove and grabbed a large cloth from the *triclinium*. He took his shawl and robe off, tucked the towel in his tunic belt, and began to speak.

"I say to you, my friends, the Son of Man didn't come forth on this Earth to be served. If your heart's desire is to be first in my *Abba's* house among men and women, you must first become their slave. Tonight, I am your servant and, as a servant, I desire to clean your feet. This is the example I expect of all my followers. Each one of you, my disciples, I will come to you and wash your feet."

Suddenly, the entire room murmured with questions about what his nephew had just said; with continued whispering as Yeshua placed the *krater* in front of himself. He then knelt in front of his inner circle of disciples.

Philip stood near Yoseph and whispered into his ear. "Master Yoseph, I am not familiar with my rabbi's new behavior. I have followed him the last several summers and before then, I was a student of Yohanan the Baptizer. I am confident he'll explain further after he finishes the ceremony."

The first three disciples he approached were Yohanan the writer, Yohanan bar Zebedee, and Andrew. He washed each of their feet, dried them, and whispered something to each one, which remained inaudible. Next, he ambled over to Philip, performed the same ceremony, finished, and Philip returned to where Yoseph stood. The big Galilean, Shimon bar Yona followed. He appeared not to have his sword and with hesitation approached Yeshua. One of the women returned, placing the empty *krater* bowl at my nephew's knees. He then poured more clean water from the ewer into the bowl. Yeshua started to wash the big man's feet. Yoseph stood close to Shimon bar Yona and noticed how dark and leathery his skin appeared, which reaffirmed to him he worked outdoors. His calloused hands were as large as small palm fronds, and he spoke to Yeshua in his loud Galilean accent.

"I am not worthy enough to let you do this," Shimon said.

He and Nicodemus looked at each other, wondering why he didn't want his feet washed.

"Shimon bar Yona," Yeshua said, "unless I wash your feet, you have no share in my Kingdom of Heaven with me."

Did he truly possess the Kingdom of Heaven? This cryptic statement didn't make any sense. Yoseph hoped he would explain its meaning as the night progressed, for his mind ached for answers.

Shimon reluctantly acquiesced yes and complied with a cracked voice to Yeshua's demand

"*Adonai*, not my feet solely, but my head and hands too!"

His nephew looked up at Shimon bar Yona and spoke, "One who has bathed does not need to wash, except for the feet, but is totally clean."

Again, Philip spoke in a subdued voice and told Yoseph. "This explains Shimon's new name, Cephus, meaning 'the rock.' Yeshua gave him that title for several reasons, but sometimes his stubbornness appears as a large immovable boulder."

Then Yeshua stood and called out to the crowd, "Not all of you are clean. *Shaytan* has a new disciple among us. A traitor sits here tonight!"

At once, the crowd uttered a gasp at what he had just said, with wide-eyed looks of bewilderment. What a strange accusation to make at a Seder dinner. Yet it didn't surprise Yoseph.

CHAPTER XXXIII

Yeshua spoke no further words as he strolled toward Yudas bar Shimon, or as Yoseph knew him, the "dagger-man." The room became silent before Yeshua started washing the Iscariot's feet. His eyes met Yudas's eyes, and he stared at his disciple with a look of sadness on his face. Yeshua shook his head as if he knew this disciple had become a great disappointment to his teachings.

Yudas's face grew crimson with anger; however, a long silence remained between the two men. Yeshua finished washing Yudas's feet, left, and approached the next disciple.

"What do you think about this accusation?" Yoseph asked Philip.

"I don't know, he has never spoken in this manner. However, Master Yoseph, one thing I do know, my *Adonai* and Yudas have disagreed many times over the past several summers. He insists that Yeshua become a military leader. Yudas has a great hatred of the Romans and thinks my rabbi will rival Yudas Maccabeus."

"If these two men haven't agreed after several summers, why does he still follow Yeshua? Also, why did he ask Yudas to join your inner circle of disciples? If he were one of my members, I would have dispatched him a long time ago with a painful departure."

"My teacher embraces peace and wants everyone to experience the love and compassion of *El Shaddai,* including Yudas. He seeks out the virtuous in all who are in his presence. Yudas came to us as a man of pecuniary abilities and because of that talent, my teacher let him shoulder the responsibility of our common fund, a position of financial trust. We elected him to manage our group's common monies. In my rabbi's eyes, he has honored him for his financial acumen and included him in his inner circle of disciples. Yeshua suffers from regret that Yudas still doesn't understand his teachings."

Once more the noise from the crowd interrupted Yoseph's thoughts. He saw Miriam of Magdala approached by Yeshua and then he placed the *krater* of clean water at her feet. The crowd's humming voices hushed at once, as Miriam placed her bare right foot in Yeshua's hands. He washed it, then after finishing one foot, proceeded with care to the other foot. She bent down as if to kiss him on the cheek but whispered something into his ear.

As Yoseph glanced at Shimon bar Yona, he noticed Shimon's face contorted with displeasure as he stared at Miriam of Magdala. Was he in league with the Iscariot man? Hadn't he brought a sword to the Seder dinner? On the other hand, maybe his jealousy of Miriam's special relationship with Yeshua provoked his ire. Now Yoseph saw new concerns popping into his mind on what further reactions he might instigate. To Yoseph's surprise, he heard his name called and saw Yeshua coming toward him. At once, Yoseph's face became hot with embarrassment and he gazed at Yeshua with a sense of unworthiness. What did he do to help Yeshua's ministry? His preparations left him speechless too, for his nephew removed Yoseph's sandals and acted as his servant. He poured the crystal-clear water from the ewer and it appeared to sparkle as he filled the silver *krater.*

His soft hands, which gave Yoseph a sense of calm, vanquished his embarrassment. His fingertips elicited a slight tingling sensation throughout Yoseph's entire body. When finished, Yeshua looked up at him and his large dark eyes revealed a deep sadness that he hadn't seen until now.

"I thank you, Yoseph, and my *Abba* and *amma* thanks you for what you have done and will do for us."

His long slender fingers reached for the towel, dried Yoseph's feet, and approached Nicodemus next. Also, Yoseph stared at Yeshua washing his worthy friend's feet and afterward saw his cheeks rise with a joyous smile on his face. He finished washing the feet of his remaining inner circle of disciples and then stood still for a moment saying a silent prayer. After finishing the prayer, his closest disciples took their seats at the *Pesach* table first, including Miriam of Magdala. Yet, before sitting down, with her graceful movements, she lit the many ceremonial candles on the *triclinium* with a small oil lamp that caused the room to become ablaze with light.

All at once, the servant men and women darted into the room bringing the *Pesach* meal and wine to all the guests who had arranged themselves on the blue-covered rugs and red-colored pillows that were scattered throughout the large open rooms. From what Yoseph observed, everyone's eyes transfixed on their rabbi and his closest disciples. All his disciples presented themselves as a powerful group of followers as they surrounded his nephew at the *Pesach* table.

Yeshua began to speak from his place at the table and said, "Blessed are You, *Eloheinu*, our *Adonai*, Ruler of the universe, who sanctified us with His commandments and commanded us to light the festival candles. Blessed are You, *Eloheinu*, our *Adonai*, Ruler of the universe, who has kept us in life and sustained us and enabled us to reach this festive season."

Yeshua sitting there, with his serene, confident image, made Yoseph proud as one of Moshe's ancestors. Now, they gathered here just as their ancient *abbas* had hundreds of *Pesachs* ago. Yeshua rose from his seat and began the *kiddush*.

"Blessed are You, *Adonai*, our *Eloheinu*, Ruler of the universe who brings forth the fruit of the vine from the Earth. Blessed are You, *Adonai*, our *Eloheinu*, Ruler of the universe, who has chosen us from peoples, exalted us above all nations, and sanctified us with your commandments."

They drank their first cup of wine. After placing the finished cup down, they washed their hands in the fingerbowls provided and then dipped their greens in the salt-water bowl placed in front of them, followed by the *karpas* blessing. After finishing this blessing, they took the middle matzah bread, broke it in half, and hid one of the pieces for the children to find later.

"Blessed are You, *Adonai*, our *Eloheinu*, Ruler of the universe, creator of the fruit of the earth," Yeshua said.

According to their *Pesach* tradition, young Yohanan bar Zebedee, the writer, stood up and asked, "Why must this night differ from all other nights?" His words were clear, and his voice had a smooth rhythmic sound to it that for some unexplained reason drew tears to Yoseph's eyes. The entire crowd became enthralled and fixated on this young man's voice. The *Haggadah* continued, with the four other questions discussed, the story of ten plagues, their exodus out of Egypt, and the significance of the Paschal lamb.

With a steady voice, they recited, "Blessed are You, *Adonai*, our *Eloheinu*, Ruler of the universe, who sanctified us with His commandments and commanded us to observe the washing of hands."

They washed their hands again before the main meal. Then, after finishing, they drank their second cup of wine, followed by the blessing of the thin loaves of matzah bread. They recited in unison, "Blessed are You, *Adonai*, our *Eloheinu*, Ruler of the universe, who brings forth bread from the earth. Blessed are You, *Adonai*, our *Eloheinu*, Ruler of the universe, who sanctified us with His commandments and commanded us to observe the eating of matzah. I am *Adonai*, your *Eloheinu*, who brought you out of Egypt as your *Eloheinu*."

They dipped their herbs in the *charoset* and then ate them. Afterward saying, "Blessed are You, *Adonai*, our *Eloheinu*, Ruler of the universe, who sanctified us with His commandments and commanded us to observe the eating of bitter herbs."

During a brief pause in the Seder, the servants rushed into the room carrying several large platters of roasted Paschal lambs and placed them on the main table, for the inner circle of disciples to eat first. The children raced around the rooms to find the hidden *Aikman* matzah bread and waited to hand it to them after the blessing. His nephew broke the first piece of bread and mixed it with the juicy-cooked, pungent-smelling herbs, and sliced lamb. They proceeded to eat, following his lead as silence overtook the room.

The lamb tasted delicious with its herbal-seasoned pepper, tarragon, and basil. All present commented on the wholesome food. The women and children ate next, as the servants hurried in once again with various platters of fruits, nuts, and fish.

Another blessing followed, and when completed, the singing and recitation of psalms commenced. The *Haggadah* continued with the drinking of the third cup of wine and its blessing. "Blessed are You, *Adonai*, our *Eloheinu*, Ruler of the universe, Creator of the fruit of the vine." With the final and fourth cup of wine poured, the door, already opened for Eliyah the prophet's traditional return, at once slammed shut from a tremendous gust of wind. Everyone stared toward the door in bewilderment. Also, the force of the wind had toppled the cup for Eliyah. What did this mean? All of their eyes looked at Yeshua for an explanation, but he spoke not a word. His face appeared in a trance, with his eyes closed. Did he know what this sign meant?

After the group had calmed down from this mysterious event, Yeshua and his disciples stood and began to sing the *Hallel*. Yeshua's voice cracked with emotion as he recited the psalms for the needy and the exodus from Egypt. Throughout the group of followers, musical instruments came forth and the music began with Miriam of Magdala strumming her kinnor. Followed by another disciple, a tax collector called Matthew, blowing his shabbabah flute in a slow and melodic sound. Each disciple either stood up and sang or reached for a musical instrument. As the tempo picked up, all present tapped their feet. Philip joined in slapping a timbrel and joyfully smiling.

The psalms grew louder and the twelve men and one woman harmonized with Yeshua as an ethereal sound came forth. Was it possible this music came from Heaven? Hebron looked at him with large eyes of wonder, and Alein Yosephe's mouth was open from disbelief. Both Yosa and Enygeus cried with tears of joy upon hearing Yeshua's singing voice above all the other voices. His face glowed, grinning as he sang, but his voice trailed off and then stopped singing. At once, everybody ceased singing and he began to speak.

"May my *Abba,* who causes peace to reign in Heaven, let His peace descend on us and all *Adonai's* chosen people. Let us meet in the new *Yerushalayim* for the next *Pesach* celebration."

What did he mean, speaking of a new *Yerushalayim*? Was this another one of his short parables?

Suddenly, Yeshua's forehead wrinkled, and with his next words, he sent another lightning bolt of disbelief throughout the crowd.

"Very truly, I say one of you at this table will betray me tonight."

Everybody gasped, followed by instant denials. Still sitting, Yeshua began to speak again.

"Woe to him who betrays the Son of Man. It would have been better for him had he not been born."

At once the big Galilean, Shimon, jumped up and said, "Not I, rabbi!" Again, many voices of denial moved throughout the room. Both Hebron and Yoseph were sure they knew the accused.

"See now the one who dips his bread in the olive oil bowl," Yeshua said after he handed Yudas a piece of unleavened bread.

Everybody's eyes darted back and forth throughout the crowd, looking for the guilty person. Then Yeshua's followers focused their eyes on Yudas the Iscariot holding the dipped bread from the bowl of olive oil.

Right away, Yudas stopped eating, looked up, and saw a room full of eyes staring at him. He looked at his fellow disciples and his face turned crimson red and the muscles in his jaws tightened as cords of rope. Yoseph observed no vexed look anywhere on Yudas's face, just guilt.

"Surely not me, rabbi, I am the man who everybody trusts with their money. Am I not your obedient student still?"

"Yudas, your face speaks of your guilt. What you have to do, do it without delay, for the evil one now uses your tongue. You need to leave our presence."

At once, Yudas jumped up, grabbed the bowl he had dipped his bread in, and threw it out the window. With his wounded arm, he scattered his food in front of him, pushing it on the floor and then turned his back to them while cursing. All ears strained to hear his stomping footsteps go down the stairway, and then Yudas slammed the heavy entrance door.

Unexpectedly, a hand reached out and grabbed Yoseph's arm. The face of his daughter gazed up at him. "*Abba*, what just happened? Why did this man leave cursing at my cousin? Why did Yeshua want him to leave? *Abba*, wasn't he one of the men with Yeshua who attended our supper in the garden of olives?"

"I can't answer all your questions at the same time, Yosa. However, you're correct in one thing. Yudas did accompany Yeshua to Gethsemane. You might remember him as the one . . ."

"The one you had a disagreement with, now I remember!" Yosa glanced toward Yeshua. "*Abba*, I sensed trouble with this man that night and he didn't sound similar to the teachings of my cousin."

"Your cousin exposed the evil spirit that possessed his body. You sensed the same suspicions the rest of us experienced, Yosa."

"*Abba*, I am scared and fear he will harm us. Do you think we are still in danger?"

"I know he was the sole person who attacked me, yet his evil strings still remain. This I am certain, and we must suspect all other possible threats. Right now, I worry for all our safety, my child. Let's see what your cousin has further to say."

Before Yeshua began to speak, a servant came in, picked up the scattered plates, food, and cleaned up the table. Everyone waited for a further explanation from Yoseph's nephew. Yeshua rose from his pillow and made another perplexing statement.

"My beloved friends, with great desire I have eaten this meal with you before I suffer. For I tell you now, no longer shall I eat until it is fulfilled in the Kingdom of my *Abba*. I shall not drink the fruit of the vine until the Kingdom of Heaven comes.

"Where two or three come together in my name, there I will reside amid you always. I am the light, which is before all things. It is I who am all things. From me, all things come forth, and to me all things extend. Split a piece of wood and I am there. Lift up a stone and you will find me there."

Next, he picked up his glowing cup of wine and gave thanks. After the blessing, he said another for the few remaining broken pieces of bread, holding one piece near his face.

"Take and eat, this is my body. Do this in remembrance of me."

He reached down, grabbed the plate, and passed to all present. Next, he raised the bronze chalice over his head and gave a special blessing for this cup of wine. At once, the room glowed with a brilliant white light with such an intense radiance that it caused all in the room to shield their eyes. Even covered, Yoseph's eyes were painful to touch as the shafts of light further forced his head to bow before the mysterious cup. After a moment of silence, Yeshua spoke again.

"This is my blood of the *brit chadashah,* which is poured out for the many for the forgiveness of sins. Take and drink it all. He who will drink from my cup will become me. I, myself, shall become he and the things that are hidden will be revealed to you. It is the glory of *El Shaddai* to conceal things, but the honor of kings and followers of the Son of Man to search out his mysteries.

"Tomorrow, my blood will flow from me for the remission of mankind's sins. I have just a short time with you; therefore, brethren, I hope you have listened with due attention to what I have said and will say.

"I leave now to prepare a place for you in my *Abba's* house. After I have made a place for you, I will come again and take you with me. And all of you know the way to the place where I am traveling."

"Rabbi, we don't know your destination," said one of his disciples, Thomas Didymus. "How can we know the 'way'?"

The faces around the room looked perplexed. What does all this mean? The room remained bright with the unexplained glow; however, Yoseph's eyes had adjusted to its intensity, letting him see with some clarity. The golden *kabod* of light remained around Yeshua's head as the chalice of wine and the unleavened bread made its way to each person in the room.

Yeshua replied to his disciple's question. "Thomas, if you had known me well all these summers, you would have already answered your own question. I am the 'way' and the 'truth' and the 'life.' No one comes to the

Abba except through me. If you know me, you will know my *Abba* also. From now on, you do know him and have seen him."

With his last words, Yeshua's *kabod* shot forth with the brilliance of the sun's rays. Once again, all in the upper rooms bowed their heads at his nephew's countenance. All around his body flowed colors of gold, silver, and purple.

To Yoseph's further amazement, Philip asked his rabbi a question, which he knew now needed no answer. "Master, show us the *Abba* and we will understand."

To Philip's incredulous question, his nephew replied, "Have I been with you all this time, Philip, and you still don't know me?"

Yeshua then addressed the entire assembly of followers. "Whoever has seen me has seen the *Abba*. How can you say, 'Show us the *Abba*'? Do you not believe I am in the *Abba* and the *Abba* is in me?"

At this point, nobody in the upper room doubted what he said or what they saw. They were all in the presence of the real *Maishiach*! Yet, Yeshua just didn't speak as a prophet for *Eloheinu*, but now before them stood the Holy Son of *Eloheinu*! The sons of Abraham and Yoseph's religion were expecting a *Maishiach*, yet not the human incarnate of *Eloheinu*. He knew to Philip, and himself, a human incarnation of their *Maishiach* was an abomination to their faith. Yohanan the Baptizer had predicted his coming and how foolish of Yoseph not seeing this in his nephew. The Son of Man lived in Yoseph's presence these past thirty-three summers and how blind of Yoseph not to see this. Yeshua continued to explain.

"The words that I say to you I don't speak on my own; but the *Abba,* who dwells in me, does His work. Believe me that I am in the *Abba* and the *Abba* is in me; but if you don't, then believe me because of the works themselves. Truly, I tell you, the one who believes in me will also do the works that I do, and, in fact, will do greater works than these because I am journeying to the *Abba*. I will do whatever you ask in my name so that the *Abba* is glorified in his Son. If in my name, you ask me for anything, I will do it. The road ahead will be deep with danger and suffering when you testify for me. When the world hates you, remember, it hated me before it hated you. Again, remember when two or three are gathered in my name, I will always reside among you.

"When I return to my *Abba's* house, the Son of Man will send another counselor to this world that will never leave you. He will touch each of you with His holy fire and this fire of love and truth will last throughout all eternity. My legacy to you, my brothers and sisters, is the peace of heart and mind. You're the fruits of my vineyard and the lambs of my flock.

"Heed my final warning, my fellow brethren. It is written that the evil one will strike down the shepherd and the sheep will scatter. All of you will desert me, except four disciples."

The entire crowd shouted a resounding "No!" with Yeshua's last statement. Shimon bar Yona jumped up first to voice his loyalty.

"Rabbi, I'll fight for you, even if it costs me my life. Just once I doubted you. I would follow you, my *Adonai*, to the depths of *Sheol* if you asked me."

"Truly, I tell you, Shimon bar Yona, this night you'll deny me three times before the cock crows."

"I will never deny you, rabbi," Shimon said, repeating his reply several times as the crowd shouted the same.

Would the evil one scatter him too? Yoseph asked himself. A sick burning sensation rose from his stomach, for Yoseph's beloved nephew had just predicted his own death to all there. Oh, what might he do to prevent this prophecy? How helpless Yoseph now felt. Yeshua continued.

"My friends, I ask that you love one another as I have loved you. No one has greater love than this, to lay down one's life for one's fellow man or woman. Always look for the virtuous qualities in humankind. I have granted you specialized knowledge to seek out this kindness. You're no longer my pupils. You are my friends, and you know what my *Abba* has told me. You'll usher forth and proclaim the forgiveness of mankind's sins. I will become the bearer of those sins. My hour draws near and my *Abba* calls, for I am leaving you after this feast. Truly, I tell you, my friends, prepare every day for my *Parousia* or return. I will come again to create a greater and more perfect tabernacle on Earth, not made with the hands of kings and prophets, but by the spirit of those who believe in me."

With Yeshua's last word, he moved from the center of the *triclinium* and came toward Yoseph and Hebron, followed by Miriam of Magdala. The rest of his inner circle of disciples remained on their pillows discussing and ruminating on what their rabbi had revealed.

"Uncle Yoseph, please follow Miriam and me outside. Let's stroll in Yohanan Marcus's fragrant courtyard and speak in private." He took Yoseph's arm and they started descending the stone steps.

"Please excuse us, Hebron, for the moment. I'll return soon and speak to you a few parting words before I leave."

What did he want to speak to him about in private? Yet, Miriam accompanied him? Yoseph's mind raced with unexpected new revelations and surged with apprehension.

CHAPTER XXXIV

As they strolled through the courtyard, he heard Miriam of Magdala's ever-present tinkling ankle bracelets and her soft shuffling sandals.

Miriam of Magdala still perplexed Yoseph. Once again, he wondered if Yeshua had made her his wife, a dedicated student, a close friend, or maybe all three? These questions had thrashed around in his head for numerous days. They were never out of each other's sight, and this moment proved no exception. Miriam bore the beauty and grace of a refined woman and her small facial features were most striking under the thin veil she wore. Her lips were full, her nose looked well-portioned for her face, and her bronze-colored skin texture appeared flawless. Her large gold bracelets, embedded with semiprecious red stones, covered her wrists and ankles. Both of her hands were small and smooth, with one large golden ring on her right finger that displayed the shape of a small fish. He knew Miriam's great wealth contributed to the disciples' common fund, which reflected her financial means. His nephew had chosen wisely his followers from all stations of life. Miriam spoke first as they strode into the heart of the courtyard.

"Master Yoseph, I understand you're writing too about my rabbi."

"Yes, but how did you know this?"

"Young Yohanan Marcus told me. He suggested that you do this in remembrance of Yeshua, which I see you took his advice. This will contribute much to my rabboni's ministry. He and Yohanan bar Zebedee are quite close and they enjoy keeping records of my teacher's life. They've a divine gift to see spiritual things, yet able to observe mankind's everyday hopes and fears. *Adonai* has blessed them with eyes and minds that can translate both of these into written words. Yoseph, we have gifts; we can honor *Adonai* and help our brethren's spirit and physical body; however, there are just a few with exceptional abilities. Those blessed by *Eloheinu* must teach this special knowledge to others. My rabboni wants to speak to you about this before he leaves."

Her long eyelashes fluttered downward as she bowed her head before his nephew began to speak. Most men saw her exceptional beauty first, yet her great intellect and most intuitive mind would still amaze them.

"Yeshua, after all you have revealed tonight, what might you say to me to reveal more?"

"Uncle Yoseph, listen with care to what I have to say. Please, hold your comments until I am finished. What I tell you here tonight comes from my *Abba*. I won't see you again as you now know me. I am traveling back to my *Abba* for the redemption of mankind's sins and the salvation of this world's souls.

"I told my disciple Matthew and my other disciples to go out and preach only to the lost sheep of our people. These are wayward sons and daughters of Abraham. You, Yoseph, and your followers will preach my words and life history to the Gentile, Jew, and these wayward sheep. Another of our old faith will preach my words to the Gentiles, but he will have great conflicts in doing so. You will be the first."

More cryptic statements his nephew now uttered.

"I am giving you the *kodesh* Seder cup and bread plate we used at the *Pesach* supper, and then I'll leave to go to the place we had supper several nights ago. There in your garden, near Gethsemane, I will pray to my *Abba* tonight, for the protection of my friends' souls from the snare of the evil one.

"You'll become one of my apostles to create a new tabernacle in my name and my *amma's* name. I charge you with converting the first of many of my new brethren. In addition, your ministry will grow quickly, comparable to mustard seeds, and will begin to challenge and change the social structure, as we now know it. You must look into yourself to find this knowledge on how to accomplish these changes. You will have a difficult *teshuva*, my dearest uncle. Recognize first what is in your sight, and that which is hidden from you will become plain to you. For there is nothing hidden, which won't become manifest.

"Remember, Uncle Yoseph, he who will drink from my cup will become me. I, myself, shall become he and the things that are hidden will be revealed to him. I shall bestow on you what no eye has seen and what no ear has heard and what no hand has touched and what has never occurred to the human mind. You'll be the teacher to let the one who seeks not stop seeking until he finds; when he finds, he will become troubled. He will then become astonished and will rule over all things.

"As one of my first male apostles and new teacher, your superior works will remain until the world ends. As a remembrance of me, all who seek the cup that I have drank from tonight, I will give my everlasting salvation. Here lies my *tiferet*. I will become the sun's rays, close and warm, but not seen. Lastly, hear my lips for a unique numerical key or *sefirot*, which accompanies my 'cup of salvation.' These numbers are . . .'"

His lips drew close to Yoseph's ear and whispered something, which sounded similar to the numbers five and eight.

"Yeshua, did you say the numbers five and eight?"

"Uncle Yoseph, your mind now fills with fear and confusion. What I said to you transcends all ordinary understanding. You must contemplate on the Seder cup I am about to give you. As time passes, all things will become clear to you."

"When and where will these clues manifest themselves? I am an impatient man and fear for my family."

Yeshua didn't answer but proceeded back up the steps toward the upper rooms. He left Miriam standing alone, as Yoseph focused his attention on her radiant face, which seemed to glow before she began to speak.

"My friend, Yoseph, Yeshua has handed you the key to following the branches of the Tree of Life. He has so honored you with his boundless love. There are many branches on the Tree of Life and a select few have the secret knowledge to know where the right limbs grow. The sacred cup he fetches for you, concentrate on its real meaning. Yoseph, not with your eyes, ears, smell, or touch, but with the beginning spark of your soul. Here rests the place of your *tiferet* and the sacred cup. Seek out this singular place. Yeshua has taught me his mysterious knowledge and bestowed on me special wisdom from *Adonai*."

"Miriam, you seem to understand what Yeshua just said, much more than I can comprehend."

"Don't despair, Master Yoseph. Yeshua has shown me many never-before-seen things, hidden in my *nous* or the rational side of my spirit. He speaks a special wisdom given to all of us by revelations from *El Shaddai*. Remember, Yoseph, I have followed Yeshua for a while, yet I am still sometimes vexed in what he teaches. The most important thing I can say, Yoseph; please, listen with your heart."

At that moment, his nephew returned with a silk purse and he assumed the enclosed bronze Seder cup.

"Uncle Yoseph, always remember me by this cup and tell how it came about. Henceforth from tonight, in your ministry to come, all will know of this cup."

Yoseph took the cup and the salver and held them close to his body. At once, warmth emanated from the purple silk cloth. He decided he wanted a closer view of the chalice and took it from its silk covering and held it in front of him. It appeared equivalent to any other yellow-bronze chalice of similar size. The sole exception consisted of numerous small-designed fish etched around its outside rim. It was similar to the fish design engraved on the box from the Isle of Britannia that his son gave to Yosa.

They embraced and then he noticed his nephew's sad eyes. His embrace seemed joyous, yet he sensed otherwise. Miriam of Magdala gave Yoseph a tight hug too, and both she and Yeshua's eyes filled with tears. Oh, how Yoseph's tears ruled him at this moment.

"Uncle Yoseph, I must leave now so I can speak to Hebron before we depart, for I have little time left. *Shalom* be with you, Uncle Yoseph."

Miriam proceeded to follow him, but paused midway up the steps, and turned to face Yoseph.

"Master Yoseph, I will say my goodbyes to your sister and Yosa before my rabboni leaves, but to you, *shalom* and may my *shalom* arise and dwell within you. I fear I might ask you for that *shalom* the next several days to sustain me, but for now, my trustworthy friend, goodbye."

She ran up the steps, then vanished into the upper rooms and left him with her baffling last statement. He stood there tired and bewildered and still not reconciling what Yeshua expected of him, other than some significant part in his ministry. When would he understand his cryptic words?

However, the steady warmth from the yellow-bronze cup gave Yoseph comforting confidence. As he waited, the voices lessened from the upper rooms, leaving him with the singular sound of the steady gurgling courtyard fountain.

His momentary contemplation ended when he heard the shuffle of sandals and saw a departing stream of Yeshua's disciples descending the steps. Most of the men were his inner circle of disciples. Yohanan the writer, left last, followed by Yoseph's sister, Hebron, Alein Yosephe, and Yosa. Yohanan Marcus and Philip approached Yoseph to say goodbye.

"Thank you, Master Yoseph," Yohanan Marcus said, "for coming to my home tonight. Now you can see why my rabbi wanted to talk to you. No one will leave here this glorious night without their life changed in some way. I know we observed a most miraculous Seder dinner, quite dissimilar to any other Seder night that I have known. My teacher wants us to stay with him tonight,"

Yohanan Marcus paused and looked up to the night sky. "I see an omen of many fallen stars in the firmaments tonight that will befall Yeshua tomorrow, yet their meanings remain hidden. As a precautionary measure, Shimon has given us a sharp sword to carry in case our Master needs protecting. He desires to pray by himself in your garden at Gethsemane. Is that permissible, Master Yoseph?"

"Yes, of course, but he doesn't need my permission."

At once, Hebron spoke up, "Is it time to leave, Yoseph? I have brought all our swords down from the upper room. We can protect him. Alein Yosephe can guard the women on the way home."

"My rabbi doesn't want you to follow him," Philip interjected. "He fears for your safety and told me he has other plans for you and Hebron. He spoke to Hebron about this matter a short time ago."

"Is this true?" Yoseph inquired.

Hebron looked uncomfortable and paused before speaking.

"Yes, Yoseph, it's true, but we must hide Yeshua, for I suspect a trap for him. Also, Alein Yosephe agrees with me."

Yoseph looked at his son for confirmation.

"*Abba*, he's your nephew and my cousin. Remember what you said about the importance of family."

Yoseph stood there, sensing indecision, but the cup helped strengthen his resolve. It told him Yeshua knew of things they didn't realize, and he must follow Yeshua's wishes.

"If Yeshua wants us to leave him in peace tonight, that's what we'll do!" Yoseph said, making up his mind. Both his son and brother-in-law's contorted faces wanted to argue, but his glare told them not to.

"My nephew speaks with great authority," he told his family, "and we must trust his decision-making. Besides, we have our own plans to execute. Hebron, we must leave at once and carry out the plan we've agreed too. Alein, please fetch your aunt and sister and tell them we are leaving at once. Again, we must follow Yeshua's wishes. Let's not discuss this matter any further."

Philip embraced him, said goodbye, and then climbed back up the steps. After the women arrived, Yohanan Marcus led all of them through his courtyard, toward the front door where they first entered. Next, he stopped and wished them *shalom*. They thanked him for his hospitality and Yoseph inquired about the safety of the remaining women in his house. He stated for him not to worry, for he knew the Roman centurion whose troops patrolled past his house with each new watch.

As Yoseph ambled out the door, his mind began to ruminate on Yeshua's miraculous powers, hearing his prophecies, and Yoseph's mysterious role in his ministry. He knew how intense Yeshua prayed about his ministry and he prayed for the same zeal.

CHAPTER XXXV

Yoseph's family followed close behind him as they exited past the porpoise-shaped doorknocker and afterward they disappeared back into the dark streets to travel home. Miriam of Magdala had kept Yohanan the Baptizer's son and would bring the boy to Yosa at Arimathea in several days. He convinced Nicodemus to accompany them for his safety. He joined the rest of Yoseph's family as they stayed close together, with their eyes searching for an unforeseen attacker. The streets were desolate and quiet as a tomb, except the sole sound of a singing nightingale.

They were almost home when they heard the stomping sound of marching men coming from the Temple Mount. The din of their thumping sandals proceeded toward the Valley of *Yehoshaphat*. How strange, Yoseph thought, for Temple guards marching this late on a *kodesh* night. A cold chill raced over his body for an instant, and he didn't want to know their destination.

Yoseph arrived home close to the end of the third watch, with a dark yellow sliver of light forming on the eastern horizon. How grateful he thought they had made it—and safe. As he touched the *mezuzah* and said a prayer, the wind started blowing through the courtyard, weaving its way through the colonnades of their home.

The lanterns swayed back and forth on their mountings as if signaling a ship of approaching danger.

There were plans to carry out before any rest and they had to implement them at once. All of them were exhausted, yet they made a weary effort to pack as many clothes and as much food as possible for their retreat to Arimathea.

They hadn't told any of the servants of their plans. Hebron approached Yoseph and said he would have one of their servants fetch the camels Eli had promised. Yoseph agreed, and Hebron dispatched someone at once.

Yoseph stumbled toward his sleeping quarters, not realizing he still clutched Yeshua's chalice. There at the foot of his bed, he opened a large spacious trunk and then prepared to pack the cup and the plate with his writing materials and personal effects. Yoseph's hands rubbed over the purple cloth sack holding the chalice, and, to his surprise, it still emanated warmth. He placed it in the small gift box from the Celtic King Aviragus, which to his amazement fit. He closed the lid and with care placed it in the trunk and locked the metal padlock with one of his many keys and took the heavy trunk to the center of the courtyard.

His children entered the courtyard and strolled toward him. "*Abba*, we have completed our tasks and we're now waiting for the camels to arrive," stated his son.

"Do you know which route we'll travel, *abba*?" Yosa inquired.

"Your brother has determined this and will tell the camel drivers, my dear."

Nicodemus approached him and said he needed to retrieve some of his personal effects and valuable scrolls from his house.

"Yoseph, my friend, I am now going home to arrange my affairs and then acquire some sleep. I will follow you late into the first watch."

In Yoseph's haste to leave *Yerushalayim*, he hadn't noticed Nicodemus's tiredness. His nervous agitation had overlooked his friend's need for rest.

"Nicodemus, one of my servants will accompany you and stay the night for your safety. At dawn, I will send one of Eli's camel drivers to secure you, after which you can follow. We'll see you in Arimathea in two evenings from now, but until then, *shalom aleichem*, my friend."

Nicodemus departed with Yoseph's servant and a lantern in his hand. The courtyard became quiet as they stood around waiting for the camels to arrive. He noticed each of his family members sitting with bent heads contemplating what lay before them.

The wind had subsided some; however, every so often an occasional gust would blow up some dried leaves, still announcing its presence. Yoseph sat on his trunk, ruminating on what strange events had transpired between Yeshua and him. His body ached from exhaustion. Yet, his mind raced with new confidence that they were making the right decision in leaving *Yerushalayim*.

In the distance, he heard an owl hooting, which seemed close, yet its cries came from all directions. He surmised its muffled multidirectional hoots confused its prey, but they grew louder in all directions. The owl's ominous hooting caused Yoseph's stomach to tense harder. Suddenly, he saw a dark flying object, which caused him to flinch. Now the owl revealed itself with its large golden orbs looking at him before it landed on a large tree limb, just outside the courtyard. There it perched, staring at him as still as a statue while voicing a low throaty sound.

At once, Yoseph sensed danger. He shivered with thoughts that something terrible had just happened. He sensed his nephew faced great peril.

Yosa rushed to him. "*Abba*, what just flew over the courtyard? It scared me so that my hands are trembling."

"My dear, a large owl just flew over stalking its prey and nothing more. Let me hold your hands and they'll stop shaking." He grasped them and they were as cold as the rings she wore on her fingers. After a short time, her hands stopped trembling and they started to warm.

Soon, the camels arrived and were making their noisy braying sounds. Then came a loud pounding fist on Yoseph's front courtyard door. He knew it was his fellow merchant friend.

"It's Eli," the booming voice announced. Yoseph ran to the

courtyard door and then unlatched the large bolts, and Eli hurried into the courtyard.

"Yoseph, I am worried. I suspect something nefarious going on at Caiaphas's house. There were many scribes, elders, and Sanhedrin members gathered there. I even saw your close friend Nicodemus standing there arguing with some unknown person as my camels passed by the windows. This sudden meeting doesn't bode well, my friend. Why did Nicodemus go there and not you too summoned before the council?"

Yoseph remained speechless. His mind reeled with disjointed responses. The words weren't coming out of his mouth, as he stood paralyzed with disbelief. After a short moment, strangled words fell from his lips.

"Nicodemus wouldn't . . . do this without me!" Yoseph exclaimed. "Eli, I suspect one of Caiaphas's guards forced him to go. We always vote similarly before the council and sway the other members to vote with us. With me absent, the council might force him to vote differently. That's why I was excluded. Especially from an emergency council meeting on *Pesach*."

"Yoseph, I don't know, but we must hurry. We'll lose our opportunity to leave *Yerushalayim* before the full light of the day. Let Eliyah and Isaiah help load your trunks. The last camels are for your family to ride. Go ahead and start mounting them to depart."

"Eli, let me retrieve something out of my trunk to carry with me," Yoseph insisted as his sons started loading the camels.

"Oh, quite well, but please hurry, Yoseph. I can see dawn forming."

Yoseph took his keys from his belt cloth and unlocked the trunk. With much care, he grabbed the small box, then stuck it in the purple samite-clothed pouch and placed that into his writing material purse that he'd prepared. Its spacious size duplicated the ones Yohanan Marcus and Yohanan bar Zebedee carried with them.

"Eli, please allow me to tell you how much your help means to us. You and your sons are risking your own safety for my family. How can I ever repay you?"

"Just hurry, my friend, and not delay anymore. I fear for you and your family's safety."

Eli's sons at once loaded their personal belongings and they said farewell to Shimon of Cyrene and their fellow servants. The tears of departing began to flow once again as they boarded their camels to leave *Yerushalayim*. Yoseph said one last prayer, touched the *mezuzah*, and climbed on his camel. Each camel rose up, braying, as Eli and his sons said something in each of the camel's ears. Yoseph took one final look back in the torchlight and saw his house, the faithful servants remaining, and Shimon of Cyrene waving farewell. Shimon promised Yoseph's family he anticipated on seeing them in several days. He had to speak to his sons before departing.

At once, the camels' fast-paced hooves raced Yoseph and his family through the empty streets of *Yerushalayim*. Yoseph still had many aching questions about his life forward, begging for answers inside his head.

As the morning sun weaved through the dark clouds, the Yoppa gate fast disappeared behind them and the Tower of David became just a speck on the horizon. They followed the Yoppa road for some two leagues and then changed to the caravan road at Gezer and from there they traveled south. About midday, as Yoseph looked back, he saw a lone rider's dust cloud gaining on them. Why was this unknown person following them? The sun, for a moment, broke through the dark clouds, giving Yoseph some daylight to distinguish the rider's form. To his astonishment, he spied Yohanan Marcus riding alone. However, Yoseph remembered he'd left with Yeshua and his followers.

Yohanan Marcus's horse glistened with white lather flying from its withers. As he gained on them, Yohanan Marcus started yelling for them to stop. Eli and his sons pulled on their reins and stopped. Yohanan Marcus pulled alongside them with his black stallion wheezing from exhaustion. To Yoseph's surprise, he wore no clothes. His entire body dripped with sweat and his naked skin had a bright pink glow from exertion.

His horse's continued wheezing made it difficult for Yoseph to hear. He shouted out one thing, which Yoseph did hear, "They have our teacher!"

Hebron dismounted from his camel, came forward, gave him a goatskin full of water, and handed him a robe to wear. His exhaustion forced his mouth to take large gulps of air, almost as fast as his horse. He took several long drinks to slake his thirst and began to speak again.

"Yoseph, the Temple guards have arrested Yeshua by order of the council, and Caiaphas wants his blood. The traitor, Yudas, has turned him in for thirty pieces of silver and has testified against him. He's saying Yeshua wants to overthrow the Temple, the Roman governor, and speaks of blasphemy against our faith.

"I escaped after the Temple guards chased me down a narrow path of your olive garden at Gethsemane. They ripped off all my clothes as I fought against their murderous grasp, but they weren't quick enough to capture me, and I escaped. Shimon 'the rock' fought with his sword and cut off one of the guard's ears. My master told Shimon Cephus to stop fighting and with Yeshua's miraculous powers rejoined the ear back onto the guard's head. All of the disciples have run away, and I think most have escaped, but I am not positive. The last rumor I heard, Nicodemus tried to stop the council from judging our rabbi for blasphemy and insurrection.

"I saw a Roman patrol near my home resting, and I stole one of their horses, which I intend to replace with a better horse when I return. Yoseph, our Lord needs your help right now! You have influence with the Sanhedrin, and I know you and Nicodemus together can obtain my teacher's freedom. Please, Yoseph, come with me. I beg you to follow me back to *Yerushalayim!*" His teary eyes begged for Yoseph to come with him.

"How did you know where to find me?"

"I rode to your home first and the man called Shimon of Cyrene told me what road to journey. Let's not discuss this any further. We need to leave at once, for I fear for my Master's life."

"Yes, I agree."

Yoseph's hand didn't release its grip of the chalice as he slid off his camel. Eli, his sons, Alein Yosephe, Hebron, and the women had heard Yohanan Marcus's explanation. Yosa and Enygeus started crying. Hebron commented first.

"Yoseph, you can't go back to *Yerushalayim* without me. Those evil and greedy sons-of-bitches, Caiaphas and Annas, are luring you into a trap. They know you will come and speak for Yeshua's defense."

"Hebron, I am aware of your concerns. However, I need you to go to Arimathea with the women and prepare for my return. I can travel faster with Yohanan Marcus and the sooner I arrive in *Yerushalayim*, the sooner I can obtain Yeshua's release. Prepare yourselves for our nephew's return. We must not speak of this affair any longer, for we have little time." Yoseph gave him a big hug, kissed Yosa, Enygeus, and at last hugged his son. All of a sudden, Eli grabbed Yoseph's arm right before he tried to mount his camel.

"Yoseph, please use my camel. He's the fastest in *Yehudah*, and Yohanan Marcus, please ride his mate. She won't let him out of her sight."

The last thing Yoseph remembered, upon looking back, were large tears trickling down Yosa's cheeks. At first, his emotions troubled him as they picked up speed, but his determination held. The tighter he clasped the chalice pouch, the more his resolve raced through his veins. It gave him strength and spoke to his inner thoughts. He knew no matter what happened, he would endure.

Their camels seemed to move at the speed of young hawks diving down between the sand dunes and rocks. Seldom did he use his long stick to urge his camel faster. Their rapid hoofbeats generated a noticeable quick cadence as both animals raced across the dry desert ground. Their constant thumping hooves caused Yoseph's ears to hear drumbeat sounds similar to an army going into combat.

The warm wind buffeted his face, but when Yoseph looked back, his face turned cold. He saw long lightning bolts coming from the dark billowing clouds behind them. They seemed to exhibit the shapes of gigantic rolling ocean waves rushing across the desert floor. The day became night, as the gigantic black clouds swallowed the sun. Several possible landmarks seemed to pass them by, which were all a blur. Late into the sixth watch, near midday, they whipped their camels, they increased their strides as if they were flying above the sandy road. It appeared the camels sensed a race for someone's life.

The closer they came to *Yerushalayim*, the road improved in quality, yet it seemed the ground began to tremble, the nearer they drew to the walled city. Suddenly, Yoseph noticed their camels weaving back and forth across the road and to his chagrin cracks formed in the dry earth. Then he observed uprooted palm trees teetering alongside the road. A thick lump of fear lodged in his throat as he thought about his family's safety.

The main road came into sight as they cleared two small hills. In the distance, Yoseph spied the Tower of David. By now, his body exhibited a muddy sweat coating and he noticed his camel foaming at the mouth, yet they didn't slacken their pace. The Yoppa road forked up ahead; one road approached the tower gate, the other traveled along the Hill of Skulls and the Necropolis.

Abruptly, hail fell like a thick curtain of ice. Their camels still maintained their unbelievable pace even when pelted with ice the size of beads. The icy stinging pellets made it difficult for Yoseph to see, but praise to *El Shaddai*, it didn't last long. The clouds at once departed, and he knew his presence at the council would see victory. Yet, his confidence fell quicker than a stone, seeing more clouds bringing darkness. What sort of portent of doom covered *Yerushalayim*?

CHAPTER XXXVI

Less than a quarter of a league from *Yerushalayim*, the hail stopped, and the clouds broke apart, revealing the sun. Yet, to Yoseph's further horror, the sun's surface seemed devoured of its brilliance. The sky changed from gray to pitch-black. The stars started appearing as the sun's final rays vanished, as if eaten by some unknown evil beast. Nighttime had arrived in the afternoon!

Both camels stopped and gave out a nervous braying groan and then refused to go another step. They were unable to force them onward, even when they whipped them with their riding sticks. The camel's anguished sounds were unusual for them. The whites of their eyes kept rolling back and forth, horrified with fear.

He and Yohanan Marcus at once dismounted and decided to run the rest of the way to the tower gate. They left the camels alongside the road and started racing toward the entrance.

Yoseph's tongue and teeth tasted the gritty desert sand as they ran toward the gate. To his left, he noticed several strange events throughout the Necropolis. The ground gaped open in numerous places, with small knots of people gathered around both burial sites and cracked stone sepulchers. Had they come out to see the strange events in the sky or something else? How bizarre, Yoseph thought, to congregate at the Necropolis, but what further drew his attention were three Roman executions taking place. His blood ran cold at the shadowy site. As they approached closer to the *Yerushalayim* wall, he saw several people dashing toward them. His gritty eyes strained to focus on them, along with the dripping sweat from his forehead stinging his eyes. Yohanan Marcus first distinguished these blurry strangers.

"Do you recognize them?"

"Yes, I see . . . Miriam of Magdala and Yohanan the writer," Yohanan Marcus answered between gulps of air

He and Yoseph stopped running, and then their bodies buckled to their knees from exhaustion. Miriam gave out a piercing scream as she came near Yoseph. Her eyes were red-rimmed, swollen, and her tunic ripped. Yohanan's face and eyes also looked swollen from crying, with his tunic too torn. He tried to speak, but not a word or sound came from his throat. Miriam kept screaming, and none of her words made sense as Yoseph staggered to his feet, grabbed her shoulders, and with what little strength he had left, tried to shake her into speaking. Her frightened eyes looked at Yohanan the writer for assistance, but he didn't reply, which increased her crying.

"Can you tell me why both of you are upset? Yohanan, I beg you to answer me!"

Yet, he still didn't reply, but fell to the ground and buried his face in the sand. Miriam kept gulping air trying to speak along with her body shaking between her moans and shrieks.

"What has happened, my dear child? Please speak to me." Yoseph implored. His mind told him that he didn't want to hear the answer that he would receive. As she tried to speak, her words come out in broken sentences.

"I never expected . . . this to indeed happen. I am not sure . . . what Yeshua expected, but, Yoseph, I can't bear it. They have . . . crucified my Lord. All of his followers . . . have abandoned him in his hour of need."

She slapped both hands over her face and then started swaying back and forth with grief. Her voice still emanated muffled moaning sounds.

Unexpectedly, from out of the sky came a bolt of lightning that struck the Tower of David, causing stones to fly off the parapet. They hunkered down and continued embracing each other, sick with their grief. What just happened in *Yerushalayim*? He had left his nephew, less than two watches ago and returned to a city racked with disaster and executions. Had the evil one seized possession of their city? All these terrible events were beyond Yoseph's mortal comprehension.

"Explain to me how this came about, Miriam. Are you sure it's him?"

Her mouth struggled to answer Yoseph as he held her in his arms.

"Yes, Yoseph . . . I wish it . . . not so. Yudas betrayed my *Adonai* for thirty pieces of silver! Now the Evil One holds sway over Yudas's soul. I knew he disagreed with Yeshua, yet not to the point that he would join in a secret plot to have him executed. My Master, my Teacher, my Love, he's no more. How will I survive, Yoseph?" A long moment of silence followed, which she didn't speak, nor did Yoseph.

"Rest your voice for now, before you continue," Yoseph told her, even though he didn't want to hear Yeshua's outcome.

"No, Yoseph, I need to tell you. I need to speak to you about my *Adonai*. His execution rips at my heart and he would want you to know. They tried him at Caiaphas's house with some of the Sanhedrin there, which, after a quick trial, they turned him over to both the Roman Governor Pontius Pilate and Herod Antipas. Nicodemus fought hard for his release, but to no avail. He had hoped you would return in time to help. He told me Caiaphas used his evil ways to trick Pilate into . . . Yoseph, what am I going to do without my rabboni? Yoseph, please help me."

"I will, Miriam. We must gather strength from each other."

"Yoseph, I can't believe my master died on a Roman cross," cried Yohanan Marcus. "Why did I leave and not try to obtain his release? I have failed my teacher." He then fell on his knees with guilt.

"No, Yohanan, we've all failed him in his hour of need."

"You don't understand, Master Yoseph; I left him and ran from Gethsemane and didn't fight and now I am a coward."

"Let's now release our grief and guilt and go do what we can to honor his name." Yoseph grasped the chalice with one hand and held

Miriam with his other arm. Yohanan and Yohanan Marcus staggered behind them with their arms over each other's shoulders. None of their small group said a word as they approached the Hill of Skulls. The name of the hill so fit it, not just for its shape, but also for the surrounding grounds, which had numerous white sun-bleached skulls and bones sticking out of the soil. As they moved closer to the three crosses, the gusting wind caused the sick-sweet smell of blood to penetrate Yoseph's senses. At once, his stomach heaved with bile, making him want to cover his eyes and plug his nose with sand.

Close to the crosses were two Roman soldiers, one a centurion and the other a legionnaire. Each wore a Roman *gladius* sword, but the centurion held a long *verutum* spear. The centurion wore what the Romans called *greaves* around his shins and calves for protection, which made a rattling sound as he paced back and forth. Also, the red cloak that he wore flapped in the wind and obscured his face. He turned around and saw Yoseph approach, then stared in his direction.

He recognized this man at once; he'd stopped both Nicodemus and Yoseph last night and identified himself as Longinus. They climbed to the top of the hillock; Yoseph saw Miriam of Nazareth and his other nieces emitting an unbearable wailing sound. Miriam of Magdala grabbed his wrist even tighter and shouted forth a moaning shriek that caused his whole body to shudder. As they approached in front of the crosses, Yohanan and Yohanan Marcus started beating their chests and further tearing their clothes.

The middle cross displayed a man Yoseph didn't recognize, though he suspected it was his nephew. Yeshua wore a large crown of sharp thorns, placed with enough force to tear his scalp, leaving his hair caked with blood. His face, distorted and swollen, hung downward and blood poured from the puncture wounds onto his forehead.

To Yoseph's horror, Yeshua's *amma* buried her face in the dirt before the middle cross. *El Shaddai,* why him? Yoseph asked himself. Why did Caiaphas and the Roman Empire want to mutilate Yeshua to where his own uncle didn't recognize him?

As much as he wanted to look away, Yoseph's eyes remained fixed. Hot blood surged through his body as his face warmed with hatred.

He kicked the dirt, causing him to fall upon the soil and then beat it with his fists. He then buried his eyes in the sandy soil and prayed that he'd suffered a fitful dream that made no sense and nothing more. However, reality wouldn't let him escape. Why did they fear a poor mason's son who was a *kodesh* rabbi? He'd loved everybody and preached for a peaceful world.

At last, Yoseph looked up and saw, to his further distress, the crossbeams held both of Yeshua's arms with bound ropes that sliced into his forearms. Bloody iron spikes pierced each wrist. Drops of his blood dripped off each wrist and fell to the ground. Strange, Yoseph thought. As each drop struck the ground, it formed a small shallow hole and then disappeared, leaving no trace. His naked body displayed deep jagged whip marks, which the Roman *flagellum* had penetrated. There were chunks of flesh and muscle hanging from the many bloody slices. He closed his eyes when he saw Yeshua's rib bones protruding from where flesh once covered them.

Each foot lay crossed in front of the other and a block of wood supported Yeshua's body weight. A long single hammered bloody iron nail penetrated through both his feet. An oozing stream of blood trickled down the wood to the base stones. With each rivulet of blood that touched the large rocks below, which held the cross upright, they cracked. Even after Yeshua's death, his miraculous blood did the unbelievable!

After the sun reappeared, Yoseph raised his arms to the sky, praying that Caiaphas, Yudas, and all the other traitors would see *El Shaddai's* vengeance today.

Without warning, both the legionnaire and the centurion shoved him out of the way, which caused Yoseph to fall. The legionnaire gripped a large iron-headed hammer in his hand ready to swing it at the first man on the cross. There came a loud cracking thud as the mallet struck both his legs, followed by the man's blood-curdling howl, after which his face contorted into a horrible grimace. Just a moment later, his head fell forward and he stopped breathing followed by his blood gushing out of a large open wound that revealed broken shards of bones.

The legionnaire next proceeded to the third man and broke both of his legs too with a single horrific blow. Their bone-cracking sounds reminded Yoseph of trees splitting in the woods from a stormy wind. The man moaned just once, and afterward his face fell forward with his chest heaving its last breath.

Once again, Yoseph became sick to his stomach and fell to his knees looking up at this unrecognizable man on the middle cross. He retched until his stomach emptied, yet the heaving continued. Tears came to Yoseph's eyes when he realized what the *naviims* Isaiah and Zechariah had foretold. To his horror, their prophecies about a future crucified *Maishiach* were true! The raging anger in his body continued to grow as he shook his fists at their invisible presence and damned them. He continued swearing, until his niece Miriam's hand touched his shoulder.

"Yoseph, I knew you would come, for you have always been there for Yeshua and me. I can't thank you enough. You are a faithful uncle, and I am grateful you supported my son."

She seemed quite serene at this terrible moment, with her red-rimmed eyes betraying her demeanor. Her hands didn't shake as she embraced Yoseph, after which she wiped his tears. Yoseph believed that long ago she knew this day would arrive and kept this impending doom locked in her heart. Why didn't she share this foretold burden with him? His family and Yoseph might have prevented this terrible day. However, it didn't matter anymore.

The centurion, Longinus, shoved all three of them backward with his spear from the foot of the cross. Yoseph gazed into the centurion's eyes and saw the full extent of the one damaged eye. Its solid milky-white color indicated blindness in that eye, which he didn't observe in last night's dim light. A large pink scar traversed from the man's brow above his eye socket, which traveled across the milky-white eye to the bridge of his nose. It didn't seem to slow his quickness, for in the time of two heartbeats he used his large *verutum* spear to thrust it into Yeshua's side, causing Yoseph to curse him too. The blood gushed forth in an arched stream and splattered against the centurion's face, followed by a loud rumbling sound coming from the shaking earth beneath their feet. Then a loud collective shriek issued forth from all gathered around this dreadful hill, with their further moaning lamentations echoing down the hillock and throughout the valley.

Longinus dropped his spear, fell to his knees, and covered his face with both hands. He tried to wipe away the blood from his eyes, then froze.

For some inexplicable reason, Yoseph pulled the bronze chalice from his shoulder sack and held it up to Yeshua's side. His blood poured forth into the cup. It made no sound as it struck the rim of the metal cup. The stream of blood at once filled his cup. Yoseph knew the spear had penetrated Yeshua's heart.

With utmost care, he lowered the cup and saw, to his shock, no liquid or blood. Not one drop of blood, moisture, or anything else resembling liquid appeared in the cup. What had happened to the blood? Did Yoseph's great anguish deceive his eyes? He then drew his attention to the centurion, Longinus, as he raised his hands. His face had no visible signs of blood on it and he held both hands to the sides of his eyes.

"I can see! I, Gaius Cassius Longinus, a centurion of Rome can see!" He shouted and then fell to his knees. Longinus jumped up and bowed before the cross and then turned to Yoseph and spoke.

"Truly, I now see the great Son of your *El Shaddai*, but . . . remorse has surrounded me this day."

Yoseph's brief presence on this hillock reaffirmed what he sensed before in his thoughts and heart; his nephew possessed greatness far greater than their foretold *Maishiach*. None of his miracles past and present had happened without a reason. With his nephew's terrible, painful death, Adam's sins and all those of past humanity cease to exist this *kodesh* day. The last words he said now struck Yoseph's brain with a jolt. He would return and create a new Kingdom of Heaven on Earth.

Miriam of Magdala ambled forward holding an alabaster jar.

"Yoseph, please help steady my hands . . . so I can collect my rabonni's blood."

Without speaking, he responded with his hands and helped her obtain the remaining blood dripping from the nail holes in his feet. Miriam, Yeshua's *amma*, strolled forward holding some small cruets that Yoseph helped her fill with her son's blood. The blood loss from the scourging, nail holes, and crown of thorns had left the cross looking as if painted dark red. Yet, it faded.

Again, to Yoseph's surprise, Miriam's jar and his niece's cruets showed no visible signs of blood once filled in their respective containers. Miriam's older sister, Miriam, wife of Cleopas came forward, revealing a small wooden bowl in her hands. With a steady reach, she held her bowl up to catch the drops of blood from each punctured wrist. Once more, after she collected the blood in her humble wooden bowl, it disappeared. They were now accepting the disappearance of his blood as a miracle. None of them questioned one another about what happened, but each knew the true Son of Man now hung before them. As they held their sacred containers, all of them knelt and prayed to *El Shaddai*.

"*Barukh, atah El Shaddai, dayan ha-emet.*"

"*Barukh, El Shaddai, hamevorakh l'damva-ed.*"

"*Oseh shalom bim 'romav, hu Ya'aseh shalom Aleinu v'al kol Y'isral.*"

After their mourner's prayer, both Miriams and the wife of Cleopas asked Yoseph to visit the *procurator*, Pilate, for the body of Yeshua. Miriam of Magdala said her *Adonai* and Master needed a proper burial, to which he agreed.

"Yoseph, as you know, the Romans will leave the bodies on the cross for all to see and use as an example. My heart can't stand to see my *Adonai* on this tree and left for the vultures."

Her painful words forced Yoseph to look up above the *titulum*; there he saw a circling kettle of black-winged vultures. Then, as he looked past Miriam of Magdala's loose blowing hair, he witnessed a venue of human vultures circling the hillock. Caiaphas led the way, followed by Annas, Summas, Datam, Gamaliel, Neptalim, and Alexander. Yoseph raised his arm and shook his fist at all of them. Then he pointed to Caiaphas, left his mournful band of friends, and confronted the son-of-a-bitch.

"You're the author of this terrible day and may *El Shaddai* place a curse upon you. The witnesses here won't forget your evil acts, which today have caused my family's horrendous suffering. Your greed and power have infected you. Now *Shaytan* possesses your soul!"

Caiaphas's lips curled as he planted his metal-tipped staff of office into the ground.

"Yoseph of Arimathea, you have brought both treason and blasphemy upon yourself. I am not the one to blame, for you have harbored malcontents, insurrectionists, and blasphemers. You have placed your reputation, life, and financial wealth at risk here today. This isn't the first time I have seen you in my arrow sights."

He raised his staff toward the sky and then slammed its tip deep into the ground. The rest of his lackeys nodded their heads in agreement.

"Go to *Sheol*, Caiaphas, with your fellow evil vultures!" He turned around and ambled back to the cross with his heart feeling as heavy as a ship's anchor. As Yoseph drew nearer, Nicodemus ran toward him crying and ripping at his robe.

"Yoseph, my friend, please . . . forgive me. I did everything possible to obtain Yeshua's release." At once he fell to his knees, bowed his head, and grabbed Yoseph's hands.

"I know you tried, my friend. We'll discuss this later; however, we must honor him by releasing him from his cross. The *Shabbat* approaches and we still have the *Pesach* to continue. I need your help when we speak to Pontius Pilate."

"I must accompany you to see Pontius Pilate, Yoseph. *Procurator* Pilate seemed quite troubled about condemning Yeshua to death. I spoke to him on behalf of your nephew, as I did before the council, but to no avail. Caiaphas and his lackeys used their wile and cunning to sway his judgment."

Yoseph asked the centurion, Longinus, if he might accompany them to see Pontius Pilate, but he didn't hear him. With his fingers touching his eyes, he remained still in shock, not realizing Yoseph stood there. Yoseph saw his clouded eye had become a clear dark brown color, which matched the other eye with perfection. Longinus still hadn't heard his request until he asked a third time. Longinus then acknowledged him with a nod and motioned for his legionnaire and them to follow him.

Yoseph knew the women would remain with Yeshua and see to it the vultures didn't defile his body.

"Yoseph, why are you leaving?" inquired Miriam of Magdala.

"Pray for our quick return. I am seeking an audience with Pontius Pilate. We will ask him for our *Adonai's* body and must convince Pilate to release it to us."

He hadn't realized he'd used the word *Adonai* until he approached Yohanan Marcus and Yohanan bar Zebedee. Truly, his *Adonai* wasn't his nephew anymore.

"Friends, we are leaving to visit Pontius Pilate, and we'll return before sundown. Please, take my purse of silver shekels and purchase a one hundred weight of spikenard and some myrrh. Also, buy some linen burial strips and face cloth for our *Adonai*." He handed his purse to Yohanan Marcus.

"But Master Yoseph, no one will sell us these items. It's still *Pesach* and the *Shabbat* will soon start."

"Rush to see Nicohseeus, the Greek merchant, close to my house. He's a Gentile and will be open."

"Also, Yohanan bar Zebedee, obtain a litter for us to carry our *Adonai*," said Nicodemus. He too handed over a purse of money to the young writer.

Yoseph's determination to see the Roman *procurator* and obtain the release of his *Adonai's* body grew more urgent with each lengthening shadow. Yet, the cup he carried gave him an overwhelming sense of confidence for a positive outcome. In addition, he had a long-forgotten secret weapon, which wasn't the *kodesh* cup, and story to persuade His Excellency Pontius Pilate to acquiesce to his request. Would it work? The Seder cup told him it would.

CHAPTER XXXVII

Both young men left at once and raced off to procure the items for Yeshua's burial. Yoseph and Nicodemus followed Longinus and his legionnaire. Longinus trotted ahead of them in martial fashion toward the Antonia Fortress, just a short distance from the Hill of Skulls. However, there were wide cracks in the earth they had to either jump over or avoid. As Yoseph looked over his shoulder, still firmly clutching the bronze chalice, he saw the outline of the hill. Indeed, it appeared in the shape of a large jaw-gaping skull. Most prophetic, Yoseph thought. As they reached the bottom of the hill, he spied Caiaphas and his henchmen. Each kept a safe distance as they shadowed them on the path to the fortress. Yoseph knew they were wondering why a Roman centurion accompanied him and Nicodemus, but he didn't care. His mind wished them all to leap into the fires of *Sheol*.

The hot winds howled once more, causing the air to form dust funnels before them. The gusts increased in speed and the dust spirals grew larger as Longinus used his brass-embossed winged *scutum* shield, as the Romans called it, to cover his face. To Yoseph's chagrin, the blowing sand covered his entire body, encrusting his eyes with its stinging particles. He fell once when his foot plunged into a large crack in the ground. Nicodemus helped pull him up and they both struggled onward. As he and Nicodemus approached the sally port of the Antonia Fortress, its high stone wall blocked the wind. Longinus shouted a loud command to open the door, after which they entered through a narrow opening. Their trek continued with no end in sight with Yoseph not knowing how long it might take.

Once again, Nicodemus began telling him what Pontius Pilate had said earlier in the day. His words caused Yoseph to hit his fist against the fortress wall because of Caiaphas's cunning and evil ways in ending Yeshua's life. Today, a *kodesh* man of peace had died, yet Caiaphas, with his dark soul, continued to spread treachery throughout *Yerushalayim.*

They continued some distance down a narrow torch-lit tunnel. On both sides of the stone walls were affixed *verutum* spears, long *pilum* spears, *gladius* swords, and many shiny suits of Roman armor, called *lorica segmentata.* The weapons were endless in quantity, which reflected the vast power of the Roman Empire.

At last, daylight appeared up ahead and he knew they'd soon leave. The sun's afternoon glare made Yoseph squint as he entered a large dusty yard of sword-practicing Roman soldiers. Right away, the men stopped fighting, and they gave the Roman Army one-armed salute across their chests to the centurion, Longinus. As he and Nicodemus walked by, the soldiers' eyes narrowed with hatred as they saw two men from *Yehudah* invading their fighting courtyard.

Suddenly, Yoseph heard epithets shouted at him and Nicodemus as they approached an arched stone doorway. One legionnaire ran up to him and spit near Yoseph's feet, hoping to provoke a confrontation. Yoseph's anger swelled, making it difficult not to respond, yet he gritted his teeth and continued following Longinus.

They were now outside of the Antonia Fortress, sprinting toward Herod the Great's old palace. As they approached a long course of steps, the personal centurion bodyguards of Pontius Pilate met them. Their red horsehair-plumed helmets appeared as a long red carpet as they ascended the white marble steps.

Many summers ago, as a young man, Yoseph had visited Herod the Great's palace. At once, Yoseph and his memory harkened back to that time, remembering his first approved contract for the tin mining business in the faraway Isle of Albion, or as the Romans called it Britannia. He'd procured it in the last days of King Herod's rule, at that time the king didn't trust anybody, not even his family. How fortunate for Yoseph to obtain this mining contract then.

Their loud thumping footsteps echoed across the large red and green-colored mosaic floor as they approached several Roman clerks and sycophants. Four of the men were congregating next to a long white marble balustrade. Each had a stylus, writing some unknown words on their Roman wax tablets. When the group stopped, the four men looked up, and Longinus said something to one of the clerks in his Roman tongue. He then started to leave.

"Noble counselors, you will wait here until His Excellency Pontius Pilate agrees to see you." He then turned and followed the clerk down a dark marble-walled hallway. Yoseph and Nicodemus moved to the balustrade to wait.

"Yoseph, I must finish telling you what happened last night."

"Yes, please proceed, my friend."

"Perhaps it isn't a proper time."

"It isn't something I want to hear, but I must know all the painful details. The words coming from you, I trust. This will help me seek out the right justice for his murder."

"Yoseph, I tried everything to help Yeshua's defense."

"I know, my friend, I know."

"A short time after I returned from your house, I heard a pounding fist on my front door. A Temple guard stood on my porch and said that Caiaphas ordered me to his house. He said I must follow him at once, yet the Temple guard acted quite odd as I followed close behind. For some unknown reason, he kept touching his ear as if confirming he still possessed it. I asked him his name, to which he replied, Malchus. After a short distance, he stated he wouldn't travel any farther and warned me of an evil cabal afoot. His dire counsel frightened me, yet he didn't divulge any detailed information.

"I traveled the rest of the way to Caiaphas's home, fearing what I might see. The first loud noises I heard were shouting voices, yet the loud voices were nothing to compare with the bizarre sight I saw. Many people were standing by the main gate, close to Annas's house, but both houses have joining courtyards, making it hard to distinguish the difference. After sneaking closer to the loud shouts, I determined they came from Caiaphas's large priestly chambers.

"As I approached the entrance, I saw one of Yeshua's disciples, the big fisherman, standing near a flaming brazier. He looked up at me as I said *shalom*, and then glanced down as if he didn't know me. I rushed through the main entrance of Caiaphas's house, glancing at young Yohanan bar Zebedee, the writer, standing at the entranceway. The wide-eyed terror in his eyes made me shiver as he told about his master's arrest. He grabbed my arm and begged me to seek his release. Was this a mistake, I asked myself? I observed a man with a dark cloth bag over his head, then I recognized our *Adonai's* birthmark. Caiaphas and his minions had tied a rope around Yeshua's neck and hands. To my horror, the Temple guards repeatedly beat him in the face with their fists while taunting him and asking Yeshua to describe the next hitter. They laughed, saying he performed miracles on blind beggars so they might see, but not himself.

"I shouted my protest, pointing my finger at each council member, stating their proceedings were illegal and an offense against *El Shaddai* and the *Pesach*. Half the Sanhedrin members were present, and Caiaphas's many guards intimidated those there.

"Both Caiaphas and Annas shouted at me in a deprecating manner. After a short period, my fists starting pounding on a table in front of me. I followed up with a violent argument with those evil dogs and demanded the scribes record my protest. This didn't stop them, for Caiaphas and the remaining members cross-examined Yeshua about his authority. With a soft voice, he said his reply to those who questioned him. '*Why have you come out with swords and clubs to arrest me as though I am a bandit? Day after day, I appeared in the Temple teaching, and you didn't arrest me.*'

"At once, Annas rushed forward, pulled his mask off, faced him, and started questioning him about his secret teaching and knowledge. Yeshua told the council his ministry wasn't done in secret and all who wanted to hear the words of *El Shaddai* were welcome. All his teachings occurred in broad daylight at the Temple or any other synagogues where he preached. At once, Annas's face turned red, and without provocation he struck Yeshua, breaking his nose. I lunged forward to prevent Yeshua from any further abuse. Right away, a Temple guard stepped in front of me and used his spear shaft to strike me across my forehead.

"I lay stunned on the floor with my blood flowing into my eyes as they dragged Yeshua from the council hall with armed guards. His family and women followers ran right behind the guards as they hurried to the *beit din*. I staggered upward, still quite dazed, while stumbling forward to follow the hordes of people through the narrow streets. Once, I fell on the cold stones, when, to my surprise, Shimon of Cyrene and his two sons saw me and helped me continue. They asked me what had happened, to which I exclaimed, 'They have our *Adonai!*' That's when they informed me Yohanan Marcus had come to your house looking for you. Shimon further said that he told Yohanan Marcus which roads you had taken and when you had left.

"When they took Yeshua to the council hall, Yoseph, I wished you, Hebron, and Alein Yosephe were there."

Nicodemus's grief and frustration were most apparent in his failed attempt to obtain Yeshua's release. Yoseph's heart ached with guilt for him and his beloved nephew.

The flapping sound of sandals on the marble floor interrupted them when the Roman clerk returned. He spoke to Yoseph first in the Greek business tongue, stating His Excellency Pontius Pilate didn't want to see them. The clerk started to convey the same reply to the centurion, Longinus, but Yoseph interrupted their conversation.

"Pardon me, your esteemed scribe of Rome, would you convey one more message to His Excellency. Tell him I met his brave *pater* many years ago on mining business in Caledonia. He spoke of his son often before he died fighting the Picti. He might want to postpone his duties for an old friend of his *pater*. Please, hand him this ring, and I know he'll speak to me."

At once, all voices ceased in the hall, with an unbelievable array of surprised looks fixed on Yoseph. He took the ring out of his money purse and handed it to the wide-eyed clerk, who at once ran back into the bowels of the palace.

"Yoseph, I never knew you were acquainted with Pontius Pilate's *abba*," Nicodemus commented.

"There were many men in that patrician family, but I didn't know they were related until the other day when Hebron and I observed him marching in with his legions. From his straight posture, and the way he rode his horse, I recognized him as Marcus Pilate's son."

"Why did he entrust you with his ring?"

"An excellent question, my friend! His *abba* gave me his ring, right before his cavalry began exploring the upper regions of Albion. The day before we met, he had a premonition of his death. He knew I had some business in Rome before my return visit to Arimathea. He feared he wouldn't return home alive and wanted his young son to have the family ring. Also, Marcus Pilate gave me some names to contact in Rome on mining business and delivering his ring.

"He appeared to me an excellent leader for the Roman Army and later died outnumbered fighting a superior horde of Picti. I spent many days in Rome trying to locate his wife and young son, Pontius, but to no avail. Later, I found out she and her son had left for Iberia several days before my arrival in Rome. The family had a large estate there that they would visit each fall. It's hard to believe, I've carried this ring these many summers. I never dreamed I would give it back under these circumstances."

"Yoseph, I noticed the ring had something inscribed on its face. What does the inscription mean?"

"The signet ring has a rider on a horse, carrying a spear that's carved into the carnelian stone. I think it's the family crest."

"Do you believe Pilate will consider it's his *abba's* ring?"

"I don't know, however, at least it could lead him to question me about it, giving us a chance to ask for Yeshua's body."

This seemed to satisfy him, and, after a long pause, he continued explaining what evil had befallen Yeshua.

"As I mentioned, Yoseph, before we were interrupted. Yeshua's presence by now had attracted a large crowd of people as we entered the Sanhedrin hall. The guards let me in through the council door but kept me at a great distance from Yeshua. Most of his inner circle of followers weren't there, except two. I did see Yohanan bar Zebedee and Miriam of Magdala. In addition, Yeshua's *amma* and the women followers were there. One thing I said, which seemed to open their ears and minds, came at the end. I shouted out for all to hear, 'If he did originate from *Eloheinu*, it will stand. If he's just a human, it will come to nothing. Similar to an arrow spent of its power by missing its target.'

"This I said to Pilate too, in his defense. Yet, there were many who bore false witness against Yeshua, but their testimony sounded as if Caiaphas had threatened them to speak against Yeshua. Their testimonies overflowed with lies, and Caiaphas twisted Yeshua's parable words about tearing the Temple down and building it back up in three days. He said Yeshua preached to zealots and insurrectionists. He further said the people of Rome and the people of *Yisrael* in the future will condemn his seditious words. Caiaphas questioned Yeshua about him as the foretold *Maishiach*. Yoseph, I am sorry to say, he replied. *'You have said so. But I will tell you, from now on you will see the Son of Man seated at the right hand of El Shaddai, the Abba almighty and returning on the clouds of Heaven.'*

"My heart sank when he said that statement. He further sealed his doom when he repeated what he said earlier to his disciples. *'I have taught my disciples that all you of the council are similar to white-washed sepulchers. Well-designed on the outside, but full of corruption and stench on the inside.'* Yeshua showed no fear on his face as his captors continued to speak their false accusations. I closed my eyes, fell to my knees, and prayed while the crowd and council yelled for his condemnation. Caiaphas at once grabbed his own cloak, ripped it, and screamed out the word, 'Blasphemer!' Still shouting to the council, he said Yeshua would proceed before the *procurator* of *Yehudah* for execution.

"At that moment, my body became paralyzed with fear as each member of the council spat on him, while passing by with their judgment vote. The shame and anger forced my fist to punch the stone wall.

"As you can see, Yoseph, I am no longer wearing my council medallion. I can't in suitable conscience belong to the Sanhedrin."

Yoseph's mind started to drift away as they waited for Pontius Pilate's reply. He knew Nicodemus wanted to tell him more details about the terrible events; however, Yoseph's thoughts were distracted by several small nests of doves. The nests were wedged on the tops of Corinthian columns below them. Two of the small eggs were starting to hatch from their little-shelled tombs. Yoseph fixated on their hatching and the constant cooing sound of the adult birds.

"Yoseph, did you hear what I just said?"

He grasped the holy cup tighter to refocus his attention on what Nicodemus further had to say.

"Still, I hadn't lost hope the Roman *procurator* would release him. Many of the faithful to Yeshua followed the Temple guards to where we now stand. Pontius Pilate listened to many testimonies in favor of our *Adonai*. The courtyard you see below teamed with many people, but they were supporters of Caiaphas and the council. Several of Yeshua's followers defiled themselves by standing in the judgment hall and gave righteous testimony for his release. One woman, named Veronica, stepped forth, explained to Pilate that Yeshua healed people with his medicine and cured her of a blood disorder. Another person told how Yeshua used poultices to heal his blindness. I spoke of his kindness and great knowledge of philosophy. Pontius Pilate tried several times to prove his innocence, but Caiaphas and his pack of cur dogs prevailed. After the council had left, Pontius Pilate had the Temple guards take him to Herod Antipas for judgment. I concluded the *procurator* didn't want the responsibility of executing a Galilean. He knew Herod Antipas ruled over Yeshua's home region, and I knew Herod Antipas wouldn't try him. As I surmised, he sent Yeshua back to Pilate a short time later.

"Once he returned, a strange thing happened. A man named Barabbas, a convicted murderer, was brought forth, and Pilate let the crowd choose which one he would release. Either Yeshua or Barabbas would have his life spared. I presumed that Caiaphas pressured the *procurator* into doing this, or he figured the crowd might condemn the murderer over Yeshua. When they brought Yeshua out first, I didn't recognize him.

"Yeshua's swollen cheeks, nose, and forehead disfigured his face. They had crowned his head with a circle of large thorns, causing his hair to mat with blood. The soldiers were mocking him and saying, here stands the new king of *Yisrael*. My poor *Adonai's* tremendous beating became a bloodlust offering to the Sanhedrin and Caiaphas.

"Pilate began to speak to the crowd again, hesitating at intervals, choosing his words with care and said, 'Behold this man! His punishment has . . . been severe.' He tried to gain sympathy from the crowd to pick Yeshua, rather than the murderer, Barabbas. However, the horrible flogging didn't elicit the crowd's favor. They started shouting, 'Release Barabbas; release Barabbas.' Yoseph, those shouting for Barabbas's release were cowards planted by the bastard Caiaphas. The crowd further screamed that if Pilate refused to obey his emperor and release the pretender king, he would regret it."

Yoseph shook his head and swallowed hard. "Nicodemus, it's still hard for me to comprehend how anybody who heard Yeshua preach in the Temple would give him over to Caiaphas and the Roman governor. He never hated anybody. Critical, yes, above all if they despised the poor and downtrodden. My nephew always sought out the smallest thread of kindness in any person, no matter how they treated him."

"Yoseph, yes, Yeshua threatened Caiaphas and his spineless friends. They feared our *Adonai's* kindness."

"I underestimated Caiaphas's monstrous ways, and I indeed misjudged him in instigating Yeshua's torture and execution. Pardon me for interrupting you, please finish telling me about Yeshua's death."

"Pilate had one of his servants come out onto the balcony with a large silver *krater* of water. There he placed it on a small table, whereupon the *procurator* with care washed his hands, dried them, and stared at the mob of fools. All the while, Caiaphas's lackeys were still shouting for Barabbas's release as Pilate began to speak again. The *procurator* had a twisted expression on his face as he addressed the crowd of bloodthirsty jackals. His final words are still ringing in my ears. '*I wash my hands of this man's guilt and I am innocent of this man's blood! His judgment falls on your heads.*' With these last words, he stared at Caiaphas and his fellow lackeys. Yoseph, I will never forget the haughty expression of accomplishment on Caiaphas's face. He puffed out his breastplate of judgment as a toad might and left the palace grounds with his pack of mongrel dogs.

"Pilate sprang from his judgment seat and left the crowd while the Roman legionnaires took Yeshua away and placed a heavy wooden crosspiece on his back. He shouldered this enormous weight all the way to the Hill of Skulls. Seven times, he fell, and seven times Roman soldiers whipped him until he collapsed. Our brave friend, Shimon of Cyrene, jumped out from behind the spectators and ran toward our *Adonai*. The Roman soldiers seized him and dragged him toward Yeshua. As Shimon reached down to help Yeshua up, he too yelled from the sting of the Roman *flagellum*. After which, both were forced to carry the wooden cross. Shimon's two sons appeared from the crowd and joined Yeshua and their *abba* to help carry the heavy crosspieces to Golgotha.

"You know the rest of the story, Yoseph, except the final words spoken by your nephew. All during this time, he never cried out in pain. Even at the moment, they drove the forearm length nails into his feet and wrists. He kept repeating saying, '*Abba, forgive them for they don't know what they are doing.*'

"Oh, Yoseph, the horrific sounds I heard from the pounding of the iron mallet as the nails cracked through bone and penetrated sinew. Yeshua's mind remained clear as they hoisted the cross by ropes and pull rings into its final position. He spoke to Yohanan, who was near the cross, and asked him to look after your niece Miriam.

"On each side of him hung a thief and a murderer, and in his last breaths He spoke to them, but I failed to hear what he said. A short time later, the skies grew dark and he cried out in a loud voice for all to hear, '*Eloi, lema sabanchthani?*' Some thought He called for *Eliyah* to come down from Heaven and rescue him from the cross, yet I knew different. I realized as He took his final breaths, Adam's sins and humanity's He now received. At that moment, He had become our 'true redeemer.'

"Before He died, Yeshua asked for a drink to quench his thirst. His captors took another spear, wrapped it with hyssop leaves, and dipped it in some sour wine. The legionnaire reached up with his long spear and then pressed the wine-soaked leaves to Yeshua's cracked lips. After tasting, He cried out, '*It is finished!*' and He died.

"Oh, my friend, I have failed all of us in protecting Him. Please, have mercy on me, for I have no excuses."

"Nicodemus, don't bear all the blame. I must share this responsibility too. You were here trying to defend Him. My nephew needed me with you; besides, I failed to stop Him before I departed for Arimathea. My ignorance and fear were far worse. Let's not fail Him this time. We'll bury Him in peace."

CHAPTER XXXIII

A loud thumping sound of many sandals came from the far end of the judgment hall, which echoed forth some distance down the white marble hallway. The noise appeared that of a marching army. Yoseph and Nicodemus moved closer to the reception hall's outer rim to see the source of the noise.

In front of a group of men marched an athletic-looking man wearing a purple-trimmed robe. Pilate's toga, which blew in the breeze with each agile step, caused Yoseph to recognize him. Ten attendants, Gaius Cassius Longinus, and another centurion surrounded Pontius Pilate.

To Yoseph's surprise, he saw a Roman woman following the group of soldiers and lackeys. All wore grim expressions as they approached where they were standing. Yoseph's worst fears began to swell.

"Are you the man who sent my *pater*'s ring to me?" Pilate asked. "I thought you would appear as a thief, but now I see you're a *Nobilis Decurio* of the Sanhedrin. You are of the same station as this man next to you who calls himself Nicodemus?"

"That's correct, Your Excellency, and we are close friends too."

"You're quite fortunate, noble counselor, to have a worthy friend. Few true friends exist these days and a reliable friend is a strong defense in times of trouble."

Pilate's face looked swollen, while displaying a cleft mark on his chin, and a prominent mole below his lip. His eyes were hazel in color and circled with wrinkles, culminating at each corner of his eyes. Also, there were dark shadows under each puffy lower lid as if he hadn't slept in several days. Pilate's hair was the Roman style of well-oiled and perfumed, to the extent it irritated Yoseph's nose.

He still had the neat and rigid bearing of a former military man from his silver festooned-strapped sandals to his clean-shaven face. Pilate maintained the assurance of a soldier, even though Yoseph detected a slight nervous twitch in his right eyelid.

Beside him stood a military man whose intense brown eyes kept gazing at Yoseph. He looked similar to a centurion; however, his dress and uniform were far more elaborate, with his red cape or *lacerna,* longer than most centurion officers. He wore a custom-fitted breast cuirass on his chest, which indicated a higher rank. Strapped on each of his shins were *greaves* covering each leg for protection, and they were inlaid with elaborately designed brass eagles. Pilate noticed Yoseph looking at the stranger.

"I guess you're wondering who stands next to me," Pilate said. "Tribune Cassius Cornelius represents the people's interests of Tiberius's empire and is my second in command. We were both in the Roman Army together."

The tribune greeted both him and Nicodemus in his Roman tongue. "*Quid agis?*"

"My centurion, Longinus, says they call you Yoseph of Arimathea and you are a rich *equite*. Is this correct?"

"Yes, Your Excellency."

They both spoke Greek and Roman, but Yoseph's Greek verbal skills were greater.

Pilate proceeded to inquire about his *abba's* ring.

"Noble counselor Yoseph, how long did you know my *pater?*"

"Just a short time. I met him in the last summer of the reign of Octavian Augustus. We had sailed to what you Romans call Britannia that summer. My nephew and I were there on a mining trip to northern Britannia. We'd contacted some of my trustworthy friends and leaders of the Silures. Their tribe had helped me with my mining interests for many summers. The mines weren't producing well and at the suggestion of their leader, we followed him to the northern regions to find new mines.

"After many days, we reached a part of the country called Caledonia by your military. The surrounding valleys lay covered with large stones, and harsh winds blew from the mountaintops with constant cold rains, making it difficult to stay warm and dry at night. Oh, how the nights were so short, and the daylight never ended. It made sleeping quite difficult and our apprehension suffered even more by the fierce Picti warriors always shadowing us.

"My Silures companions had great respect for this dangerous tribe of blue-painted men, and we tried to avoid them where possible. One day we came upon a Roman cavalry-scouting unit, which totaled about a hundred men, led by your *pater*. They gave us some food, water, and your *pater* befriended both my nephew and me. For some reason, he took a great interest in Yeshua. Somehow, it appeared they both knew their destinies were intertwined, for reasons at that time I didn't understand. I think your *pater* longed to see you, for he spoke about you the entire day. My nephew had just lost his *pater* and they both had companion needs to fulfill. Before departing, he asked me to convey his ring to Rome and deliver it to you. He knew we would arrive in Rome at the same time, me there signing new mining right contracts. Your *pater* said that the next day he would leave the camp and negotiate a treaty with the leader of the Picti. Also, he told me that the night before a terrible omen had appeared in his dream. In this dream, he would die in the barren wasteland of the Picti and wouldn't see you again."

Yoseph noticed Pilate's eye twitching faster and then he spoke.

"My *pater* always had dreams; however, it never deterred his bravery. Honor to him was everything. He feared no enemy, but, *Nobilis Decurio*, please finish your story."

"Thank you, Your Excellency. The next morning, as the Roman soldiers prepared to leave, we left. We found the mines the following day and proceeded to return to our ship and Rome. My nephew said something at that time, which I thought strange. 'The life of one son would live for eternity and the other would prosper and die.' At the time, I didn't understand the complete meaning of what my nephew meant, but now I do.

"Sometime later, I heard your *pater* died in combat, resulting in a significant battle in northern Britannia. Still to this today, the Silures speak of the enormous courage of a Roman horse officer and how many Picti he killed. When we arrived in Rome, after many inquiries, I found you had left with your *amma* or *mater* to travel to your estate in Iberia. We had to sail home at once, because of the approaching start of the winter storm season. This left us no choice, but to set sail for Caesarea. For many summers I've carried his ring. Several days ago, I saw you ride into *Yerushalayim* with your legions and I knew you were Marcus Pilate's son."

Pontius Pilate stood there in complete silence after Yoseph had finished. He seemed frozen in deep thought. Yoseph feared the setting sun would race ahead of them if Pilate didn't soon respond. The sun's rays had already cast its long shadows on the frieze designs of the judgment hall, indicating the *Shabbat* and *Pesach* would start soon.

"Noble Yoseph," he finally said, "you aren't here to deliver my *pater*'s ring but to obtain your nephew's release, am I correct?"

"Yes, Your Excellency. I beg you to release his body to me before sundown. It's customary to bury our people before the *Shabbat* begins."

Yoseph's throat tightened at once, knowing he saw his real motives for his presence. A hopeless fear gripped him, and he knew he wouldn't give his approval. However, to Yoseph's surprise, he signaled his scribe to come forward and in logical Greek words dictated his command to release the body to Yoseph and Nicodemus. After finishing, he placed his magistrate's ring on the wax tablet, approving their request. He looked up, stared straight into Yoseph's eyes.

"Yoseph, neither one of us has gained anything here today. We can't undo what has happened. My *pater* died and also your nephew. All we have are painful memories. Your nephew, an itinerant rabbi from Nazareth, died a horrible, but honorable death. The two times

I had him behind the judgment curtain, he left me with more questions than answers. Your people are most strange. They want to crucify a doctor of healing, who performs his work on your *Shabbat*, and instead demand the release of a cold-blooded murderer. Your nephew had a different way of speaking than most men I have known. I assumed he was a prophet or soothsayer."

He paused for a moment of silence as he placed his long narrow finger across his hairless arms. Pilate then stared in the distance as if contemplating his thoughts before he spoke further.

"How can a rural itinerant rabbi speak with such abstruse words and have such a command of philosophy? Did the Greeks train your nephew? I understand his *pater* practiced stone masonry and carpentry. Maybe his family once lived among the Greek philosophers?"

"Yes, you are correct, his *pater* knew masonry and carpentry, but I don't think the Greek philosophers trained my nephew, Your Excellency. Many say our *Elohim* gave him unique gifts at his birth and even his own brothers never understood him."

"Several strange things happened while we talked. Each of my legion standards kept falling over my judgment seat. However, the oddest happening occurred when the Imperial Fasces kept jumping out of its stone mount. My servants were afraid to replace the standards and fasces to their upright position. I had to have my centurions remount them because the servants refused."

Yoseph noticed the shadows growing longer but knew better to interrupt.

"I asked him many questions to catch Him in a lie," Pilate continued, "but to no avail. The first one I asked, 'Are you the true king of *Yisrael*?' To which he replied, 'What proof do you have or are you listening to other people who have betrayed me?'

"From there I examined Him about tearing down the Temple and rebuilding it in just three days. He revealed to me that many years ago as a boy he helped repair the Temple with his *pater*. Nevertheless, he didn't advocate a physical destruction and rebuilding of the Temple; however, he meant building a new spiritual Temple and Kingdom not of this world, he explained. 'If my Kingdom reigned over this world, wouldn't my army of followers be fighting in the streets? Wouldn't they have prevented me from coming before the Sanhedrin and the judgment seat? My army reigns in Heaven, and I can summon it at any time for my greater glory. I came into this world to proclaim the truth of my *Abba* for mankind's sake!'

"What is the truth?" I asked him. He replied, 'Truth resides in Heaven and I am the King of Truth.'

"Then I asked, 'So you are a king?' The last answer he gave surprised me, 'You have said so.' And he spoke no more. The crowd continued to shout for his execution, but I saw no reason to comply. I tried and found him innocent four times, but the will and wrath of the people became overwhelming."

Pilate then turned to Longinus and inquired if Yeshua had succumbed to his crucifixion. To which he replied, "Yes, Your Excellency. I used my spear to confirm His death."

Yoseph noticed he didn't look Pilate in the eyes but appeared quite sullen and contrite. The young tribune, Cornelius, seemed to notice this too. He glanced in Yoseph's direction with his eyes searching for more answers.

During a slight pause in their conservation, a young woman, whom Yoseph had noticed earlier, stepped forward and introduced herself to him.

"I am Claudia Procula, granddaughter to the holy Octavian Augustus and wife of the governor of *Yehudah*. Yoseph, *Nobilis Decurio,* may I speak to you in private?"

"Yes, but with Your Excellency's permission." Pilate gave his nod of approval, and they moved from the large hall to a small alcove.

Her shaking hands displayed an awkwardness. Her station and bearing made it difficult for Claudia Procula to stand in the presence of a Jew. He surmised by her smooth pale skin, that her age totaled about twenty-five to thirty summers. Her shiny black hair revealed several streaks of gray color and she wore it in the Roman fan style with a small golden tiara within.

Claudia Procula's red-rimmed eyes were puffy and the black liner around her lashes had dripped down onto her partially exposed chest. Around her neck, she wore a magnificent garnet necklace with diamonds between each stone. Claudia's blue stola enveloped her slight build.

Her large hazel-colored eyes spoke of more transpiring thoughts about the *procurator*, which he didn't know.

"I fear for my husband's life. I pleaded with him this morning not to try this seer. The last three nights I've experienced fitful dreams of an unknown lake in the mountains. There, my husband's bloated body floated in that lake. In addition, I kept seeing an image of your nephew's swollen face each time I have had this dream. You have influence with your people. Please, I beg you not to condemn him for what has happened here today."

Yoseph's mind recoiled with surprise at what she asked. How dare her to ask such, he thought. Above all, after her husband had sentenced his nephew to a horrible torturous death, yet she and Pilate weren't solely to blame. The author of this great tragedy wore a high priest's tribal vest plate surrounded by his mob of jackals. Hadn't Pilate found his nephew innocent four times? Still, he engaged his executioners.

What might he tell her that would help alleviate her distress or should he?

"My dear princess, I will speak to my nephew's closest followers and have my friend talk to them too. We will convey a truthful accounting of what has transpired this terrible day. They'll render their own judgments. I can speak and write the truth and nothing more."

Yoseph's reply seemed to satisfy her, for she clasped his hands with her ring-filled fingers and thanked him. Her eyes still held their sadness as they left the small marble stone alcove to rejoin the others.

"I hope my wife hasn't bored you with her dreams and silly premonitions," Pilate said as they approached. "I am sometimes amazed at what she predicts, but the gods might deem otherwise." He turned to his centurion.

"Gaius Cassius Longinus will supply you with a ladder and tools to remove His body from the wooden post."

"Thank you, Your Excellency." Pilate turned and addressed his centurion, who at once saluted Pilate and left.

"Yoseph of Arimathea," Pilate said. "I hope you will keep your attention on the priest, Caiaphas. If I were you, I would henceforth guard my back, for I fear we are both condemned men. We Romans have a saying, '*alea iacta est*' or 'the die is cast.' *Nobilis Decurio*, this die, we now own. Also, far worse men than me will follow in this office."

After his last prophetic statements, Pilate left with his soldiers and sycophants. He walked a short distance, stopped, and looked back at Yoseph.

"Thank you for my *pater*'s ring." Then he proceeded down the judgment hall with his men and disappeared from sight. Both Yoseph and Nicodemus stood there ruminating over the dire warning. They both knew the evil nature of Caiaphas, but his political power didn't rival Rome's, or did it? Why had Pilate condemned himself?

CHAPTER XXXIX

Joseph didn't want to return to the cross and see Yeshua's body but knew he needed to hurry, for several urgent reasons: first, there wasn't much time left to bury Yeshua under Jewish law, and second, the sun indicated the closeness to the twelfth hour. The day of preparation and *Pesach* would soon start. Yeshua deserved their honor and respect. Yoseph's duty required him from leaving their new *Adonai* on a gnarled wooden cross, letting the buzzards peck away at his bloody flesh. They ran past the many red-caped centurion guards, while he and Nicodemus headed for the *praetorium* exit.

They reached the central marketplace, with each of them wheezing from exhaustion. Then they started uphill toward the Hill of Skulls. Suddenly, the crowds stopped at the Yoppa gate, for no apparent reason. As they waited, Yoseph heard several marketplace vendors discussing the sacred Temple curtain. They said, for some unknown reason, the curtain tore itself in half. How odd their conversation, yet nothing seemed normal this tragic day. As the crowds continued to gather, a rather tall man began speaking about seeing opened tombs, with no explanation of what caused them to open. Again, another bizarre event as Yoseph's impatient hands twisted with the unbearable waiting.

Once through the gate, Golgotha loomed a short distance down the Yoppa road and from there a short trip climbing the skull-shaped hillock. As they rushed up the hill, he observed both Yohanan bar Zebedee and Yohanan Marcus were wearing dirt marks of mourning on their foreheads. Each of them held the purchased burial supplies.

The women were still moaning and wailing and also had placed black dirt marks on their foreheads. On further observation, to show their grief, they'd ripped their robes in several more places. He didn't see Longinus, but surmised he'd taken the shortcut through the Antonia Fortress, because a ladder and tools lay on the ground. Next to the cross were the two spears used at the crucifixion. Yohanan Marcus held the litter poles waiting for Yoseph's directions while Yohanan bar Zebedee and Miriam of Magdala each held light green-colored alabaster jars of spikenard. The burial cloths, shroud, and a facial napkin lay folded next to his niece Miriam, who clutched a lambskin satchel.

"I am relieved to see you didn't have any trouble buying the burial supplies we needed," he stated to Yohanan bar Zebedee.

"No, Master Yoseph. The Gentile accepted your money. I pray you have excellent news from the procurator. We saw the centurion return with a ladder and tools, but he didn't say anything."

"Yes, Yohanan, Nicodemus and I bring good news. Pilate did consent to let us remove him from the cross and bury him as our forefathers have commanded."

"Praise be to *El Shaddai*, he has consented," Miriam of Magdala said. "However, where will we bury him, Master Yoseph? We don't have a burial site for him."

"We'll use my not-long-ago constructed tomb. He's of my brother Yoachim's line, and it's more than fitting we honor his memory with my unused tomb."

Yoseph reached down and grabbed a handful of dirt and charcoal, which were the remnants of the centurion's campfire and rubbed it across his forehead, which was their custom. Nicodemus did the same as they prepared to start the deposition.

Young Yohanan bar Zebedee took the ladder and adjusted it against the cross. He reached down, grabbed the pliers, and proceeded to climb up the rungs. Yohanan Marcus took a small iron prying bar and positioned himself behind the cross and then pried the bent nail tips straight. He reached down, grabbed the heavy iron mallet, and started hammering the sharp end of the nail, followed with horrific pinging sounds that echoed throughout the valley. After finishing, and not too soon for Yoseph, Yohanan pitched the iron mallet and bar to Yohanan bar Zebedee, letting him pry the nails from the front. Each blow from the iron hammer brought more tears and shrieking from the women standing at the foot of the cross. Yoseph's heart skipped a beat with each pinging blow and once again hoped this would end soon.

Yeshua's feet were now free and he placed the large nail on the ground. Yohanan Marcus pitched the pliers back to Yohanan bar Zebedee and, after some difficulty, he extracted both nails from Yeshua's wrist. Each nail fell to the ground with a loud thud, forming a triangle design with the first nail.

All of their eyes transfixed on the equal-sided geometric shape. Did each side represent the *Abba*, the Son, and the holy spirit? The sides were aligned with each other in a triangle symbol. Yohanan bar Zebedee broke their focus when he yelled for someone to retrieve a knife. He needed to cut the ropes on Yeshua's arms to lower his body. Yohanan Marcus shinnied up the cross behind our *Adonai* and handed him a small dagger to cut each set of ropes. At once, his swollen limp body heaved forward and fell across the shoulders of Yohanan bar Zebedee. Yohanan Marcus jumped down just in time to grab Yeshua's knees and helped lower the body to the ground, whereupon Yeshua's body slid into the lap of his *amma*. Miriam started rocking him back and forth and cried out, "My baby, my baby, Yeshua, what have they done to you?"

At that heartbreaking moment, all those present ripped their clothes further and said prayers of lamentation for their *Adonai*. Miriam of Magdala came forth, fell on her knees, and wiped Yeshua's face with a wet cloth she had soaked in drinking water.

With care, she used the knife to gently pry off the crown of thorns with some difficulty. She rubbed his hair of matted blood and placed the crown of thorns into her lambskin leather sack.

Yoseph draped a clean linen cloth over their *Adonai's* naked body while Nicodemus retrieved the stretcher, and then returned. Salome took the nails and placed them in her robe after the blood vanished. Before they lifted their *Adonai's* body, his *amma* gave Him a final kiss on His cheek. The men placed Yeshua's body on the cloth stretcher, said a prayer, and thereafter grabbed the poles to lift Him.

Yohanan bar Zebedee ambled in front and Yohanan Marcus followed behind, holding the stretcher as they stumbled forth toward Yoseph's sepulcher. Yoseph looked back once, as they proceeded down the hillock of the skulls and saw the two remaining crucified men. The vultures landed and were devouring their eyes as they made their way to Yoseph's new tomb.

Their short journey seemed to last forever, yet the distance was close from the Hill of Skulls to his sepulcher. A short time ago, he had the tomb extended that stood next to his late wife's ossuary, and its larger size provided for the burial of several people. In memory of his wife, he'd spent a considerable amount of money on landscaping a garden surrounding the tomb. Now, he realized the new tomb wouldn't suffice for a new *kodesh* king.

Along the way, several people stood by and viewed their sorrowful procession, but didn't show any grief. Some were too busy making their way home for the *Shabbat* and *Pesach* to look. How strange it seemed, less than five days ago, His nephew's admirers heralded Him as the *Maishiach*. Where were they now to mourn His death? Fear can make the faithful vanish as fast as a lightning bolt in the clear blue sky. Oh, how weak their faith!

The sight of the garden pleased Yoseph, even though their small group bled with tears. The green from the grape leaves and the smell of the fig blossoms helped to temper the anguish raging in his body. As the sunset neared, small animals and birds rustled around the trees and grounds and told him of their evening hunger.

The last yellow rays of the sun had given his polished white tomb a golden ivory color, making it appear as solid gold when they approached the opened entrance. Yoseph believed the stonemason had left it open before rushing home to the start of *Shabbat*. Both

Yohanans stopped and then lowered the body of their *Adonai* to the ground. Yohanan bar Zebedee first looked into the small outside window shaft and from there proceeded to enter the sepulcher. A short time later, he came out and said the interior of the tomb didn't have any standing water or pests. Yohanan bar Zebedee and Yohanan Marcus descended the stone steps into the antechamber and then laid their rabboni's body on the stone-chiseled floor. The women, Nicodemus, and Yoseph followed behind.

Once inside, he thought they wouldn't fit, but the precise stone-masons proved Yoseph wrong. They'd penetrated deep into the rock, allowing their party of mourners to stand with ease. This allowed them sufficient room to prepare the body and place it into the *locus*.

Nicodemus handed the alabaster jars of spices and ointment to the women. They at once started preparing the body for cleansing. Yoseph and Nicodemus took the burial cloth and cut it into strips, using Yohanan Marcus's small dagger.

Out of the corner of Yoseph's eye, he saw Miriam of Magdala weeping and shaking as she applied the ointment from one of the alabaster jars. Her teardrops mixed in with the sweet-smelling aloe and spikenard as her hands glided across Yeshua's pale chest.

As the women worked to clean their *Adonai's* naked body, something inexplicable occurred. Yoseph noticed the swelling had disappeared from Yeshua's face and the grievous wounds he'd sustained appeared to be healing. Was it the aloe and myrrh ointments working on his skin and nothing more? Yeshua's body looked healthier, yet His blood still seeped from the spear puncture hole on His side.

As she did at the cross, Miriam placed a small alabaster jar beneath the seeping blood. It would fill with crimson liquid, similar to the other containers at the cross, and then vanish. After Miriam had rubbed additional ointment onto Yeshua's side, the blood flow stopped.

When the women were finished, Yoseph pulled the shroud over Yeshua and they carried him into the inner tomb. They placed the cloth stretcher on the dry floor and proceeded to wrap the linen strips around his body. The smaller interior tomb caused them to bend over to complete their dire task, as everyone's stone-faced gaze watched them. Nicodemus started wrapping the strips around Yeshua's feet and then came a gasp from him as he pointed to the nail holes in Yeshua's feet. Were his eyes deceiving him? To Yoseph's disbelief, the holes were closing in his wrists, his sides, and forming dark indented scars too.

"Yoseph, do you see what I see?" Nicodemus whispered. Yoseph nodded his head in agreement, as they finished wrapping Yeshua's body.

"Is . . . everything all right, Yoseph?" Miriam of Magdala whispered.

"Yes, we're about finished and will soon place his body in the *locus*."

With care, he and Nicodemus lifted the wrapped body from the stretcher onto the stone bed. Yoseph's hands wedged a linen cloth under his head and placed the remaining shroud over him. Strangely, the body seemed warm to the touch, even through the linen wrappings and shroud. They stood there for a short time and recited several passages from the book of Psalms, at which time Yoseph's mind wandered back to what his nephew had once said. "*The foxes have holes and the birds of the air have nests, but the Son of Man has nowhere to lay His head*," but now indeed he had a place to rest.

Even though grief left Yoseph with emptiness, he had arranged an honorable place for Yeshua to lay his head. By now, the sweet, pungent smell of frankincense had permeated the whole tomb. He and Nicodemus stepped down into the antechamber and observed Yohanan bar Zebedee burning an offering to his rabbi. The time had come to say the mourner's *Kaddish* and praise the life of Yeshua bar Yoseph.

Yoseph started reciting the memorial prayer, "*El maleh rakhamin*," followed by Nicodemus saying the final *Kaddish* verse, "*Oseh shalom bimromav, hu ya'asch shalom Aleinu v'al kol Yisrael, Omein*." Miriam of Magdala, with hesitation, stepped forward and offered praise of her beloved rabboni.

"In darkness, Yeshua came into this world under the light of a great star. His *kabod* of countenance has led many to his beacon of salvation. He took me out of the darkness of demons and showed me the 'way.' My body and mind were once lost in the night and doubt, as were some of you now standing here. My teacher taught me more things than were possible to see or hear and his sacred light now penetrates our souls, in the place of the *tiferet*, where our spiritual and physical realms meet. The chains of death don't bind his love, and let's bear witness here to what has happened and teach his love to others. We are now sons and daughters of his ever-present light."

She stood there for a short moment and didn't speak further. Yoseph observed tears rolling down her cheeks. They'd been changed this day. How, he didn't know, yet he knew it determined a new life and a new future. One at a time, they started moving into the inner chamber to say their own personal prayers. His niece entered first with the crown of thorns in her hand, and then said her prayer, followed by her placing the crown of thorns next to his head. She returned and put both her cruets into Yoseph's palms.

"Yoseph, my beloved uncle, please accept these in remembrance of my son."

Miriam of Magdala followed next, placing one of the small alabaster jars next to his arm. She said her prayers too, after which she shook and moaned with broken words. Miriam Salome and Miriam, the wife of Cleopas, decided not to enter alone, but to hold each other as they prayed. They placed their wooden bowls at their *Adonai's* feet.

Yohanan bar Zebedee, strolled alone, stopped, fell to his knees, and prayed for his teacher. He wept louder than a crying baby, which echoed throughout the tomb, causing a lump to form in Yoseph's throat. At once, his tears raced down Yoseph's cheeks, as an uncontrollable shaking sob took over his body.

Nicodemus then embraced him and whispered in his ear.

"Yoseph, remember what Pontius Pilate said about friendship?"

"Indeed, I do remember, Nicodemus, and I am glad for your presence here this terrible day."

Yohanan Marcus, the last to enter, trudged into the inner chamber. He stood before their *Adonai* and once again ripped his robe, followed by raising his arms in a lugubrious manner, and he beat his head with the palms of his hands. At last, Yohanan Marcus let his anguish pour out too.

"*Barukh ata Adonai Eloheinu Melekh ha'alam dayan ha emet,*" he wailed. Then he stood in silence for a brief moment; afterward, he knelt down and kissed the arm of Yeshua. This ended the honoring of their departed teacher, leaving Yoseph with a sickening finality as they stumbled out into the final rays of the sun. Four of them grabbed the large round stone and started pushing it over the entrance to the sepulcher. It wouldn't move at first, but after several attempts, it started rolling on its downward stone track. The grinding sound of stone against stone caused Yoseph to shiver. At last, the large round stone came to a thundering stop. Each of their mournful party came forward and said thanks to Yoseph. With a sorrowful heart, he embraced each with Miriam of Magdala coming last.

"Yoseph of Arimathea, our most blessed counselor. I thank you for what you did for my teacher, and for me too. We'll meet again, and I now leave you with these parting sacred words."

Her lips kissed him on his cheek, then she whispered into his ear, "I leave you with these sacred Greek numbers, *penta* and *octa*. I must depart and return to Yohanan Marcus's house. His sister is watching young Zechariah." Miriam turned from Yoseph and strolled down the path with the other women and the two Yohanans. She left him mystified with her numbers that she'd just whispered into his ear. Were these the words Yeshua whispered to him after the *Pesach* supper? What did these Greek numbers mean?

He and Nicodemus stood there in silence as they viewed their friends' departure down the garden path.

"Well, Yoseph, what do we do now?"

"I think I am returning home to say my evening prayers and then catch up on some much-needed rest. In several days, I'll seek out my family. After our reunion, I'll then write about what occurred here today.

"There were many terrible and strange events, which have ensued the last several days. I need time to think about their meaning; and find reason in their causes and most important, how to seek out *El Shaddai's* justice."

CHAPTER XL

Before Yoseph turned to leave, a sudden flapping sound of wings caught his attention as numerous birds swooped by him. Then he heard the thumping cadence of marching soldiers advancing toward them. He recognized the loud *clanking* sounds created by the Roman legionnaires' *scutum* shields.

Through the branches of the flowering fig trees, Yoseph spied them marching toward the tomb carrying their long-shafted *pilum* spears. Out in front, leading his men, marched the centurion, Gaius Cassius Longinus. Yoseph counted eight soldiers with him, the smallest unit of men who performed guard duty.

Longinus stopped in front of them. "Noble counselors, I've been instructed by the governor to seal this tomb and guard it. Several of the *contubernia* will stay the night and for the next several days."

"Has the high priest, Caiaphas, visited your procurator?" Nicodemus asked.

"Yes . . . but I won't testify to what I say here. I know the dead man in this tomb made me see. I have heard your people say he practiced medicine and performed healing miracles. And yes, his splattered blood performed a powerful miracle on me." His long index finger pointed to his healed, clear eye. However, he returned to the business of his ruler. "The procurator has ordered me to place the string seal of his office and the emperor of Rome on this stone door."

Longinus reached into his tunic and out came a bronze metal stamp, a small container of soft red wax, and several strings. Then with quick military fashion, he approached the round stone. He spread the wax on the edge of the stone covering the sepulcher, placed the twine across the entrance of the round stone, and with one swift motion, he stamped the wax. To Yoseph's horror, the wax seals had the image of the imperial Roman eagle.

"Blasphemy!" Yoseph shouted. "You can't place a graven image on my nephew's sepulcher! I won't allow it!"

Swiftly, Yoseph lunged toward the centurion with both his hands reaching for Longinus's throat. At once, eight *gladius* swords appeared from their scabbards and the circled soldiers pointed them at Yoseph. Nicodemus grabbed him around his waist and pulled him away. Yoseph continued shouting the words "blasphemy," followed by damning the Roman Army and Caiaphas. Nicodemus kept a cooler head and verbally interceded on his behalf.

"You must excuse my friend's behavior; he has suffered a most grievous sorrow today. He hasn't slept in two days. However, I'll escort him home for some much-needed rest. We'll leave right now and not cause any more trouble."

"I will overlook this threat because of his grief, but both of you must stay away from this tomb. I hope I have made myself clear," Longinus insisted.

Nicodemus nodded his assent, and Longinus ordered his men to step aside, letting them leave. Yoseph picked up his chalice pouch, afterward clutching it close to his heart as they exited his garden. Their swords were still drawn as they proceeded down the path onto the road. The chalice helped calm Yoseph's anger and dolorous heart as he started for home.

"Yoseph, you need some rest so you can stay focused on your departure from *Yerushalayim*. I'll send for the camels that you left at the foot of Golgotha. One I'll keep and send the other to your home. After we're both rested, I'll meet you and then we'll journey to Arimathea."

Yoseph didn't disagree with him as they trudged through the Yoppa gate and then parted company. Yoseph shuffled along with exhaustion, making each of his feet as heavy as sacks of grain, with his ankles pushing them forward with each step.

As he scuffled homeward, he saw just one stranger, while his sorrow longed for a solitary evening. The Gentile merchant started to close his tent but turned and stared at him with derision. Yoseph guessed he looked like an unwanted beggar.

Nearing his house, the horizon had swallowed the sun, with three stars now visible in the sky for *Shabbat*. Exhausted, his fingertips touched the *mezuzah*; next, he unlocked the courtyard entrance door, pushed it open, and then entered. With stinging eyes, the courtyard's darkness caused him to stumble on some loose tiles. The servants were surprised to see him, still thinking Yoseph and his family were resting in Arimathea. A few courtyard leaves made a scratching sound as a cold breeze blew through the colonnade.

His last remaining surge of energy told his feet to move faster for some overdue rest, even though *Shabbat* meant staying awake. Slowly, he made it to his bedroom door, opened it, and then entered. He took off his dirty clothes and with his patting hands touched the foot of his bed; there he placed the cup. He told his servants not to disturb him.

His tiredness forced him to plunge onto his bed and, at the same time, he recited his prayers. Sleep came right away and so did the fitful dream. In his dream, he saw the *kodesh* cup floating in front of him while he raced toward it. Both his hands were forever reaching out to grasp the chalice, but, for some unknown reason, he never reached it. One time he looked back and saw the bloodied image of his crucified nephew. Neither the chalice nor his crucified *Adonai* appeared to move out of his sight. Both were always the same distance away from him, followed by a ground-shaking earthquake under his feet. In his nightmare, the path in front of him would split wide open with a terrible ripping sound; thereafter it would close back up as he raced forward.

In the middle of the night, he bolted straight up in bed wide awake. Moonlight caught his eyes as it streamed through an open window and left him restless. As he sat there in bed, his thoughts caught the image of his good friend Nicodemus. He prayed he didn't face any trouble on his way home. The rest of the night, Yoseph worried about his family, Nicodemus, and his nephew's followers.

The morning sun seemed to never rise, but once it did, his entire body ached with soreness, accompanied by a hazy veil covering his mind. His servant, Hezekiah, rushed into his room with food.

"Master Yoseph, I thought you and your family were in Arimathea. Why did you return?"

"I don't want to discuss this right now. Please leave the fruit, and I want nobody to disturb me." In Yoseph's current emotional state, he didn't want to see anybody.

Also, the same fitful dream continued itself over the next several nights. On the third morning there came a loud pounding noise, arousing Yoseph from his terrible dream. The sound echoed from the main courtyard door. Remnants of his nightmare left him dripping with sweat as he put his feet on the floor. At once, Hezekiah breathlessly ran into his room, announcing the Temple guards were outside his courtyard entrance.

"Master Yoseph, they are saying if you don't open the door right now, they'll break it down. I estimate there are a dozen guards outside the main door." Hezekiah's trembling hands tried to drape a clean *tallit* over Yoseph's shoulders. Without warning, Yoseph heard wood cracking that told him they'd breached his thick courtyard door and gate. He rushed out to the center courtyard, as the stream of Temple guards came crashing through the doorway.

"Who ordered this?" Yoseph shouted as they circled around him. "You have no right to break into my house and destroy my property!"

A big man with rotten teeth approached him and asked his name.

"I am Yoseph of Arimathea and a member of the Sanhedrin. What rank or privilege do you have to break into my home?"

"The high priest, Caiaphas, has ordered me to arrest you for blasphemy and high treason."

"This isn't so!"

"You are to come before the *beit din* for trial. Now leave with me at once, or I will have to use force."

Again, Yoseph protested, "Caiaphas has no authority to do this. He's no more than a jackal, even lower than a jackal! We are celebrating a *kodesh* time, and all of you are the true blasphemers. Now leave my house and tell Caiaphas to go to . . ."

The hilt of the guard's sword hit his head, and everything went black.

Later, a swirling light brought Yoseph out of his unconscious state as he was thrown down a flight of stone steps. Then he saw a group of men standing before him.

With radiating spots swirling in his line of sight, he sought to concentrate on a group of flickering images. To his right, Nicodemus lay on the stone floor next to him. He too had his hands tied behind him. In front of Yoseph lay his trusting servant, Hezekiah, with blood flowing from a jagged hole in his head. His chest didn't move as Yoseph grew horrified they'd killed him. It appeared he'd fought in Yoseph's defense, for his knuckles were bloodied and broken. He wondered how many more people he loved would die today.

Sitting there in the judgment hall were the same jackals he saw on the Hill of Skulls four sunsets ago. Caiaphas rose up from his stone seat with a crooked smile on his face and began reading the charges. They accused him of defiling a tomb, stealing a corpse, breaking the imperial seal of Rome, and beating up several Temple guards.

"Caiaphas, you are mad!" Yoseph shouted. Was he still dreaming? However, a trickle of blood ran down over his lips, with its salty taste giving him a dose of reality.

The Sanhedrin charged Nicodemus with the same accusations, but when Nicodemus asked witnesses to testify on his behalf, none came forward. His face then glared, exposing his gritted teeth toward each member of the Sanhedrin, followed with each person looking away as though he didn't exist.

Yoseph demanded Caiaphas to explain why he instigated this during a *kodesh* time. "Why are you breaking the laws of Moshe and trying us today? Haven't you drawn enough blood from my family? Is it now a crime to bury a family member in my own sepulcher?"

"Yoseph of Arimathea and Nicodemus, you haven't just brought the wrath of this council on both of you, but also the empire of Rome down on your heads. I have read the charges as stated against both of you and they speak for themselves. A trial won't commence here today, because of the laws of Moshe. You and Nicodemus will stay in the dungeon until the *Pesach* festival ends. At that time, both of you will come before the full council for the aforementioned crimes. I am quite certain a guilty verdict will keep both of you in prison."

Caiaphas took his staff of authority, raised it, and motioned for his guards, who grabbed Nicodemus first, cinched a rope around his neck and hands, and then led him away. Two other Temple guards draped his servant's body in a burial shroud. One guard then bent down, picked up his bloody body, and slung Hezekiah's limp arms over his shoulder. He left the council chamber while the big guard with the rotten teeth stepped forward. He grabbed Yoseph's chain necklace Sanhedrin medallion and yanked it off his neck. He threw it on the stone floor and stomped on the medallion with his sandal until it broke into many pieces. Afterward, he also tied a rope around Yoseph's neck and hands and pulled him in the direction of the prison.

Soon, he found himself in the interior bowels of the *beit din*, which he'd only known by name. The guard yanked him down a spiral set of slippery damp steps that smelled of mold and urine that terminated at the bottom of a stone passageway stinking of feces. The hallway had thirteen wooden doors, with numerous groans emanating from behind them. Similar to Yoseph, how many of these past poor souls suffered unjust imprisonment? His mind's eye visualized these poor wretches dragged from their homes on fallacious charges and not heard from again. Why hadn't he seen these horrible injustices carried out earlier by Caiaphas?

The guard halted at the end of the passageway, took out his ring of keys and unlocked a large wooden door. Three giant brown rats scurried out and ran over Yoseph's sandals as the guard pushed him into a vile pungent-smelling cell. The door slammed shut in front of him, followed by the *clanking* sound of the lock and then came the total darkness of a tomb. Was this place now his final sepulcher? At once, the bile of desperation came over him and he retched. However, he had to pull himself out of this hopeless sensation.

Had his total life's history come down to this terrible place? Was Yeshua mistaken about what he saw in his future just a few days ago? A dark, hopeless doom crept into his heart. At that same moment, he realized he didn't have his sacred chalice. What happened to his precious cup? Did the Temple guards give it to Caiaphas? "No!" he screamed. "Oh, Yeshua, I've failed you!" He fell to his knees.

His body shook with mixed emotions, one of anger, the other grief, all culminating at the same time. Once again, he remembered a Psalm and said the verse aloud. *"Blessed be El Shaddai, my strength, which teaches my hands to war, and my fingers to fight in battle; my fortress and my tower; my deliverer and my shield, in whom I seek refuge."* Saying these words aloud gave him some assurance to fight back and not fall into a deep state of despair.

Hampered by the rope around his wrists, he struggled to sit up. However, when he leaned against the door, his arm touched a sharp piece of metal protruding from a large hinge. It took just a moment to use the pointed-shaped metal to saw through his rope shackles. He finished and with numb fingers, he untied the rope around his neck. As Yoseph's fingers touched his neck, it burned. Yoseph gave thanks to *El Shaddai* for his life, then prayed for his poor servant. He knew his health and sanity were on a precarious edge. He must create a plan with solutions to cope with his horrible predicament.

He groped around the walls to measure the dimensions of his cell. Yoseph's palms and fingertips collected a sticky unknown liquid that covered most of the cold stone floor. To his surprise, the cell seemed larger than what he would have expected, with a narrow stream of light coming from a thin crack in the door threshold. He remembered that the hallway outside his cell had two window openings at each end of the passageway. Also, there were several unlit torches stationed around for nightfall. With this information, he could determine the day's beginning and end. He hoped to find something to draw a mark on the walls. His hands moved along the bottom of each wall until he found a sharp nail. How fortunate thus far with his new discoveries, he thought. Unknowingly, his captors had left him with some small necessities.

At once, he made his first mark deep into the damp stone, pushing and restriking his rusty iron nail on the wall next to the door. After finishing, his fingertips touched the depth of the indentation and this gave him reassurance about starting his calendar. How does one adjust to a dark, stinking, and foul room? It never occurred to Yoseph that Caiaphas would starve him to death, yet the damned bastard called himself a priest. With his stone-cold heart, he used it to crush the people who blocked his way.

After four days or marks had occurred, the hope of a trial vanished. By now, his body had become quite weak from the lack of food. The guards hadn't fed him or poured him any water during the time of his imprisonment.

On the fifth day, he awoke from his sleep-induced weakness by the squeaking sound of his door hinges. A blurry-imaged guard placed something on the floor. Blinded by the passageway's sudden light, his eyes kept him from seeing where he put the object. His hands moved along the cold and sticky floor until he found the tray.

Two of the objects on the tray were bowls, which held water and cold barley gruel. With the ravenous hunger of a wild animal, Yoseph's fingers poked the gruel down his throat. To his horror, the gruel chunks were moving! The contents of his bowl wiggled with some type of unknown vermin. He threw the wooden bowl down, spit out the gruel, and shouted. "You bastards!" Yoseph heard no movement, nor did anyone reply, just silence.

He sat there contemplating what to do next, when unexpectedly he had to vomit. To keep up his strength, he had to eat and drink. No matter what his captor brought him of a vile nature, they would never starve him. "Never!" Yoseph shouted. Today, however, his determination didn't matter, it provided little nourishment, but he must do whatever necessary to stay alive. Maybe someday justice would prevail.

Grabbing his water dish, he now realized he should have reached for it first. Yoseph gulped down the gritty, thick liquid. In the dark, he found the bowl he'd thrown away; now comprehending he had to eat the gruel, even with its infestation. The strength Yoseph needed to stay lucid and robust had started ebbing from his body. Most of the cold sticky gruel hadn't spilled. He proceeded to pick out most of the maggots and then swallowed the entire bowl's creeping contents.

After about twenty marks, things started to resume a bizarre daily routine. He knew that after every fifth mark, he would receive the same gruel and dirty water. Between those days, he supplemented his water allowance from the water seeping out of the mortar between the stones. His additional food supply consisted of morning and nighttime forays of insects found on the cell floor. They would enter and exit through the door threshold, where he would set his traps, using a few leftover morsels of barley gruel for bait. To his surprise, it worked every time. The taste of these insects ranged from almonds to figs. After pulling off their legs, they were easy to chew and swallow.

His nose always told him when the *Shabbat* arrived, by counting the number of times he smelled the burning torches lit each day. Yoseph would then mark his calendar with a T-shaped symbol. Other days he would pace around his cell for exercise and kept his area as clean as possible. Praise be to *El Shaddai*, for these activities kept him from losing his mind. Although, if his children saw him pacing in feces-stained clothes and his wiry, caked hair, they wouldn't recognize him. Each day, Yoseph feared insanity.

The guards, who gave him his food every fifth day, were the sole noises he heard, other than the moans of his fellow prisoners. Yet, he never saw their faces. Each day he looked forward to the changing of the guard, that's when they would exchange gossip about the Temple priests, Caiaphas, and their families. Late one night, he had an unexpected little furry visitor. It started as a scratching sound at his door and then a low audible squeak. Through the crack in the doorway squeezed a small brown mouse. At last, a companion! His faltering mind pondered what to do next, when he remembered, whenever a guest visits, one offers hospitality. The discarded legs of Yoseph's insects were all he had to offer. The mouse, at first, would come and eat the legs that he provided; however, sometimes Yoseph would startle him and he would scamper away.

After several nights, he would place some tidbits of leftover gruel to supplement the mouse's food supply. It didn't take long before he would return and munch on Yoseph's meager offerings. It seemed ironic; they both had much in common, for each of them needed the other's companionship to survive. Yoseph detected him each day by his two shiny eyes staring at him from the light. He carried on a daily dialog with his mouse friend on Yoseph's accomplishments. After which, his furry friend scurried to Yoseph's palm and ate the small pieces of gruel, then leave. Yoseph looked forward to his regular visits, which made him a reliable little fellow. He hoped one day to tell Nicodemus about his new friend; he knew both were loyal and faithful. What a laugh they would have! Nicodemus, his supporter. Wherever he was, he prayed he was alive and well.

Yoseph had an everyday routine; however, on the thirty-ninth day, things didn't seem the same as they'd been in days past. The insects didn't come to his baited trap, the guards weren't present, nor did his furry little friend come to keep him company. The total silence was odd. And he wondered what the change meant.

CHAPTER XLI

Discouraged, Yoseph crawled to his stone-floor bed and lay down. He started to drift off to sleep, when suddenly a radiant buzzing orb of light and a rose fragrance permeated his cell. The pleasant smell took the place of the putrid stench of his waste. At first, he thought his guard had opened the door. A blinding light emanated from the corner of his cell, next to his door, causing his eyes to burn. Then a loud voice announced, "Behold the Lamb of *El Shaddai* who takes away the sins of the world!"

Yoseph's eyes still pained from the pulsating white orb and tears of irritation rolled down his cheeks as the great light spoke once again.

"I am the spring that offers water to all who are thirsty."

On each side of the burning orb appeared another separate, intense white light. The luminous center light seemed to form a human shape, yet all that Yoseph saw were scarred feet suspended above the stone floor. As Yoseph's blurry vision tried to recognize the human apparition, now two spiritual beings started forming. The one on the right held Yoseph's missing bronze Seder cup and the Last Supper paten! The one on the left grasped a spear and a sword in one hand and the cruets from his niece in the other. Great fear caused Yoseph to step backward. Then a shiver shot down his spine, thinking a demon might have possessed him.

"Yoseph, my beloved uncle and apostle, we are not evil spirits. You're in my *Abba's* heavenly grace. It's I, Yeshua, who has come to you from my *Abba's* Kingdom. Fear me not, for I have come to you as your Savior."

This was an illusion and not his nephew, for they'd buried Him in Yoseph's tomb! The radiant center light became whiter than white mountain snow, and then diminished as He continued speaking. His white raiment radiated yellow beams of light and Yoseph saw His head encircled by a brilliant golden-colored *kabod*. Once again, it made it difficult for Yoseph's eyes to focus on his nephew's features. The voice he recognized, but he wanted to see His face clearer to confirm Yeshua's identity.

Yeshua made a hand gesture to each *malach* spirit, after which they placed their objects on the stone floor. As they completed their task, another unbelievable event occurred. Both *malachs* moved backward, not touching the ground, and faded into the stone wall, leaving Yoseph in awe. Their disappearance helped him refocus his vision, thus, indeed, he recognized his deceased nephew Yeshua!

"Yoseph, I have returned to show you the spear of death doesn't extinguish my light nor the whip beat down the Son of Man. The Roman cross can't stop my teachings nor a tomb hold my spirit captive. I am about to journey to my *Abba* and your *Abba's* Kingdom. I am leaving you with spiritual gifts in my remembrance. Each has its own unique hallowed purpose, but I bestow on you one gift above all, which will exalt the Son of Man for all eternity."

After He had said this, to Yoseph's great surprise, He handed him a lamp and his writing satchel.

"My beloved uncle, the weapons of my warfare aren't of this earth, but I have the divine power to destroy all who are evil and those who might challenge my *Abba* and His hosts.

"You will finish a grand *kodesh* book about my Last Supper and the chalice I drank from for the remission of mankind's sins. This same chalice will remind you to write and tell of my teachings. Yoseph, now journey to the lost sheep of the house of Yáakov and tell of my lessons. After this, show my 'way' to the Gentiles, for they thirst for the waters of salvation.

"Uncle Yoseph, you have weapons granted to you by my *Abba*, which are far greater than any army might possess. Remember what I have said and done. Write these things down to show that we are all my *Abba's* children. This holy cup signifies your battle standard, guard it well.

"Remember this, Yoseph. The nearer you are to the threat of the sword, the closer you are to my *Abba* and me, for we are your shield. Beware, my uncle, of the *maddiah*, the evil one, who will lead the faithful of my flock astray. He'll come in many disguises. Always watch for him, my beloved uncle, for I appoint you the first apostle to speak in my new temple. Remember the names of Bezalel, Oholiab, and the glory of Solomon. They're the forgotten architects of my new Kingdom, please follow their example.

"Uncle Yoseph, I have always known the love in your heart that you have kept for me and my *amma*. Have the same respect and love for the Cup of Salvation."

He also handed Yoseph the paten from the *Pesach* supper and then His floating image touched Yoseph's hands, feeling like the solidness and warmth of a mortal body. The touch of His fingers gave Yoseph's hands a sudden jolt of euphoria that coursed throughout his body.

"Remember what I said when I drank from this *kodesh* vessel," Yeshua continued. "You'll now serve this redemption meal in my remembrance and you are now the new 'fisher king' for my flock. Just three guardians will follow, protecting this chalice until I come again. Yoseph, always hold this chalice up to honor our *Abba*, the Son of Man, and the *Kodesh* Spirit. With these three powers, they'll act as one.

"Choose wisely who will guard and honor this cup in remembrance of me when you're no more of this earthly world. You now possess other *kodesh* objects, use them in my name and remember my secret knowledge and the words I have imparted to you." His shimmering hand pointed to the sword, spear, cruets, and paten.

"My beloved Miriam from Magdala knows the secrets of my heart. She will comfort you and support you in times of trouble.

Also, you must do the same in her times of trial. Both your strengths and wisdom will slay all foes. If you need me, just say my prayer."

"But, Yeshua, I don't know this prayer. I haven't heard you say it."

"Yes, twice, Uncle Yoseph. The first time at the Temple Mount, when we were cleansing ourselves at the *mikveh* bath and at the *Pesach* dinner at the home of Yohanan Marcus. I spoke secret words into your ear of many things. Pray on what these words were, and you will find them hidden in your heart.

"I must now leave and soon travel to our *Abba's* house. I leave you with special parting words and sacred numbers. A great *ruah* or wind will come to you in ten sunsets. Embrace this wind, for a holy fire will descend on you and then baptize you with its power. Afterward, you'll go forth and feed my sheep, for they will thirst and hunger for what you have to say.

"The numbers that I tell you are the keys to my house and my *amma's* house. You'll become the first among men and nations to construct this home. You will build a house of remembrance and salvation to enclose the hallowed gifts, which I just gave you.

"The sacred numbers are *octa* and *penta*. Remember them well and contemplate on the *octa* thrice. Pray and search your heart again for their meaning. Stay alert, Yoseph, for my final coming. The throne of my *Abba* will have many places for it to reside before I come again. Look for me descending from a cloud to usher forth the end of days and afterward reigning upon the throne of a *New Yerushalayim* for a thousand years. My coming will seem like a thief in the night. Not even I know the hour, day, month, or summer. However, my *Abba* knows when the *Parousia* will come."

Yeshua's *kabod* grew brighter in intensity as He spoke about His second coming. Once more, His radiating light burned Yoseph's eyes to the extent he failed to see.

"Yoseph, I will stay with you and in your heart, through all eternity."

His flaming white light undulated throughout Yoseph's cell, forcing his eyes to squint as Yeshua moved toward the wooden door.

"I am the doorway to the truth. All who seek this door will see salvation! For all that is born, all that's created, all the elements of nature are interwoven and united with one another. All that is composed shall become decomposed, for I am the Alpha and Omega."

After His last word, Yeshua vanished through Yoseph's prison door. The room became dark again, except for the lit oil lamp, and Yoseph sat there in a numb state of disbelief.

He didn't know what to think. His mind gushed with a river of thoughts, which had overflowed its banks. However, the sacred numbers He'd mentioned were the same words Miriam had revealed at the burial tomb. What did these *kodesh* numbers mean? Did they have a purpose or use? He had to pray and contemplate the power of these gifts that Yeshua had bestowed on him. This he did right away, with his lips quivering, as the first words came from his mouth.

"Truly you are the *Maishiach*, son of *Eloheinu*. Please, always remember me, my *El Shaddai*, as you reign in your Kingdom."

After finishing his short prayer, nothing came into his mind to reveal the meaning of the Greek numbers. However, the reality of his dank cell still stood before him. Yet, there were several tangible reminders of what just happened radiating their presence to Yoseph. They gave off an iridescent orange-yellow light, the brightest of which came from the chalice. At last, he saw his prison cell surroundings and the bronze cup beckon him to grab it. The orange glow surrounded Yoseph as he sat there and held the Last Supper chalice, reminding him forever of the last meal he had with his *Adonai*.

Sitting there, he wondered about Yeshua's cryptic plans for him. He didn't specify but spoke in His usual parable phrases, still leaving Yoseph with uncertainties. How did these individual Greek numbers create a home for Yoseph's ministry?

As he gripped the chalice tighter, his strength returned. To his surprise, he saw wine or blood filling the cup as Yoseph gazed into its interior. Seeing the garnet-colored liquid forced him to empty it in one swift gulp. He didn't care if the contents contained wine or blood, for the liquid broke his mind's chains of obfuscation.

At once, his inner eye saw the hidden meaning in what Yeshua had just said. He was to build a new type of synagogue for Yeshua's nascent faith and a new prayer in the remembrance of his nephew.

Yet, where would this synagogue be built? What about the numbers *octa* and *penta*? Yoseph believed the numbers were keys to help travel to a future new kingdom. Again, to his surprise, the miraculous metal paten filled with coarse bread that had a yeasty smell of just-baked bread. His hunger tore into it and devoured one large crusty piece. After satisfying his appetite for the endless supply of food, he turned to the chalice for more wine. How strange, Yoseph thought, the cup always refilled itself to the brim after he swallowed its contents.

Once full of a meal, his clear thoughts reconciled all of Yeshua's hidden meanings, which had vexed him. Yoseph, was now a teacher, builder, scribe, and apostle of our *Maishiach*. His life as a member of the Sanhedrin and a wealthy tin merchant no longer existed. He knew from that moment forward, he had just one master named Yeshua, his *Adonai*. One concern did lodge in his mind, the safety of his family and the fear of the evil Caiaphas and his henchmen harming them. Yet, right away, now his faith in *Adonai* helped dismiss these thoughts.

After nine sunsets and one *Shabbat*, Yoseph checked his crude calendar and saw tomorrow started the beginning of the festival of *Shavuot*. He was now in the month of *Sivan* and his prison time totaled forty-nine days. He remembered Yeshua's prediction of a great wind and fire that would visit him. Yoseph sensed an anticipation of happiness on what tomorrow would bring, yet he knew not why. He laid his head down and drifted off to sleep.

The next thing he heard was the thumping of sandals, indicating the changing of the guards. Their footsteps signaled the start of a new day and the festival of *Shavuot*. He took his rusty nail and made another mark on the cell wall to indicate the beginning of this *kodesh* day.

His cell always remained quiet and that made any new sound out of place. So, to his astonishment, came a weak rumbling sound that grew louder with a slow piercing roar. He didn't know from whence the sound emanated. However, the roar stung his ears. At once, Yoseph fell backward from a great gust of wind. Where did it originate? He was belowground, surrounded by stone walls. He found himself on both hands and knees trying to rise when a large narrow shaft of fire appeared above him. It hovered over the top of his head as he straightened to stand upright. His entire body stung, in what he thought was a swarm of stinging bees, but he saw no whelps or sensed any pain. Yet, instead, a light tingling sensation coursed throughout his entire body. The odd awareness he didn't recognize, for every part of his person produced a pleasant warmth. However, the greatest intensity centered near his heart.

The flame above him stayed suspended for a moment and then disappeared without a trace. The euphoria remained and an inner voice drew him to his writing satchel. He picked up his writing pen, dipped it in the dark ink clay jar, and started writing.

Yoseph stopped keeping track of the days and months and wrote each day until he fell asleep. His nourishment and strength never ceased, always replenished by the *kodesh* chalice and paten. Time seemed meaningless as the never-ending divine supply of ink, parchments, and quill pens helped complete his writing each day.

One night as he started to fall asleep, he thought he heard his daughter and son crying over him. Doubts raced through his mind, yet he knew his great *kodesh* book neared its completion. However, he doubted he would ever share its story and meaning with mankind. What about seeing and embracing his children, his sister, Hebron, and Nicodemus? How many future summers and winters would he not see them? A tear trickled down his cheek as he drifted off to sleep.

His last whisper to himself, he said, "*Adonai,* please grant me forbearance and hope."

PART FIVE

Not the End

CHAPTER XLII

Pyrénées Mountains
Late Fall
Anno Domini 1190

After completing Squire Hughes's investiture as a *chevalier* and now-acknowledged Templar, his cheeks and lips were blue-colored. I knew his days with us would be short, and I chose to spend it with him in some way, which I knew he would enjoy. I continued reciting to him about my written narrative of Joseph of Arimathea and the painful events of our Lord. From the beginning of our quest, Squire Hughes had shown a passionate interest in the holy written words of the saint. Young Hughes lay next to the fireplace with a slight smile on his face. His eyes focused on my lips as each event unfolded. Abruptly, Hughes stopped me to inquire about what Yeshua had meant when he said, "*I leave now to prepare a place for you. I'll come again and take you to myself, hence where I am there you'll reside also.*"

"Young Hughes, what He is telling us, if you believe in Him, there's a place in His *Père's* house for all eternity."

This seemed to satisfy his mind, for afterward he drifted off to sleep. I gazed at his shallow breathing for some time, as I finished the final pages of the *Sangraal* book. *Chevalier* Hughes died the next morning.

I observed Gilbért's pale face slump forward with grief. He crossed himself and mumbled an unrecognizable prayer, as did the other men. The remaining *frères*, including Commander de Érail, struggled to stand and see to their departed fellow *chevalier*. I ran outside and motioned for Muhammad to confirm Hughes's death, but I knew his spirit now belonged to God. Muhammad grabbed his limp wrists and gave out a dolorous sound of "*morte*." His peace had come at last with a place in *mon Père's* Kingdom for this brave and unselfish lad.

The other two sergeants toiled to come close, one with a make-shift crutch and the other hobbling on his sword, and both followed by Commander Gilbért. Each man stood in silence, showing his respect for a true Christian martyr. Hughes now stood tall among the Warriors of Christ.

EPILOGUE

I glanced at Commander de Érail before Muhammad and I prepared *Chevalier* Hughes's body.

"I need to speak to you in private, Lord de Borron." I helped him walk in the slushy snow toward the back of the cabin. Once we stopped, he began to speak.

"I curse the day we met up with that evil de Tournay. He has caused us a great deal of suffering; however, I have a confession to declare, Lord de Borron." He motioned for me to come closer. "I haven't told you all the facts as to why we are risking our lives to pursue the next set of *Sangraal* parchments.

"When fighting in the Levant, during the reign of King Baldwin IV, the Grand Master made me the commander of Jerusalem. This occurred before our terrible defeat to Saladin Yoseph Ibn Job at the battle of Hattin. We were in the second excavation of the Temple Mount to expand our stables. One day, one of my *chevaliers* brought me an ancient Hebrew scroll from the excavation. He said he found it hidden in a room, behind a wall sealed with quarried stones. The small room had numerous parchments stuffed in an olive wood box. In addition, one parchment edge revealed itself in a stone mortar crack. After a vain attempt to read it, what little he translated, it did reveal the next codex's whereabouts.

"My chaplain tried reading the many parchments pages that were contained in the box. To his amazement, after some difficulty, he found that Saint Joseph of Arimathea wrote all the pages. Much of the text he didn't understand, but he knew they were holy parchments about our Lord and Savior, Jesus the Christ.

"All who dug at the excavation, I had them swear an oath not to divulge what we had found. My chaplain and his fellow priests bound the parchments into the *Sangraal* book you read back at the commandery monastery. The holy book always stayed near me, secured in a separate vault from the commandery treasury in Jerusalem. My chaplain, without much success, did translate just a small portion of its main contents. Some day in the past, Saint Joseph of Arimathea meant to come back for this book or left it there for some future disciple of Christ to discover. My chaplain did confirm a separate note found in a mortar crack, which fell out during the digging. He said Saint Joseph would write a future set of parchments about his ministry to the Gentiles.

"He further said Saint Joseph's family had escaped to his birth town of Arimathea after his imprisonment. His hometown lay about seven or eight leagues northwest of Jerusalem, which I traveled there by myself to investigate. I spoke to several local Saracens about Saint Joseph, and they directed me to a cave on the outskirts of town. When I arrived, I saw an old man living in the cave and he confirmed that, indeed, Saint Joseph once lived in the ancient cave. He further said the army of Muhammad had conquered this region hundreds of years ago and some in the army had left Arimathea for northwestern Africa. The old man thought they became the empire of Almoravid rulers.

"I knew the caliphs of Almohad had conquered a large portion of the Iberian peninsula, and I believe the next *Sangraal* parchments might still exist, perhaps in the city of Toledo. Toledo became the greatest learning center since the glory days of Alexandria. I suspect the elusive holy parchments are hidden in one of the libraries there."

Divulging this new information caused his breathing to sound raspy, but he wanted to complete his story to me.

"Lord de Borron, please bring me a cup . . . of *vin* from the skin."

Quickly, I returned inside to fetch it and a bowl. Afterward, I poured the red liquid into a wooden bowl and handed it to him. He gulped it down and proceeded to finish his story in a voice difficult to hear.

"I planned to seek out the other set of parchments, but our Grand Master Arnaud de Toroge died. The priory rumors spoke of me as the next elected Grand Master of our entire order. After the funeral of our deceased leader, I found out that one of his close *chevaliers* and the priests who helped me with the parchments had betrayed me. Grand Master Toroge had approved of my plan to pursue another set of Saint Joseph's parchments but wanted me to keep it a secret. He feared someone in the Roman Curia would use it against our order. *Chevalier* Gérard de Ridefort told the patriarch what we had found and my secrecy to my former Grand Master. He had me discredited among my fellow *frères*. This affected the outcome of my election and Gérard de Ridefort became the new Grand Master.

"He obtained his position by nefarious means and nothing else, but far more dangerous for our order and faith, he exhibited a reckless nature. The man knew nothing of military tactics or the Saracen mind. Gérard de Ridefort sacrificed several thousand Templar *chevaliers* and Christian soldiers at the battle of the Horns of Hattin. We lost Jerusalem to the Saracens and the Holy Sepulchre. I had left before this shameful day came about, by requesting a transfer back to Provence. I suppose if I hadn't, I would have died with my martyred *frères*, but God willed otherwise.

"I took the book with me before I left and brought the men you now see here. Gérard de Ridefort met his long-deserved end, along with the patriarch. Yet, before the patriarch died, he sent a letter to the Curia telling them I took something of importance when I left Jerusalem. I appealed at once to Pope Celestine III to keep the book, but several cardinals persuaded him to rule against me. Somehow, Cardinal Folquet suspects there's the possibility of a second set of parchments. My chaplain, who translated Saint Joseph's note, fell to a murderer's dagger right before the fall of Jerusalem. It's my belief that Cardinal Folquet had found out what he knew and then killed him. Now you know why I want to see him ruined and disgraced. He has earned his place in Hell, and I plan on throwing him into its fires."

Although, I didn't say it, my vengeance too told me to find the hottest place in Tartarus, for both him and his evil puppet, Marcel de Tournay. I knew Commander de Érail possessed great courage, honesty, and religious conviction, making it difficult for him to kill a man for revenge. However, my heart had turned to stone and I knew how many innocent people Marcel de Tournay had killed. Once again, Commander Gilbért's presence, along with his fellow *chevaliers,* made me proud.

Commander de Érail said he appreciated that I had left my home on such a short notice and given up the comforts of hearth and family. He further stated the search before us included many more unknown dangers. However, he wouldn't think less of me if I decided to return to my family at Borron.

"Lord Robert, you have demonstrated to me that you're brave, righteous, and a true warrior of God, despite the fact you're a troubadour. It isn't in your nature to shy away from difficulties; however, I want you to know you have fulfilled your promise to me."

I nodded and smiled at him. "I will forgive you from pulling me away from home. I gave you my word and won't renege on it just because of some harsh times. I am quite grateful you would approve of my actions if I decided to journey back home. However, I intend to follow your men where our holy quest might lead, even to the ends of the earth.

"The hand of God has preordained me to seek out further *Sangraal* parchments and tell their stories. I promised I wouldn't disappoint you in any way, and furthermore, I don't want to speak of this matter again."

"*Merci*, Lord Robert, I am not surprised by your response. I apologize and honor your request. You are a *bon* man, Lord Robert de Borron."

The deep snow had given us a mixed blessing by delaying Marcel de Tournay and his men. The next morning of our eighth day in the cabin, the snow stopped, and the weather warmed. Commander Gilbért said Marcel de Tournay and his men appeared lost, and the deep snow had made it difficult for them to track us. Besides, Marcel de Tournay needed additional *chevaliers*.

Muhammad packed our remaining horses and afterward prepared the *traîneaus*.

He helped me load the rest of my *frère* monks onto the sleds to leave. Due to Muhammad's superb medical treatments; my fellow *chevaliers* were mending quite well, while moving with less assistance. I treasured our newfound relationship that the Saracen prince and I had developed. Thinking back on how we had worked together in nursing the men, feeding them, and their recuperation, never again would I question the loyalty of Muhammad. He had exceeded my expectations more than once, even when he didn't have to. Because of our new relationship, I now saw into his honorable heart. However, my initial prejudices had still left me with a sense of guilt.

I draped a blanket over young Hughes's face, tied him down tight, and we left the cabin, with the rest of my companions looking for a suitable burial place for Hughes. I rode next to Muhammad, who didn't say a word, and I knew something troubled him besides Hughes's death.

"You seem bothered, *mon ami*. Am I correct?"

He looked at me and nodded his head.

"Do you care to let me know?"

His hand reached down from his horse and pointed to the melting ice that had formed small rivulets of water across our path. Just as I understood what he meant, I heard the loud noise of rushing water, some distance away. At that moment, our horses panicked, as they reared on their hind legs. Muhammad shouted at each one to move faster, but his magical words didn't speed them forward. With rolling white eyes of fear, each horse crept forward up the steep path. To my horror, right before my eyes, not too far in front of us, the snow-capped peaks disappeared, followed next by a thunderous roar. It took everything we had to calm the horses and start them moving.

At last, we reached the summit of a rock-strewn plateau, where we stopped and allowed our horses to rest from their frightened uphill climb. Abruptly came a loud "boom," and the earth began to shake beneath us. The air around us started vibrating as we hurried onto the plateau.

Muhammad yelled something in his native language, and we spurred our horses forward. We raced a short distance across the high rocky *montagne* plateau and came upon a snow-free open meadow. I stopped and then looked back to see our cabin had disappeared under a *montagne* of snow. Much bewildered, I listened to the avalanche's echoes rumbling back and forth through the snow-covered peaks.

"May peace and blessings be upon the prophet *Isa*, for our protection," Muhammad stated. To my surprise, he praised *Isa* or Jesus. Once again, I thought, God had intervened to protect us on our holy quest. I followed this with a silent prayer to Heaven asking for continued protection. I finished just as Commander Gilbért prayed aloud.

"God has led us here and offered His Almighty protection during this avalanche, Amen! Soldiers of Christ, I can't think of a better place to bury our fellow *chevalier*!" he said. Then he motioned for me to come near his sled or *traîneau* as he called it.

"Lord de Borron, let us inter our *frère* Hughes here. Our Lord can easily see this spot." At once, I dismounted my horse, took my helmet, and started digging. Along with Muhammad's help, the muddy soil gave way in large chunks.

While digging, I indeed did notice the sanctity of this spot to bury young Hughes de Montbard. His eternal resting spot now faced close to Heaven and God's grace. Also, our Savior's white-tipped *montagne* crown would surround our fallen hero.

The grave depth grew suitable to place young Hughes's body into the narrow pit.

To my surprise, Sergeant Jacque de Hoult strolled forth, carrying a large piebald flag.

"Our battle standard, the *beauséant*, befits his bravery."

I helped him drape the battle flag on Hughes de Montbard's lifeless body; afterward, Muhammad finished covering the body with soil. I placed numerous smooth stones over the mound of dirt. The wind started blowing from the west, as we put Commander de Érail's fitchée metal cross at the foot of the grave.

We each took turns and said a psalm. After completing our psalms, we stood in amazement as Muhammad knelt on the ground, facing east, and said the word *shahid* four times. Commander Gilbért said this means that young Hughes had become a holy martyr in Muhammad's thinking.

"Observe well, Lord de Borron. He's reaching for his *tasbih*, which are his prayer beads," Commander de Érail further said.

We focused our attention on Muhammad as he took out a string of black beads from his tunic belt and started counting them, saying the words "*La ilaha illa Allah*" in repetition.

"Muhammad will maintain this chant until all ninety-nine beads are counted." Muhammad then paused and said something, which sounded similar to one of our prayers.

"The Saracens have a prayer for the dead, it's recited four times, and called a *takbir*," Commander de Érail continued.

Some of these words I had heard before, for he said "*Allahu akbar*" in a steady drawn-out cadence of four lines. His reverence and grieving touched my heart, while showing me his loyalty to his compatriots and me.

Before each warrior-*moine* left the burial site, he made the sign of the cross and tossed a handful of soil over the grave of his martyred *frère*. I didn't want to leave him alone, hesitating to say *mon au revoir*, yet I had to say something more, "*Pax vobiscum, mon ami*," I uttered. Somehow, at that moment, I knew he would later assist and protect us from his spiritual post on our holy quest.

Muhammad bowed several times with admiration toward the rocky mound, and then approached his horse, wedged his boot into the stirrup, swung himself upon his saddle, and prepared to leave. I mounted my steed while realizing I must put the past behind me. Where was Marcel de Tournay? Halfway down the *montagne*, Muhammad answered my thought. He pointed to a gulley, where we observed a huge pile of snow. Sticking from the peak were dead horses and men. Near the bottom, stood the cardinal's standard draped over de Tournay's body. A sense of satisfaction coursed through my body, followed with a verbal sigh. He now burned in Hell for all eternity.

We now proceeded in our holy pursuit of the next set of *lé Sangraal* parchments, if they still existed. Also, I prayed to discover the meaning of the numerical clues written by Saint Joseph de Arimathea. What cryptic meanings did the numbers *penta* and *octa* have to do with Miriam of Magdala's Tree of Life? What dangers would we confront in the mysterious land of Iberia? Were there more obscure hidden parchments of the Cup of Christ and the forgotten disciple? Where were they leading us?

GLOSSARY

Latin Terms

Contubernia—squad of eight soldiers

Dominus vobiscum—the Lord be with you

Equites—wealthy business class

Flagellum—Roman lead-tasseled whip

Gladius—Roman sword used by a legionnaire

Greaves—Roman soldier metal shin guards

League—unit of measure equaling three miles

Lorica segmentata—Roman soldier breast armor

Nobilis Decurio—noble counselor

Non nobis Domine, non nobis, sed nomini tuo da gloriam—Not unto us, O Lord, not unto us, but to thy name give glory (Psalm 115:1, KJV) —Knights Templar battle cry

Pater Noster—Lord's Prayer

Pax vobiscum—peace be with you

Pilum—Roman javelin like spear used by legionnaires

Quid agis—How are you?

Scutum—Roman soldier's shield

Titulum—name-titled sign

Verutum—heavy jabbing spear

Frankish Gaul Terms

Abbaye—abbey

Abbé—priest (father)

Affectueux—loving

Amant—lover

Ami—friend

Bâtard—bastard

Bell-soeur—sister-in-law

Bienvenu—welcome

Bon—good

Bon ami—good friend

Bonjour—hello

Bonsoir—good evening

Coeur—heart

Comte—count (title)

Duc—duke

Église—church

Épouse—wife

Frère—brother

Le Sangraal—the Cup of Christ (the Holy Grail)

Mari—husband

Mère de Dieu—Mother of God

Mère—mother

Mes fils—my sons
Moine—monk
Mon cheri—my dear or darling
Mon fils—my son or sons (des fils)
Monsieur—mister
Montagne(s)—mountain or mountains
Morte—death or dead
Père—father
Roi—king
Royaumes—kingdoms
Seigneur—lord (title)
Soeur—sister
Traîneau—sled
Très bien—very good
Vin—wine
Vis-à-vis—compared to

Jewish and Aramaic Terms

Abba—father
Adonai—our Lord
Amma—mother
Beit din—judgment hall or religious court
Ben or *bar*—son of
Birkat ha-mazon—the prayer blessing for food after the meal
Brit chadashah—new covenant
Charoset—Seder herbs
Ein Sof—without end
El Elohim—deity
El Shaddai—The Almighty
Hosanna—our greatest glory comes from the House of David
Kabod—halo or bright light
Kinnor—musical-stringed instrument
Kodesh—holy
Maddiah—evil one
Maishiach—anointed one (The Messiah)
Malach—angel
Mezuzah—Hebrew sacred doorpost with selected Torah verses
Mikveh—ritual baths
Navi—prophet
Omein—amen or so be it
Parousia—the Second Coming
Pesach—Jewish Passover
Ruah—spiritual wind or holy breath
Seder—order for Passover service
Sefirot—emanations or attributes
Shabbat—Jewish Sabbath

Shakharit—morning Jewish prayer
Shalom aleichem—peace be with you
Sheol—hell or burning pit
Shofar—religious ram-horned trumpet
Spikenard—ointment (perfumed) from the Himalayan mountain used in burial rites
Teshuva—repentance or being transformed
Tiferet—balance or harmony
Ya'akov—name for James
Yahweh—sacred name G_d (Tetragrammaton)
Yehudah—Judea
Yerushalayim—Jerusalem

Muslim Terms

Alaikum al salaam—I return the peace unto you
Allah akbar or Allahu akbar—God is great or greatest
Baraq—Prophet Muhammad's mare horse who took him to seventh heaven from the Dome of the Rock
Baraka—blessing
Insha Allah—if Allah wills it
Isa—prophet Jesus the Christ
Jambiya—dagger with a curved blade
Misbaha—prayer beads
Mujahedeen—holy warriors
Rusul—one who is divinely sent
Salaam alaikum—peace be upon you
Shahid—martyr
Takbir—prayer for the dead
Tasbih—prayer beads

Medieval Terms

Aketon—long quilt-padded shirt covered with chain mail
Apse—rounded alcove behind a church altar
Bailey—castle courtyard
Barbican—gateway or outer works defending a drawbridge
Beauséant—piebald-colored flag of the Knights Templar
Coif—hood of chain mail
Crenellations—battlement openings at the top of a castle wall
Destrier—medieval combat horse
Keep—heavily fortified tower in the interior of a castle
Mandorla—church almond-shaped stone-chiseled structure with a Virgin Mary design enclosed
Narthex—large foyer or entryway of a church
Nave—central part of a church
Portcullis—heavy wooden-grilled gate that can be raised and lowered
Presbytery—part of the church lying east of the choir where the altar is placed
Quarrel—thick metal tip of a crossbow arrow

Refectory—common hall where monks eat

Romany—Gypsies

Sacristy—room in a church where sacred vestments and vessels are kept

Saint Michaelmas—holy feast day celebrated on September 29th

Sally port—small hidden door to a fortress

Scutage—knight's fee paid to his lord in lieu of military service

Tympanum—area of a church between the lintel of a doorway and the arch above it.
    May have biblical scenes carved in this area

WRITER'S NOTES

My story goes back to periods of time still lacking historical information. As a young boy, my dad and I had interests in Arthurian legends and "the forgotten people of history's mysteries."

The time of Christ and the medieval periods were often entwined with miraculous saints, apocryphal biblical stories, and supernatural happenings. Some of these events and people were from the Holy Bible; however, many other books were written about those times after the life of Jesus the Christ. Between the years of 1100 and 1300, several secular authors wrote stories about the quest of the Holy Grail and its sudden appearance and disappearance.

Lord Robert de Borron was a romance writer who lived in the latter part of the twelfth century. Where today romance writing involves love stories, in the twelfth through the fourteenth centuries, they wrote, sang, and memorized ballads about heroes and unrequited love. Lord Robert lived in the Northern Burgundy region, which now includes France. His benefactor was Count Gautiér de Montbéliard, who was his brother-in-law and helped him publish his stories of Merlin, Sir Perceval, and Joseph of Arimathea.

I have put Lord Robert on a fictitious quest in *The Cup of Christ and the Forgotten Disciple*, which he might have followed. I gave most of his literary-created traveling companions fighting experience in the Levant during the Crusades. One of his associates was *Chevalier* Gilbért de Érail, a Knights Templar who actually fought in the Outremer and later was elected twelfth Grand Master of the Knights Templar order. Their true story has been lost over time, so I decided to present one possible version of their history.

During medieval and biblical times, numbers were important sacred symbols to the clergy and secular community, but everyone was aware of the importance of how numbers were utilized to construct ancient temples, cathedrals, and monuments. Numerical figures were also used to tell stories, to prophesy, and to garner power. In my story, the numbers five and eight play important clues to Joseph of Arimathea and Lord Robert de Borron's quest. Each number has a significant religious connotation, which encompasses Jewish, Christian, Muslim, and Druid beliefs.

The ancient art of numerical divination called gematria was used by the Greek and Jewish communities. Its alpha-numeric representations concealed or revealed important names, words, and directions. Those cultures elected certain individuals from priestly classes or secret societies to make use of geometry and mathematics. Who gave them this original secret knowledge? Was it a higher spiritual being? It is said that God is the great architect of the universe.

Along with secret power comes the temptation of evil intent. Lord Robert must make serious choices between family, friends, and his Roman Catholic faith. His religious confidence is undermined by powerful and not-so-powerful individuals in the Roman Catholic Church. A cardinal by the name of Folquet lived close to the same time period and used his power to kill people and confiscate property of the ever-growing gnostic Christian sect called the Cathars, who once lived in Southern Gaul now called France.

Joseph of Arimathea is mentioned five times in the canonical New Testament and Mary Magdalene is mentioned eight times. Legends say that Joseph of Arimathea was a great uncle to Jesus the Christ, from his brother's side of his family. Both these numbers are significant in the Old and New Testaments.

The ancient Jewish tabernacle construction had five as its pervading design number. Most every measurement of the tabernacle was a multiple of five. The tabernacle had the five-letter word "grace" stamped on it. The pillars that held up the tabernacle were five cubits tall (a cubit is an approximate length from a man's elbow to the fingertips). The whole of the outer curtain was divided into squares of twenty-five cubits (five by five). The measurement of the brazen altar of the burnt offering was also the same size.

There are five books in the Pentateuch (the Law of Moses).

There are five books of Psalms totaling 150 chapters. The Star of Bethlehem purportedly had five points. The first sum of even and odd numbers two plus three equal five. To the early Christian mystics, the pentagram was a sigil of Jesus the Christ. The square of a five-pointed star, contained in a pentagon with a side measuring one unit, is equal to 2.368 square units. The number 2368 is the gematria equivalent to the total letters of Jesus Christ in the Greco-numerical alphabet. King Solomon's sigil was a five-pointed star that he legendarily used to construct the first Jewish temple. Jesus the Christ had five inflicted wounds while hanging on the cross.

Eight also has an arcane and religious significance. The baptismal font was always eight-sided. The square cubits of the first tabernacle to house the Ark of the Covenant measured 8,000 cubits. King Solomon's temple was eight-times greater. Add three eights to equal twenty-four, the total number of letters in the Greek alphabet. In the Islamic faith, the eight-point star represents eight regions of paradise. Eight angels support the throne of Allah on Judgment Day and the eight-point star of the Seal of the Prophets. When eight is written on its side, it becomes the symbol for infinity.

I hope this story transports the reader back to those times to realize how the people lived, understood their surroundings, and felt pain and joy in the context of their customs. Readers are encouraged to keep an open mind and to not be judgmental. What would you do if confronted with the same difficult decisions to protect your family under these ancient cultural restraints?

The following books and spiritual philosophies are excellent reading sources if readers are interested in where I obtained my reference materials for this beginning series.

The Apocryphal New Testament, compiled by Dr. Montague Rhodes James, includes sections of *The Gospel of Nicodemus*, or *Acts of Pilate*; *The Assumption Narrative of Joseph of Arimathea*; and *The Acts of Thomas*.

The Gospel of Thomas, *The Gospel of Philip*, and *The Gospel of Mary Magdalene* are part of the great gnostic metaphysical series redacted by Jean-Yves Leloup.

Magdalene's Lost Legacy: Symbolic Numbers and the Sacred Union in Christianity by Margaret Starbird.

Merlin and the Grail: Joseph of Arimathea, Merlin, Perceval: The Trilogy of Arthurian Prose Romances by Lord Robert de Boron, translated by Nigel Bryant

The Universe Speaks in Numbers: How Modern Math Reveals Nature's Deepest Secrets by Graham Farmelo.

> *Tolle numerum omnibus rebus et omnia pereunt.*
> Take from all things their number and all shall perish.
> —Saint Isidore of Seville

Coming Soon

The Tree of Life

The second book in The Cup of Christ trilogy series finds Joseph of Arimathea and Lord Robert de Borron on their continued epic journey. They will further travel through Southern Gaul and ancient Iberia still searching for the fulfillment of their holy quests.

Thank you for reading the first book in my trilogy series.

jackmholt.com

CPSIA information can be obtained
at www.ICGtesting.com
Printed in the USA
LVHW050305261020
669798LV00022B/605/J

9 781735 528304